THE GREAT WORK

THE GREAT WORK

SHELDON COSTA

This is a work of fiction. All names, places, and characters are products of the author's imagination or are used fictitiously. Any resemblance to real people, places, or events is entirely coincidental.

Library of Congress Cataloging-in-Publication Data
Names: Costa, Sheldon, author.
Title: The great work / Sheldon Costa.
Description: Philadelphia : Quirk Books, 2025. | Summary: "In the post-Civil War Pacific Northwest, Gentle and his nephew hunt down a legendary giant salamander in an attempt to resurrect Gentle's best friend using alchemical knowledge"—Provided by publisher.
Identifiers: LCCN 2024061286 (print) | LCCN 2024061287 (ebook) | ISBN 9781683695059 (paperback) | ISBN 9781683695066 (ebook)
Subjects: LCGFT: Paranormal fiction. | Western fiction. | Novels.
Classification: LCC PS3603.O8663 G74 2025 (print) | LCC PS3603.O8663 (ebook) | DDC 813/.6—dc23/eng/20241230
LC record available at https://lccn.loc.gov/2024061286
LC ebook record available at https://lccn.loc.gov/2024061287

ISBN: 978-1-68369-505-9

Printed in the United States of America

Typeset in Adobe Garamond Pro, IM Fell English, and Winsel Variable

Designed by Andie Reid
Cover illustration by Maryann Held
Illustrations on pages 15, 47, 129, 201, and 273 from *Elementa chemiae* (1718) by Johann Conrad Barchusen. Select images courtesy of the Science History Institute.

Quirk Books
215 Church Street
Philadelphia, PA 19106
quirkbooks.com

Quirk Books' authorized representative in the EU for product safety and compliance is Easy Access System Europe, Mustamäe tee 50, 10621 Tallinn, Estonia, gpsr.requests@easproject.com.

10 9 8 7 6 5 4 3 2 1

"What the Mediterranean Sea was to the Greeks, breaking the bond of custom, offering new experiences, calling out new institutions and activities, that, and more, the ever-retreating frontier has been to the United States directly, and to the nations of Europe more remotely. And now, four centuries from the discovery of America, at the end of a hundred years of life under the Constitution, the frontier has gone, and with its going has closed the first period of American history."

—FREDERICK J. TURNER,
The Significance of the Frontier in American History

"For there never was any dead thing in the cosmos, nor is there, nor will there be."

—BOOK XII OF THE *Corpus Hermeticum*

CONTENTS

Prologue

The first sighting of the Dragon of Dalton Lake occurred in May, five months before Washington officially joined the union. Joe Fisher, a Klallam man who lived alone in a shack on the northern shore of the lake, stumbled into the Wolf's Den saloon one night and began screaming about the creature he'd just seen. Though Joe was generally a reserved man, visiting town once or twice a month to quietly sip whiskey in a corner of the bar, that night he couldn't stop talking about the giant lizard, some monster with skin as white as the moon that had risen from the waters beneath his boat and nearly capsized him while he was out trying to catch trout.

The creature had only shown itself briefly, Joe said, surging up from the depths and disappearing a few seconds later. For a moment, the old man thought it might be a log that had dislodged itself from the lake sediment, but the beast lingered long enough for Joe to make out four fat arms with giant, webbed fingers, and a wide, triangular head. The monster studied him with dark, marble eyes, as if trying to parse out whether the fisherman was friend or foe, before it dipped back beneath the waves.

Few believed Joe's story. He was ancient, and by all accounts had spent the bulk of his life as a recluse. And anyway stories of giant monsters were as common on the peninsula as sawdust. Most figured Joe would move on from his tale in a day or two, maybe exhume it every few years when the man felt like spooking some newcomer at the bar. But Joe didn't move on. He returned to the Wolf's Den every night for the next week, looking worse and worse every time he stepped through the door. His eyes sank to two dead embers hidden in the leathery folds of his face. He twitched and shivered in his seat, slapping at the air around him like he was being pinched by phantoms. If he talked at all, he spoke only of the dragon. How it came to him in dreams. Showed him things. If anyone bothered to ask him what these things might be, he only gnashed his teeth and whimpered, as if the very act of speaking of what he'd seen was too painful. The townsfolk began to give him a wider berth.

Two weeks after Joe's encounter with the dragon, he stopped coming to town. At night, no light emanated from his little cabin across the lake. When the sheriff, Mac Dalton, went to investigate, he found the old man hanging from the branches of a dead tree in his front yard. At his feet, he'd left a sheet of paper neatly folded beneath a rock. Two words were scrawled on the page in letters that had been retraced again and again, as if Joe was afraid they might be missed: DEEP WATERS.

Soon other people began reporting their own sightings of the dragon. A colossal white body crushing through the trees behind their homes. The flash of a giant tail disappearing beneath the lake's water. A low, throbbing roar that shook the trees in the middle of the night. With these encounters came more nightmares, more desperate townsfolk gathered in the Wolf's Den, their faces winnowed down to the same expressions of exhausted hopelessness that had haunted Joe's features in his final days.

A few followed his lead and took their own lives. They hung themselves and shot themselves and hurled their bodies off the nearby cliffs. Some left town, loading up whatever belongings would fit on their old carts and leaving the rest behind. Some simply disappeared.

Those who didn't see the creature weren't safe from its influence, either. The water from their wells took on a strange taste, a blend of coal oil and copper that refused to dislodge itself from their throats. Livestock that were once plump and docile became ornery, refusing hay and slop even as their ribs pressed up through their skin. Crops that had stood tall and healthy drooped and rotted on their stalks. When rumors reached Dalton Lake about strange occurrences along the coast, where the turbid waves kept belching up horrible fish with blind eyes and human teeth, the news was almost banal.

By the time the sheriff realized Dalton Lake was headed toward a crisis, it was already too late. He dubbed the phenomenon "lizard fever" and forbade all mention of the monster. Yet the town had become obsessed with the creature and what its presence might mean. The most devout among them proclaimed that the monster was a sign of the end times, a beast straight from the pages of Revelation. The local priest, finding his pews increasingly packed on Sunday, did little to dissuade them. He was the one who'd dubbed it a dragon in the first place: one of hell's scaley minions, come to test their faith there at the edge of the civilized world.

As for those who thought themselves immune to apocalyptic

theatrics of this sort—those who'd seen, over the years, how every drought and famine and flu became evidence that the end times were at hand—even they could not deny that Armageddon was in the air. If they saw no dragons in their dreams, old nightmares they'd thought long forgotten slipped back into their heads. And if they could not turn to prayer they turned, instead, to drink. They locked their doors, clutched their bottles, and waited for this new and terrible thing to pass.

I

Prima Materia

Three days after his best friend, Liam O'Kelly, was murdered by the Dragon of Dalton Lake, Gentle Montgomery discovered he was an uncle. He received this news while huddled on the floor of Dalton Lake's one and only jail cell, where he'd been tossed the night before after the sheriff caught him trying to exhume Liam's corpse from the mossy graveyard behind Our Holy Mother of Immaculate Miracles Church. Though the sheriff had accused him of graverobbing, Gentle found this hyperbolic: He'd barely managed to dig three inches into the freshly turned dirt before Mac cracked him in the head with the butt of his shotgun.

He'd tried to explain that he hadn't been robbing anyone. The real thief, he said, was Father Eli, who'd buried Liam in one of the shallow plots behind his church. If Gentle had been around when Liam was dredged up from the river he never would have allowed the priest to dump his friend's body in the dirt like so much unwanted rubbish. Unfortunately, Gentle was so drunk at the time that the words had gummed up in his mouth. So Mac just tossed him into the cell and went home.

Mac did not return until early the next evening. Gentle had just closed his eyes and felt himself drifting toward a cold, unpleasant slumber when the rusty grind of the jail's front door lurched him awake again. Mac entered first, his derby hat askew on his head and his face ruddy from drink. Looking, as he habitually did, with an embalmer's eye, Gentle perceived the sheriff not so much as a fellow human being but as a future subject of his trade: the length and width of his coffin, the gallons of embalming fluid required to fill the swelling paunch of his belly, the bottles of powder needed to return some semblance of youth and virility to his jaundiced face. He could even say with some confidence, based on the sheriff's monthly visits to a particularly squalid house of ill-repute in Port Townsend, that the man was likely to expire from a disease of the venereal nature. This was the talent—or the curse—of the embalmer. To see, in every living creature, the lurking specter of their inevitable demise.

"Your nephew has come to take you home," Mac said, just as Gentle finished calculating how much stitching would be necessary to return a bit of dignified rigidity to the sheriff's sagging jowls.

"I don't have a nephew," he replied.

"Sure you do," Mac said, using the voice he reserved for only the most belligerent of drunks, a syrupy coo somehow laden with menace, like a hard candy with a razor in its center. "This young man has come all the way from Ohio to look after you."

Hearing the word *Ohio* stiffened Gentle's spine. As his supposed nephew stepped into the jail, Gentle squinted to see him more clearly in the dark. He was a pitiful-looking creature, maybe fourteen years old, with a shaved head and a black bruise around his right eye. He wore a rumpled dress shirt two sizes too large for his thin body, some dusty gray trousers, and a pair of black loafers that, despite their scrim of dirt, were far too fancy for Dalton Lake's muddy boulevards. With his bruised eye and ill-fitting clothes, the boy reminded Gentle of a starving raccoon that had gotten caught in some dapper gentleman's clothesline.

"Uncle Sampson?" he said, in a voice so faint Gentle could barely make it out over the wind buffeting the jail's walls.

"There is no one named Sampson in Dalton Lake," Gentle croaked. His head still throbbed from the sheriff battering his skull the night before.

"That's what I told him," Mac said. "But he's got a letter with your address on it."

The boy dug into the slim leather bag that hung from his shoulder and pulled out an envelope, its edges yellowed by time. He hesitated, as if Gentle were some unruly animal whose domestication was in dispute, before handing the envelope to him through the bars. Gentle took it and rotated it in his hands, knowing, even before he slipped the letter out, what he would find inside.

My dearest mother, the note began, in that crooked, loping script Gentle had never been able to fix, even after two decades of Liam's calligraphy lessons. He remembered the rest of the letter without needing to read it. The tormented apology for failing to send any correspondence for so many years. The brief inquiry regarding her health. The hope that this letter found her well, and that someday soon she might make the trip out West to see him. After many years of adventuring, he had written, he'd finally settled down in a place called Dalton Lake, where he had helped set up a laboratory with a man named Liam, a genius who'd dedicated his life to the study of natural philosophy. The work they were doing, he'd explained with the burning certainty of youth, would soon complete the labor of countless generations of human beings: the conquest of death itself.

He remembered how he'd felt, writing that letter. The foolish conviction that he was finally putting the shame of his departure from Ohio to rest. That his mother, overjoyed by the news that he was still alive after all this time, would board the first wagon train west and hurry out to find him.

And he remembered his brother's reply, delivered on a slip of their family's stationery some months later, MONTGOMERY BEEF emblazoned atop the page in pretentious script. Those swooping letters—which looked as though they should be announcing the dates of a royal marriage—informed Gentle that his mother was dead. Had been dead, in fact, for many years. They asked that Gentle refrain from sending any more letters and requested back the ten dollars he had stolen from the family safe before he set out on his *little adventure west.* Gentle acquiesced to only one of his brother's demands: He never tried to contact his family again.

"Where did you find this?" he asked.

"In my father's lockbox. I'm Emmanuel's son." The boy spoke slowly, as though he were afraid Gentle might not be able to make the connection himself. "My name is Kitt."

"Odd name," Mac mumbled from his corner of the room, where he'd begun to tap his boot impatiently.

"It's short for Christopher," Kitt said apologetically.

"Is my brother dead?" Gentle asked.

"What? No. Of course not."

"That's a shame. Why are you here, then?"

The boy blushed. He must be freezing in those clothes, Gentle thought. November in the Olympic Peninsula was no time to go around without a coat.

"I wanted to meet you," he said. "My father told me you died in the war."

"Well, you've met me," Gentle said, and rose from the floor. He stepped forward and watched that familiar amalgamation of fright and wonder rearrange the features on Kitt's face as the light fell upon him, revealing the fat, crooked scar that curved in a crescent arch from the bottom of his left ear down to the tip of his chin. He was a large man, more wide than tall, with the stocky frame and apish features, Liam liked to say, of a *noble simian*. His night in the cell had only intensified his feral appearance, he was sure: The stink of booze and sweat hung over him in a fetid haze, mingling with the tang of the chamber pot in the corner of his cell. When he ran a hand through the dark bramble of his hair, his fingers were quickly knotted up in its greasy curls.

"I'm looking for a place to stay," Kitt said, his gaze hovering over Gentle's scar.

"The Wolf's Den has rooms for rent," Gentle said. "Not the sort of lodgings you're accustomed to, I'm sure, but the best you'll find around here."

Kitt was silent. Gentle stared at him, searching for Emmanuel's face in his. But the boy must have taken after his mother: He had none of Emmanuel's ugly ruggedness. He was all angles, with the high cheekbones and long lashes of a porcelain doll. Even his black eye, a perfect circle of marbled blue, seemed more like some elegant birthmark than an actual bruise.

The boy mumbled something, but Gentle couldn't hear him.

"Speak up," he said.

"I was hoping to stay with you," Kitt said, finally looking at him. "Just for a little while."

"Not possible."

"Why?"

Gentle leaned forward, the old bars of the cell groaning against his weight. He caught Kitt's eyes—and here he finally found his brother, peering out at him through two bright spheres of startling blue—and let his gaze linger there for a long second before he spoke again. This heavy stare was a trick Liam had taught him years ago: a surefire way to penetrate a person's skepticism and make even the most absurd claims sound like common sense.

"I'm heading upriver," he said. "To kill a dragon."

Of course, Gentle wasn't Liam. He had none of his friend's preternatural charisma. When he entered a room, people did not gravitate in his direction, desperate to catch themselves in the wide arc of his orbit. His scar was a natural repellent, a fact he had appreciated for much of his life. He slipped into his own coarseness, he'd always felt, like a knight slipping into a suit of armor.

And now, without Liam there to clarify, with some charming aside, how this seemingly delirious proclamation was less mad than it might first appear, Gentle was just a large, smelly drunk mumbling about mythological monsters.

Mac's eyes sharpened to slits. "That's enough, Gentle," he said.

Kitt frowned and looked between the two men, as if trying to decide whether they were making a joke at his expense. "Did you say dragon?" he asked.

Mac lumbered forward to unlock Gentle's cell, with the denial he'd been repeating for weeks in his abortive effort to maintain some semblance of sanity in town: "There are no dragons in Dalton Lake."

"Call it what you want," Gentle said. "Whatever it is, it killed Liam."

Mac swung the cell door open and shook his head with what looked like genuine sadness. "The man drowned, Gentle."

"He was a strong swimmer."

"Water gets mighty cold this time of year."

"A fact Liam knew well."

Mac sighed and slipped his thumbs into the loops of his belt. "Liam was acting strange all summer."

"Whole world's been acting strange," Gentle said.

Mac scratched despondently at his moustache. "Maybe so," he said. "But I'll have order in Dalton Lake."

"What order? Half the town is dead or disappeared, you dolt."

The sheriff's face reddened. He swept aside his coat, revealing the Colt he always kept in his holster. The threat was not a hollow one: Gentle had seen the man shoot people for far lesser crimes than digging up the dead. "Tell you what," he said. "Since our little town no longer agrees with you, why don't you go on back to Ohio with your nephew here?"

"I'm not going to Ohio."

"I don't care where you go. I want you out of town by tomorrow morning. If I find any bodies missing from that graveyard, I'll string you up myself. We'll have no more of you or Liam's necromancy in Dalton Lake."

Gentle bristled at the man's mischaracterization of Liam's work. He was tempted to remind the sheriff that he'd had no qualms about Liam's medical techniques when it came to his own health: Just a few weeks earlier he'd appeared at their door, one hand clasped painfully around his crotch, to request a mercury rub from Liam to help assuage his *manly troubles*. But then he remembered what Liam had always said about nonbelievers—*more worthy of pity than contempt, for their eyes are closed to the glory of mankind's greatness*—and the thought of his friend's kindness filled him with such unspeakable despair that he bolted past the sheriff and toward the door, stopping just long enough to lean over a slack-jawed Kitt and growl, "I never asked for a nephew," before heading out into the dusk. If he spent another second in that still, rancid air, he thought, he would begin weeping and never stop.

Even though he and Liam had lived there for twenty years, their cabin looked much the same as it did when they'd first arrived at Dalton Lake: a slumped structure of unevenly stacked logs with a crooked brick chimney. Like everything else in town, the house had a mossy, rain-beaten look about it, even in the drier months, as though it might melt into a pulpy sludge at any moment. It had once belonged to the town midwife, a woman named Mildred Cox who now occupied a much sturdier home in Port Angeles. Liam had been more than willing to look past the rugged exterior on account of the expansive herb garden Mildred had cultivated in the front yard, and the stone root cellar dug into a hillock just a few yards from the front door, the perfect location for his laboratory. Liam had also approved of its location, perched on a rocky outcropping beside the lake at the southernmost edge of town. Close enough that people wouldn't have to travel too far if they needed to buy a tincture or request an embalming, but far enough away that no one would make a habit of interrupting their work.

As Gentle stepped up onto the porch and caught sight of the jagged ouroboros carved above the doorframe—Liam's first addition to the house, a clear sign to all those who'd studied the secret wisdom that this place's occupants were devotees of the hermetic arts—he felt a lump grow in his throat. He reached out to trace the symbol with his fingers, but stopped when he heard a sharp intake of breath from somewhere behind him. He turned to find his new nephew standing a few yards away, staring in amazement at the far corner of the front yard, where Abe—named after Liam's favorite president, on account of the creature's massive stature and melancholy eyes—had wandered out from behind a strand of pine trees.

"Your horse is huge," the boy said.

"Mule," Gentle corrected, though it was a fair mistake. Liam often bragged that Abe was the largest beast of burden in the western hemisphere, a tawny brown descendant of the giant donkeys gifted to George Washington by the king of Spain. "Why are you following me?"

Kitt tugged nervously at the leather strap of his bag. Even when he was standing still, the boy emanated self-consciousness, fluttering his hands about as if he were trying to tuck various parts of himself away for fear of taking up too much space. "I told you. I need a place to stay."

"You heard the sheriff," he said. "I'm to be out of town by tomorrow morning."

"Can I stay with you until then?"

"Why?"

"I don't have anywhere else to go."

"How about home?"

The boy shook his head firmly. "I'm never going back there."

"A runaway. Just as I feared. Does your father know where you are?"

Kitt's shoulder slouched, and one of his little hands crept up his cheek to massage the dark circle around his eye. "I certainly hope not."

Gentle's stomach roiled. He hadn't eaten since the previous night.

"So can I stay with you?" Kitt asked again.

"I would rather you did not."

"Okay," Kitt replied, nodding with a sort of mercantile solemnity, as if he and Gentle were hammering out the price of a cow. In this gesture, too, Gentle spied traces of his brother. The only time he ever remembered seeing Emmanuel smile was at the end of a favorable transaction.

Abe clomped over to the boy and gave his shoulder an inquisitive nudge. When Kitt, terrified by the creature's interest, nearly toppled over from the shove, the mule turned his head to Gentle and gave a desultory shake of his shaggy mane, as if to say *this thing does not belong here*. Standing next to the animal, Kitt looked even smaller and more pitiable than he did in the jail, a shivering collection of delicate limbs draped with skin so pale it was nearly translucent. Gentle couldn't fathom how his brother, who had devised all manner of torturous calisthenics during Gentle's youth to ensure his younger sibling did not develop a "feminine physique," had produced such a child.

"Fine," Gentle said. "Come in, then. Before we both freeze to death."

The boy followed him inside. The cabin's interior was sparse, though not nearly as barbaric as some of the dirt-floored hovels Gentle had seen men living in at the lumber mills and mining camps that dotted the peninsula. Liam had great contempt for squalor. A man who could not care for himself, he liked to say, was no man at all. In service of this ideal, he'd conscripted Gentle's help in sprucing the place up over the years. They laid down pine boards over the cabin's earthen floor and installed an iron woodstove beneath the chimney's flue, flanked on either side by a pair of rocking chairs Liam had accepted as payment for embalming a carpenter's wife. They built a wall of shelving to hold their pickled goods and strung a wire over one side of the room where they could dry bundles of their herbs. In front of the cabin's solitary window, over which they hung a simple white curtain, Liam had placed a small table, just large enough for the two of them to eat their dinner comfortably, so long as one of them faced his knees toward the wall and the other turned his out toward the center of the room. They even had their own rooms. With the addition of a few panels of thin wood in the back of the cabin, they had shaped each man a cubby just large enough for a simple bed, though the added walls did little to stop Liam's formidable snoring from keeping Gentle awake most nights.

"This is where you live?" Kitt said, failing to hide his dismay.

"Liam and I, yes. Disappointed?"

"It seems very cozy," Kitt said, and then, as if to prove the earnestness of this claim, dropped his leather bag to the floor and sat down in one of the kitchen chairs.

"I suppose Emmanuel still has you living in the old farmhouse," Gentle said. As he recalled, his family home, with its square two-story frame and white wood-paneled walls, was fairly humble by Ohio standards. Even after Emmanuel had started amassing his wealth, he'd done very little to improve the place, as he considered such extravagancies a waste of money. Still, compared to even the nicest house in Dalton Lake, the drafty old homestead would have been the height of luxury.

The boy nodded stiffly, as if even the briefest mention of his house caused him intolerable discomfort.

"Suppose you'll be wanting some food," Gentle said. "Our

meals are just as *cozy* as our accommodations, I'm afraid."

He went to one of the cupboards in the kitchen and surveyed its contents. A few jars of flour, some old, hardened biscuits, a wrapped hunk of cheddar cheese, and a half-empty tin of coffee. He grabbed the biscuits and the cheese, taking a moment to carve off a few slices of mold from the latter, and set them on the table. Then he grabbed his bottle of whiskey from its hiding place behind the stove—an unnecessary subterfuge, now that Liam was no longer around to harangue him—as well as a slim brown vial of his friend's Sweet Vitriol. He'd ransacked Liam's supply of the stuff the night he found out about his death. His nightmares had returned alongside his grief, as if they could sense the weakness of his resolve, and two drops of the tincture were enough to send him into a blissful darkness so impenetrable that even his most troubling memories had no hope of reaching him. One drop merely calmed him down.

"So," he said. "You going to tell me why you're here?"

But when he turned he found the boy seated at the table, nibbling on the block of cheese while he flipped through Liam's Liber Alchimiae with his greasy fingers. Gentle had left it there before heading out to the graveyard the night before.

He lunged forward and yanked the journal out of his nephew's hands. Kitt flung up his palms to protect his face.

"What the hell are you doing?" Gentle said. "Put your damned hands down."

"I'm sorry," Kitt said. Slowly, he peeked out from behind his knuckles. "I was just looking at the pictures."

Gentle pressed the leather journal to his chest like a father cradling his firstborn child.

"These are not pictures. They're codes."

"Codes for what?" Kitt asked.

"Alchemy."

"Alchemy," Kitt said, pronouncing the word slowly, as if testing it out. "Is that some kind of medicine? Are you a doctor?"

"The alchemist shares with the doctor his zest for healing," Gentle said. "But he diverges from him in matters of the spirit. The doctor forsakes the metaphysical world for the material one. The alchemist sees them as intrinsically conjoined."

Liam's words, verbatim.

"So you aren't a doctor," Kitt said.

"A good farmer cares about more than how high his plants have grown on any given day. He considers the soil. He tracks the seasons, the movements of the stars, the minerals in the water. So it is with alchemy."

The boy frowned. "I don't think I understand."

Gentle didn't blame him. It had taken him twenty-four years to memorize Liam's riddles. Even now their meanings could prove elusive. There was no point trying to explain them to a child.

"First you show up and demand a place to sleep," Gentle said. "Then you rifle through my things. What is it you're doing here, boy?"

"My father and I had a dispute," Kitt said.

"About what?"

"My mother."

"Your mother. Right." Gentle settled into his seat and poured himself a glass of whiskey. He put a single drop of Sweet Vitriol in the drink and swirled it around. "Hard to believe Emmanuel got married. Never showed much interest in romance when I knew him."

"He still doesn't," Kitt said, and for the first time since his arrival, Gentle thought he saw the faintest tug of a smile at the edge of the boy's mouth. "He and my mother slept in separate rooms."

"Slept?"

Kitt's smirk disappeared. "She's unwell."

"Sorry to hear it," Gentle said. "What ails her?"

"Nerves," Kitt replied bitterly. "A *melancholic disposition*, according to the doctors. They sent her to the hospital back in June."

Gentle had seen such institutions—usually further east, though he'd heard rumors of one down near Tacoma, too. Imposing structures of stone that looked more like prisons than any place of healing.

"Sounds like you dispute their diagnosis," Gentle said.

"My mother was perfectly healthy," he said. "She was just a bit sad, is all. It's not easy, living with my father."

"Of that I am certain," Gentle said.

"I didn't know where else to go."

"Your mother doesn't have any relatives in Ohio?"

"I've never met her family. Father says they're below our station. All I had was the address on that letter."

"And what if you hadn't found me?" Gentle said.

"I would still be away from him. That would be enough."

"Brave," Gentle said. "And stupid. Especially now. Statehood has people acting strange."

"On the way here, I met a man who told me there were monsters in the woods. Animals with the bodies of men. Said the roads weren't safe anymore."

"There's always been talk of monsters in these woods," Gentle said. "Liam and I once spent a full month tracking down rumors of a werewolf. When we finally found him, he turned out to be a particularly stout lumberjack with bad hygiene and uncommonly abundant body hair."

When news of the dragon first reached them, Gentle had tried to tell Liam as much. Tried to remind him of all the times over the last two decades they'd spent chasing rumors of ape men and thunder-spitting eagles, certain these tall tales were in fact misattributed sightings of phoenixes and homunculi. But it had been useless: From the moment he'd sat down across from Joe Fisher and heard his story, Liam could think of nothing else but the dragon.

"But he's right," Gentle allowed. "It's dangerous for a boy your age to be traveling all alone out here."

"Father always said I should start acting like a man. Guess I finally took his advice."

"Is that why he did that to your eye?" Gentle asked. "Because you weren't acting like a man?"

Kitt's fingers traveled up to his face and traced the edges of the bruise. "It doesn't matter," he responded, and Gentle saw, in the tightening of his features, that he would get no further explanation regarding whatever had happened between them.

Gentle could imagine all sorts of reasons his brother might have hit the boy. When they had lived together, Emmanuel had taken great joy in finding cause to punish his younger brother for what he called *emasculating habits*. He'd once forced Gentle to run laps for hours under the hot Ohio sun because some of the ranch hands had seen him picking flowers for their mother.

"The sheriff told me about your friend," Kitt said, rushing to change the subject. "I'm sorry for your loss."

"My loss?" Gentle said, and all at once he remembered that Liam was dead. It was like he was hearing the news for the first time again, Mac standing uncomfortably in his doorway, his hat in his hands and his eyes downcast as he told Gentle that they had found Liam's body in a creek a few miles northwest of town and buried him behind the church.

Buried. Before Gentle could even see what the salamander

had done to him. Buried. All alone beneath the earth, with no one but the worms for company.

Gentle brought the whiskey up to his lips and drank, the glass clanking painfully against his front teeth. Thanks to the addition of the Sweet Vitriol, the calming effects were nearly immediate, muffling the screeching roar of his grief into a harmless whimper.

"I suppose you can sleep here tonight," Gentle said. He stood up from the table, wavering a little as the drink turned his legs to rubber. "I'll make up my bed for you. I won't be needing it this evening."

"Why not?"

"Still need to dig up Liam's body."

If Kitt was surprised by this admission, he didn't show it. "The sheriff told you to get out of town."

"Exactly. Which is why Mac will never suspect me of running right back to the cemetery. He thinks I'll spend the night packing."

"I thought you said you were going to kill a dragon."

"I am," Gentle said. "But first: Liam's body. Need to embalm him."

"Embalm?"

"Stifles the process of decay. That's what Liam did during the war—embalmed soldiers so that they could be sent home to their families."

"Is that why you want to dig him up? To send him to his family?"

"No," Gentle said. "Liam was an orphan. Both his parents died when he was still a toddler, on the boat over from Ireland."

"Why didn't you embalm him before he was buried?" Kitt said.

"Because they buried him *without* me," Gentle said. "I was up in Port Townsend when he died, embalming the remains of some rich boy so they could ship him back east."

"But what's the point of preserving him now?"

Gentle hesitated before answering. Without Liam there to explain things more elegantly, Kitt would think he was insane. But maybe, Gentle thought, this was for the best. Perhaps the boy would be easier to shake if he knew what Gentle planned to do.

"I'm going to bring him back from the dead."

It might have just been the Sweet Vitriol, but Gentle found a strange comfort in this wild proclamation. Last night, when the idea had first struck him, it had arrived with all the hazy uncertainty of any other drunken delusion, which was why he hadn't even bothered to bring a shovel to the cemetery. But Gentle had had all night in the frigid jail cell to ponder his plan, and even after the whiskey had worn off, the idea continued to burn in the center of his thoughts, shining out at him from the dark sea of his despair like a lighthouse's blazing bulb.

Kitt stared at him for a long time, as if waiting for Gentle to elaborate. When he didn't, he asked, "How?"

Gentle placed the Liber Alchimiae back on the table and opened it to the page he'd bookmarked the night before. It was in an earlier section of the journal, where Liam had recorded some of his first visions. There, drawn by Liam's very own hand, was a crowned royal with two heads, one with a beard and the other with long, flowing hair, stabbing a leering skeleton with a curved dagger. Above the figure, a sun and a moon jostled for prominence in the sky, while down below its legs disappeared into a bubbling cauldron, beneath which four animals—a raven, a lamb, an owl, and a salamander—writhed in a bristling sphere of flames.

"This," he said. "The Magnum Opus."

The boy leaned across the table and studied the drawing with surprising intensity, his blue eyes skittering over the page.

"What's the Magnum Opus?"

"The Great Work. The dream of every alchemist. The creation of the rebis. Though you may know it by its more conventional name: the philosopher's stone."

Kitt looked up from the page. His curiosity had been replaced, now, by a look more familiar to Gentle: the casual disregard of the skeptic. The sort of expression you expected to see on a parent's face when their child proclaimed they'd spotted pixies in the garden.

"You're talking about magic." Kitt said.

"Of a sort."

"Like from fairy tales," Kitt said.

"Fairy tales are stories," Gentle said. "What I'm talking about is *real.* Something men have studied for thousands of years. Look here."

He jabbed a finger into the book. "This picture is a recipe. The two-headed royal is the rebis, the blessed hermaphrodite, humanity in its most purified state. The moon is dissolution, the sun is coagulation. This means I'll need to refine the substance many times for it to reach its purified state. Just as man, in life, must suffer, again and again, on his path to enlightenment."

The whiskey was really running through Gentle, now, and with it came a warm, golden excitement. How proud Liam would be, he thought, to hear him explaining it all so well.

"See how the rebis stabs the skeleton?" Gentle said. "So, too, will the stone let us conquer death. But first we need our base materials." Gentle's finger slid down the page to the animals boiling beneath the cauldron. "The raven represents the first stage, nigredo. Putrefaction. Simple enough: Any rotting material will do. The lamb is albedo. Purification. The application of a strong acid, most likely. The owl represents citrinitas, the solar light and the awakening of knowledge. In this case, that might mean a nugget of sulfur. And the salamander—well, that stage is the most important. Rubedo. The culmination of the great work. For this, you need blood. But not just any blood. The blood of the dragon. A primordial substance. Prima materia."

Kitt stared at Gentle for a long time, his eyes moving back and forth from his uncle's face to the book on the table. "So the dragon is a salamander?" he said quietly.

"Indeed. A very old one, Liam reckoned."

The title of *dragon*, Gentle knew, was a historical misunderstanding. In many texts the salamander was depicted with wings, and over the ages this had caused many to confuse the creatures with their mythological cousins. But any learned alchemist would recognize that the presence of the wings was not to be taken literally. It was an instruction that the salamander should be boiled, its vapors harvested for further refining.

"And you're going to kill it?"

"That is generally the best way to get something's blood, short of asking politely."

"How?" Kitt said. He studied the shelves of dried goods, as if he expected to find the weapon capable of killing such a beast—an enchanted sword, perhaps—hanging nearby.

Gentle waved the question away. "I'll stop in Cedarville and hire some men with a greater aptitude for violence than myself. Plenty of fellows on the peninsula who love a good hunt."

"You really think you can just shoot it?"

"I've yet to meet an animal that can't be put down with a bullet."

Though this was, Gentle knew, a profound obfuscation. In just a few months, the monster's mere presence had managed to drive most of the town insane. And those who'd kept their heads—who, like Gentle, had managed to ignore the foul taste in the water, and the disturbing sounds that drifted through the trees at night—had done so only by retreating into a stubborn obliviousness, like animals nibbling at bait while the jaws of a trap closed slowly around them. How Gentle planned to kill such a thing was unimaginable.

And yet, far from dissuading him, this only made Gentle all the more certain of what he must do. This would be his final gambit, he thought as he sipped his whiskey. One last stab at salvation before perdition took its due. The sort of grand conquest, he mused, that the alchemists of old would not have hesitated to pursue. If bullets would not kill the thing, then he'd use knives. And if knives could not pierce it, he'd hurl rocks on its head. And if rocks could not crush it, Gentle would lumber into the river and wrestle with it himself, like Jacob and his angel. And like Jacob, he would receive his blessing or die.

"You really believe it will work?" Kitt asked. "That you can bring back the dead?"

"Liam believed," Gentle said. "Enough to go after the damn thing when I was out of town and get himself killed. He'd been keeping track of the sightings. Decided it was headed upriver, toward the peninsula's interior. But I'll need to make sure Liam's body is preserved before I go. No point trying to resurrect a rotting corpse."

Kitt's hands wrestled in his lap, though Gentle couldn't tell if they were animated by discomfort or excitement. He got his answer just seconds later, when Kitt asked, "Can I help?"

Gentle was surprised. He'd figured Kitt would be a shrewd materialist like his father. Emmanuel, in all the years Gentle knew him, had shown absolutely no interest in metaphysical matters.

He never missed a chance to mock their mother—herself a devout Christian—by proclaiming that religion was a delusion concocted for the benefit of the poor.

Yet Kitt appeared to have none of his father's disdain for the otherworldly. In fact, he looked ready to march out to the graveyard and unearth Liam's corpse at that very moment. Gentle knew that any good, sane man would refuse to involve a child in his scheming. But the task of digging up Liam's body would be much easier with two people, especially given Gentle's precarious sobriety. Plus, there was a pleasurable irony in the thought of conscripting his brother's son in the completion of Liam's work.

He picked up the bottle, took a swig, and let the booze, which always induced an optimistic view of things, decide for him.

"I take it you know how to use a shovel?"

Three hours later they were back, covered in dirt and sweat, with Liam's body swinging between them. Thankfully Gentle's friend was a diminutive man, barely five feet—otherwise he doubted Kitt, who looked as though he might keel over from exhaustion at any minute, would have managed to hold up his end of the corpse all the way home.

"Quickly now," Gentle said. "Into the root cellar. We've only a few hours before dawn."

They carried the body down the stone steps into the cellar. It was warmer down there than up on the surface, and as Gentle lit the coal oil lamp near the entrance, the room ignited with flickering golden light, so that every surface seemed to sway and tremble with quiet anticipation.

There was a time when the shelves that ran along each wall of the cellar had been packed with Liam's alchemical supplies. Bottles of gold flakes and silver shavings, packets of nitrate and salt. With the money he'd made embalming soldiers during the war, he acquired for himself a seemingly inexhaustible supply of every mineral and chemical compound known to man, lest he find himself lacking when inspiration struck. But as the years passed, and their money disappeared in a steady trickle, Liam's supplies had grown scarce, until the only objects left on the shelves were a few disparate chunks of charcoal and iron and his gangly legion of glass beakers, whose names—lute, alembic, cucurbit—forever eluded Gentle.

Kitt and Gentle carried Liam's body to the wooden table in the center of the room and laid him flat. They stood there panting, the smell of their sweat mingling with the scent of clay and stone in the air. Now that Liam had been brought into the light, Gentle could finally take a good look at his friend. Though Gentle had spent the better part of his life handling dead bodies, the sight of Liam's corpse, still dressed in the grimy cotton shirt and suspenders he'd been wearing the last time Gentle had seen him, made him hesitate. It wasn't simply the image of his friend's frail, stiff body that disturbed him. In the years he and Liam had been in business together, Gentle had become intimately familiar with all the different ways death could dispatch a person on the frontier. He'd seen torsos riddled with bullets, crushed by falling trees, and torn apart by wild animals. And while he sometimes handled folks who'd died peacefully in their sleep, more often than not he preserved the bodies of those who'd died long before a single gray hair had sprouted on their heads. Sometimes even children no older than a few hours, who'd barely had time to squint their eyes against the bright and dreadful light of the world before slipping back to the cool darkness from which they'd emerged.

By now, Gentle considered himself an unsentimental soldier in humanity's eternal war against mortality. Yet faced with Liam's corpse he found himself suddenly unable to move. What distressed him was the fundamental *wrongness* of seeing Liam lying there on the table. Liam had always seemed more like a force of nature than a man, and to be faced with the reality of his death was like being told that a mountain or a sea had died. Such nonsense strained against the universe's most fundamental truths. He certainly didn't look like someone who should be dead. At forty-three, only a few stiff wrinkles had taken up residence at the edges of his green eyes, and the effect of this was to make him look more, not less, vital. Like a man who'd already weathered the worst of life's troubles and come out stronger on the other side. He was still handsome, too, with his high cheekbones and pouting lips, which seemed perpetually poised to break out into one of his self-effacing grins.

"Are you all right?" Kitt said.

"Of course I am," Gentle replied. As if to prove this, he heaved Liam's body onto its belly and began striking him fiercely on the back, stopping every now and then to tilt Liam's head to the side and inspect his mouth. Kitt gaped at him from the corner of the room, horrified.

"I knew it," Gentle announced triumphantly. "Not a drop of water in his lungs. And they expect me to believe he drowned. Imbeciles."

Just to be sure, Gentle repeated the technique a few more times.

"Doesn't look like he was killed by a giant salamander," Kitt said.

This was true: Liam, so far as Gentle could tell, appeared unharmed. There was no obvious evidence of violence anywhere on his body.

"Unsurprising. The salamander's primary weapons are likely psychospiritual in nature."

"Psychowhat?"

Gentle waved him away. "You can go back to the house now. The embalming will take some time."

"I'd like to watch," Kitt replied, "if that's all right with you."

"It will be bloody," Gentle said.

"My father is a rancher," Kitt replied. "I'm no stranger to blood."

"Then go get me some water from the well," Gentle said, pointing at a bucket by the door. "We need to wash him. Grab me my whiskey, too."

While Kitt was gone, Gentle went about removing Liam's clothes. His heart sank at the sight of his friend's pale, naked form, curled like a starving fawn on the table. Scars lacerated his chest and pelvis, remnants of a cannon blast from the war. Liam had been spared the bulk of the canister's shrapnel, but a smattering of his compatriots' bones and viscera had blasted into him like so many bullets, lodging themselves in his flesh. The surgeons had done their best to clean him up, Liam said, but bits of his fellow soldiers were too small, and driven too deep, to be removed entirely.

Sometimes, when his thoughts turned somber, Liam liked to point at the scars and say: "I am pregnant with the deaths of many men."

To have survived so much, Gentle thought, and wind up like this?

He heard the cellar's door creak open. Kitt stood at the top of the stairs, a bucket of water swaying in one hand, the bottle of whiskey in the other. The wet smell of cedar followed him down the steps. When his eyes readjusted to the dark and recognized Liam's naked form, a flood of crimson rushed over his cheeks.

"Shouldn't we cover him?" he said, looking away.

"Why would we do that?" Gentle yanked the bottle from Kitt's hand and wet his mouth with the cold alcohol.

"It's more dignified."

"There is nothing more dignified than the human body in its natural state."

Gentle grabbed a rag from a nearby shelf and dunked it in the bucket of water. Quickly, he scraped the wet rag over Liam's body, scowling at the gray tide that formed in its wake. The priest hadn't even bothered to wash Liam before shoving him in a coffin.

When this was finished, he grabbed his leather embalming case from the shelf. Two fasteners on the case's side unclipped and allowed it to fold out flat on the table, providing Gentle a comprehensive view of the scalpels, vacuum pumps, razors, and skin dyes that were essential to his trade. Technically the wrinkled leather bag belonged to Liam, but in the past few years, as Liam's lab work began to take up most of his time and the embalming was left to Gentle, he'd come to consider the case his most sacred possession.

As he slipped a scalpel free, he felt Kitt hovering just behind his shoulder.

"Planning on cutting him up yourself?" Gentle said.

"Sorry," Kitt mumbled. He stepped back and leaned against the wall. "I just wanted to see what you were doing."

Kitt managed to observe the work for nearly an hour, much longer than many of Gentle's usual clients, who generally fled the room at the first sight of his tools. Once Gentle took out his trocar and began draining his friend's belly of gas, though, the boy's face took on a decidedly sickly shade.

Gentle had been counting on this. He handed Kitt a bottle of a tincture he'd prepared while the boy was collecting the water.

"Drink this," he said. "It will help you calm down."

"I'm fine," Kitt mumbled.

"Just drink it."

The boy took a tentative sip. Once he seemed to recognize the sweetness of the brew, he glugged down the rest in one gulp.

"What's this?" he said.

"Chloral hydrate and sugar. Very calming."

"Yes," Kitt said. "I think I feel it working already."

After fifteen minutes or so, the tincture had completed its work. Kitt slumped to the floor, fast asleep.

Gentle moved quickly after that. He set down his tools and hoisted the boy's limp body over his shoulder.

"Sorry, kid," he said.

He carried him up the stairs and back outside. Dawn was just breaking, and the day looked to be as dreary as one might expect from the peninsula in November. The sky overhead was a flat, untextured slab of gray, like a tombstone suspended above the tips of the nearby trees. In the house he laid the boy on his bed and tucked him under the quilts, then went to the kitchen and grabbed a slip of parchment paper and a grease pencil from one of the cabinets.

Apologies for the abrupt exit, he wrote. *Thank you for your help. When the sheriff comes by, give him this money and tell him to get you on the next train east.*

Gentle struggled to find the proper words with which to end the letter. Should he offer some sort of ancestral wisdom to the boy? Some profound truth he'd sifted out of the gray wastes of his own life? Liam, he knew, would know exactly what words Kitt needed to hear. But Gentle's mind could conjure up no comforting insights, so instead he finished the letter with one of Liam's favorite quotes from Paracelsus, an adage he was fond of delivering whenever times were tough: *Be not another, if you can be yourself.*

He hoped Kitt would find some comfort in this. The boy didn't seem so bad.

He left a stack of bills on top of the letter—a few dollars from the Port Townsend job, minus the money he'd need on the road—and returned to the cellar again, where Liam's body was waiting for him on the table. He lifted his friend off the table and carried him up the cellar steps, then set him back on the ground and headed around to the back of the house. There, beside the stack of firewood he kept a small, miserly casket, cobbled together from thin cedar and rusty nails, that he normally used to transport bodies from rural areas to the nearest train station or port. He carried it over to the small shed where Abe lived, a tilted hut that smelled perpetually of wet hay and shit. The mule was already awake and waiting, his massive head thrust through the shed's solitary window. Gentle led him out of the structure and over to Liam. At the sight of his owner's body, Abe's steps quickened, and Gentle watched, his heart slithering up to the back of his throat, as the great beast leaned over Liam's tiny body and tousled his hair with the tip of his snout. When Liam didn't respond, Abe nudged him again, a bit more forcefully, and when this, too, failed to wake him, the mule gave a distressed whiny and trotted fretfully back and forth beside him.

"I know," Gentle whispered, tossing some oilcloth he'd grabbed from the shed over the mule's shoulders.

Even after Liam had been placed in the casket, the combined weight of his body and the box was light enough that Gentle was able to heave the casket on top of the cloth and perch it on Abe's broad and muscled back. The mule seemed aware of Gentle's aims, and even widened his stance a little, so that the casket remained stationary while Gentle ran a rope over its top and under Abe's belly half a dozen times, careful to ensure that it was tight enough to keep the casket in place but loose enough not to cause the mule any unnecessary discomfort.

He ran a hand through Abe's shaggy mane after he was finished. "How do we feel?" he asked. "Think you'll manage?"

Abe tossed his head back and forth in what Gentle could only interpret as excitement.

"Just one more thing," Gentle said.

He descended the stairs into the cellar, where he grabbed his leather bag of tools—they were too precious to leave behind—and Liam's remaining tinctures, including the final three bottles of Sweet Vitriol, nestled in their tin box at the back of one of the shelves. After these had been safely secured, along with his camping supplies, he gave his breast pocket a conclusive slap, just to make sure Liam's Liber Alchimiae was still safely in place above his heart.

With this, he had everything he needed to finish Liam's work.

Or, rather, nearly everything.

The final ingredient was still out there, rushing headlong through the cold waters of the river, the old earth made manifest in glistening skin and gaping maw. All Gentle had to do now was track it down and bleed it dry.

The sun had finally breached the edge of the mountains, burning off the overcast and hurling a wave of gold over the landscape. As he led Abe around the house, Gentle noticed a buck standing in the distant trees, its lower body hidden behind the ferns. Taken with the warming glow of the first real sunshine Gentle had seen in weeks, the animal was an unmistakably good sign. The stag, Gentle knew, was a symbol of spiritual regeneration. The harbinger of the sun, and new beginnings. Liam had often left out food for them in the winter.

The animal jerked toward him as he approached the road. Gentle stopped, not wanting to startle it, but it was too late. The creature's unblinking eyes studied him for a moment. Then, it stood up.

Not on four legs. But two.

As it rose the forest floor seemed to come with it—a blanket of leaves and sticks swaddled around the buck's body like a green blanket. By the time the stag had come to its full height, it must have been at least six feet tall. It continued to stare at him, unmoving.

Dread prickled Gentle's skin. He did not understand what he was seeing. He remembered what Kitt had told him. Monsters on the road. Animals with the bodies of men. Was it possible the Sweet Vitriol was making him hallucinate? Liam had always told him the tincture should only be taken in low doses. He clenched his eyes shut and held them there for a few moments.

When he opened them again, the stag was gone.

He reached a trembling hand into his coat and removed the Liber Alchimiae from its place against his chest. When he had returned from Port Townsend, he'd found the journal sitting on their kitchen table. Upon seeing it, he'd immediately begun to suspect something was wrong. Liam never let it leave his side. Even when he slept he kept it clasped to his chest.

Liam had left a note on top of the journal. When Gentle read it, he knew. Hours before the sheriff showed up at his door, hat in hand, he knew. Before Mac led him to the graveyard and showed him the hastily dug pauper's grave, he knew. His friend was dead.

Am following the salamander upstream, the note read. *If our work still means anything to you, come find me in the deep waters.*

As Gentle led Abe out of town, he whispered those final words—*come find me in the deep waters*—to himself. He repeated them once, and then twice, and then again and again, until they sounded like a prayer.

II

Nigredo

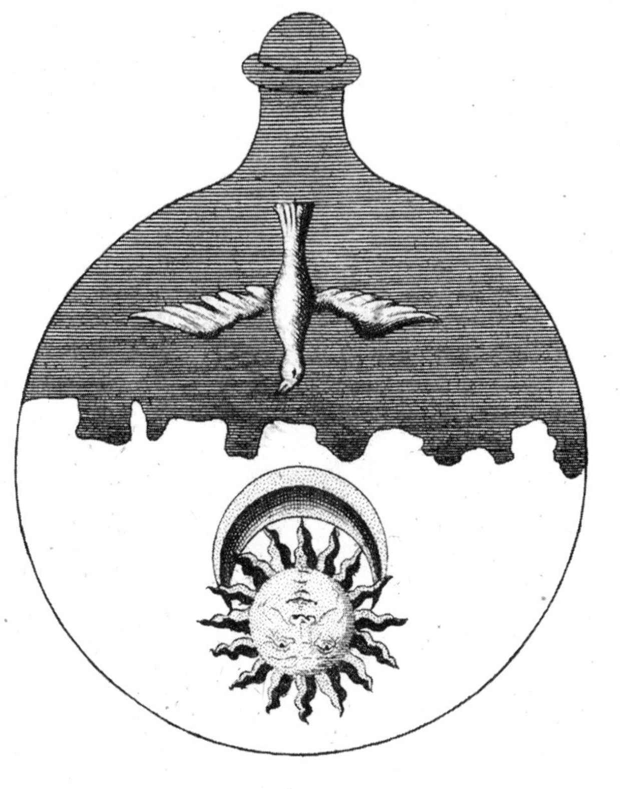

Gentle was halfway to Cedarville when he realized he was being followed. His first thought when he heard the footsteps sprinting through the mud was that he should run: He'd been on edge all morning after he'd seen the strange buck in Dalton Lake. Despite his many attempts to tell himself it was nothing but a bleary illusion caused by sleeplessness, he'd been unable to shake the feeling that something was watching him through the trees.

Yet he was too tired from hiking all day to flee. So when he heard the footfalls behind him he leaned over and grabbed a large stick from beside the trail and swiveled around, brandishing the pitiful branch before him like a spear. But instead of seeing the buck lurching up through the woods he saw only Kitt. The boy's face was red, and he was breathing rapidly. He must have spent the whole morning running just to catch up. He wore Liam's old frock coat, a flimsy jacket checkered with so many patches and strips of stitching that it looked more like a giant chessboard than a cohesive piece of clothing. It fit him surprisingly well. Gentle dropped the stick and kicked it aside, embarrassed.

"Who the hell said you could wear that?" he asked.

"I was cold," Kitt said. He grasped his knees and leaned over, huffing desperately as he tried to catch his breath. "That tonic you gave me was drugged."

"It appears I should have used a higher dose."

"Why would you drug me?"

"I had a feeling you were the persistent type. Clearly I was correct."

Gentle watched as the boy gagged and coughed. It had begun to snow, and his breaths formed a tiny armada of floating clouds in front of his mouth.

"I'm coming with you," Kitt finally said.

"No," Gentle said. "You are not."

With that, he began to walk again. He'd gone maybe fifteen yards before he realized Abe was not with him. He turned again and saw the mule standing beside Kitt, sniffing at his coat. He must have recognized Liam's scent on the garment.

"Abe," Gentle said. "Get over here."

The mule ignored him. Kitt reached up and scratched behind his ear. "I don't have anywhere else to go," he said.

"Go back to your father."

"He doesn't want me," Kitt said.

"Don't be dramatic. You've had a fight is all. Apologize and be done with it."

Though Gentle doubted things would be so easy with Emmanuel. Once, when Gentle was fourteen, he'd watched his brother beat a horse to death for the unforgivable crime of bucking him. Gentle had been playing in the upper rafters of their barn one afternoon when Emmanuel led an elegant Missouri Fox Trotter into its stall and began hissing furious curses into its face while twisting its ears. Then, he grabbed a hammer from a nearby stack of tools. Gentle never forgot the horrible sound the creature made when his brother brought down the first blow, on the hard ridge of bone right between its eyes, or the grim smile that flashed across Emmanuel's lips when the first streak of blood slashed across his face.

"I don't want to apologize. I want to go with you. I want to find the salamander."

"You have no idea what you're talking about," Gentle said, pointing west, where the snow-streaked peaks of the peninsula's interior loomed, jagged formations that cleaved up from the earth like the remnants of some cataclysmic explosion. "I'm walking into some of the most inhospitable territory in the whole country. It's never even been mapped."

"Mother was very fond of hiking," Kitt replied. "I'll be fine."

"You will not."

"I made it here, didn't I? It took me nearly a week."

"By *train*," Gentle said. "This is true wilderness I'm talking about. Full of dangers you cannot imagine. Wild animals. Frigid mountain passes. Ferocious native hunters!"

This final threat embarrassed Gentle. The Native people, he'd long observed, were not nearly as dangerous as his fellow white men, who seemed to have no depths of depravity to which they would not lower themselves in the pursuit of their own greed. But they remained a reliable boogeyman for Easterners.

"Mother says the Indians are just as much children of God as the rest of us."

"And what of your mother?" Gentle said. "How will she feel, wondering where her baby boy has gone?"

"I'm not allowed to see her," Kitt said bitterly.

"Your father might change his mind."

The boy shook his head, his eyes glazing over with hurt. Abe seemed to sense his distress: He leaned his head into Kitt's fingers, rolling his neck in pleasure, as if to remind him that there were more important matters at hand than the recounting of painful memories—namely, the scratching of ears.

"I can't protect you," Gentle said.

"I can look after myself. And I'll be useful. I know how to cook and sew."

"I said no. That's the end of it."

Kitt pointed at the casket on Abe's back. "We dug up a dead body together," Kitt said. "I'm an accomplice to your crimes. I can't go back now."

Gentle scoffed. "Mac wouldn't hold you accountable. Just tell him I forced you to do it."

"Or maybe," Kitt said, "I could go straight to the sheriff and tell him where you plan to take that body you stole."

There it was, Gentle thought. The boy really was a spawn of his brother.

"You don't even know where I'm going."

"Cedarville, right? That's what you said yesterday."

Gentle cursed. Of course. How else could the boy have known which road to take out of town? He marched back down the trail and scowled down at his nephew, ensuring his scar was on full display.

"Are you threatening me?" he said.

But Kitt, who'd been so meek the day before, only looked up at his uncle and cocked an eyebrow.

For a few tense seconds they stood there, Gentle scowling down at Kitt while the boy scowled right back at him. Just when it seemed like Gentle might have to take a swing at the child, Abe placed himself between them and began sniffing at Liam's coat again. He turned to Gentle and snorted.

Gentle sighed and unclenched his fists. He tossed his pack onto the ground. "You'll carry my bag," he said. "And if I hear you complain, even once, I'm tying you to a tree and leaving you for the wolves. Now button up that damn coat. This snow will give you a cold."

Kitt grinned and heaved the pack onto his shoulders. It was nearly as large as him, but, to his credit, he offered no objections. He did, however, stare quizzically up at the sky.

"I don't think that's snow," he said.

"Of course it's snow," Gentle said. But when he caught a few flakes on his palm he realized the boy was right. It wasn't snowing. The air was full of ash.

They reached Cedarville just in time to see the hanging.

The fire had already been put out by then, but the inferno's passage could be seen all over town. Cedarville, a ramshackle smattering of clapboard houses surrounded by miles of cleared forest, had always looked like an open wound on the landscape. Even on the best of days, the cookfires and chimneys of the sawmill's workers spewed black smog into the air, which whirred endlessly with the grind of saw blades and the tectonic thundering of timber being dragged up from the river. Gentle often found himself called there to stitch up the dead bodies of men who'd lost limbs to the mill's blades or been crushed like insects in the frothing morass of logjams.

Now, half of the town was a smoldering ruin of charred wood, and the mill, a cavernous structure that could chew through entire forests in a month's time, was only a tangled skeleton of black bones, like some rotting animal whose belly had been picked clean by vultures.

They learned about the fire from a man near the edge of town. He sat on one of the endless stumps that surrounded Cedarville, his clothes and face covered in a slick sheen of soot. The fire had started early in the evening, the man explained, and had grown quickly, fed by the piles of lumber waiting in the warehouse beside the mill. Half the town had burned to the ground before the mill workers finally managed to put it out.

"How did it start?" Gentle asked.

"A couple of madmen. Won't even deny the crime. Said the animals told them to do it."

"The animals?"

"Animals that walked and talked like men."

"That's impossible," Gentle said, heart ramming against his sternum.

"Like I said: madmen," the man replied. "Reverend Judge says they're only pretending to be crazy. Says they're Harmonites, trying to sabotage his business."

"Harmonites?" Kitt asked.

"A couple of overeducated city folk who showed up a few years back and built a little town up in the mountains," Gentle explained. "Called it Harmony. Last I heard they mostly keep to themselves. Never took them for arsonists."

The man shrugged. "Doesn't matter. Either way, they'll be dead soon." He stared at the smoking carcass of the town. Gentle wondered if his home was one of the ones that had burned.

"I'm sorry to ask this," Gentle said. "But I'm looking for an animal. A giant salamander. It's been sighted in the rivers around these parts. I don't suppose you've seen it?"

The man's demeanor abruptly changed. He winced, as if Gentle had pinched him. He jumped to his feet.

"Don't know anything about that," he said. Before Gentle could say any more, the man shoved past him and began heading back down the road toward the forest.

"They're just going to hang them?" Kitt asked. "Won't there be a trial?"

"Why bother?" Gentle replied. He was still watching the man walk away. The man glanced back at Gentle over his shoulder a few times before disappearing into the trees, his face pale. "They already admitted to the crime. They're lucky a hanging is all they're getting."

"How so?"

"You familiar with the term *pound of flesh*?"

"Sure."

"Well, the man who owns this mill—Malcolm Crane—takes it quite literally."

"What does that mean?"

"Means if he catches you stealing from the company store, he'll take the hand that's done the deed."

"That's barbaric."

Gentle shrugged. He grabbed the leather rope hanging from Abe's neck and began to guide the mule toward the muddy path that led into town. "Welcome to Washington."

The boy was silent. But when they reached the edge of Cedarville and found the weary, sooty townsfolk gathered around a makeshift gallows, he stopped to watch, even after Gentle had told him they should keep moving.

"I want to see," Kitt said, barely audible above the voices of the men around them—it was mostly men in Cedarville—who were shouting all manner of profanities up at the gallows. The mill workers were creatures for whom life was brief and brutal, and they prized their scars and broken bones the same way others might cherish a family heirloom. In a way, they lived for moments like this, when the raw viciousness that had been turned against their own bodies for so long could finally be flung back at the world in one roaring burst. The galvanized hum of these events, which Gentle had witnessed far too many times, always seemed to end the same way: with someone, usually anyone unlucky enough to not be a white man in a white town, strung up in a tree or battered in the street.

The last time Gentle had felt it was three years ago, when a mob in Seattle had dragged the city's Chinese residents from their homes and tried to force them into ships bound for San Francisco. There were no Chinese in Dalton Lake, but even there Gentle had listened to residents grumbling at the Wolf's Den about how the sheriff who'd put together a posse in Seattle to halt the forced exodus was a *traitor to his race*. Gentle heard the raw desire in their voices: how terribly they wished they'd been in that crowd. It frightened him, the ease with which they drifted into that sort of talk, as if forming a lynch mob were no more disturbing than trying out a new brand of tobacco.

From this distance, Gentle couldn't identify much about the men on stage. The mill workers had already gone to work on them, and their features were lost beneath a pulpy mess of bruises and blood. Their ages were mostly indistinguishable, but both men appeared to be white and in their early twenties, with long beards and filthy hair.

A third man, dressed in a frock coat and crooked top hat, stood beside them, hands clasped behind his back. He appeared to be an authority figure of some kind—when he began to speak, the crowd briefly quieted down.

"And your names?" he asked the two men.

The shorter of the two men stepped forward.

"We have no need of our old names," he said in a voice of disconcerting confidence, as if he were entirely unaware of the noose dangling mere inches above his head.

"Noted," the man in the top hat said distastefully. "And you admit, here, to your crimes?"

"We started the fires," the man announced, eliciting another ferocious round of insults from the crowd. "But this was only the beginning. The spark that will ignite a great inferno."

Gentle, who'd spent so much of his life repeating Liam's theorems, could easily identify the clumsy cadence of a rehearsed speech.

"Then by the power invested in me by the Reverend Judge Malcolm Crane, I condemn you to hang for your crimes," the man in the top hat said. "I will give you a moment to make peace with your God."

At this, the short man looked back at his companion. The taller man had begun to fidget, a look of fear steadily creeping over his face. The short man muttered something to him, and his companion seemed to relax at the words.

"We have seen Leviathan. The beast that will swallow the world," the short man shouted. "We have joined with the beasts of the forest and earned our place in the green country. We have seen the deep waters and did not avert our eyes!"

A chill slithered through Gentle. Deep waters. He knew those words.

The man said more, but Gentle couldn't hear him over the crowd, who'd grown increasingly agitated with each new word that left his mouth. When it became clear that they would not listen to him, the man stopped speaking and stared over their heads at the sharp rim of the Olympics in the distance.

As the man in the top hat stepped forward to slip a noose around each man's neck, Gentle tried to pull Kitt away again. "Come on," he said.

The boy didn't budge.

"I said come on."

"Just wait," Kitt said. "Please."

Gentle watched the man in the top hat gesture to someone behind the gallows. There was a crack, and the doors beneath both men opened. Their bodies were just beginning to fall when Gentle looked away. He stared at the mud beneath him, churned into a sloppy mess by the boots of the crowd.

When he looked up again, he saw that the short man was already dead—had died, most likely, at the first drop. But the other one still kicked at the air, his eyeballs bulging out of his face like two bright eggs. The crowd was quiet now. In the silence, they could all hear the desperate gurgle and heave of the man as he fought against the noose's strain.

It took him nearly four minutes to die. Gentle knew because he counted the seconds.

By the time the hanged man had finally gone silent, a glob of foamy drool swinging from his bottom lip, the men in the crowd had grown bored with the spectacle. They passed around a bottle of whiskey and spoke amongst themselves, while the fellow in the top hat stepped down from the stage and began announcing the formation of a posse, declaring that the Reverend Judge was willing to pay a good daily wage to those brave enough to join something called the Army of the Olympics.

So far as Gentle could tell, Kitt never once took his eyes off the dead man.

Cedarville's one and only hotel had been spared by the fire, but was stuffed wall-to-wall with the mill's former employees: a weary brigade of dirty, broken men nursing their hurt over tankards of watery ale. This meant Gentle and Kitt would need to sleep elsewhere, preferably a good distance away from the roving bands of belligerent drunks that now patrolled Cedarville's streets. Before they left, though, Gentle gave Kitt a list of supplies and a stack of cash and sent him to the building's attached general store, while he headed over to the hotel bar to inquire about the salamander.

Gentle pushed through the batwing doors and announced that he was looking for news of a giant river monster in the area, and that he was willing to pay fifty dollars to any man willing to track it down. He figured this offer would be met with great interest. After all, most of these men were now unemployed, and fifty dollars was far above the market rate for hunting down an animal, no matter how large. But instead of the line of candidates he expected, he was met with glares of unmistakable hostility from every dingy corner of the packed room. Those not staring at Gentle with outright disdain hunched their shoulders and frowned into their drinks as if they were about to be struck. Even the bartender, an old woman Gentle had once watched beat a man near to death with an axe handle after he insulted her pour, pinched her lips and stared helplessly down at the glass she was polishing behind the bar.

Only one man showed any interest in speaking to Gentle. A grizzled little elder swaddled in stinking furs beckoned frantically from the far side of the room, eyes skittering around suspiciously.

"If I were you I'd cease all mention of that creature," he whispered after Gentle approached. "Unless you aim to see yourself gutted."

"Why's that?"

"Most of these fellows think the monster's cursed."

"So you've seen it, then?"

"Not myself, no. But many have. Get me a drink and I'll tell you the whole of it."

Gentle bought the man a beer and watched him sip it down with agonizing lassitude, licking the sudsy fizz from his mustache after each slurp with the unhurried indolence of a cow chewing its cud. When he finally finished, he leaned back in his chair, unleashed a tremendous belch, and told Gentle all that he knew about the river monster.

Men had first started reporting signs about a month prior. These accounts sounded similar to what Gentle had heard back in Dalton Lake. A massive shadow surging beneath the water's surface down by the mill. A low, miserable moan that rebounded over the rooftops at dawn. Lumbering footsteps from the deep forest so loud they seemed to rattle the town's foundations. And, of course: nightmares. Even before the trees started bleeding, the old man said, the men at the mill began complaining about strange dreams and sleepless nights.

"What do you mean bleeding?"

"I mean the trees started bleeding," the old man replied. "Every single one they brought to the mill. Moment the sawblades touched the wood, blood started gushing out of the trunks."

"You mean sap?"

"I mean blood. Human blood, by the look and the smell of it. Though I guess there's no telling the difference between a man's effluents and a beast's. End of the day the whole place looked like a slaughterhouse. After that folks didn't much want to hear about the creature. A hunter showed up here about a week ago asking about it and they nearly ran the fellow out of town."

Gentle's pulse quickened. "A hunter?"

"That's right. Biggest fellow I've ever seen," the old man said. "Traveling with an Indian. Said he was gonna set up camp a couple miles out of town—'bout two days hiking west of here—and anyone who had news of the beast should come and find him."

Gentle was so thrilled by this information that he bought the man another drink, as well as one for himself. While he guzzled the sour brew, he learned everything he could about the location of the man's camp. Once this was done, Gentle rose to head back outside, but before he could leave the old man reached out and grabbed his arm.

"Tell me," the old man said, looking at Gentle with sudden intensity. "What's your interest in the monster?"

"It's a scientific matter," Gentle replied. He tried to pull his arm away, but the man's grip was surprisingly strong.

"So you aim to study it?"

"In a sense."

The man snickered. "*As you do not know the way the Spirit comes to the bones in the womb of a woman with child, so you do not know the work of God who makes everything.*"

"Pardon?"

"You're not afraid?"

"No," Gentle said, surprised by his certainty. "I'm not."

The old man's fingers unclenched from Gentle's arms. The strange intensity drained from his eyes, and he went back to sipping his drink. "Best of luck to you, friend."

Gentle returned to the street outside, rubbing the place on his arm where the old man had gripped him. Night had fallen and Cedarville, normally alive with the belligerent chaos of men seeking consolation after a long day at the mill, lay all around him in black, silent devastation. Kitt stood with Abe beneath a solitary oil lamp, the casket on the mule's back now cushioned with bags of cornmeal, coffee, and salt pork. Beneath Liam's patchwork jacket, Kitt now wore a flannel shirt and wool pants. His loafers had been replaced by a pair of old boots.

"I didn't tell you to buy new clothes," Gentle said.

Kitt handed him some bills—the leftover money from the supplies. "I traded in my old ones for these."

Gentle counted the money. Forty dollars. "You could have gotten twice this for the shoes alone."

"I didn't want them anymore," the boy said firmly. "Is this where we're staying?"

"No room. Probably for the best."

"And the salamander? Any news?"

"A hunter. A few miles west of here. We'll camp outside town and find him tomorrow."

They headed out into the scorched remains of Cedarville. As they walked, Gentle continued rubbing his arm where the old man had touched him, the memory of that fierce hold clinging to his skin like sap.

They were at the very edge of Cedarville, a few yards away from the collapsed pile of cinder and sheet metal that was once the mill, when they heard the scream. High and shrill, the sound of it cut through Gentle like a cold knife. But he kept walking. Kitt, of course, stopped immediately.

"Someone's in trouble."

"Someone who is not us," Gentle said. "Fights happen all

the time in towns like this. Probably a couple drunks disputing a hand of poker."

"Didn't sound like a couple of drunks."

"Kitt."

But the boy was already heading away from the road, toward the mill's remains. Gentle noticed the faint glow of light emanating from the other side of the wreckage. He called out Kitt's name a few more times in a hissed whisper, but the boy ignored him. With an enraged sigh he tied Abe to a nearby tree and started scaling the rubble in pursuit of his nephew. When he caught up with Kitt, he grabbed his shoulder and pulled him back.

"Stay behind me," he said. "And be quiet. If there's trouble, we run. Understand?"

"I understand."

They crept up and around the bulk of the burned wood to a portion of the mill's wall that had managed to remain standing. From there, Gentle could peer down into the interior of the mill, which the fire had reduced to a blackened crater, while remaining hidden from whoever was beneath them. Gentle peeked around the wall and gasped.

There, standing in the center of the crater, was a small assembly of monsters.

Gentle knew of no other way to describe what he was seeing. The only light came from a single torch held by one of the monsters at the edge of the crowd, but Gentle was able to see that the creatures wore clothes woven together from ferns and filthy scraps of cloth, their shoulders and chests armored by plates of what looked to be femurs and vertebrae. Though they had the bodies of regular men—some tall, some short, some fat, some muscled—each neck ended in the head of an animal. Among the contingent Gentle spotted wolves, bears, bison, and boars. Some carried guns, while others gripped weapons of a more makeshift variety. Spears. Knives. Clubs. Shears. Even a farming scythe, blackened with a curdled edge of dry blood.

A man kneeled in the dirt at the center of the crowd, his hands tied behind his back. It was the Judge's executioner from earlier in the day, Gentle realized. He'd lost his top hat, but Gentle could identify him by his fancy clothes. He whimpered and sobbed beneath the vacant faces of his captors, who appeared entirely unmoved by his lamentations. It looked like a scene from the Liber Alchimiae, Gentle thought. The creatures of the forest standing in righteous judgment over the sins of mankind. Some veiled coda on the necessity of balance in the natural world.

Kitt, who'd been a little ways behind Gentle, tried to maneuver around him to see, but his uncle pushed him back.

"Stop," he said—and despite the boy's assertiveness just moments before, the fear in Gentle's voice made him freeze.

When Gentle looked back down, the man had shuffled forward on his knees. He twisted and jerked against his restraints.

"Please," he whimpered, though there was a lack of fortitude in his words, as if he were an untrained actor reciting lines he'd only just learned. "I am a representative of the Reverend Judge Malcolm Crane."

One of the creatures stepped forward. It was a deer—the same buck from that morning, Gentle was sure—with antlers branching from its head like two great, black hands. It leaned down toward the man in the frock coat and placed a hand on his cheek, almost gently. The man jerked his head away, but the stag tightened its grip, yanking the man's face closer. It reached out with its other hand, so that it could grab both sides of the man's face, and for a moment it almost looked as though it planned to bring its snout down and kiss him. Then it brought a thumb over each of the man's eyes and dug its nails into the sockets.

Gentle had heard many screams in his life. But he had never heard one like this. Impossibly high-pitched, like a kettle at the height of its boil. The crowd of monsters, hearing this, started to scream, too. They neighed and squealed and bellowed, drowning out the man's screams beneath their own bestial chorus.

"What's happening?" Kitt said. Gentle spun around and clamped his hand over the boy's mouth. The boy's eyes bulged above his hand. Gentle pulled him closer and whispered in his ear, hoping the boy could hear him over the screaming animals below.

"Bad men," he said. "They've got the Judge's executioner, and they're hurting him. If they hear us, they'll hurt us too. So we don't make a sound, understood?"

The boy was trying to speak. Gentle pulled down his hand.

"Shouldn't we help?" he whispered.

"There's nothing we can do," Gentle said.

Kitt looked like he was about to start arguing again when a new round of screaming reached them from behind the wall.

"Ready?" Gentle said. The boy nodded.

Gentle took his hand and led him carefully back down through the scraps of burned timber and away from the mill, testing every step before putting his weight down for fear of making a noise. When they reached the dirt again they sprinted away from the structure, not stopping until they reached the road.

"We need to get out of here," Gentle said. He was trying to untie Abe's lead from the tree, but his hands were shaking too fiercely. Despite their caution, Gentle could hear footsteps making their way up and over the mill's remains. Some of the creatures must have heard them creeping through the rubble. The light from their torch grew brighter as the monsters neared the top of the heap. Gentle cursed as his fingers, slick with sweat, slipped off the lead again.

It was Kitt who eventually reached around him and undid the final knot.

They rushed into the woods, the man's screams still echoing in the air long after they'd left Cedarville behind.

They did not stop walking until late the next day. Only then, after the sun had risen and started to set again, did Gentle feel certain that they weren't being followed. On a bluff where Gentle had a good sight line on the road behind them, they dropped their bags to make camp for the night. Gentle told Kitt to make them a fire and was mildly astonished when the boy pulled a tinder box from his leather bag and went about expertly igniting the small heap of wood he'd stacked in the dirt.

He noticed Gentle's surprise. "It's my mother's," he said, tapping the wooden box. "We'd go camping sometimes, in the woods outside the ranch. Mother liked being outdoors."

"A nice escape from Emmanuel, I imagine."

"Yes," Kitt said, more somberly. He began unpacking some of their supplies, slipping a cast-iron grill over the flames. "There was that, too."

It was the first time they'd spoken since the night before. Gentle had taken the boy's silence for terror, but seeing Kitt's face now, he wasn't so sure. As he went about cracking some eggs into the skillet, Gentle noticed that Kitt moved with an unexpected excitement that did not seem fitting for someone who'd nearly been killed a few hours before.

"Is it always like this?" Kitt asked.

"What do you mean?"

"The West," Kitt said, gesturing toward the surrounding wilderness. "I've read novels, of course. But Mother always said those books were fantasies. She said the West was cruel and ugly and a testament to the sordid nature of men's souls. Not some thrilling adventure."

"A fairly accurate summation, I'd say."

"Yet last night *was* thrilling."

The memory of the buck digging its thumbs into the man's eyes flashed in Gentle's mind. He reminded himself that Kitt had not seen the act—yet the boy had certainly known they'd been in mortal danger. He'd heard the man's horrible screams, same as Gentle. "We could have died."

"But we didn't," Kitt said. He flipped the sizzling eggs in the cast iron with a metal spatula. "Though we might have helped that man if we'd had some guns."

"Two days on the peninsula and you already want to play sheriff," Gentle said. "What the hell do you know about guns?"

"Father had me practice with his rifle every Sunday. It seems dangerous not to carry one."

"Listen to me," Gentle snapped. "There are few things in this world quite so dangerous as a gun. If it bothers you so terribly to travel without one, you're welcome to go back to your father and his rifle."

Kitt's face dropped. He stared down at the eggs. "But you must have used guns in the war."

"I didn't fight in any war," Gentle said. He riffled through his bag and found his flask.

"But my father said that's why you ran away," Kitt said.

"He told you I died, too. Yet here I sit."

"You didn't fight at all?" Kitt said.

"Sorry to disappoint you. Lord knows I tried."

"What happened?"

"Bad timing," he said. "I left home in the middle of the night. Figured I'd stay off the road in case Emmanuel went looking for me. Ended up getting lost in the woods. Six days later I stumbled out of the forest, starving and half dead, and tumbled into a ditch. Cracked my face wide open on a rock. That's where Liam found me. Told me the war had been over for three days. He was carrying the body of some boy who'd died in battle to his family out West. Said he was on his way to the Washington territory. Wanted to go somewhere *unsullied by the tireless march of progress*. Somewhere to finish his work."

"And you just went with him?"

"I did," Gentle said. Because to explain the real reason why he'd agreed to Liam's offer would mean telling Kitt the truth about those six days he spent starving in the woods. And there was no one, no one other than Liam, who'd ever heard that story.

"Weren't you afraid?"

"Not with Liam," Gentle said.

The boy looked at him expectantly, waiting for him to elaborate. Gentle did not. Kitt slid some eggs onto one of their plates, along with a hunk of the bread they'd bought at the general store, and passed it over to his uncle.

"Why do you think those men did what they did?"

"Men?" Gentle said. Because the things he'd seen the night before were not men. All night the gruesome scene replayed in his head, but his mind could land on no logical explanation. No explanation but the salamander, that is. If the creature could give men nightmares and make trees bleed, why couldn't it make beasts walk upright? Why couldn't it let them carry out their vengeance on the men who hunted them down and ravaged their forests? Gentle, with his quest to bring Liam back, was hardly in any position to decide what qualified as rational.

"The ones who killed the Judge's man?" Kitt said.

"Right." Gentle began to eat. The eggs were frustratingly delicious. He tried to think of a story that would make sense to the boy. "Perhaps they were friends of those fellows he hanged. Wanted revenge."

"And the arsonists? Why would they try to burn down Cedarville in the first place?"

"You'd have to dig them up and ask," Gentle said. "They mentioned Leviathan. I suspect they were referring to the salamander. Perhaps the monster has driven them mad."

Or perhaps, Gentle thought, the creatures from Cedarville had once been men, too. Transformed by the salamander into its devoted foot soldiers. Maybe those men on the gallows would have been turned into monsters, too, if they hadn't been caught first.

"*Thou brakest the heads of Leviathan in pieces, and gavest him to be meat to the people inhabiting the wilderness.*"

"What?"

"It's from the Book of Psalms," Kitt replied, as if this were obvious. "One of Mother's favorites. Why would the salamander make them burn down a mill?"

"I don't know," Gentle said. "Back in Dalton Lake its presence had a strange effect on folks."

Gentle told him about the spate of suicides that followed the salamander's first appearance. The boy's response to this news was surprisingly dramatic. He dropped the fork that was currently carrying eggs to his mouth.

"Why would it make them kill themselves?" he said urgently.

"Not sure," Gentle said. He took a drink from his flask. "When Liam first heard from Joe about the lake monster, he told me some story about an alchemist in ancient China who'd once encountered a giant salamander like this one. Supposedly this alchemist was one of the emperor's closest advisors, and when the ruler found out about the monster he asked the alchemist to brew him a potion from the creature's blood, believing that the elixir would allow him to live forever. But the alchemist was untrained, and he made some mistake in his measurements—the potion did not grant eternal life. Instead, it showed the emperor terrible visions, specifically concerning the fall of his empire. The emperor had the alchemist buried alive, and then threw himself off the roof of the tallest tower in the city. A cautionary tale about the hubris of the young. When you're dealing with something as powerful as prima materia, anything is possible."

The boy was silent for a few moments. The fire spat up sparks in the air between them.

"Is that what you think happened to Liam?"

It was Gentle's turn to drop his fork. "Excuse me?"

"I only mean that you didn't find any wounds on his body."

"No man loved life more than Liam," Gentle said. "He dedicated himself body and soul to the usurpation of death. Suicide is a vulgar insult to everything the alchemist believes. An abnegation of the world that Liam found profoundly disgusting. To imply that Liam would do such a thing is not an insult I will suffer to hear again. Am I understood?"

Tears began to gather in the boy's eyes, but he didn't argue. Gentle stood and tossed the rest of his eggs into the fire, where they bubbled and blackened into a repulsive husk. He'd lost his appetite.

"We should get some rest," he said. "We'll head to the hunter's camp early tomorrow. Should only be a mile or so away."

Gentle offered to let the boy sleep beside him in the tent. But his nephew, perhaps hoping to prove his hardiness, said that he'd stay beside the fire and keep it burning through the night. Gentle shrugged; if Kitt was so dull headed as to think that freezing to death made one a real man, there was no point in trying to tell him otherwise.

Because he'd had no Sweet Vitriol before dozing off, Gentle's nightmares came for him in full force. As always, he was drowning, swept along in the cold, dark river. His fingers slipped over wet stones and jammed themselves against the twisted roots of sunken logs. The water held him down with malevolent force, his head only ever surfacing for a brief moment, just enough time for a few frantic breaths before he was pulled back into the depths again.

As always, hopelessness wore him down to a raw nub. Despair stretched him to a single filament, a throbbing wire of anguish. Just when it seemed like he could bear it no longer, two hands surged through the water and took hold of him, dragging him up out of the cold and tossing him onto the wet bank of the river.

As always, a moment of relief. A second to catch his breath. And then the sight of the boy who'd saved him. A boy missing half of his face—the upper right quadrant of his head scooped into a half-moon of bone and brain matter. A boy fractured beyond repair, and yet in Gentle's dreams he moved as easily as any living person, kneeling over Gentle's chest and circling his hands, almost tenderly, around Gentle's neck. Smiling his crooked smile, the sinews of his jaw visible as his lips stretched upward, he pressed his full weight against Gentle's throat. Gentle began to struggle, but to no avail. Despite his thin arms and pale complexion, the boy was as heavy and unyielding as a block of iron.

Normally, this was when Gentle woke up, fingers clawing at his neck and throat gasping for air. But that night, as he lay there on the riverbank, thrashing helplessly in the boy's hands, the iron grip around his neck suddenly slackened. Gentle watched as the boy's mangled visage rearranged itself: The skin healed into a featureless plane, which quickly grew into a softly rounded head bisected by a thin, wide maw. Two black eyes bulbed out from either side of the white flesh, staring down at Gentle with an indifference that made his skin crawl.

The salamander pointed one hand—still the boy's hands, Gentle noticed—off farther into the Ohio forest. As Gentle sat up and looked in that direction, he found himself crawling, not through trees, but through a winding tunnel of ice. As he approached the end of the tunnel, he saw that the ice formed a circular window, through which light was pouring. After Gentle's eyes adjusted, he found himself staring out over a vast valley of incomprehensible splendor. A plain of green grasses extended in all directions, rising and falling in glossy waves with every gust of wind. In the center of this valley was the largest tree Gentle had ever seen, its trunk so wide and tall it seemed to be holding up the heavens. Every branch was flush with fluttering leaves, and nestled beneath these were numberless blue-black fruits, each with its own peculiar, rounded shape.

Despite the salamander's unblinking gaze upon him, Gentle felt a profound peace wash over his body. He knew this place—he'd seen it, redrawn and reimagined under different names in the pages of Liam's Liber Alchimiae. Paradise. The Promised Land. Arcadia. Elysium. Eden.

What could that great golden tree be, then, but the tree of life?

Gentle was surprised to feel warm tears running down his face. He tried to rise to his feet, but the salamander boy held him back. Gentle looked up into the creature's face, and it pointed once more at the valley, as if it thought Gentle had misunderstood something. As if it wanted him to look closer. So he did.

A deep unrest began to nibble away at Gentle's contentment. At first he couldn't understand why—so far as he could tell, nothing about the scene before him had changed. But the longer he stared at the tree, the more certain he became that something was wrong. And then he understood: It was the fruit. The strange, misshapen fruit hanging from every branch.

It wasn't fruit at all.

It was heads.

Human heads. Heads of men and women. Heads of children and infants. Heads of every race and age. Gentle's vision skittered over the golden branches, unable to look away, until it froze on a face that he recognized.

Liam.

His face was a mask of incomprehensible pain, his red hair greasy and caked with mud. His lips creaked apart like the walls of a tomb being pried open, and out of them came two words, which he repeated again and again, louder and louder, until Gentle realized that every head on the tree was doing the same, their voices filling up the tunnel until Gentle could hear nothing else, even as he pressed his hands over his ears and began to scream.

Deep waters, they said.

First with sorrow, then with rage, and then with desperate desire, like every head was suffering from some unquenchable thirst.

Fire began to flicker along the tree's base. It swarmed through the valley in a red tide, rushed up the tree's trunk and crawled along the branches in a horrible blaze. The heads writhed where they hung, begging Gentle for deep waters while the fire turned the green valley into a sea of flames. Smoke flooded the icy cavern. Gentle tried to crawl away from the fumes, but he was smothered in a black cloud, his lungs wheezing against the blasted particles he inhaled with each breath. Suddenly he was drowning again—not in water, but ash.

Gentle lurched up in his bedroll, gasping. He clawed his way out of the tent like some savage beast ripping itself free from the womb, then collapsed onto his knees in a shivering, sweaty pile. It was still night. Despite Kitt's promise to keep watch, he was now snuggled up against Abe on the ground, both of them fast asleep. The fire was a bed of glowing coals.

Gentle rose shakily to his feet. A peculiar susurration drifted through the air, a ceaseless clicking noise that Gentle could not attach to anything he'd ever heard in the forest. Knowing that sleep would likely be impossible now, he decided to investigate. He grabbed a lantern from the saddlebag and lit it with a match.

The noise was coming from a nearby creek. As Gentle crept down the sloping hill toward the water, the clicking got louder and louder, until it felt as though he had stepped within the chittering gears of some impossibly huge clock. Gentle held the lantern out toward the water and beheld what appeared to be a kind of living carpet: a thousand chitinous legs scrambling over the rocks in the shallow creek, hardened beaks and antennae probing between curled hillocks of slimy tentacles and bulbous, ebony eyes. Within the slithering mass Gentle recognized a few species of crabs and eels, but the majority of the creatures frothing in the water were a mystery to him. Many of them resembled giant insects and snails, with curled shells and armored limbs. Some seemed particularly ill-equipped for the river march, carried along more by the flopping gyrations of their fellow creatures than by any locomotive intention on their part.

The smell of brine wafted off the creek water in abrasive gusts. Despite the chaos, Gentle could tell that all of the strange creatures were moving in the same direction. Upriver. His eyes followed their squirming migration off toward the edge of the lantern's glow, where the creek curved away into a wall of black so abrupt that it seemed to swallow the light. And though Gentle could see nothing beyond that point, his skin suddenly prickled with the awareness of some horrible *immensity* staring back out at him from the forest. He tried to move his legs, to creep closer, to hurl the clarifying light of the lantern's flame upon whatever was waiting for him beyond the creek's bend, but fear held his limbs in such rigid paralysis that he wondered, for a moment, if he was still dreaming.

Was it the salamander? He felt it must be. Some primeval instinct in him seemed to recognize the monster's eyes upon him, refused to allow Gentle's brain to overpower his body's certainty that any movement would bring the salamander's jaws soaring out from the dark to devour him. He had no choice but to stand there—for how long he didn't know—with his muscles aching from the strain, until he heard, above the raucous clattering of the creatures in the creek, the moaning snap of trees bending and twisting around some massive body as it retreated farther into the dark. The creatures slithered on in pursuit, disappearing into the night.

Gentle's muscles relaxed when he was sure that the creature—whatever it was—had gone. He turned away from the creek and made his way back to camp, tripping over roots and stones like a fevered drunk, and crawled back into his tent. He found the

Sweet Vitriol among his bags, uncorked one of the bottles with shaking hands, and took a great gulp before blowing out the lantern's light.

For a moment, while his head was still muddled by the lingering glow of the Sweet Vitriol, Gentle imagined that Liam's death was nothing more than a bad dream—that his friend was crouched on the other side of the canvas flap making his favorite meal: heaps of pancakes and bacon slathered in syrup and butter. Though a lack of funds usually meant that he and Gentle rarely ate much beyond corn cakes and oat porridge, Liam insisted that they sit down for this hearty breakfast at least once a month, since he considered it the *quintessential American meal* and *a great redeemer of the human spirit.*

But when Gentle emerged from the tent it was just Kitt he saw, cooking biscuits over the rekindled fire. Abe's head hung over his shoulder, sniffing at the aromas wafting off the skillet.

"Cold night?" Gentle said.

Kitt patted the mule's rump. "Abe kept me warm."

"Awful kind of him," Gentle murmured. He rooted around in his pack, searching for his flask. When he found it, he took two long, desperate glugs, savoring the warm trickle down his chest. He caught Kitt staring at him strangely when he brought it down again—the same puzzled frown he'd seen on Liam's face whenever his friend caught him turning to the bottle.

"Did you have trouble sleeping?" Kitt asked.

Gentle's strange encounter at the creek turned hazy in the fresh light of morning. Had it actually happened? Or had it just been another nightmare? He could no longer hear the ticking march of the nocturnal crustaceans, and a quick scan of the creek below revealed the same trickling stream he'd seen the day before.

"No more than usual," he said.

"You kept whimpering. Like you were having a bad dream."

Gentle grunted. He grabbed one of the biscuits off the skillet, tossing it back and forth in his hands until it was cool enough to place in his mouth. It was warm, buttery, faintly floral. God. The boy hadn't been lying—he could cook. He finished it in two bites and reached for another. "What's in these?"

"The usual. And some rosemary."

"They're good."

The boy blushed. Gentle wondered if it ever made him dizzy, all that blood rushing to his head every few seconds. "My mother's recipe. It's all she was able to teach me before Father made her stop. He says it's unbecoming in a man to cook."

"Nonsense," Gentle said. "Cooking is a cousin to alchemy. Liam always said a man who couldn't cook was no man at all. He said you could know everything about a person based on what they chose to cook for guests—told you more about them than their name, even."

"Speaking of names," Kitt said. "There's something I've been meaning to ask."

"Ask, then."

"Why Gentle?"

"Just an old joke between Liam and me," Gentle replied. "When we first started working together, I was clumsy with the bodies. Had a knack for dropping them. Liam was always yelling at me—*Gentle, boy, gentle!* After a while he decided it was a more fitting name than Sampson. So I kept it."

"It's very peculiar."

"More peculiar than Kitt? Odd shorthand for Christopher."

"It's not actually short for Christopher. It's short for Kitten. That's what Mother called me when I was young. Father hated it."

Gentle laughed. "My God," he said. "I bet he did."

The boy smiled bitterly. "The first time I ever saw him hit Mother was when she used it in front of him."

Gentle stopped eating. Before he could decide how to respond, the boy stood up and went to fetch some water for their coffee.

They'd been walking for an hour when the unmistakable boom of a rifle shot fractured the calm of the forest. Gentle's first thought was of Cedarville—perhaps some of the Reverend Judge's men had returned to the mill to hunt down the creatures that had killed his executioner. But the gunshot was too close to have come from Cedarville, and it echoed from the opposite direction—the northwest, where the hunter's camp was supposedly located.

Gentle grabbed Abe's lead and shouted for Kitt to hurry. He was so anxious of the possibility that the hunter might have found the salamander and killed it without him that he did not stop to realize that he might be rushing them toward the very same monsters he'd seen back in Cedarville until ten minutes later, when they rounded a bend in the trail and came upon the camp. But by then it was too late for caution—they'd arrived at the source of the gunshot.

The hunter had pitched his camp just off the trail, in a flat expanse that ran up against the gnarled side of a nearby cliff. Gentle didn't know how long the hunter had been at the camp, but he'd clearly had time to settle in: A giant, circular canvas tent had been constructed at the base of the cliff, as well as a smaller lean-to built from sticks and canvas, the two structures separated by a large cookfire still smoking from breakfast.

In front of the tent stood the largest man Gentle had ever seen: a hulking, nearly seven-foot figure wearing a fur cape that ran from the collar of his tasseled jacket down to his belt. A prodigious beard hid most of his face, but beneath the mess of dark hair Gentle could see the hunter was a handsome man, maybe in his late twenties, with chiseled features and dark brown eyes. In his hands, he held a rifle of similarly gargantuan proportions, with a barrel that must have been nearly three feet long, and a wooden stock as thick as Gentle's thigh.

He was pointing the gun at the camp's second occupant—a middle-aged Native woman with pockmarked cheeks and two tight braids of black hair running down her shoulders from beneath a wide-brimmed hat. She was dressed like a man, in a heavy wool coat buttoned up to her throat and a pair of muddy trousers, and sat on the ground with her back against a pine tree. Her own firearm, a simple revolver, was trained on the hunter. Despite the comparatively minuscule size of the weapon in her hand, the woman seemed much calmer than her opponent, and Gentle thought he saw the faintest trace of a spiteful smile tugging at the edges of her chapped lips. On the tree behind her, just a few feet above her head, the bark crumpled into a fist-sized crater. Gentle surmised the mark had been made by the gunshot they'd heard earlier.

Abe whinnied at the sight of a short brown mule on the far side of the camp, which drew the attention of both the hunter and the woman. They turned their heads to glare at Gentle and Kitt without dropping their firearms.

"What do you want?" said the hunter. His voice, despite its distinct Texas twang, was less gruff than Gentle had expected, with the nasally modulation of a banker.

At the sight of the guns, a cold terror darkened the edges of Gentle's vision.

"Well?" the hunter said.

Kitt stared at Gentle, waiting for him to respond. But Gentle's mouth kept filling with saliva, and he had to keep swallowing it back down. Kitt interceded on his behalf. "We're looking for a hunter," he said.

"You've found one," the hunter said. Gentle noticed a familiar slur in the man's speech. He was drunk.

"We're searching for a river monster."

The hunter turned to look at them more closely. Gentle had a clearer view of the rest of his strange outfit, now. His coat and chaps, stitched together out of tanned hides, hung over his body in rigid plates, like the carapace of a giant beetle. On his feet he wore a pair of high-ankle cattleman boots made of alligator skin. The hunter had kept the alligators' snouts and fangs intact, so that each foot ended in a snarling reptilian sneer.

"You've information about the monster?"

"We're looking for it, too," Kitt said.

"Why?"

"Revenge," Gentle said, the words finally emerging from his throat like a hardened clump of congealed blood. "It killed my friend."

The hunter jerked his chin at the casket on Abe's back. "He the one in the box?"

"Yes."

"How long's he been in there? Must reek."

"He's preserved," Gentle replied. He swiped a lock of greasy hair from his face, careful to make sure the hunter could see his scar. Such men, he knew, had great respect for bodily mutilation.

"I promised his family I wouldn't lay him to rest until I'd put the creature down."

Gentle's ruse worked—the hunter bobbed his head reverently, softened by such manly commitment. "I've been following the creature for weeks. It's a savage thing. Wily, too. Like the worst kind of Indian."

At this final word, the hunter shifted his gaze back to the woman, who'd been watching this all unfold without muttering a word or lowering her gun.

"We'd like to help you find it," Gentle said.

"I'm not one for sharing a kill."

"We don't want the kill. Just proof that it's dead."

"Doesn't matter what you want," the woman said, finally speaking. "No one is tracking down any monsters until I get paid."

"Maybe we could put the guns away?" Gentle said. But the two didn't seem to hear him.

"We had an agreement," the hunter said.

"You hired a guide," the woman said. "Not a soldier. You saw the smoke. The woods aren't safe. You want me back in that forest, you'll need to up my pay something considerable." She pointed at the gunshot in the tree behind her. "Shooting at me isn't liable to change my mind."

"You're talking about Cedarville," Gentle said. "The fire. We were there."

The two looked at him again.

"Well, what the hell happened?" the hunter barked.

The beast-men gouging out the executioner's eyes flashed in his mind again. "Some lunatics tried to burn the place down," he said. The truth would only make him sound insane.

"See?" the hunter said. "Just a couple of degenerates up to no good. Hardly worth calling off our hunt."

The woman shook her head. "And who's to say there aren't more of them prowling around the peninsula? Back in Cedarville we heard rumors about people getting kidnapped off the roads. Now folks are setting mills on fire? I'm not risking my life for forty dollars."

"How much do you want?" Kitt said suddenly. Gentle tried to catch the boy's eye—they had barely sixty dollars to their name—but Kitt ignored him.

"At least two hundred," the woman said without hesitation.

"Robbery!" the hunter said.

"We can pay," Kitt said. Gentle watched in amazement as the boy pulled a heavy stack of bills out of his pocket. "Half now, and half when we find the salamander. Does that seem fair?"

By way of answer, the woman holstered her revolver and rose to her feet. She strode over to Kitt and held out her hand. "Manon," she said.

"Kitt," the boy said. "And this is my uncle, Gentle."

Kitt counted out a hundred dollars and placed it in Manon's open palm. Manon folded the money in half and slipped it into her jacket pocket. "Pleasure doing business with you, Kitt," she said. "We'll resume our search tomorrow."

Hatred burned so fiercely on the hunter's face that Gentle feared he might pull the rifle's trigger again. But after a few seconds he let the weapon's barrel drop. A glob of spit, hurled from his lips into a nearby bush, served as his only response. Manon turned away from the group and strolled toward the wooden lean-to on the other side of the camp, whistling.

After she'd disappeared inside her shelter, the hunter turned back to Kitt and Gentle and gestured toward the tent behind him.

"Join me for a drink," he said, not bothering to pretend it was a request. Despite the tent's colossal proportions, the hunter still had to lean down to his waist just to fit through the front flap.

Kitt began to follow, but Gentle grabbed his shoulder.

"That money," he whispered harshly. "Did you steal it from your father?"

"My payment for working on the ranch," Kitt said. "I've been saving it for some time."

"I find it hard to believe that Emmanuel would pay his own son for doing his chores."

"Money," the boy said coldly, "is about the only thing my father has ever given me."

He ducked out of Gentle's grip and headed for the tent.

Hercules Belmont was unlike any hunter Gentle had ever met. The peninsula was full of all manner of beast-slaying men, but they tended to be rough folk, raised under the brutal tutelage of frontier life, where failing to kill one's quarry might mean starving to death. Hercules, on the other hand, had been born in New York, the son of a wealthy financier and a much-respected socialite. He'd been homeschooled by some of the east's greatest minds—by twelve, he could recite the entire Declaration of Independence in Latin, and by fifteen he'd visited every capitol in Europe, as well as a variety of exotic locales scattered throughout Asia and Africa.

He slurred off these accomplishments within fifteen minutes of their entering the tent, whose interior was as extravagant as his biography. The stiff fur of a skinned grizzly covered the floor, while the rest of the space was heaped with trunks and crates and what appeared to be a full-sized bed swaddled in heavy silk sheets. In the center of it all was a squat drafting table, upon which Hercules had laid out a small battalion's worth of rifles, pistols, knives, and ammunition, all of them arranged in tidy rows, as if placed there by a museum curator. Hercules shoved the weapons away and motioned for Gentle and Kitt to sit, while he elaborated on how revolted he'd been by the *decadent femininity of the old world's cities*. Gentle's mind wandered to contemplating where Hercules kept his drink.

"Which is not to say my younger years were easy," Hercules said, cracking his knuckles with such ferocity that Gentle was snapped back to attention. "I was a sickly child. Like your boy here."

He pointed a beefy digit at Kitt, though the man was so drunk that his finger merely pirouetted in front of his face, as though he were tracing out some symbol in the air.

"All skin and bones. Doctors said I had bad lungs. Said I'd be bedridden my whole life. Didn't stop me, though. I could hike and hunt with the best of them. Not that I complained! Because the suffering *healed* me, you see—the more time I spent outdoors, the healthier I became. That and diet, of course. I only eat meat."

"No vegetables at all?" Gentle asked.

"Not if I can help it. Some greens every now and then to keep my bowels regular."

"Do you suffer from rashes?"

Hercules scowled, as if the mere suggestion of such a thing was a grave insult. "Not at all. Healthy as an ox."

"Strange. A diet rich in salts usually requires a counterbalance of the vegetable variety." Liam had once cured a man whose body had broken out in red pustules by prescribing him a simple tincture of lemon and spinach oil.

"Nonsense," Hercules said. He opened one of his trunks and retrieved three small glasses, as well as a bottle of whiskey, his leather vest squeaking with every movement. "The secret to good health is a carnivorous diet. Just look at nature. Which animals are the largest, the strongest, the most fearsome? Bears. Lions. Wolves. Why should man be any different?"

"What about elephants?" Kitt asked meekly.

"Pardon?" Hercules said. "Raise your voice, boy. I've heard mice squeak louder."

"Elephants," Kitt said, his voice still barely more than a whisper. "Elephants don't eat meat. And they're quite large, aren't they?"

For an instant, Hercules looked stupefied, his brow wrinkled into an accordion of ridged muscle. Then, he laughed—a roar that rose up from his belly and sent a painful rattle through the inner cavities of Gentle's ears. "Elephants!" he said, as if Kitt had delivered a clever joke. "I've hunted elephants, you know. Eaten them too. Taste a bit like elk."

"Liam always said," Gentle mumbled, unable to look away from the bottle, "that ground elephant tusk improved one's virility."

"One's what now?"

"I'm not very fond of meat," Kitt mumbled.

Hercules set the glasses on the table and poured a thimble of whiskey into each one. "I can tell," he said. He shook his head mournfully at Gentle, as though he were responsible for Kitt's skimpy frame. "Your son is thin as a rail."

"Nephew," Gentle corrected, and downed his whiskey. When Kitt reached for his own glass, Gentle snatched it up and drank it, too. The heat of the liquor calmed his nerves. Men like Hercules made him anxious. The hunter moved with the brutal assurance of someone who'd never had his sovereignty questioned, slamming his giant fist on the table at the end of every sentence as if the act of speech was a kind of combat. His physical dimensions—his broad shoulders, his enormous biceps and thighs, his shockingly white teeth, each one the size of Gentle's thumb—connoted a lurking, predatory *hunger*, whether it was for meat, or space, or simply air. Even preparing such a man for burial, Gentle thought, would be a trial. How many miles of stitching, how many gallons of embalming fluid, would his prodigious frame require?

"I'd like some whiskey, too," Kitt said.

"That's the spirit." Hercules tilted the bottle toward Kitt's glass again, but Gentle thrust his own glass out instead.

"Boy's too young," he said.

"Nonsense. Had my first drink when I was ten. Puts fire in a man."

"Father let me have wine on holidays," Kitt said.

"I said no."

"Have it your way," Hercules said, filling Gentle's glass. But Gentle could tell, by a subtle shift in the man's tone, that Hercules's estimation of him had suffered. "Let's talk business, then. Before we begin, I'd like to make something clear: Though I appreciate your financial investment in this enterprise, I still intend to be the one to kill this beast. I hired Manon first, after all."

"That's fine," Gentle said. "I've no skill for hunting anyways."

"Very good. So what do you know about the river monster?"

"Salamander," Gentle said.

"Never seen a salamander this size."

"So you've laid eyes on it?"

"No. But I've met those that have. They say it's bigger than any animal they've ever seen. Sound like a salamander to you?"

"Stranger things have happened on the peninsula."

"That I believe. Met an Indian woman farther downriver who was so terrified by the sight of the thing that she packed up her whole family and decided to move inland. Said it was some sort of spirit. A god, even. But you know how easy it is to spook an Indian."

Gentle didn't dignify this final comment with a response. He drank his whiskey, savoring the alcohol's warm, enveloping glow.

"Hell, maybe it *is* a god," Hercules continued. "If so, all the better. How many men can say they've killed a god?"

Kitt gasped.

"Settle yourself. Only joking. I'm a Christian man, same as you. I only mean that this monster is something far beyond your average beast. Maybe the last truly wild animal on the continent. Makes one a bit melancholy, doesn't it? Used to be that the West was full of wild things worth hunting."

Hercules's voice quivered with a strained, almost childish self-pity. He took another long glug of whiskey and burped, his eyes glazed with a gummy film. Gentle squirmed in his chair. The sight of a man in the weepy throes of his own drunkenness always stirred up unfortunate recollections of all the times Liam had been forced to go and collect him, soiled and whimpering, from whatever dank corner he'd slithered into to drink away his nightmares.

"Well," Gentle said, standing. Much as he longed for more whiskey—his own flask was already growing disconcertingly light—he did not intend to listen to yet another drunk eulogy about the end of the frontier. Ever since it was announced that the Washington territory would join the union, every tavern and bar Gentle visited hosted at least one foul-smelling trapper, barely recognizable as human beneath his tattered assemblage of rank racoon pelts, who loudly mourned the end of the West. "We've had a long day's walk. Best set up our tent and get some rest."

"Certainly," Hercules said. "And don't worry about Manon.

I've heard her father was a white man, so she's only half Indian. She came highly recommended."

"I've no concerns," said Gentle coldly.

Hercules nodded. "Hunt like this won't be easy. But I'm sure a man like you is no stranger to violence."

Gentle, who'd already begun heading for the tent's exit, stopped.

"A man like me?" he asked.

"Fought in the war, didn't you?"

Before he could stop himself, Gentle nodded.

Hercules slapped his knee and grinned. "I knew it! You're just the right age. And you've got that scar. Which side you fight for?"

"I am a great admirer of President Lincoln," Gentle said—knowing, as the words left his mouth, that this was a stupid thing to say. Even now, after twenty-four years of peace, an incautious word regarding one's wartime allegiances could easily boil into violence.

Some of the enthusiasm drained from Hercules's face. "A Yankee, then."

"Didn't you say you were born in New York?"

"Born there, sure," Hercules said. "But I own property in Texas now. I've seen firsthand what the Republicans have done to their Northern cities. Man can walk the whole length of Manhattan Island without spotting a single white face. Bet you've seen some glorious battles in your time."

"No," Gentle said.

"Pardon?"

"I never fought. I embalmed the dead."

Hercules looked disappointed. "I suppose there's still dignity in that. I don't blame the Northern soldier for the moral decrepitude of his masters, by the way. Honor on both sides of that war.

One of my greatest regrets was that I was born too late to serve."

Gentle was surprised by the rage that burned inside him. His fingers dug into the rough flesh of his clenched fists. "Only an idiot would dream of being a soldier."

The hazy film that had fallen over Hercules's eyes dissolved. The muscles along his jaw twitched into sharp lines. "Is that so?" he said, his voice suddenly sober.

"Good night," Gentle said. As he led Kitt out of the tent, he felt the hunter's eyes drilling into his back, piercing him like two hot irons.

"Why did you lie to that man?" Kitt asked.

He and Gentle were lying in their bedrolls, listening to the rain patter intermittently against the tent's oilskin roof.

"How do you mean?"

"You didn't tell him about the philosopher's stone."

"That's our business," Gentle said.

"And what about the war? I thought you said you didn't serve."

"I didn't."

"But you told him you did."

"Men like Hercules have a special affection for war."

"So you wanted to impress him," Kitt said thoughtfully.

"Something like that."

"Then why insult him?"

Gentle didn't know why. It was true that he had sometimes allowed men to think he was a veteran when he thought it might serve his interests—while Gentle generally kept his opinions about the traitorous South to himself, he was not above letting some fellow buy him a drink because he assumed, as Hercules had, that he'd obtained his scar in glorious combat. But this had been different. He'd pushed things further than he needed to, lost whatever respect he might have gained by lying about his service.

"Have you ever heard of Andersonville?" Gentle asked.

"No."

"It was a prison camp for Union soldiers down in Georgia. Liam was captured and sent there near the end of the war."

What Liam experienced at Andersonville had so disturbed him, Gentle explained, that he rarely ever spoke of it, though when he did he painted a terrifying picture: a patch of deforested swamp crammed with forty-five thousand men, their only source of water a sluggish river used as both a latrine and a drinking font. The prisoners were not allowed to build any structures to protect themselves from wind or rain, so they wasted away beneath the cruel, open sky, subsisting on rotten cornmeal and raw meat. Most of them died from starvation, but those who didn't spent weeks waiting for death in the muck, tortured by dysentery and typhoid, or murdered by their fellow inmates, who'd organized themselves into competing bands that routinely attacked one another with makeshift weapons. Life in the prison was so wretched that the men sometimes walked to the bottom of the surrounding walls—a stretch of forbidden earth called "the dead line"—so that a guard's bullet would free them from their misery.

The only thing worse than the sight of all those skeletal men piled atop one another like the moldering dead, Liam had once told him, was the stench. The stink, he said, could only be described as the *opposite of life*. A mortifying reek no human being was ever meant to smell. The only reason Liam had survived the place was because it had been liberated a few weeks after his internment. But even such a short indenture had scarred him beyond imagining.

"Andersonville was where Liam had his first vision," Gentle said. Liam had been lying in the muck, dying of hunger and thirst, when he looked up into the sky and saw the Virgin Mary, suspended in the air, her body the size of a mountain and draped in cerulean, her bright red heart pulsing with a crimson light that rivaled the sun's. The heart had been pierced by a golden sword, yet it still pumped with all the vigor of life, and as it did so brilliant red droplets of blood, sparkling like rubies, spurted from the wound and arced across the sky like falling stars. Liam knew, immediately, that to touch one of these glimmering droplets would relieve him of all his suffering—would save not only his soul but the souls of every man in that prison camp. But the blood couldn't reach him, because as it gushed toward the earth it hit an invisible barrier and slid away, as if a glass sphere surrounded the planet. Mary, seeing this, closed her eyes and wept.

"Liam said that was the horrible truth of his realization at Andersonville," Gentle said. "That hell was *here*. Not in some netherworld of burning lakes and cackling demons, but all around us. The barrier he saw, the thing holding back the Virgin's mercy, was just like the walls that kept him and those men trapped in Andersonville. The world is a prison built to punish us."

Kitt was silent for so long that Gentle began to wonder if he'd fallen asleep.

When he spoke again, there was sadness in his voice. "You really believe that?"

"I'd be hard pressed to imagine a place more like hell than this country."

"My mother doesn't believe in hell," Kitt replied. "She says God is too merciful."

"And yet he was still cruel enough to put us here," Gentle

said. No doubt Kitt's mother was one of those naive Evangelicals who prattled on about the beauty of God's creations while she held court in her husband's perfumed tearoom, safely cloistered away from the violence and filth that gushed over the nation each day like a foul wave. It was a story he'd seen repeated throughout the West: rich men opining on the godly glories of progress while their workers toiled away in mines and lumberyards, their minds diluted with drink and the false promise that their endless labor would one day build a paradise on earth.

"Do you really hate the world so much?"

"Asks the boy who crossed a continent just to get away from his own father."

"Not everyone is like him," Kitt said. "My mother isn't."

"Then tell me this: If my brother is so terrible, why did this wonderful mother of yours marry him?"

"She said he was charming when she met him."

"Charming," Gentle said. "Yes. I suppose I could see that."

There were times, when they were boys, that Emmanuel could be kind. More than kind, even—there was a certain charisma, a beguiling allure, that he could exert on people when he wished. Gentle remembered when his brother had taught him how to ride. How he never mocked Gentle for struggling to mount the horse, never raised his voice when he failed to keep the animal under control. Gentle had been surprised to learn that his brother's quiet respect could leave him dizzy with joy, even if he knew that Emmanuel, just a few moments later, might beat him with a strap of leather for failing to clean his saddle properly. In some ways this made him even more frightening: Gentle could never be sure which version of his brother he'd encounter at any particular moment.

"I suppose I just wanted to put that man in his place," Gentle said, returning to Kitt's original question. "Foolish to wish you'd been there."

"But didn't you run away to join the war?"

"I did. And I was a fool. I was fourteen when I left to join the effort. Wanted to avenge my father."

"Grandpa fought?"

"Of course he did. I suppose Emmanuel never mentioned it. He was never fond of Father's convictions."

"He said Grandfather was a drunk."

"A drunk?" Gentle said. "Eliza Montgomery was a hero. He died at Bull Run."

"Father said he got them run out of half a dozen towns before they settled in Ohio. And then abandoned them."

"I think we've verified that your father's version of events leaves much to be desired. Now go to bed."

Gentle wasn't surprised by Emmanuel's deception: Growing up, the only thing his brother disdained more than their abolitionist father was the war that had killed him, which he blamed for *throwing the nation's markets into disarray*. That is, until a beef contract with the Union army made him one of the richest men in Ohio. After that he liked to joke that he hoped the war would never end.

Gentle waited until he heard Kitt's breaths go deep and steady, and then he reached into his bedroll for one of his vials of Sweet Vitriol. He poured two drops of the medicine into what was left of his whiskey and was about to drink it when he noticed Kitt's eyes shining like silver coins in the dark.

"Why do you drink so much?" he asked. There was no accusation in his tone, just genuine curiosity.

Gentle lowered the flask.

"Helps me sleep."

"But you drink during the day, too."

"I suppose that's true."

"Have you always been this way?"

"Not always, no. Had to be much more careful when Liam was around. He didn't approve."

"But now he's not around."

"Right."

"Does it make you feel good?"

"It's more like it makes me not feel anything."

The boy made a thoughtful noise. "Father didn't like to drink," he said. "He told me that drinking was the favored pastime of men without conviction."

"Liam might agree with him on that point," Gentle said. "He hated it when I drank. Said no man ever reached paradise by dulling his senses. Called it the coward's tonic. I suppose that's what he thought of me in the end. That I was a coward."

"I don't think you're a coward," Kitt said. "I think what you're doing is very brave."

"We need to sleep," Gentle said. "We have a long day ahead of us."

"Goodnight, Uncle."

"Goodnight."

Gentle turned away from the boy and drank from his flask. The Sweet Vitriol's effects were immediate and delightful—a soft darkness that drifted through his body like a warm black tide.

The land surrounding the hunting camp was largely swamp, the lowland forest giving way to a tangled mess of stagnant water and overgrown logs. Hiking through the mucky shallows would be a pain, but according to Manon the valley's pervasive wetness would make an appealing home for an aquatic monster, while the mountains to the northwest would form a natural barrier to the creature's progress upriver. It was the perfect spot, she explained, for the salamander to have made its home.

On account of the soggy terrain, it was decided that the mules would be left in camp, with Kitt to watch over them. The boy was not pleased by this turn of events. He even threatened to pull his financing from the entire endeavor if he was not allowed to go with them, until Gentle sat him down and calmly explained that Kitt was the only one he trusted to look after Liam's body. This recognition of his importance clearly pleased him, but he persisted in his complaints until Gentle promised to leave the Liber Alchimiae in his care and assured him that they would return to the camp each night to report their findings.

From the moment they began their search that first day, it was immediately obvious that locating the salamander would not be a straightforward task. Apart from the fact that there were no established trails through the muck, there was also a deeper sort of wrongness permeating their surroundings, a kind of sour unease Gentle tasted in the air the moment their camp fell out of sight. At first, he attributed this to his own paranoia. He had not forgotten about the creatures he'd seen back in Cedarville. He imagined the monsters hiding behind every bush and bramble, ready to leap upon the party the moment they let their guard down. But there'd been no sign of the beasts since they'd entered the swamp, and after an hour or so of stumbling through the sludgy terrain, Manon stopped walking and frowned up into the treetops.

"Something's not right," she said. "Listen."

They stood there for a moment in silence. Gentle was thankful for the break. Already his thighs burned from wading through the ankle-deep waters and sucking mud.

"I don't hear anything," Hercules said.

"Exactly," Manon said. "There's nothing. No insects. No birds."

She was right. All around them the damp forest was deathly still. There was no creak of trunks settling themselves against the shifting temperature or leaning in the wind. No rustle of wings flittering through the treetops, whose skirts of mossy branches stood as rigid as plaster. Even the nearby creek was quiet and unmoving, its surface a spotless window through which Gentle could see a miniature tableau of petrified grasses and stones.

It looked, he thought, more like a painted scene than any living landscape. A forest ripped from the real world and trapped in oil.

"So what?" Hercules said. "It's winter. Woods are quiet in winter."

"It's fall," Manon said. "The peninsula is not quiet in the fall. The elk should be mating. There should be salmon in the river."

"Maybe the salamander scared them off," Gentle said.

"Maybe," Manon said. But her voice did not sound certain.

Now that she'd pointed out the silence, Gentle could focus on nothing else for the remainder of the day. As they marched over decaying logs and squelching peat, he yearned for any sound—the snap of a twig, the snort of some unseen beast retreating into its hovel—not produced by their own passage. More and more the woods felt like a stage of some kind, the set for a play in which he and his companions were the unfortunate actors.

When they returned to camp, hours later, they'd found no evidence of a giant river monster in the woods—just mile after mile of wet, still wilderness. Kitt was seated by the mules, peacefully drawing a picture of Abe in what appeared to be a small sketchbook.

"How'd it go?" he asked as they approached.

"Where's our dinner?" Hercules said before any of them could reply.

Kitt looked around the campsite, as if the meal might be hiding somewhere among the tents and bedrolls.

"I haven't started cooking yet," the boy replied.

"Clearly," Hercules said. "You seem occupied by more important endeavors."

Kitt glanced guiltily down at the sketchbook. The drawing of Abe, Gentle noticed, was quite good. "I was only passing the time," he said.

"Maybe pass the time cooking us some food, then?"

"Of course," the boy replied. He dropped the sketchbook and rose quickly to his feet. He began unpacking the cooking supplies while Hercules lumbered off to his tent and Manon settled down on a stump to smoke. Gentle joined the boy by the fire and tried to help him set up the grill, but Kitt waved him away.

"I said I'd do it," he said.

"Pay that man no mind," Gentle said. "He's just angry we didn't find the salamander today. Not a very patient fellow, I take it."

"He's right," Kitt said. "I promised to look after the camp."

Gentle winced at the boy's deferent tone. He could sense, in Kitt's quick switch to subservience, his brother's violent presence.

"What's on the menu?" he asked, trying to lure the boy back out of himself.

"Just beans and biscuits. Nothing special."

"I suspect they'll be the best beans and biscuits I've ever had."

The slightest hint of a smile formed on Kitt's face. Gentle was surprised by how pleased he was to see it.

Over the next few days, Manon proved herself an efficient guide. The woman skillfully led them through what seemed at first glance an impenetrable bog, always managing to locate a slim trail that allowed them to slip easily through the moldering carcasses of titanic trees and around sudden cliffsides that—had she not been there to guide them—Gentle would have easily slipped down and broken his legs.

On the second day they began to find their first evidence of the salamander's presence. A tunnel of cedars bent at odd angles, as if some giant shape had been forced through them. A stretch of earth that seemed suspiciously flat, like a long, tubular belly had been dragged over its surface. And most exciting of all: a black, sticky mucus they occasionally found draped on rocks and along the flanks of trees. The first time they came upon the stuff, Gentle had tried to collect some in an empty vial, but Manon slapped his hands away.

"Some salamanders excrete poison," she admonished. "I wouldn't risk it."

After she'd turned away, Gentle still tried to scoop some of the phlegm off a tree with his knife. But as he leaned in to scrape at it, his throat began to burn as if he were inhaling toxic fumes. He jerked back, and as he did so he noticed that the bark around the mucus was beginning to peel and crack, like a scab swelling from infection. Stepping back, he noticed that the whole plant seemed sick. A pile of gray leaves had fallen from its branches and lay scattered around its roots, while its trunk slumped unnaturally to one side. The tree looked as though it might liquify at any moment. After that, Gentle made sure not to go anywhere near the black gunk when they encountered it.

At first these signs of the salamander were exciting—each time they came upon one, a surge of energy bolted through the group, hastening their steps. The salamander was just around the corner, it seemed. And yet, every clue inevitably led them to some dead end, with the trail plummeting suddenly into a deep ravine or ending in a sheer wall of rock, as if the salamander had somehow untethered itself from the material world and disappeared entirely.

They were following one such fruitless trail when they came upon one of their strangest discoveries. It was their third day in the swamp, and they'd been chasing a trail of trampled ferns through the undergrowth when they emerged from the swamp into a compact river valley at the edge of the mountains. Above them, wedged between the lower slopes of the two peaks, was a peculiar stone structure, a kind of concrete barrier. A blasting fume of white water crashed through a gap in one end of the wall, while a multistory building rose beside the other end, connected to the thing by a series of huge metal pipes.

"What the hell is that?" Hercules said.

"It looks like a dam," Manon said. It was the most obvious explanation, yet Gentle had never seen a dam of such titanic proportions. A network of scaffolds, cabling, and smokestacks covered the structure in a dizzying complexity whose purpose Gentle could not even begin to understand. Compared to this mountain fortress, the mill in Cedarville—easily the most exceptional piece of human engineering on the peninsula before it had been burned down—looked like the work of simple-minded apes.

"You mean you've never seen it before?" Gentle asked.

Manon shook her head.

"Must be one of the Reverend Judge's new projects," Hercules said. "That explains the lack of animals. Workers need food. Probably hunted every bit of game within ten miles."

"Impossible," Manon said. She seemed unnecessarily shaken by the dam's presence. "I was here three weeks ago and there was nothing up there."

"Wonders of American engineering," Hercules replied, less confidently.

"No," Manon said. "That thing looks like it's been here for decades. It's falling apart."

She was right. Gentle had been so impressed by the scale of the dam that he'd failed to notice the leaking cracks along its walls, or the thick mantle of vines clinging to its foundation. The window slots in the attached building were full of shattered glass panes, while the metal silo on its roof was encrusted in rust. Considering its disrepair, Gentle was surprised it was able to hold back the river at all.

"You must be confusing this for another valley," Hercules said.

"I'm not confused. I know exactly where we are," Manon said. "It's impossible for that thing to be here."

"Well, it's here," Hercules said, and the incontestability of the statement left them all standing in dumbstruck silence for a few minutes.

"Should we go inside?" Gentle eventually asked.

"No," Manon replied almost immediately. "I don't want to be here."

Gentle felt it too. Looking at the dam made him feel unwell. The longer he stared, the more the edges of his vision seemed to blur, as if his eyes were trying to erase the image before him. His heartbeat quickened and his palms began to sweat. The hair on his arms and neck rose to attention. It made no sense—it was only a dam. Yet every instinct urged him to turn around and run. His head began to throb terribly, and he had to sip some of his Sweet Vitriol to stave off the pain.

"She's right," Hercules said. The man was pretending to wipe some dirt off his alligator boots, but his face was nearly green with nausea. "It's just a building. Not likely to find a salamander up there."

Gentle offered no complaints. As they descended back the way they'd come, none of them stopped to look back at the impossible building, and the farther they got from it, the less and less real it seemed. By the time they returned to camp, Gentle could almost believe that they had never seen it at all.

But that night Gentle dreamed of the dam. He stood at its base, staring up at its yawning height. He heard the whirring hum of unseen machinery hammering within, felt the electric sting of some immense power throbbing inside the wall like the thunderous heart of a god.

Below him, in the torrential roil of the river, he watched innumerable salmon hurl themselves at the unyielding stone. He felt their despair at finding this unmoving thing standing between them and their spawning pools. In the flurry of thrashing tails and gasping mouths some of the salmon were flung onto the surrounding banks, where Gentle watched them slowly suffocate, their wide eyes staring uncomprehendingly up at the world that had suddenly forsaken them.

Rage rumbled inside Gentle. Rage for the salmon, who would keep thrusting themselves against the wall until exhaustion killed them. Rage for the river, which had been robbed of its ancient flow, strangled to a meager drip. As his rage grew the ground around him seemed to shake. Cracks began to form in the dam's formerly seamless wall, sprouting jets of water and stone into the air. All at once the dam broke and the river rushed out in furious freedom, sweeping Gentle up and carrying him downstream in a whirling chaos of bubbles and foam.

Again he saw the tunnel of ice, the green valley, the burning tree. But these were followed by new sights. A sea of black tar churning its greasy waves over a shore littered with mounds of dead fish. A landscape of twisting, labyrinthine machinery, where the warped tubes and pipes coiled around each other like the rusty veins of some infernal engine, jutting from the nightmare landscape in spires that belched gouts of fire into the sooty atmosphere. A desert crusted in cracked earth and swirling dust, where the only protection from the unrelenting glare of the sun was the spindly, crooked remains of trees that dotted the landscape like so many spent matches.

Coiled in the center of each desolation, the salamander waited for him, staring at Gentle with unmistakable hatred, its white skin so bright it blinded him. The monster opened its wide mouth and Gentle heard its howl, booming over the landscape in a deep, mournful voice.

Deep waters, it cried. *Deep waters. Deep waters.*

For the rest of the week, the hunting party's trips became increasingly tense affairs. The silence of the forest continued to feel like a warning. Though it never rained, the air was thick with moisture. Gentle was no stranger to the perpetual damp of the Pacific Northwest—he and Liam had passed many mornings sitting on their cabin's porch, watching the rain descend over the mountains in a hazy curtain—but this constant wetness, which seeped through his clothes and left his skin red and chafed, felt somehow predatory, as if the landscape itself were trying to soften him up for eventual consumption. More than once Gentle felt so dispirited by discomfort and exhaustion that he felt like his body might simply surrender, slumping down into the mud and waiting for the forest to devour him. He shivered at the thought of what he knew came next: the animals and insects picking his flesh clean, the mushrooms sprouting from the loamy pockets of his eye sockets, the ever-patient roots slithering over him like so many twisting eels, poking and prodding his corpse for lingering bits of fertile mulch. He knew how hungry these forests were—how little time it took for them to disassemble a living thing into another layer of soggy soil.

They returned from these trips cold, damp, and depleted. They developed coughs, runny noses, strange rashes. The water in their canteens, Gentle noticed, began to take on the same sour tang that had infected the wells back in Dalton Lake. No matter how long they sat by the fire, none of them seemed to be able to get dry.

Kitt tried his best to keep their camp in order. But the boy had a knack for distraction—most days they returned to find he'd wandered off to draw some interesting mushrooms or burnt their beans after leaving the skillet over the flames for too long. He was especially entranced by the Liber Alchimiae, and often spent dinner peppering Gentle with questions about the alchemical arts. Gentle did his best to impart what he'd learned from Liam. He explained the basic rules of the universe, how all things were either stable or volatile, how each one was a combination of earth, fire, air, and water. Using a stick to draw diagrams in the dirt, he elucidated how these elements could further be divided into the two fundamental natures of all creation: wetness and dryness. The feminine and the masculine. The spiritual and the material. All of these elements were present in the human body, Gentle explained, and with proper knowledge of their arrangement, one could conceivably counteract any illness by reestablishing harmony between them. Even death, which was simply the point at which the body's internal balance became so thoroughly disordered that the spirit was expunged like a spectral butterfly from a moldering cocoon.

Gentle found himself calmed by these lectures—reenacting Liam's lessons for Kitt was a comforting reminder of the long nights he'd spent listening to his friend's stories about the alchemists who'd come before them. Egyptian alchemists who received the secrets of metallurgy from white-winged angels. Hebrew alchemists who imbued life into clay golems. Chinese alchemists who pulverized precious stones into pigments and powders that let men and women live for thousands of years. All those incredible people, scattered across the globe, who'd dedicated their lives to the simple belief that mankind did not have to accept its lot in life. That the arrangement of the planets and stars, the plants and minerals, was not random, but held together by a divine thread that could be teased free and reshaped however they liked.

Of course, Kitt's real interest lay in the Liber Alchimiae's enigmatic iconography. Gentle was not surprised; he himself had spent many nights flipping through those pages—after receiving Liam's permission, of course—and marveling at the drawings within. Phoenixes plummeting from swirling clouds into the waiting arms of bejeweled maidens. A muscled hound spewing fire into a bowl of coals. A legion of demons—a seething mass of curled horns, scaled hides, and engorged members—trapped in a glass flute, brandished toward the heavens by a stately emperor in furred robes. Animals of every shape and size paraded over those pages, rams and cocks and wolves, peacocks and whales and tigers, alongside creatures pulled straight from dreams: an elephant whose trunk ended in the head of an axe, a snake whose neck split off into a hundred heads. You could spend your whole life looking through the Liber Alchimiae and still find some new mystery scribbled in its margins.

Kitt wanted Gentle to explain these strange images to him—how could any curious child not?—but Gentle had to admit that his knowledge of the leatherbound journal was limited: It had been given to Liam by his mentor, a mysterious woman named Zelda who had adopted him when he was still a feverish orphan scrounging for scraps in New York. After spending a decade teaching Liam everything she knew about alchemy, she'd passed along the journal to him before dying peacefully in her sleep at the ripe old age of—so she claimed—two hundred and twenty-seven. Even Liam had not entirely understood the book's many hidden meanings. And like any good alchemist, he knew that his understanding might change from day to day, for the alchemist's own place in life—his attitude, his beliefs—could influence an experiment just as easily as his ingredients.

Of considerable interest to Kitt was a drawing in the Liber Alchimiae depicting the world's creation: a sphere hovering in the cosmos, suspended between the primordial waters that preceded Genesis and the light of God's presence. Within the sphere stood the divine hermaphrodite, a broad-shouldered figure with the prodigious organ of a man and the breasts of a woman.

"Do such people exist?" Kitt asked one night near the end of the week.

"Liam says they are exceedingly rare," Gentle replied. "But

there was a time when all of humanity looked this way."

"What about Adam and Eve?" Kitt said.

"Mere metaphors. Adam and Eve are names for the same being. The first rebis. A figure in perfect harmony with itself."

It was only after our fall from grace, Gentle explained, that men and women were torn asunder, forced to wrestle for traces of that ancient unity through acts of what Liam described as *debased coupling*.

"Father always said that men and women were like different species," Kitt said.

"An unsurprising simplification," Gentle said. "The sexes are physical manifestations of a deeper, spiritual disharmony. The more we divide them, the further we stray from the natural order of things."

"He said a man is like a farmer, and a woman is like his field."

Manon, who'd been smoking on the other side of the fire, snorted mockingly. This was a mistake: For most of the week, the woman had managed to avoid Kitt's attention. Now the bright blaze of Kitt's interest swept over her like a spotlight.

"I suppose you prove that isn't true, Miss Manon. You're a lady, but you dress like a man."

The woman looked down at her pants, smoke drifting from her nostrils. "Wouldn't make much sense to hike through the peninsula in petticoats, would it? You can just call me Manon."

"Manon," Kitt repeated. "That's a peculiar name, isn't it?"

"You mean for an Indian," the woman replied from across the fire.

"I only meant I've never heard it before," Kitt said.

"My father named me. He was a Frenchman. A trapper."

"And your mother?"

"Chemakum. She died when I was very young." She pointed

to the scars on her face. "Pox. Almost took me, too."

"A dreadful disease," Gentle murmured. "Liam reckoned it had something to do with the body's dispensations of yellow bile. Could never work out a proper tonic for it, though."

"I'm sorry," Kitt said.

Manon shrugged. "Happened a long time ago."

"Did you grow up here on the peninsula? Is that why you know the woods so well?"

The woman grunted in affirmation.

"Just you and your father?"

"Till I was twelve or so. Then he got sick, too. After that I looked after myself."

"You mean you lived all by yourself in the woods?"

She nodded. The shadows carved little nests into her face.

"Must have been lonely."

"Never very fond of people," she replied pointedly.

"Me neither. Sometimes my father invited his business partners over for dinner, and he would always make such a fuss about the party preparations. He'd spend all week getting things ready, and then when the guests arrived, all they did was sit around smoking cigars and discussing the price of beef. I never wanted to attend, but my father insisted. Said I needed to *learn to assert myself among men of repute*."

Gentle smiled to himself as the boy deepened his voice in mockery of Emmanuel's inflated way of speaking. What he lacked in physical presence, Gentle thought, he more than made up for in conversational tenacity.

When Manon didn't reply, Kitt continued, undeterred. "I suppose your father was very interesting. Is he the one who gave you that necklace?"

Manon's head shot up. Quickly, as though she expected Kitt

to lunge across the fire and steal it, she wrapped her fingers around the strange trinket strung around her neck, a spiraled bit of stone that Gentle had assumed was some kind of charm.

"No," she said. "It belonged to my mother. My father wasn't much for gifts."

"Mine neither. It's a fossil, isn't it? Some sort of sea creature?"

"Yes," she said.

"My mother took me to a museum once, in the city. They had ones just like that, though they were much larger."

"They're all over the mountains if you know where to look for them," she said. For the first time all week Gentle heard something like enthusiasm in her voice. "It's mostly sea life around here. Fish and crabs and other aquatic oddities. I do business with a man back East who pays well for any I bring him."

"How do you think they ended up there?"

"My guess," she said, "is that this whole peninsula used to be underwater. An ocean, most likely."

Gentle snickered, thinking the woman was joking. She glared at him.

"Something funny?"

"I know it rains a lot around here," Gentle replied. "But I'd hardly call it an ocean."

"Not now, of course. The water receded millions of years ago."

Gentle dropped the bottle of whiskey he'd been nursing. The memory of all those slick, crawling things he'd seen in the river after they escaped from Cedarville returned to his mind.

"You can't be serious."

"Are you familiar with the works of Mr. Charles Darwin?"

"He the one you sell those 'fossils' to?"

Manon laughed. It was a short, clipped sort of noise, with a hint of the accidental in it, as though it had slipped from her lips without her permission. "No. He's a scientist. An Englishman. Died seven years ago."

In a rush of words—more words than Gentle had heard the woman speak since they met—Manon outlined Mr. Darwin's theory, which she called *natural selection*. It was the most patently absurd assortment of fantasies and half-truths Gentle had ever heard. The earth, according to this fellow, was old beyond imagining, and every living thing upon it—every bird and beast and fish and flower—had arisen, not through the careful design of some creator, but through the vicissitudes of random chance, growing legs and wings and all varieties of feathers and scales over the course of countless generations. The fossils hidden in the earth, she explained, were the calcified remains of ancient creatures who had roamed the planet long ago, strange monsters who were in fact the ancestors of the ones that lived today, as though God himself were some aspiring chef forever trying out new recipes, discarding fins and adding legs and fingers in pursuit of the perfect dish.

And though it wasn't the strangest of such theories Gentle had heard—a man in Port Angeles had once passed an evening trying to convince him that he'd seen a tribe of giant ape men deep in the woods—Gentle still huffed derisively after Manon had spent a good ten minutes explaining the "evidence" Mr. Darwin put forth in defense of his thinking, which, so far as Gentle could tell, consisted entirely of measuring the beaks of tropical birds.

Manon, who'd been speaking excitedly about how all the animals in the woods around them had originated from just a few distinct species, noticed Gentle rolling his eyes. The smile dropped from her face. "What?"

"I am simply impressed by the lengths some people will go to lend credence to their delusions."

"You doubt Mr. Darwin's theory?"

"More than doubt. I deny it, most vociferously."

"On what grounds?"

"If a man told you the sky was purple, what position might you take to argue against him?"

"I might point to the sky and the obvious truth hanging above us. Mr. Darwin has done so in his book, which anyone can read. How many books have you written?"

"None. But I happen to have in my possession the only one that matters."

"Which is?"

"The Liber Alchimiae."

"You mean your little book of magic?"

Gentle laid his hand protectively across the Liber Alchimiae's cover. "There is more wisdom in a single page of this book," he said, "than in a thousand of your Mr. Darwin's dusty tomes."

"Care to enlighten me?"

"We are mirrors of divinity," Gentle said, trying his best to enunciate clearly despite all the whiskey he'd drunk. "Reflections of God himself, originally placed on this earth to revel in the splendor of his creations. To hear this Darwin fellow tell it, you'd think humanity had crawled out of the dirt by mere chance."

"Uncle," Kitt interjected. "You yourself told me that change is the fundamental rule of the world."

Gentle scowled at this betrayal. He'd been so proud of his explanation of alchemy earlier in the week, yet now the boy appeared to be using it against him.

"While it's true that change is the rule of the *material* world," Gentle said, "in the spiritual one, change itself is unnecessary, because there is only harmony."

"And where is your evidence of this claim?" Manon asked.

"The evidence is all around us," Gentle said. "Tell me, what is more beautiful: a broken egg, or an unbroken one?"

Manon furrowed her brows. "I don't understand the relevance of the question."

"Sure you do," Gentle said. "Anyone would admit that an egg looks best before it is shattered. It is the same with the world. Unbroken things are superior to broken ones."

To Gentle's consternation, Manon laughed again.

"You find this humorous?"

"I'm only thinking," Manon said, "that a man who believed such a thing would have a difficult time making an omelet."

Gentle felt his face redden. He'd bungled the metaphor somehow, he thought, even though he'd heard Liam successfully make this very same argument a thousand times before. But before he could try to articulate his position more clearly, a horrible sound erupted from the far side of camp, where the mules had been tied to trees and left to graze. They rushed over to see what was wrong, and found Abe thrashing in the dirt, bellowing and screeching like someone was jabbing a hot poker into his belly. His flanks were milky with froth, as if he'd been running full speed for miles, and his entire body radiated such heat that, even from a foot or so away, the air around him was hot. Though his eyelids were clenched shut, Gentle could see the frantic movement of his eyes beneath.

"What's wrong with him?" Kitt said. "Is it a seizure?"

"Bad dreams," Gentle replied, carefully maneuvering himself around the huge equine's wheeling hooves. When he got close to his head, he kneeled down and began massaging the mule's snout.

"Wake up, old man," he whispered in Abe's ear. "You're all right now. Just wake up."

He continued stroking Abe's forehead, trying to ignore his

own racing heart. Abe could be ornery, but Gentle had never seen the mule acting this way. He was thinking of the lifeless swamp he'd been hiking through all week—how the land itself seemed rotten somehow. Had that same sickness come for Abe, too? When the animal's pulse finally began to slacken, and he drowsily opened his eyes, Gentle released a tremendous breath he hadn't known he'd been holding in.

"You scared us," he said, scratching Abe's ear. "Eat something that didn't agree with you?"

But Abe did not seem to hear him. He rose shakily to his legs and turned toward the forest, his eyes staring unblinkingly into the night. Gentle followed his gaze, but there was nothing to see but trees and ferns half glazed with light from the fire. Abe's hooves took slow, dragging steps toward the dark, stopping only when he reached the end of his lead. And even then he kept trying to move forward, the leather tensing to a tight wire.

Gentle reached a hand under Abe's head and tried to lure him back toward camp, but the mule was unyielding, his whole body leaning toward the forest like a compass's needle angling toward north.

"Snap out of it," Gentle said.

Abe grunted and jerked forward, practically choking himself on the rope, which had begun to dig into the flesh around his neck.

"Kitt," Gentle said quickly. "Go to my bag and grab the green bottle from the front pouch. Quickly." While Kitt ran off, Gentle turned to Manon. "I need you to help me hold him still."

Manon did not ask him to explain. She stepped forward and wrapped her arms around Abe's head, tugging him back as best she could. Kitt returned with the bottle and held it out to Gentle, who uncorked it and began splashing it against Abe's mouth, slipping his fingers into his lips and rubbing the fluid against his gums, since the animal's teeth were clamped shut. He used nearly the entire bottle, the sweet bite of its contents singeing the air in Gentle's nostrils, before the mule finally began to relax. His shoulders, cables of taut muscle just seconds before, finally dropped, and Abe snorted with sudden excitement, sticking out his tongue to lap up the remaining fluid in Gentle's hands.

"What was in that bottle?" Kitt asked. "Some kind of elixir?"

"Peppermint cordial," Gentle said. "Abe's favorite."

Abe followed them back to camp, plodding happily along as though nothing had happened. But Gentle could not forget the way the mule had yearned toward the forest—how something out there had seemed to entrance him. If Gentle had set him free, he wondered, where would the mule have gone? That night, he dragged his bedding out of their tent and laid it beside Abe. He barely slept, afraid the animal would rise again and try to leave. If he did, Gentle suspected he might not be able to stop himself from untethering Abe's lead and following him wherever it was he was being called to go.

The next day they found where the salamander had been hiding.

Nothing about the morning suggested it would be any different from the rest of that miserable week. They'd been stalking through the woods for three or four hours, hiking through the same wet, listless scenery, when Manon suddenly stopped moving and held up a hand. "I hear something," she said.

It took Gentle a moment, but soon he heard it too: a low hum in the distance, so quiet he might have mistaken it for a bit of tinnitus.

"What is it?" Hercules said.

"Let's find out," Manon replied.

The noise led them to a canyon of sorts, carved out between two rocky hillsides. A feeble trickle of water oozed along the bottom of the cracked ravine, leading deeper within.

"Doesn't look like the sort of place a giant salamander would loiter," Hercules said.

But Manon seemed more intent on ignoring him than usual. She gestured for them to follow. "Keep your voices down," she said.

They spent maybe another hour following the riverbed deeper into the canyon, sticking close to the edges so as not to twist their ankles on the loose stones heaped in the ravine's center. As they walked the sound grew louder and louder, until it seemed to surround them, vibrating in the air like so many thrumming strings. And yet still Gentle could not understand what it could be coming from: It sounded like the hissing of one of Gentle's vacuum pumps as it cycled embalming fluid into a corpse, but much louder. There was a smell, as well. Saccharine, like fruit left too long in the sun, and strong enough to bring tears to Gentle's eyes.

Finally, as they turned a corner and came upon a depression that might have once been a small pond, they discovered the source of both the noise and the stench. After all the horrors of the last few days—the monsters in Cedarville, the lifeless forest, the impossible dam—Gentle had begun to think himself inoculated against whatever new terrors the salamander's trail might have in store for him. And yet none of it had prepared him for what he was looking at now.

There, flung atop one another in a pile of fur, antlers, feathers, and claws, like some savage ziggurat erected for a bloodthirsty deity, were the rotting bodies of the forest's missing animals.

Hanging above the grisly monument was a dense cloud of flies, their buzzing so loud now that Gentle almost couldn't hear the sharp gasp Manon emitted, or the strangled "Christ" Hercules choked out at the sight.

Among the bloated, stinking corpses Gentle spotted every variety of peninsula wildlife: elk, bears, wolves, marmots, crows, and, strangely enough, otters, whose presence there, so far from the coast, made no sense. The animals near the bottom of the pile were in an advanced state of decay, their gaping mouths and weeping eye sockets alive with wriggling maggots.

The group made a slow circuit around the mound, hands clasped over their noses.

"Did hunters do this?" Gentle asked. Manon and Hercules shook their heads.

"No gunshot wounds," Hercules said. "Or knife marks, for that matter."

"Then how?" Gentle said—though the answer was obvious. Giant webbed footprints passed through the mud in front of the mound, leading to a cave jammed into the side of the canyon. The group peered inside the cavern, which extended ten or fifteen meters into the earth. Water trickled through the damp soil in its farther reaches, forming a shallow reservoir in the space where a massive body had cleared out the cave's center. The same black mucus they'd been following all week clung to the cave walls in gummy streaks.

"I don't understand," Gentle said. "Why carry their bodies here, but not eat them?"

"Maybe it prefers the taste of carrion," Hercules said.

"Maybe," Gentle said. But he had the sense that none of them believed this explanation.

Hercules began to wrestle with the straps that secured his

enormous rifle—which he had lovingly dubbed Bertha—to his torso, but Manon stopped him.

"Settle yourself," she said. "It won't be back anytime soon. It's nearly evening."

"How do you know?" Hercules said.

"If it's really a salamander, it'll be most active at night. It won't return till dawn."

"Then we lay a trap and wait."

"And leave our scent all over its nest? We've already got the wind at our backs. Better to come back in the morning, when it's resting. I know a better spot on the other side of this canyon—higher up, where you can shoot at the thing from a safe distance."

"I'm staying," Hercules said. "This might be our only chance."

"Stay if you want," Manon replied. "I'm heading back before the rain starts."

"What rain?" Gentle asked.

As if the question had summoned it, a cold drop of water struck Gentle's forehead. Within seconds, a minor deluge was falling from the sky.

Manon began walking back the way they'd come. Hercules, frowning beneath his dripping fur hood, scowled as he watched her go, then snorted violently and followed her.

Gentle lingered, unable to pull his eyes away from the giant indentation in the cave. Frustration ran riot within him. The salamander might have been there just seconds before and they'd missed it. But he was happy, too; happier than he'd been in days. The presence of the den was just more proof that the salamander was real.

A bit of movement near Gentle's feet caught his attention. Staring down, he saw a rabbit hopping between his boots, its long ears twitching against the rain. The little creature looked as though it were starving—Gentle could see its ribs beneath its matted fur—and showed no fear at Gentle's presence. It shuffled over to the pile of dead animals with uncharacteristic lethargy, stopping every now and then to sway back and forth, as if fighting the urge to fall asleep. As it reached the bottom of the heap it began to climb over the corpses in a sort of daze, slipping every so often on the remnants of the creatures that had come before. When it finally reached the top, it closed its eyes, shuddered, and went limp.

The hunting party arrived back at camp in a wet frenzy, peeling off their drenched coats and shoes and hanging them over the large fire Kitt had prepared under a tarpaulin. As they huddled around the flames, Hercules told Kitt about the den and their plans to return to it the next morning.

"Tomorrow's the day," he said. "I can feel it. A hunter always knows."

Kitt responded to all this with an expression of muted indifference. He'd been uncharacteristically quiet since they returned. He stared into the fire, unblinking, as Hercules wondered aloud about how the salamander's meat might taste, and how long it would take to stuff the thing. He had the perfect spot for it at the top of his staircase back in Texas, he said. The beast would be the first thing a visitor saw upon entering his house.

Kitt's voice interrupted the man's revelry. "What if we don't kill it?" he said.

Hercules laughed. "That's rich."

"I'm serious. You said yourself that it might be a god. What happens to someone who tries to kill a god?"

"It's just an animal," Hercules said.

"We need the blood," Gentle said.

"I've thought of that," Kitt said. "Maybe we could trap it somehow. Just long enough to get the blood."

Frowning, Hercules swiveled his gaze from Gentle to Kitt. "What's this about blood? You said you wanted revenge for your friend."

"Blood. Revenge," Gentle said. "It's all the same."

"Seems mighty specific."

"Something's not right," Kitt said.

"What are you talking about?' Hercules replied.

"I know you can feel it," Kitt said, turning his attention to the rest of the group. "I can hear you at night, you know. All that muttering and groaning? You've been having bad dreams. All of you. About the salamander."

This surprised Gentle. He knew about his own nightmares, but he hadn't suspected the others were suffering from them, too. Looking at Hercules and Manon, though—how they avoided Kitt's gaze, staring instead at the fire with eyes sunken with exhaustion—he had no doubt the boy was telling the truth.

"It's just an animal," Hercules said again.

Gentle felt Kitt's eyes on him. *Tell them*, the boy seemed to be saying. *Tell them what the salamander really is*. But there was no point in trying to explain. People like Hercules and Manon did not understand the intricacies of the hermetic arts—would only laugh at the thought that the salamander's death might have greater, cosmic ramifications. The boy might be right, for all Gentle knew. If the salamander's blood truly was prima materia, if it was really the key to overthrowing death, who could say what effect it might have on the ones who spilled it? Liam had told him plenty of stories about alchemists who'd been struck with strange illnesses—or turned to stone or driven mad—after tampering with forces they didn't understand.

But the stakes were too high. This might be their only chance. He looked at Kitt.

"You're the one who begged me to take you on this hunt," he said.

"But—" Kitt began.

Hercules cut him off. "I haven't spent the last month chasing this beast through hell and high water just to give up because of some bad dreams. The lizard is mine."

"Amphibian," Manon said, breaking her silence.

"What'd you call me?"

"*Amphibian*," Manon said again. "Salamanders live on land and water. So: not a lizard. An amphibian."

"Do you think we should kill it?" Kitt asked.

Manon shrugged, her face inscrutable.

"You're paying me to track the animal. What you all do with it is your business."

"Then let me clarify my intentions," Hercules said. He was looking at Kitt, now, with troubling intensity. "Tomorrow, I'm killing that monster. And if anyone tries to stop me, I'll kill them too. Understood?"

Kitt flinched.

"No need for threats," Gentle interjected. But Hercules ignored him.

"I said, do you understand, boy?"

The Texan twang in Hercules's voice, Gentle noticed, had disappeared entirely.

"I understand," Kitt whispered.

Hercules smiled. He turned to Gentle, the fire's reflection dancing in his eyes. "And you?"

"All I want is the blood," Gentle said.

"Oh, you'll get your blood. Don't you worry about that."

Gentle, Manon, and Hercules left a few hours later, just before dawn. The storm had passed, but a wetness lingered in the air, the forest glistening like a polished stone beneath the moonlight. Hercules forbade Kitt from making a fire—he didn't want the smell of the smoke on them—so they quickly ate some leftover corn cakes from the night before and set out into the darkness. Gentle thought Kitt might fight with them about wanting to come along, but the boy, who looked haggard after another night of restless dreams, didn't utter a single word all morning.

Manon guided them into the woods, stopping every now and then to stare up at the purple patches of sky visible between the treetops. They did not speak as they traveled, so the only sounds they heard were the rhythmic grunting of their breaths and the cracking of sticks snapping beneath their feet. The world seemed poised on the edge of some precipice, suspended over a bottomless pit. By the time the sun began to brighten the sky, the sense of expectation had become intolerable. Gentle's nerves felt so strained that he was compelled to sneak a sip of Sweet Vitriol. The bitter liquid burned away the rigid structure of his distress like one of the acids Liam used for melting down metals, leaving behind a golden slag of euphoria so calming that Gentle started humming, though he stopped when Hercules spun around and glared at him.

Just as Manon promised, the trail hugged the edge of the canyon they'd been hiking through the day before. They must have been a good fifteen feet above the riverbed, now swelled with muddy runoff, their presence mostly obstructed by a thick border of pine trees. This meant that they would have a good vantage point for spotting the salamander, yet they themselves would be hidden among the foliage.

When they reached the spot Manon had told them about—a perch above the canyon carved beneath a great boulder, where they could kneel in the shadows and survey the nest just a few yards away—the salamander was nowhere to be seen. Hercules, who'd settled down into a firing pose with Bertha the moment they arrived, glared at Manon.

"Where the hell is it?" he said. "You told us it slept during the day."

"Calm yourself," Manon replied. "The sun's barely up."

"I swear to God, woman, if we missed our chance, I'll make you pay."

"Strong words for a man whose gun is just as liable to explode in his hands as it is to fire a shot."

The hunter's face bloomed with purple rage. He'd spent most of the week bragging about the giant weapon, which he'd personally designed and constructed himself. "I fired her half a dozen times during testing. She's sturdy as a cannon."

"Right," Manon said.

Gentle could see Hercules gathering some bitter insult into his mouth, but the expression that flashed on Manon's face stopped him. It was a look so alien to the woman's features that Gentle nearly didn't recognize it.

She was afraid.

"Feel that?" she said.

For a moment, Gentle could feel nothing except the steady drumming of his heart. But it soon became clear that the thrumming he felt in his limbs was not his heartbeat at all. The rhythmic thumping was coming from the dirt beneath them. And it was growing stronger.

"God above," Hercules said.

Gentle saw it, too: the great bulk lumbering through the early morning fog. The beast was larger than he ever could have imagined, its body as long and wide as the front carriage of a train engine, though it moved with a careful grace that defied its size, climbing slowly up the rocks leading to its nest with the studied concentration of an old woman navigating a perilous staircase. It matched Joe Fisher's description: a fan-shaped head and short, stubby arms, each easily the size of a grown man's torso, all of it sheathed in rubbery flesh a pale shade of white that seemed, somehow, to be the absolute opposite of all colors, as if the amphibian's body was not a physical presence but a kind of gap in the landscape. A shifting, salamander-shaped incision in the earth that revealed the impossible emptiness behind the world's deceptive heft.

Staring at it, Gentle felt blinded, like the salamander's skin was spreading over his vision, blotting out his sight until all that was left was that singular, depthless whiteness. Any excitement at finally seeing the monster was dwarfed by the paralyzing immensity of his fear. He felt that if he moved even an inch some final defense within him—some glassy protection, like the crystal sphere that surrounded the globe in Liam's drawings—would shatter, and he would be engulfed and washed away by the white swell.

When he finally managed to glance away from the salamander, he found both Hercules and Manon similarly stupefied, staring slack-jawed at the animal as it lumbered past the pile of dead animals toward its den, where it curled up in the damp indentation and tucked its snout into its belly.

They stood there, mesmerized, for a long time, before Hercules took a long, shaky breath and held up his rifle.

"One bullet," he whispered. "Right between the eyes."

It would not be a difficult shot. From their spot, they could see the entirety of the salamander's body in its den. The monster was one huge, white target.

"Stop!"

They turned to see Kitt dashing along the trail behind them, waving his arms wildly through the air. Abe galloped at his heels. The boy must have been creeping along the trail behind them all morning.

"Quiet!" Hercules whispered. "You'll scare it off, for God's sake."

"Please," Kitt said. He was staring, pleadingly, at Gentle. "You can't kill it."

With a scoff, Hercules turned away from the boy, settling into his firing pose again. The salamander, still slumbering in its nest, had not heard them.

"I don't have time for this," the hunter said. He raised his rifle. But Kitt threw himself at Hercules and held on to his arms. Hercules lowered Bertha and frowned at Gentle.

"Control your boy," he said. "Or I'll put a bullet in him."

An icy indifference had slipped into the man's voice. Gentle did not doubt that he was speaking the truth.

"Kitt. Get out of the way."

"I will not," the boy replied. Despite his trembling, Kitt's eyes were blown wide with devotion, like a man lost in the craze of religious revelry.

"It's going to get away," Hercules growled.

"Good," Kitt said.

Gentle saw it right away: that look of terrible calm that settled over Hercules's face. As though the man had suddenly turned to stone. He recognized it for what it was: the cruel detachment that filled some men before acts of violence, a shrugging away of their duties as moral creatures. This look had haunted his childhood, always hiding behind Emmanuel's smirks and snarls, a subterranean cruelty that could shatter the landscape at any moment. Like the time he punished Gentle by holding his little brother's hand over a candle's flame until he began to sob and beg for his forgiveness. His face then had looked the same as Hercules's did now. Entirely impassive, like a monster no longer pretending to be human.

Hercules raised Bertha over his shoulders. Gentle knew what was coming—could see, in his mind, the rifle's stock crashing down into Kitt's bald head.

Gentle's body, acting on no recognizable thought or impulse, hurled itself forward. His arms took hold of Bertha's barrel and for a few terrifying moments, the two men struggled wordlessly on the forest floor. Hercules, being younger and larger than Gentle, was undoubtedly the stronger man, but his efforts to extricate the massive rifle from Gentle's grip were hampered by the fact that Kitt had clamped onto his head like a bear cub attempting to scale a tree, his fingers scrambling to find purchase around the hunter's mouth and eyes.

They wrestled like this for some time, Abe prancing back and forth beside them in nervous indecision, until Kitt leaned forward and clamped his teeth around Hercules's ear. With a swift jerk of his head, Kitt yanked a chunk of the ear free. Hercules gave a shrill cry and let go of Bertha so that he could bring his hands up to his head, and in doing so, allowed Gentle to tumble backward with the rifle in his hands.

Hercules stood at the edge of the canyon, one fist clamped

against his temple, hissing steam through his clenched teeth and glaring at Gentle, who stood just a few yards away, rifle cocked against his shoulder. Kitt, blood dribbling from his lower lip, spit the morsel of Hercules's ear onto the patch of earth directly in front of him, then stared at the pink lump as though he still couldn't quite believe what he'd done.

Manon, who'd watched all this in silence from a few yards away, whistled admiringly.

"Enough!" Gentle said. The gun shook in his hands.

Hercules was staring at the chunk of ear on the ground. Already, a battalion of ants was busy surveying the gory shred of flesh. "My ear," the man said. "You bit off my fucking ear."

"I'm sorry," Kitt said, sounding genuinely remorseful.

Hercules made a move for the boy, but Gentle held up the rifle and shouted his name.

"Stay back," he commanded, hoping Hercules wouldn't notice how the weapon swayed uncertainly in his grip. "Let's talk this out like civilized men."

"Says the one holding the gun," Hercules spat.

"I'd happily set it down if you promise to be reasonable."

Hercules held up his hands in surrender. "You've my word. Now put my Bertha down."

"Don't do it," Kitt said. "He's lying."

Maybe so, Gentle thought. But holding the gun made him nauseous. Bile crept up the back of his throat, scalding his mouth. All he wanted to do was drop the weapon and take a long swig of his Sweet Vitriol.

"You give me your word?"

Hercules pressed his hand to his heart.

"Don't," Kitt said.

Gentle lowered the rifle to the ground. By the time he'd

leaned back up, Hercules had already reached under his coat and grabbed one of his spare revolvers, which he now trained on Kitt and Gentle.

Hercules shook his head, amazed. "You might be the dumbest man I've ever met."

"You gave me your word," Gentle said.

"He bit off my fucking *ear*."

Hercules cocked the gun. But before he could fire, Abe, who was standing just a few feet away from the hunter, gave a dignified snort and reared onto his back legs. The man managed to swing his body back before Abe could plant both enormous hooves on his chest, but the motion tipped him off his balance. He toppled off the edge of the path and down into the canyon below.

After a minute of stunned silence, during which Abe wandered off to munch on some sweetgrass, Gentle sprinted over to the edge of the trail and peered down into the ravine.

"Is he dead?" Kitt asked from behind him.

For a moment, it looked to be so: Hercules was completely still, sprawled in a tangle of ferns at the base of the mound of rotting animals. But then a cough rattled his chest, and the giant's bloodshot eyes sprang open. He rolled on the ground, taking low, wheezing breaths, and scratched at the dirt with his gigantic hands.

"He's alive," Gentle said, relieved.

"Gonna kill you," Hercules moaned. "Gonna kill the both of you."

"Uncle," Kitt said. He was standing beside Gentle now. "The salamander's gone."

He was right. The salamander's nest was empty. The gunshot must have scared the creature away. Strange that they hadn't heard it escape, given its size.

"Damn it all," Gentle said. "Manon, how much farther does this trail go? Do you think we can catch up to it?"

Yet when Gentle turned around, the woman was nowhere to be seen. He called out her name but there was no response.

"She's run off," Gentle said. "She's abandoned us."

"I think we should go," Kitt said. "Mr. Belmont doesn't seem very pleased."

Gentle peered down into the canyon again. Hercules was on his knees, staring down into the earth. Drool hung from his lips in thick strands. He tried to use the mound of animals to steady himself, but his fist slid into the rotting belly of some unidentifiable creature. "Lord," he groaned, jerking his arm out of the corpse and releasing a gush of gore from the cavity it had left behind.

"Stay where you are," he said. "I'm coming back up there."

The canyon's walls were too steep to climb, even for a man of his height. If he wanted to enact his revenge, Hercules would need to double back down the ravine for a mile or so before he reached the upper path. More than enough time for Kitt and Gentle to make their escape.

"We'll go after the salamander ourselves," Gentle said.

"But we don't have a guide," Kitt said. "Or a gun."

Gentle ignored him. A manic energy was surging through his body. Nothing mattered except following the salamander—they couldn't lose it now. Not when they were *so close*. He grabbed Abe's lead and began marching in the direction he thought the salamander must have gone. They still had a whole day of light left, Gentle told himself, and the weather was clear and bright. They would find it. They had to.

But within thirty minutes of their leaving Hercules in the canyon, a legion of black clouds invaded the sky and rain began to fall. First a drizzle, and then a downpour so heavy that Gentle could barely see more than a few feet in front of him. For the rest of the day—during which they found not a single trace of the salamander's existence—the rain did not stop.

III
Albedo

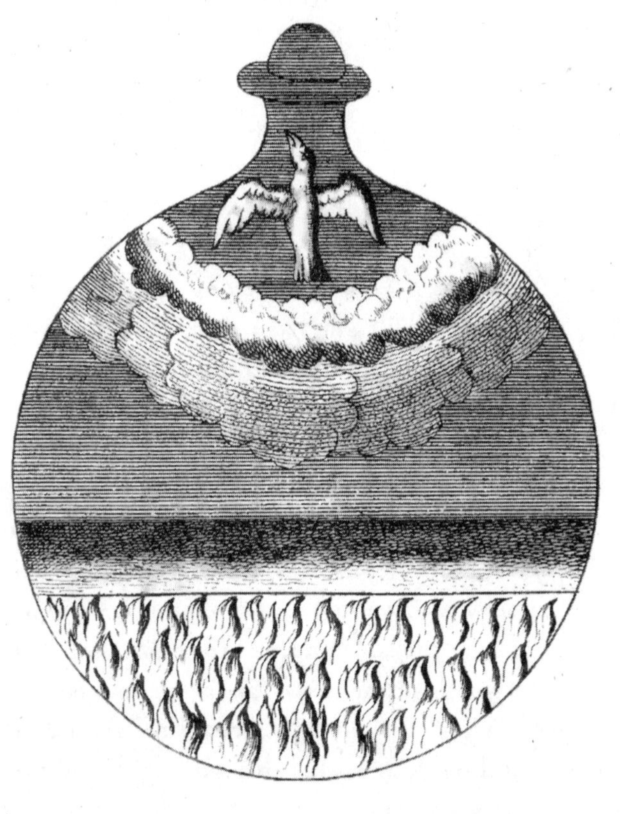

The last time Gentle saw Liam alive, they'd had a fight. It was at the end of October, after months of growing tension in the house—rooted, of course, in the appearance of the salamander.

Liam had been one of the first to hear Joe Fisher talk about the dragon. From the moment he'd heard the old man's tale, he'd become obsessed with seeing the creature himself. Yet Gentle had been skeptical when Liam initially relayed this news to him. Joe was hardly the most reliable source of truth in Dalton Lake. No one had ever gotten a clear answer on his age, but based on the depth of the wrinkles in his face and his glacial pace of moving, Gentle had put it somewhere between eighty and two hundred. Sometimes, during his visits to the Wolf's Den, Gentle had caught the old man fielding intense, whispered debates with his own drink that lasted well into the night.

But these qualities, Liam said, were exactly why he believed

Joe. The man had lived on the lake his whole life—had already been there, in fact, when Mac's father, Gregory Dalton, trekked south from the coast and founded the town, luring a dozen or so unlucky families to the lake by spreading rumors that gold had been found on its shores. If anyone in Dalton Lake could be trusted, Liam reasoned, it was Joe, who'd made his living trading salmon and cedar beer with the hapless townsfolk during their first grueling winters on the peninsula.

Liam's certainty was no surprise to Gentle—his friend had a preternatural conviction that Native people were beings of impossible spiritual and moral purity. His reasoning was simple: Since their customs required them to live in harmony with nature, not unlike Adam and Eve in the garden, they were uniquely protected from modern man's spiritual decay. And no matter how often he was proven otherwise—like the time a Makah man pulled a gun on him after Liam wouldn't stop pestering the fellow about his people's burial practices—he refused to accept Gentle's own theory, which was that Native folk, being people, were capable of all the same virtues and deceptions as the rest of mankind.

Joe's suicide—and the strange behavior of the other townsfolk who encountered the salamander—only solidified Liam's belief that they were dealing with genuine prima materia. All summer Liam searched for the monster, paddling out onto the water in their rickety canoe and spending hours in Dalton Lake's numerous tributaries. But as summer dropped off into fall, Liam became increasingly distressed by the fact that he still hadn't encountered the salamander. Sometimes he disappeared for days, only to return home late in the night, silent and dismayed. A sudden paranoia took root in him, one Gentle had never seen his friend exhibit. Gentle caught him muttering about how the salamander was playing games with him, leading him in circles and laying down false trails. He'd become so preoccupied that by October Gentle couldn't speak to him for longer than a few minutes without the conversation spiraling into Liam's bitter ruminations.

Gentle had entered the house that night with a renewed conviction that he could rescue his friend from this slump. He had received a letter from one of his contacts up in Port Townsend, which was currently enjoying a booming trade in land speculation on account of some rumors that a railway terminus would soon be built there. A young man—another Eastern dandy hoping to make a name for himself out West—had run afoul of some Russians during a poker game and got himself stabbed, and his parents were willing to pay a tidy sum to see their beloved boy returned intact to Pennsylvania from the feral reaches of the West. The owner of the establishment was anxious to throw in some extra cash, too, if Gentle and Liam could get the body out of his cellar by the end of the week.

"It's enough to keep us well-fed through the winter," Gentle said. "Maybe even enough to restock some of the materials in your lab."

But his friend, who was currently hunched over the kitchen table surveying a map of salamander sightings he'd been drafting over the last few months, did not reply.

"Liam," Gentle said. "You hear me? We've got a job."

Liam did not look up. "No time," he muttered.

"What do you mean no time? We haven't made a dime since March. If we don't take this job we'll be eating boot soup come Christmas."

"By then," Liam replied, "hunger will be a thing of the past."

"Well, in the event that you don't achieve immortality by then, perhaps we could make sure we've something in the larder?"

"I do not care about the larder," he said.

"It's just another rumor, Liam."

"A rumor that has driven half the town to hang themselves? A rumor that has fouled the water, the air, our food? Are you really so blind to the world around you?"

Gentle sat down next to him at the table.

"Do you remember, back in seventy-six, when half of Dalton Lake got sick with the flu? Remember how scared folks got? And how it made them crazy? Martha Robinson drowned her infant, thinking she was sparing the babe a more painful death. Peter Miller said a coven of witches was the source. This is no different."

Liam grabbed Gentle's wrist. "But it *is* different," he said. "Can't you see? Look—look, here."

Liam pointed at the Liber Alchimiae, which lay open above his map. The page depicted a man kneeling before a ball of flame encircled by jeweled rings. The man clutched his face, as if to hide his eyes from the sight of the burning sphere.

"In scripture," Liam said, "why do the angels always say *be not afraid*? Because the sight of anything so pure, anything so unsullied by the corruption of the material world, is liable to drive the weak-minded mad. Whatever this creature is, it must be having the same effect. For the unlearned, the sight of prima materia is like staring into the sun. It's like thrusting your hand into an open flame. This is why the ancient alchemists hid their teachings behind symbols and riddles. The uninitiated do more harm than good when they try to tamper with forces they don't understand."

Liam's eyes shifted back to his map: a chaos of lines and dots that looked more like the scribbles of an angry child than any genuine effort at cartography. His voice grew softer as he spoke, as if he didn't care whether Gentle heard his words. He closed his eyes and began to massage his temples, something he always did just before one of his migraines began.

"When was the last time you slept?" Gentle asked. "Or ate a meal?"

Liam waved away the question and reached into the pocket of his vest. His hand returned with a vial of Sweet Vitriol. Liam had used the tincture to treat his headaches for as long as Gentle had known him, but that summer he'd been using the medicine far more frequently. Gentle had even caught him sneaking drops into his morning coffee.

"Hitting that a little hard, don't you think?" Gentle said now.

Liam did not open his eyes. "I should think you know better than to lecture me on the proper dosage of one's medicine. I can smell the whiskey on you."

Gentle blushed. It was true he'd allowed himself a drink or two at the Wolf's Den that afternoon, to celebrate the news of the job up north. He'd chewed a sprig of mint on his way home in hopes of hiding the scent.

"Listen," he said. "The job won't take longer than a few days. It'll do you well to get away from Dalton Lake for a little while. We'll get a room at a hotel and treat ourselves to a feast."

Liam slammed his fist down on the table and turned to look at Gentle. There was a sneering disgust in Liam's tired eyes that Gentle had never seen before. His lips, nearly obscured beneath the mangy red beard he'd allowed to sprout in patches around his cheeks, twisted into a snarl somewhere between anger and agony, as if this expression—so novel on Liam's normally inviting features—extracted considerable pain for each second it remained on his face.

"Who *are* you?" he said.

"What?"

"You heard me," Liam said. "Who are you? And what have you done with my dear friend Gentle? Where is the boy I found in that forest? The one who refused to die—who *clung* to life despite the miserable, meager allotment of joy the world had allowed him thus far?"

"You're being absurd."

"You're being absurd!" Liam said, shouting now. "For twenty years we have toiled away in this damp corner of the world, and what do we have to show for it? A thousand bodies stitched up and shoveled into the earth? We were meant to conquer death, not serve as its handmaidens. We're running out of time, for God's sake!"

Liam had begun to tear at his hair. Gentle felt frightened. His friend was prone to fits of melancholy and bouts of despair, but he'd never seen him so thoroughly racked. He reached out and grabbed Liam's shoulder, shuddering at how thin his friend had become.

"We've plenty of time," he said.

Liam jerked away from his touch and jumped to his feet, kicking over his chair.

"We do not have time! Take a look around, Gentle. Look what this country has done. What it's *becoming*. All of the death, all of the horror. It's mere prelude. You weren't in the war. You don't know. You simply don't know."

"The war is over, Liam."

"No," he said. "Oh, no. The war marches on. Look what we've done to the natives. And when we've finished putting them to the sword, we'll find someone else—more bodies to shovel into the furnaces. More flesh left to rot in the sun. It will go on and on until the whole blasted planet is one putrid battlefield. Unless we fix it. Unless we *end* death. Finish the Great Work. If we don't, what has any of this been for?"

With these last words Liam threw back his arms, encompassing the whole of their little cabin—and with it, the cumulative years that he and Gentle had spent living there. Gentle felt a deep pang in his chest over the ease with which Liam had reduced their lives to something pointless.

"We've helped plenty of folks in our time," Gentle said.

Liam let out a hateful laugh. "Bouts of indigestion? Rashes and toothaches? Is that to be our mark on the world? If that's enough for you—by all means, go north and collect your silver pieces. Maybe I've misunderstood the sort of man you are."

Gentle rose to his feet. He was surprised to feel a heaviness gathering behind his eyes. He told himself that Liam did not mean these things. That he was just tired, and hungry, and sick—and that it was Gentle's job, as his friend, to lure him back to earth so he could recover his strength. Hadn't he done it a million times before? Hauled him from the lab to his bed when he'd gone days without sleeping? Stitched together his clothes after he'd torn them tromping off into the wilderness in search of odd herbs? Risen groggily from bed in the early morning to record the ingredients of some tincture Liam had seen in a dream? Boiling a pot of coffee and staying up with him through the long winter nights when memories of the war kept him from sleep? Wasn't that his sacred role in this arrangement? The sturdy, steadfast foundation upon which Liam could build his crystal palaces.

He knew that he should tell Liam that he had not lost his faith. That there was still no one else in the world that he admired as much as his friend. That if Liam wanted to drag him through the swamps and rivers of the peninsula he would go—of course he would go. But something stopped him. Some stubborn embarrassment over the way Liam had disregarded their decades together as if they were no more than a passing fancy he'd suddenly grown tired of.

"Yes," he said. "Maybe you never understood me at all. Or maybe you're just an old fool who's wasted his life chasing his own delusions."

And then he left, hiking up to Port Townsend on his own. When he finished with the dead man, he stayed an extra week at the port just to spite Liam, using a portion of the money from the job to get a room at a new hotel and indulge in one of the most heroic bouts of drinking he'd undertaken in years.

Only later would he learn what had happened. According to the sheriff's report, Liam headed south a few days after Gentle's departure, to the last place the salamander had been seen. There, he rented a boat from a farmer and paddled upriver, where the waterway split into a twisted snare of smaller channels. He promised to have the boat back by evening, but never returned. The farmer, afraid he'd been swindled, alerted the sheriff, and the next morning they set out in search of Liam. It didn't take long to find his body, tangled in some roots in a small creek half a mile or so from the farmer's house. The boat was discovered farther downstream, its hull mysteriously intact. The sheriff—finding no signs of struggle on Liam's body, and his pockets full of empty vials of Sweet Vitriol—had, of course, deemed it a suicide. But Gentle knew better. He knew his cruel words had whipped Liam into a frenzy—had driven him to put himself in danger and make some grave error in his encounter with the salamander, just to prove him wrong. Gentle knew, without a doubt, that his friend had died because of him.

After their fight with Hercules, Gentle and Kitt charged headlong into the woods, following the trail along the gorge until it descended back to the riverbank and was reabsorbed by the forest. From there, they hugged the edge of the river, moving fast over the slippery ground, even as the wind grew so fierce that it threatened to topple them with every gust.

"We can't lose it," Gentle said, shouting over the roar of the storm. "Not now. Not when we're so close."

But the salamander, despite its size, was either very fast or in possession of some special form of camouflage, because by the time night arrived, they hadn't seen a trace of the pale monstrosity anywhere.

Even then, drenched and shivering, Gentle wanted to keep going. He doubted they'd be able to keep tracking the salamander without Manon's help. And since the woman had clearly forsaken them, they had no choice but to continue pursuing it before it disappeared again.

There was the problem of Hercules, as well. Gentle saw the man's shadow looming behind every wind-thrashed tree, heard his alligator boots hunting them in every squelch of mud. He had no doubt that the giant was fast in pursuit, Bertha in hand, ready to enact his revenge for the loss of both his prey and his ear. Kitt seemed equally hesitant to stop their progress, despite being clearly exhausted—perhaps because he, too, feared what would happen if Hercules caught up to them.

It was Abe who made the choice to rest. Just after dark, when the moon emerged as a feeble glow behind the striated bands of clouds overhead, the mule refused to go any farther. No matter how hard Gentle and Kitt shoved against the animal's muscled haunches, Abe could not be compelled to continue. Instead, he turned around and stood beneath the wide boughs of a nearby fir, waiting for Gentle to slide the casket off his back.

Though the tree protected them from the worst of the rain, it was still too wet to make a fire, so Gentle and Kitt peeled off their wettest garments, huddled up against the damp trunk beneath their tent's oilcloth, and ate a few stale biscuits they were able to find at the bottom of one of the saddlebags. Though Kitt had remembered to strap the casket on Abe's back before following the hunting party into the woods, he hadn't packed the rest of the food. With nothing to cook, and no way to dry their clothes, they hunkered miserably beneath the tree's branches and attempted to sleep through the worst of the storm.

After an hour or so of tossing and turning, Gentle gave up on rest and began drinking from his flask. Which was when he heard Kitt's whimpering. The boy was only a few feet away, curled up against Abe's side, his shoulders shaking from the force of his weeping. Gentle shifted a little closer, so Kitt could hear his voice over the wind.

"Come now," Gentle said. "None of that. You'll only tire yourself out."

Kitt straightened immediately, as if caught committing some unforgivable act, and brushed the tears off his cheeks.

"This is all my fault," he said hoarsely. "I should have let Mr. Belmont shoot the salamander."

"We'd certainly be much drier if you had."

Gentle's joke prompted a fresh round of blubbering.

"I just felt like we couldn't kill it," Kitt said. "It felt *wrong* somehow. I thought that if we killed the salamander something terrible would happen. It was stupid of me."

"Hercules might have denied us the creature's blood. Didn't seem the generous sort, given how quickly he turned on us. Perhaps your interception was a blessing."

"You're just saying that to make me feel better."

But this wasn't true. Gentle remembered the awe that had

overtaken him when he saw the salamander. He'd been afraid, then, at the thought of what would happen when Hercules took a shot at that vast, incomprehensible whiteness. Some part of him had wanted to stop the hunter, too.

"I suppose you wish you'd managed to leave me in Dalton Lake," Kitt said. "I don't blame you. Father always said I was a magnet for calamity. Like my mother."

"And yet," Gentle said, "if it weren't for you and your money, we never would have enticed Manon to track down the salamander in the first place."

"My father's money," Kitt said.

"I didn't see his name on it."

A tremor passed through Kitt—not quite a laugh, but some frail relative.

"Liam always said that everything happens for a reason," Gentle went on. "To an alchemist, nothing in the cosmos is random. Everything leads us back to the Great Work, whether we like it or not."

"Even the bad things?"

Gentle's heart ached at the heavy hope hanging in Kitt's words. His nephew sounded like a condemned man begging for clemency at the executioner's block.

"Especially the bad things. Liam said that our suffering on earth served an essential purpose—when paradise finally arrived, we would remember our pain. We would remember what it was like to live in a broken world, beyond hope, living and dying like common animals. And in remembering, we would not take our salvation for granted."

"Liam sounds like a smart man."

"Not just smart. Wise," Gentle said. Despite the cold and the rain, he felt something warm bloom inside him. But grief, always prowling nearby, infected the memory of his friend, souring the flavor of his life with the bitter aftertaste of his death. "Even after all the horrors he'd seen, he never lost faith. He knew we were put here for a greater purpose."

Kitt bolted upright and turned to Gentle.

"Let's make a deal," he said.

Gentle laughed at the boy's sudden seriousness.

"All right. What kind of deal?"

"I won't lose faith in our mission again," Kitt said. "If you promise to start being honest with me. No more slipping drugs into my drinks. From now on, we're a team. All right?"

"Fine," Gentle replied. Because what else could he say?

"Promise?"

"Promise."

Soon Kitt was asleep. Gentle leaned his head back against the tree trunk and stared down at his nephew, who looked so peaceful curled up against his shoulder.

The Sweet Vitriol burned less that night as it slid down his throat. And though its effects were noticeably muted—the softening of pain that had brought Gentle so much joy in the last few weeks now arriving more like a dull suggestion of happiness—Gentle felt a faint stirring of hopefulness. He lay an arm over Kitt and closed his eyes, waiting for sleep to finally come.

It did, just a few minutes later, dragging Gentle down like a powerful undertow.

The next morning, after a few more hours of fruitless, hungry wandering, they found a dead soldier hanging by his feet from the low branches of a tree.

Gentle assumed he was a soldier because he wore the gray, high-collared jacket of an infantryman, and he assumed he was dead because his throat had been slit, the wound frowning down at them like a second mouth. The man had been killed recently: The blood on his face was bright red, and his body dangled in the breeze with the unmistakable rigidity of rigor mortis. Someone had removed his eyes and stuffed the empty sockets with soil.

"Don't look," Gentle said. But it was too late.

"Lord have mercy," Kitt murmured. "Who would do this? Indians?"

"No," Gentle said. He was thinking of the monster in Cedarville. The buck jamming its thumbs into the executioner's eyes. The last few days had produced so many new outrages that he'd almost forgotten about them. "We need to go."

"We can't just leave him up there," Kitt said.

"It isn't safe," Gentle said.

"You're an embalmer. You have a duty to care for the dead."

"It's a profession, not a duty. And this man doesn't look to have any money."

"I'll pay you myself, if that's really the issue," Kitt said.

"Whoever did this could be nearby."

But the boy had already started fiddling with the ropes tethering the corpse to the tree. Abe stopped as well, staring at Gentle with droopy, equine disappointment.

"Give it here," Gentle snapped. He detached the ropes from the trunk of the tree and the man's body thumped to the ground.

"All right," Gentle said. "Let's go."

"We should cover him with something," Kitt said.

"Kitt," Gentle said. "We need to go. Whoever did this could be nearby."

"It won't take long," Kitt said.

Gentle sighed and cast a glance into the surrounding woods. The rain had finally stopped, but it had been replaced by a milky fog that rendered sight impossible beyond a few yards. Gentle spied no human-shaped shadows in the murk, but that was hardly assurance that they were alone. Still, he helped Kitt drag the rigid corpse off the trail. They spent the next five minutes or so stacking stones and branches over the body, until they'd obscured him beneath a mound of debris. Once this was finished, Kitt hung his head and recited a quiet prayer, the particulars of which were lost to Gentle, who was busy searching for his flask in Abe's saddlebags. Upon finding it, he took a long drink and turned around to find Kitt staring at him.

"Anything you'd like to say, Uncle?" he asked.

"Death is the midwife of very great things," he said quickly, slapping an "amen" at the end of the phrase for good measure. Kitt did not seem impressed.

"What does that mean?" he said.

"Just something Liam used to say." He took another drink. "Can we go now?"

But just then Gentle heard a rustling in the fog behind them. He spun around, half expecting to see a very angry Hercules leveling Bertha in their direction.

Instead, he saw a wolf.

Or rather, the head of a wolf, standing on two legs, its body covered by a robe of woven greenery, its chest encircled by a bandolier of bones. It was holding a revolver.

Gentle grabbed Kitt and turned to run. But he stopped when the wolf began to speak.

"Halt!" it shouted, in a distinctly human voice. The voice of a young man, in fact—though muffled, as if he were speaking through a mask. The reason for this was obvious: The wolf's jaws did not move as it spoke. Because it *was* a mask. A hodgepodge assemblage of fur and teeth, stitched together so clumsily that Gentle could actually see bits of the man's skin beneath. Seen for just an instant—as he had back in Dalton Lake—or in the darkness of night—as he had back in Cedarville—Gentle could understand why such a costume might be mistaken for the real thing. But now, in broad daylight, with a few extra moments to study its shoddy construction, Gentle was so relieved that he would have laughed, if he had not very quickly remembered that this man was likely the same one who'd butchered the fellow they'd just cut down from a tree.

"You with the Judge?" the man in the wolf mask asked. Gentle noticed that his other hand, the one without the gun, was clasped around his side. Blood seeped through his fingers.

"We're not with anyone," Gentle said. "We're just lost."

"We're all lost," the man said.

"We aren't looking for trouble."

"Have you seen the dream?"

"What dream?"

"You have eyes, but you choose not to see," the man said. There was a haggard strain to his voice, Gentle realized, likely due to the wound in his belly. The gun had begun to loosen in his grip, but as Gentle took a tentative step forward, he jabbed the pistol forward and began to shout. "Don't come any closer!"

Gentle threw up his hands. "Please," he said. "We don't have any weapons."

"We are all weapons," the man mumbled. "Some are honed. Some are dull. I can tell by the look of you that you're the latter. I ask again, and for the final time: Have you seen the dream?"

"You're hurt," Gentle said. "I have tools. Tinctures. I can help."

"You think I'm afraid to die? I long to see the green country," the man said. But Gentle could hear a tremor. He knew very well the fevered uncertainty that slithered into a person's voice when they refused to accept that they were losing their life. "But you'll see it first."

He cocked the revolver. Gentle threw up his hands, tried to shield Kitt's body with his own. But the boy stepped around him.

"We've seen it!" he cried. "We've seen the salamander. It showed us the dream."

The man's body straightened.

"Tell me," he said. "Tell me what you saw."

"A green valley," Kitt said, in a tone that sounded far too reverential for Gentle's liking. "And fires. And floods."

"What else?" the man said.

Pain took hold of Kitt's features. "Bad things. Ugly things."

Finally, the man lowered the gun. "True things," he said. He reached up and pulled off the wolf mask. The face below was even younger than Gentle expected—he couldn't have been older than nineteen. His skin was a sickly shade of yellow, and his dark hair was stuck to his head by sweat. He looked exhausted.

"You say you have medicine?"

Gentle nodded. "I can stitch up your wound."

"Follow me."

They had no choice, of course. The man led them, gun still drawn, to an overgrown section of forest where he'd cleared away just enough ferns and moss for a small fire and a bedroll. He told them to tie Abe's lead to a nearby spruce and then sat himself down on a rotting log to watch them. Not once did he allow the gun to drift from their direction, though as Gentle squatted down he noticed the man grimacing.

"I've something you can take for the pain," Gentle offered. The man snarled out a laugh.

"Something to knock me out, you mean," he said. "Not a chance."

"That wasn't my intention," Gentle said—though it was, in fact, exactly what he'd been planning to do. His mind was racing to think of some way to get him and Kitt away from the armed lunatic, who was sure to kill them the moment Gentle had tended to his wound. If he could not knock the man out with a strong dose of chloral hydrate—the same strategy he'd used with Kitt back in Dalton Lake—his only other option was to try and disarm him when he'd gotten close enough to stitch up his wound. But Gentle doubted the man would be foolish enough to let his guard down.

As he began rooting around in his embalming bag for some stitching, the man shouted for him to stop.

"Bring me the bag," he said.

Gentle did as he was commanded. After he'd set the bag down, the man told him and Kitt to sit across from him in the dirt.

"Keep your hands where I can see them," he said.

Gentle looked at Kitt, who was staring at the man with an odd, calm sort of concentration. The man began to toss things out of the bag—syringes, makeup kits, empty glass vials—with his free hand, his eyes flickering down just long enough to analyze each item before he flung it to the ground. When his hand returned with the Liber Alchimiae Gentle jumped to his feet. The man fired a shot into the air without hesitating. Kitt yelped in fright at the sound. Abe jerked at his lead and, when this proved fruitless, tossed his head back and forth and began stomping his giant hooves in distress.

"I said sit the fuck down," the man said. Gentle was suddenly glad he'd eaten so little in the last few hours.

He sat down again and watched the man flip roughly through Liam's book.

"What is this?" the man grunted.

"Just pictures," Gentle said.

"I've seen this before," the man said.

"What?"

The man held up the journal so Gentle could see. He was on the page that showed the recipe for the Great Work, with the leering skeleton and boiling salamander.

"I've seen this," he said again. "In the dream."

"Impossible," Gentle said. "Liam copied down that picture nearly two decades ago."

"I said I've seen it," the man said. Before Gentle could explain that, unless this man were secretly an alchemist himself, there was no way he could have seen such an image before, the man dropped the Liber Alchimiae to the ground with the rest of the bag's contents.

"What do you need to fix me up?" he asked Gentle.

"Bit of thread and a needle," Gentle said. "And some lint for packing."

"Get to it, then. And be fast."

Gentle shimmied over on his knees and grabbed the required materials. As he approached, the man tugged up his woven cloak and displayed the wound. It was an ugly looking thing: two red, puckered lips of torn flesh smeared with fresh blood and dirt. As Gentle leaned forward to study the damage, he felt the man press the barrel of the revolver against the back of his head.

"Nothing funny," the man said.

"I'll need to clean it with some water," Gentle said. "To see if there's a bullet in there."

"Get on with it, then."

"It'll sting."

"You don't say."

Gentle dribbled some water from his canteen over the wound, aware that all it would take was a flinch of the man's finger to send a bullet through his skull. The man hissed, and his abdomen tightened, but he refrained from pulling the trigger.

"I'm not seeing any bullet," Gentle said. "You're lucky."

"Luck has nothing to do with it. The Sons of Adam are Leviathan's chosen. The beast protects us."

"You'll still need stitches," Gentle said.

"Who are the Sons of Adam?" Kitt asked suddenly.

"Those who have seen the dream. Those who will burn away the filth from the land and sow the seeds of the green country."

"The green country," Kitt said. "You mean the place from our dreams?"

"Eden," the man said. "A new frontier."

Gentle, who'd just finished threading the needle, interrupted them. "I'm going to start stitching you up," he said.

"Do it," the young man said.

Gentle jabbed the needle into the ridge of flesh. The man gasped in pain. After a few seconds he gestured at Gentle to continue.

"Why are you killing people?" Kitt said suddenly. There was an innocence in the question, as if he were asking the man why he preferred one brand of tobacco over another.

"Why does a farmer burn his field before laying down a new crop? The land is full of rot. You've seen the dream. You know."

Gentle tried to focus on slipping the needle back and forth

through the wound, but the images from his nightmares—the tree of screaming heads, the black beaches, the grim landscape of steel and fire—flickered behind his eyes.

"It's only a dream," Kitt said. "You can't kill people over a dream."

"Can't you?" the man said.

"Thou shalt not kill," Kitt said. "It's in the scripture."

"And yet we do," the man said. "Every day. Every minute. Every second. If not men, then beasts. If not beasts, then the trees. If not the trees, then the crawling things that live beneath them. Killing is life's greatest necessity. If God's laws govern the earth then we are all condemned. Adam knew. That's why the beast chose him."

"Adam?" Gentle said.

"The first of us, the best of us. Adam Lee."

Some distant bell of recognition rang in Gentle's memories. But he couldn't place it. Adam Lee. Where had he heard that name before?

"Who is Adam Lee?" Kitt asked.

"Soldier. Frontiersman. Martyr. Prophet," the man said. "He is all of these, and none."

"Wait," Gentle said, finally remembering. His needle hovered over the wound. "He's the one the Judge hired to map the peninsula last year."

Gentle had heard the rumors: Last fall, a man had shown up in Cedarville with a small army and bought up most of the town's supplies, announcing that he had been hired by the Reverend Judge to conquer the nation's last great wilderness. Such expeditions were nothing new—Gentle had heard of half a dozen such endeavors over the last two decades. Each one ended the same way: with its assortment of spirited adventurers limping back to civilization after losing their way among the ice-shorn peaks and crumbling glacial valleys. The only reason this particular excursion warranted any note was Adam Lee himself, a grizzled old adventurer so arrayed in myth and legend that he seemed more like Paul Bunyan than any living man. His appearance on the peninsula had carried with it stories of his exploits in the Indian Wars and his adventures leading pioneers over the Oregon Trail. It was said he had singlehandedly killed two hundred Sioux before being discharged by his scheming superiors for questioning their orders. It was said that he had fought off packs of wolves with nothing more than a skinning knife, and carried whole families over frigid mountain passes on his back, porting mothers and fathers and their kin on his shoulders like so many sacks of feathers. When word began to circulate, a few months after he headed into the backcountry, that Old Lee and his men had disappeared, it had served as final proof that the Olympic Peninsula would never be conquered by mortal men.

"What do you mean?" Gentle asked. "That the beast chose him?"

The man's body went rigid again, and he shoved Gentle, who had nearly finished the final stitch, away. Gentle threw his hands up in front of his face, but when he peeked around his fingers he saw that the young man was pointing his gun at the woods behind Kitt.

"Quiet," he said.

Voices reached them from between the trees. Two men—one boyish and frantic, the other old and gruff—seemed to be arguing about something.

"I'm telling you," said the younger one. "I heard a gunshot."

"Probably a tree falling," said the other.

"I see something!"

Two figures emerged from fog hanging between the furs. They were dressed just like the soldier Gentle and Kitt had pulled down from the tree, though their clothing was significantly more tattered. Their coats were missing half of their buttons, while their flat gray caps slanted on their heads like squashed loaves of moldy bread. The rifles they clutched in their hands looked more like antiques than weapons of war. Upon catching sight of them in the clearing, the younger of the two raised his gun and cried out in excitement.

"There!" he said. "Enemy combatants!"

"Put your damned gun down," the other man said wearily. His face, Gentle noticed, was dominated by a scar very much like Gentle's own, a white vein curved across his forehead like a shooting star. "They don't even have any weapons."

This surprised Gentle, given that the man in the wolf mask was leveling a pistol at them. But when he turned around he saw that the man had taken his mask and disappeared, the only evidence of his presence the bloody bandages crumpled on the log where he'd been sitting moments before.

"You!" the younger soldier shouted at Gentle. "Explain yourself."

"My nephew and I are lost."

"A likely story," the young man said.

"Relax, Milo," the scarred man said. "He has a kid with him, for God's sake."

"That's *Private* Milo," Milo said. "What about the bandages? There's blood on them."

"I'm a doctor," Gentle said. "Some fellow in a wolf mask held us at gunpoint and demanded I stitch up his wound."

Milo tensed and began scanning the surrounding woods with his rifle.

"Hear that, Private Boris? Aiding and abetting the enemy."

"Open your ears, idiot," Boris said. "They didn't have a choice."

"They could have refused."

"And gotten themselves killed?"

"Better that than helping the Sons of Adam. That's a crime, I reckon. We should go after the one they helped. He can't have gotten far."

Boris shook his head. "He's long gone. We should take these two back to camp. Judge might have use for a doctor."

"I'm sorry," Gentle said. "But who the hell are you people?"

Milo finally lowered his rifle. He puffed out his chest and tipped back his hat, looking like a child's roughed-up tin infantryman. Boris rolled his eyes.

"We are soldiers in the Reverend Judge Crane's Army of the Olympics," he said proudly. "And you are under arrest."

They smelled the Army of the Olympics long before they reached their camp: a smoky miasma of cooking meat that left Gentle's guts wrangled in a desperate knot.

"That'll be the feast," Private Milo said, sniffing the air in greedy gulps. "We staved off an assault by the Sons last night. The Reverend Judge is throwing us a Thanksgiving dinner to celebrate."

Gentle hadn't bothered to argue with his arrest—he was more than happy to allow the soldiers to take him where they wanted, so long as there was a hot meal and a dry bed waiting for him. With news of the feast, visions of roasted hams and steaming pies jostled any lingering anxiety out of his mind.

Private Boris dismissed Milo's pride with a snort. "Hardly a sterling military success. A few of them snuck into the camp and made off with some of our supplies. Even dragged one of the men into the woods with them. They're still out looking for him."

Kitt looked up at Gentle uncertainly.

"We may have run into him," Gentle said.

He explained how they'd come upon the soldier. "We cut him down," Gentle said. "Buried him under some stones and such."

Private Milo shook his head. "Private Johnson was a good man."

"Private Johnson was a drunk," Boris said. "Who liked to fondle little girls. Sounds like he got what he deserved."

"We killed a few of them. And captured one of their scouts," Milo said, ignoring him. "With the information we get out of him, it'll be no time before we put all this ugliness behind us."

"We captured a crazy old man. They probably left him behind on purpose."

"He'll be an essential asset," Private Milo continued. "When the Reverend Judge is done with him, we'll know exactly where the Sons are hiding."

"You mean they're going to torture him," Gentle said.

"Torture is too kind a word for what the Judge will do to him," Private Boris said.

"The cruelty of war makes Private Boris squeamish."

"What war?" Private Boris barked. "The Reverend Judge has no military credentials to speak of. Nor do any of the men he's conscripted into his little army. It's the blind leading the blind."

"Why join up with him, then?" Kitt asked.

"Same reason this fool did," Private Boris replied, jabbing a finger at his fellow soldier. "The Sons burned down the mill that employed me. Judge is offering five dollars a day to anyone willing to join the fight. It was this or the poorhouse."

"Well, *I'm* not doing it for the money," Private Milo said. "It's my Christian duty."

Private Boris groaned. "Here we go."

Milo turned and leaned closer to Kitt, as though fearful they might be overheard. "The Sons of Adam are serpent worshippers. Like the old Israelites. That's why they're burning down the Judge's mills. The scout we captured wouldn't stop talking about it. Leviathan, he calls it. *The beast that will swallow the world.*"

"Nonsense," Boris said.

"I heard it with my own ears! That's why they're working with the Harmonites, you know. It's just as the Reverend Judge says—they've all succumbed to the snake's minestrones."

"*Ministrations.*"

"It's a salamander," Kitt interjected. "Not a serpent."

The two soldiers stopped and looked down at him.

"You've seen it?" Boris said.

Kitt's cheeks reddened from the sudden attention.

"Just a few days ago," Kitt said. "We tried to follow it, but we got lost in the storm."

Private Milo crossed himself. "See, Private Boris? It's real! Just like the Reverend Judge said. Satan incarnate, slithering through these very hills."

Private Boris stared at Kitt with unsettling intensity.

"What did it look like?" Private Milo asked excitedly. "Was its skin as black as coal? Did it spew fire from its mouth? Did it speak with the voice of a voluptuous harlot, offering you untold riches if you pledged your soul in its service?"

"It was beautiful," Kitt said. "The man we were traveling with, a hunter, he said it was a god. That's what it looked like—a god."

Gentle's skin prickled at his nephew's tone. Was that veneration he heard? Devotion, even?

"A god?" Private Milo said, sounding disappointed. "What sort of god commands its disciples to sow devastation throughout the lands of honest, Christian men?"

"We should get going," Gentle interrupted. There was no point in telling these strangers the rest of the story. It wouldn't reflect well on them to explain what had happened to Hercules. "Unless you want to miss your feast."

They continued in silence, the air thickening with the smell of roasting meat, until suddenly the forest fell away. All around them the plant life had been systematically cleared—the trees cut down, the underbrush burned—as if the forest itself had been beaten back in some ferocious battle. At the end of this scorched valley rose a long wall of logs cemented together with pitch, their tips sharped like the ramparts of a fort. As they approached the fortification, Gentle felt himself withering beneath the scope of a soldier who aimed his rifle at them from atop a guard tower built above the wall's gate. Thanks to the eradicated wilderness, there was nowhere to hide from the man's sight.

When they reached the gate Milo waved up at the guard. The guard glared at the young man for a few moments, then leaned over the rail behind him and shouted something down below. A few seconds later the great doors of the gate swung open with a splintering groan.

Gentle marveled at the sight of what awaited them on the other side. A manicured valley of Arcadian splendor sprawled out before them, an oasis so verdant and lush that it seemed, for a moment, that they had slipped out of the peninsula entirely and been transported to the pristine green plain of Gentle's recent dreams. Fields of downy grass covered sweeping hills of fenced pastures and dewy meadows. A road of cobbled stone ran through them, weaving between herds of fat, docile cows, until it reached a village of sorts composed of twenty or so bright white houses, each one pumping a dense column of smoke into the sky.

"Workers' housing," Private Milo explained, as they began following the road toward the buildings. "Though the Reverend Judge has been kind enough to convert them to barracks for the soldiers."

"I'm sure the workers appreciate that," Gentle said.

"It's a bit cramped, I'll admit," Private Milo replied. "Some of them were lucky enough to get moved to the main house."

Private Milo pointed toward the structure in question—not that it was easy to miss. Rising above the square like a cathedral presiding over a medieval hamlet was the Reverend Judge Crane's mansion, an imposing fortress so huge it seemed less like a building and more like a natural feature of the landscape. Though it resembled a log cabin in style, with walls of stacked timber and a roof of split shag, its stained-glass windows and four-story wings left no doubt as to the owner's wealth. The mansion's structure was odd, though—rather than rising to a point, as one might expect, the building grew larger on either side, so that it resembled a bow tie or a ribbon.

"That shape," Gentle said. "Is it . . ."

"An axe-head." Private Boris nodded. "Reverend Judge loves to remind folks how he made his fortune."

"Strange place to live," Gentle said. "Out in the middle of the woods like this."

"This is just his summer home," Milo said. "He winters over in Tacoma. Got a house out there three times as big as this one."

They'd reached the barracks, where the valley's bucolic qualities were dampened by the sight of a burning pile of peculiar-looking logs. They were thin and black, like twisted rods of scorched iron, and scattered among them were pinpricks of white, as if someone had inlaid the wood with square bits of ivory. Staring at one of the rounded logs, which jutted up from the flames like a swollen boil, Gentle's eyes fell upon a stretch of wood that bore an uncanny resemblance to a human face, with a gaping slit that could have easily been a mouth and two round hollows that might have once held eyes.

Gentle noticed more of these charred visages in the pile. The realization seemed to hit him and Kitt simultaneously, because they both stopped walking. Those were not logs in the fire. They were bodies. And that smell in the air? The one that had sent Gentle's stomach groaning in hunger?

He felt a tide of bitter bile rising in his throat. He swallowed it down.

Milo noticed them halting on the path.

"A few Sons of Adam," he explained. "We caught them trying to escape after the raid. A fitting end for arsonists, don't you think?"

"They should have Christian burials," Kitt said, not looking away from the fire.

"Only Christians deserve Christian burials."

Kitt cupped a hand over his nose. It occurred to Gentle that, despite the soldiers' hospitality, they were no less a danger to him and Kitt than the man in the wolf mask. He gave his nephew's shoulder a squeeze—to comfort himself or the boy, he wasn't sure.

Gathered around the burning corpses, chopping wood and cleaning rifles and playing cards, was the Army of the Olympics: a ragtag squadron of thirty or forty dour-looking men nearly indistinguishable from the bloodthirsty crowd of weary laborers Gentle had seen back in Cedarville. They wore the same uniforms as Private Milo and Private Boris, gray rags that looked as though they had only recently been wrestled off the stiff bodies of the dead, and went about their labors with sluggish brutality, slapping logs into piles and shoving ammunition into cartridges as if punishing the objects for some prior slight.

"Afternoon, gentlemen," Private Milo announced, saluting the stinking assemblage of soldiers, most of whom ignored him. "Anyone in need of medical attention? Boris and I wrangled up a doctor."

"You're three hours too late," one of the men replied, not even bothering to look up from his cards. "Miller died this morning. One of the Sons got him in the gut during the raid. You should have heard the way he was howling at the end."

"I've a nasty rash on my ass," said another man, a skinny fellow whose bottom lip was fat with tobacco. "If you'd like to take a peek, doc."

This elicited a hearty round of chortles from the rest of the soldiers, whose disproportionate mirth at the joke was explained just moments later when the sweet stench of whiskey wafted over from their direction.

"We'll take him to the Reverend Judge first," Private Boris said. "His ass takes priority."

The men seemed to find this even more hilarious, and the sound of their laughter, high-pitched and desperate, followed them all the way up the hill to the door of the Judge's stronghold.

A pale man in a white three-piece suit opened the front door, a towering slab of polished oak twice as tall as Gentle.

"How many times do you I have to tell you brutes that I'll ring the bell when dinner is ready?" he said. "Pestering me will not speed up the preparations, you know. Is it not enough that the Reverend Judge has done you the kindness of opening his home to you?"

"We're not here about the food, Jenkins," Private Milo said, pressing an arm against the door and shoving it open. The little man gave a yelp and shuffled backward. "We've brought a doctor. Figured the Reverend Judge might be interested in meeting him."

"The Reverend Judge is very busy," Jenkins said uncertainly. "Maybe after dinner."

"They've seen the serpent," Private Milo said.

"Salamander," Kitt corrected.

"They've seen the *Leviathan*. The one the prisoner keeps babbling about. Certainly, the Reverend Judge will want to hear about that. Or would you prefer that we withhold important military information until the Sons have another chance to attack?"

Jenkins dismissed them with a flutter of his hand. "All right, all right. I don't have time to argue with you. I've a banquet to prepare. He's in his study. But don't come whining to me if he puts you in the stocks for interrupting his work."

Jenkins stepped back to allow them inside the house. A strip of lush red carpet led into an expansive foyer with wood-paneled walls and a giant, gleaming staircase that encircled a ten-foot marble bust of what appeared to be George Washington, his prodigious dome flanked by two of the largest American flags Gentle had ever seen. Above them, a chandelier composed of entangled antlers glowed with the combined light of countless candles.

The place was a hive of activity. Members of both sexes—all of them dressed like Jenkins, with the men in bright white suits and the women in white bonnets and voluminous petticoats—hustled down the stairs and across the hall to the massive dining room that connected to the foyer. They moved with a tense, mechanical urgency that reminded Gentle of puppets being jerked about by strings, an effect only intensified by the fact that some of them looked to have been the victims of the Judge's famous retaliatory amputations: Gentle noticed a man expertly balancing himself on a wooden leg while pouring wine into a crystal bowl and a woman feathering dust from a mantel with a hand missing three of its fingers.

Running parallel to the stained-glass windows was a table large enough to seat at least a hundred people. Silver platters of steak, roasting cauldrons of oil-slicked gravy, and wicker baskets of hot biscuits lay in sumptuous rows all over the table, interspersed with glass jugs of coffee and whiskey. Though the smell of the bodies burning outside was still fresh in Gentle's nose, he found his mouth shamefully filling with saliva at the sight.

Jenkins gave a haughty little tut and nudged him toward the staircase. "Don't get any ideas," he said. "We'll eat when the Reverend Judge is finished with his sermon."

They headed up the staircase and down a long hall, passing rooms stuffed beyond comprehension with all manner of luxuries: towering armoires and gold-framed paintings and beds large enough to fit three or four fully grown men, all of it polished and scoured of any possible evidence of human touch, as though the entire house had just been shipped to the peninsula from some factory back east. Gentle was acutely aware of his own filthiness—his muddy boots leaving a trail of dry brown muck in the soft red carpet, his unwashed body pumping off such evil fumes that he noticed Jenkins pressing a silk handkerchief to his nose and gagging with overembellished disgust.

Gentle loathed these sorts of places. They reminded him of his childhood with Emmanuel. The only thing his brother prized more than a swelling bank balance was a tidy house, and one of his favorite justifications for torturing Gentle was his failure to maintain their home's immaculate equilibrium. Even now, decades later, Gentle found himself tensing up in preparation for some strike whenever he noticed a smudged fingerprint on the side of a glass or some dry crumbs wedged between the floorboards in the kitchen. Judging by the way Kitt held himself as they walked along the hall—with both arms pinned tightly against his chest, as if he feared that the lightest brush of his dirty coat against any part of the house might cause the whole thing to crumble to the ground—his brother's violent retributions for uncleanliness had not slackened with age.

Given the ostentation of the rest of the house, Gentle was surprised to discover that the Reverend Judge's office was an austere, almost spartan affair. A gargantuan desk dominated the center of the windowless room, and the closest thing to decoration was a single steel crucifix hanging on the wall. A balding man sat hunched over the desk, the crooked arch of his aquiline nose pointed down at the sheet of paper he was busy filling with small, neat writing. He wore a white suit so clean and pure that it seemed to emit its own light. One of his hands hovered over the page, attacking the sheet with an ink pen, while the other—an elegantly carved fist of lacquered pine—lay impassive beside a stack of papers.

The general outlines of the Reverend Judge Malcolm Crane's biography were well-known throughout the peninsula. The only heir to the illustrious Crane logging empire, a nation-spanning institution that had been carving away at the continent's evergreen forests since the arrival of the *Mayflower*, Malcolm had caused some minor controversy in his younger years when he'd announced his plans to shrug off the family business and pursue a life of the cloth. But when his father died of gout before producing another heir, young Malcolm—fresh out of seminary and preaching perdition in the mining camps of Montana—returned to the peninsula and took control of the family's extensive network of mills and timberland. The Reverend proved to be a surprisingly ruthless businessman, and within a few years he'd either absorbed or eradicated most of the competition, until there wasn't a stretch of woodland between Seattle and the Pacific that hadn't been claimed by the Cranes. The title of Judge was a recent addition; just two years previous, Malcolm had run for the position on a platform that highlighted his business acumen and propensity for law and order, arguing that the territory's resources could never be properly utilized until its *criminal elements* were brought to heel. He ran unopposed, since his only rival, some lawyer out of Tacoma, was found murdered just two days after announcing his candidacy. His head had been caved in and his body dumped in a ravine. Just more evidence, Reverend Malcolm lamented that Sunday, that the peninsula needed a firmer hand to guide it.

As for the Reverend Judge's wooden fist: Some said that he'd lost it when he was a young man, working in one of his father's lumberyards. Others spoke of the young Reverend's religious visions, and how he had chopped off his own hand after being commanded to do so by God as a test of this faith. Either way, the wooden prosthesis had became a weighty symbol of his reign as the owner of Crane Lumber. Apart from the horror stories Gentle had heard about the Reverend Judge slicing off his workers' fingers and toes for various indiscretions, the man was said to have no mercy for anyone who impeded his ravenous consumption of the peninsula's forests. While he was never caught committing any crimes, the people who stood in his way—farmers who refused to sell their lands, labor organizers who tried to drum up discontent among his workers—tended to find themselves stabbed in bar-room brawls or drowned in creeks. The Reverend Judge's heart, it was whispered, was as hard and cold as his wooden fist.

Having heard such rumors over the years, Gentle had always assumed that the Reverend Judge would look like Emmanuel: a broad-shouldered brute of a man, pompous in his bearing and quick to fits of violent temper. So he was surprised to find before him a bookish, diminutive fellow, who responded to their interruption with a weary, almost sleepy disinterest. He peered up at them without moving, and when he spoke his voice was soft and chiding, as though he were a schoolmaster whose lesson planning was now being disrupted by a group of rowdy pupils.

"Gentlemen?" he said.

"Apologies, sir," Private Milo said. "We found a doctor while we were out on patrol. Thought you might have some use for him."

"*This* man is a doctor?" the Reverend Judge replied. He looked over Gentle as though he were something he'd recently pried off the bottom of his exceptionally white shoe. "Where did you study?"

"My uncle learned his trade in the war," Kitt interrupted. "The battlefield was his university."

The Reverend Judge set his pen down. He brought three long fingers to his pink lips and tapped them contemplatively.

"We could use a doctor."

"They've seen the serpent," Private Milo added abruptly. "It's real, sir. The Leviathan. Just like the old man said."

"I thought I'd made it clear," the Reverend Judge said, "that I'd suffer no mention of heathen monstrosities in my presence."

Private Milo flinched. "Of course, sir."

"Your names?" the Reverend Judge asked.

"Gentle and Kitt," Gentle said.

"Montgomery," Kitt added.

Intrigue flared in the Reverend Judge's eyes. "Any relation to Emmanuel Montgomery?"

"My brother," Gentle said. "Kitt is his son."

"Ah!" The Reverend Judge clapped his wooden fist on the desk. The change in his person was disarmingly swift. He leaned back in his chair, swept out his arms, and grinned with the tender sincerity of a merry shopkeeper welcoming back his favorite customers. "Is God not good, my friends? Does he not provide for the righteous in their time of need?"

"God is good," Kitt agreed, though the boy looked just as confused as Gentle felt.

"I've never had the pleasure of meeting Emmanuel, but I know of his exploits back east. A titan of the beef industry! Tell me: Is your presence here confirmation that my prayers have been answered? Is Montgomery Beef thinking of doing business here in Washington?"

Kitt and Gentle stared at each other, dumbfounded.

"Yes?" Kitt said.

"That's why we were in the woods," Gentle added quickly. This could be the first time in his entire life, he realized, when his relation to Emmanuel might serve some benefit. "Scouting out property. Unfortunately, we were abandoned by our guide and got lost. One of those lunatics in the animal masks took us hostage, but your men here were kind enough to rescue us."

Crane shook his head. "And yet here I am, interrogating you, when all you need is a warm meal and a bath—if you'll pardon my saying." He waved his good hand at Privates Milo and Boris, still posted by the door. "Go and tell Jenkins to bring up refreshments for these fellows. Have him check the cellar for something good."

As the two soldiers left, a slim sapling of happiness sprouted within Gentle. The Reverend Judge was bound to have some fine spirits in his cellar—leagues better than the rotgut he was used to imbibing.

"You'll have to pardon my lack of hospitality, gentlemen. These are dark times on the peninsula, as I'm sure you know. Men of righteous spirit find themselves wrestling with vipers. Those thugs in the forest have been trying to recruit my mill workers. Spreading lies and pagan deceptions. It's hard to know who to trust. We recently caught some Indian woman trying to sneak through the nearby woods. And then there was all that nasty business the other night. I'm sure you've seen our little campfire out by the barracks. As civilized fellows, you may find my methods barbarous. But I assure you barbarism is the only language these Sons of Adam are fluent in."

"Indian woman?" Gentle said.

"Indeed. Dressed like a man. I've placed her down in the stockade with that scout we captured. So far neither of them has revealed the location of the arsonists' base of operations, but I've no doubt they'll start talking once I've applied some additional pressure."

A grim smile tugged at the edges of the Reverend Judge's lips.

"We have a group of rabble-rousers who've taken root in the nearby mountains," the Reverend Judge continued. "They call themselves the Harmonites. No doubt they're aiding the arsonists, though they deny it, of course. Even those godless heathens aren't stupid enough to face me directly. Like any snake, they choose to strike from the shadows, filling my ranks with spies and informants."

A knock rattled the door.

"Come in, Jenkins," the Reverend Judge called.

The little man entered, balancing a tray in his hands. He placed it on the desk between them, and Gentle's heart sank at the sight of what it contained: three tall, slim flutes of milk, surrounded by sweating hunks of white cheese. The Reverend Judge raised one of the flutes to his lips, tipped it to Gentle and Kitt, and drank it down in one long gulp. The wet membrane of milk clinging to his upper lip after he set the glass down gave him the unmistakable appearance of a giant baby.

"Please," he said, waving his wooden fist over the bland buffet. "I'm sorry not to offer you any water, but it seems our well was contaminated by those miscreants during their raid—stuff tastes like rust and lantern oil. I've had to ration our uncontaminated reserves to the soldiers. No matter, though: Crane Dairy's milk is a far superior alternative."

Gentle forced down a mouthful of milk out of politeness. The buttery, warm drink seemed to curdle immediately in his stomach. "I thought lumber was your trade," he said, stifling a gag.

"My father's trade, and his father before him. A respectable business—but one not meant to last. Tell me: What happens when all the trees are gone? Could we not put these cleared lands to better use as pastures? That is my dream for the future, gentlemen. Dairy cows as far as the eye can see. A land of milk and heifers, just as the good book promised."

"You mean milk and honey?" Kitt said. He'd begun nibbling on some of the cheese. Judging by the expression on his face, it was about as appetizing as the milk.

"A common mistranslation," the Reverend Judge replied. "Hence my joy at the news that Montgomery Beef has set its sights on this edge of the continent. I believe our families could do great things together. Once the last of this peninsula's untamed quadrants have been cleared away, of course."

"Is that why you hired Adam Lee?" Gentle asked, hoping to change the topic before any earnest business discussions could get underway. "We heard he's connected to these—what did you call them?—Sons of Adam."

A quiet gasp escaped Jenkins's lips, though the man quickly covered his mouth with one of his hands. A blue vein twitched on the Reverend Judge's forehead. He pointed at the exit. "Leave us," he said to Jenkins.

The attendant shuffled quickly back out the door, closing it quietly behind him. The Reverend Judge leaned forward, tapping his wooden fist methodically against the tabletop. "Who told you this?"

"The masked man who captured us in the woods," Gentle said. "A slander, perhaps. Meant to confuse us?"

"It's no slander," the Reverend Judge admitted, surprising Gentle. "I did indeed hire Adam Lee to scout the peninsula last year. And I know, without a doubt, that he is the leader of the arsonists."

"Then why are you blaming the Harmonites?"

"Oh, I'm sure those anarchists have been helping him. They probably concocted the whole mill-burning strategy themselves. They've been rabble-rousing in my lumberyards ever since they settled in these mountains. Brutes like Old Lee are tools—easily swayed by flattery and the promise of grand acts, no matter how nefarious. Which is why I prefer to keep his role in all this quiet. I take it you're aware of his many accolades?"

"I've heard stories."

"Then you know he's a much-beloved figure among this country's common folk. How might they feel if they found he'd lost his mind and started burning down mills? Most people are simple, as you know. If a man they admire starts spewing drivel about

Leviathans and the *end of days*, they're liable to see some sense in his madness. I've never romanticized such figures myself, mind you. You know he was dishonorably discharged, yes? Disobeyed orders and gunned down some Indian village full of women and children. Not that I've any sympathy for the average Sioux—but a man of his station should always defer to his superiors. Otherwise, what's to differentiate him from the savages?"

The Reverend Judge squinted at the far wall, and his tone became grand.

"Men like you and I, Mr. Montgomery, men of *means* and *vision*, look at places like this peninsula and see a hurdle: a frustrating impediment to the grand march of progress. We can calculate the untold riches that may hide there—the miles of fresh-cut timber, the rich soil waiting to be seeded with grain—and we can drive ourselves mad with this knowledge, knowing those treasures are so tantalizingly out of our reach, kept from us by nothing more than a few hazardous mountain passes. Yet therein lies our problem: Those of us gifted with the wisdom to build nations are stifled by our own intellect. The same mind that conceives of the grand purposes for which those resources could be used is also bent on preserving itself, and as such is wary to put itself in danger to secure them.

"Men like Adam Lee are untroubled by such fears. What they lack in foresight they make up in raw yearning. Their single-mindedness—their blunt, animalistic urge to hurl themselves at danger and discomfort—makes them effective tools for overcoming such obstacles. Which is why I hired him. Despite his history. And his eccentricities."

"Eccentricities?"

"His religious convictions."

"An odd complaint," Gentle said. "Coming from a reverend."

"Not so odd, actually," the Reverend Judge said. He hoisted himself out of his chair and turned his back to Gentle and Kitt, so that he could contemplate the iron crucifix on his wall. "Religion, law, and business are three spokes of the same wheel. Properly balanced, they are the means by which civilization propels itself through history. With their support, we glide over the ruts of our baser instincts. But allow one to dominate the others, and the wheel shatters. Adam Lee is such a man—I saw it the moment he walked into this office. He spoke of the *last frontier* like it was some sort of Goliath put on this earth for the sole purpose of being slayed by him. Yet there was a most unbecoming bitterness about him, too, as though this triumph would signal the end of some great journey he'd embarked on long ago."

Gentle's head was beginning to ache. He had the distinct sense that the Reverend Judge thoroughly enjoyed the sound of his own voice. "The man who captured us said some strange things," he said. "He seemed to be under the impression that the world is ending."

"One hears such things from all the old, grizzled frontiersmen these days, does one not? As though the cultivation of these wild lands is some grave injustice. I sent Lee into the peninsula with forty of his men—stocked to the gills with all the supplies they'd need to forge a path through the wilderness—and in one year he's transformed them into a roving pack of heathens. Three mills burned to the ground in a single month. Untold losses in timber and manpower. In just a few weeks, Lee and his Harmonite conspirators have set my plans back by years. Which is why I've put together this army, you see, rather than conscripting the local authorities, who aren't good for much beyond breaking up the occasional bar brawl. This is *my* cross to bear—my pride and arrogance made manifest, so that my faith might be tested. I am not surprised by all this talk of a giant serpent: The devil himself seeks to test me. But he will find in me a most unyielding opponent."

When the Reverend Judge had finished this speech and turned back to them, his face was flushed and self-satisfied. He peered at Gentle and Kitt expectantly, as though awaiting applause.

"But it isn't a serpent," Kitt said. "It's a salamander."

"Salamander, serpent, what's the difference? It's a beast that crawls on its belly and whispers dissent into the hearts of weak men. My purpose is clear: Strike down the vile demon and all its followers. Lay low the scheming Harmonites and bring order back to the peninsula. You've arrived at an auspicious time. Tomorrow, I'll begin my interrogations of our prisoners in earnest. And when they tell me what I want to know, the Army of the Olympics will begin its march into the peninsula in pursuit of the heathens. I'd hoped to amass a larger force before taking any dramatic actions, but Lee's men have forced my hand. During their raid they made off with a significant quantity of dynamite, and I tremble to think of what evil purposes they plan to use it for. The time to strike is now."

"You were storing dynamite here?" Gentle said. He recalled a story he'd heard, years ago, about one of the Reverend Judge's timber competitors, an old-timer who'd refused to sell his operation to Crane, only to die a few weeks later when a freak explosion burned down his mill. "Why?"

The Reverend Judge waved away the question. "I use it to clear out stumps on the property. Much easier than digging them up. Regardless, it's imperative that we bring the fight to Adam and his men before they use the explosives for some nefarious end. Tell me, doctor, how are your skills with a suture?"

"I've stitched up a body or two in my time," Gentle said.

"And the boy?"

"A fine assistant," Gentle said.

"Very well. Jenkins will set you up in one of my rooms here in the house. No need to bunk you with the common soldiers."

"Much obliged," Gentle said. As he rose from his chair, a plan began unfolding in his mind. He and Kitt would stay through dinner, filling up their bellies and indulging in the Reverend Judge's hospitality. Then, after the feast had ended, and the bulk of the army, drunk and drowsy from their gorging, had settled down to sleep, Gentle and Kitt would collect Abe and make their escape. He could already tell, from the Reverend Judge's pontifications, that Private Boris was right: The man had no idea what he was doing and was liable to get himself and the rest of his men butchered in the forest—that is, if they didn't get lost and starve first. Gentle had no intention of joining them. His only concern was resuming his search for the salamander.

"Oh, and gentlemen," the Reverend Judge said, lowering his voice. "I'm sure this goes without saying, but please don't mention the river monster again. The men are on edge as it is. Rumors of a giant lizard are liable to make them nervous."

"Amphibian," Kitt said.

"What?"

Before the boy could respond, the sound of a thundering crash shuddered through the house. It was followed immediately by shrieks and hollers and the shattering of plates. The heavy tread of footsteps clamored up the stairs, straight for the office. Gentle, seeing no other exit, grabbed Kitt and hunched down behind their chairs. Meanwhile, the Reverend Judge pulled a gold-plated gun from his desk and aimed it at the door with disquieting calm, as if such events were a regular a feature of his day.

"Stop this instant!" Gentle heard Jenkins scream from the other side of the door. "You can't—" The man's words were cut off by a garbled grunt and a heavy thumping noise. A second later, the door to the office exploded inward, followed by the boot that had kicked it in: a mud-speckled, snarling alligator snout.

At the sight of Gentle and Kitt, Hercules's bloodshot eyes blew wide. "I knew it!" he said. "I knew it was them the moment I saw that mule!"

The man was panting, his leather jacket creaking with every breath. Jenkins lay sprawled out on the ground behind him. It appeared Hercules hadn't bathed since their last encounter—the creases of his clothes were gummed with dirt and grime, and a dry streak of blood still clung to the fibers of his beard. The missing chunk of his ear had been reattached with a few thin threads. Whoever had performed the operation had done a miserable job. Judging by the bright red flesh swallowing up the strands and glistening with pus, infection had already begun to ravage the wound.

The Reverend Judge raised the gun. "What is the meaning of this?"

Hercules held up his hands. "Whoa there, Judge," he said.

"That's *Reverend* Judge. Now tell me why you've broken into my house."

"Meant no disrespect, Reverend Judge. Name is Hercules. Hercules Belmont."

"Of the New York Belmonts?" the Reverend Judge asked. Gentle rolled his eyes. Had this man memorized the surnames of every rich family in the country?

"The very same," Hercules said. "Nathaniel Belmont is my father."

The Reverend Judge lowered the gun. "I've done business with him. Charming fellow. I was saddened by news of his financial troubles. Have his prospects fallen so low that his son has taken to common frippery?"

Hercules frowned down at his reptilian boots. "My apologies," he said. "It's only that I couldn't hesitate, sir. You're harboring a fugitive."

"Fugitive?" Gentle said, peeking up from his place behind the chair. "Did Mac Dalton tell you that? I am well within my rights to do with Liam's body what I think is best!"

"Not you," Hercules said. "The boy. Wanted for attempted murder. And theft. Nearly beat his father to death, and stole a fair bit of money from him, too."

"Impossible," Gentle said—but already he could see the color draining from Kitt's face.

"You have proof of this claim?" the Reverend Judge said.

Hercules's lips peeled back into a grin. He stepped to the side, revealing a second figure who'd been hidden behind him. He was a smaller man, and a fair bit older, dressed in deceptively simple clothes: a black canvas jacket, a frumpy pair of cotton trousers, a rounded derby hat. His face was so discolored from bruising, and his nose twisted at such an odd angle, that Gentle did not immediately recognize him. But then he saw his eyes, pressed deep into the folds of his wrinkled face—so impossibly blue, like the cold heart of an iceberg.

"Sampson," the man said, in a low voice that chilled the blood in Gentle's veins. "Been a while, little brother."

Gentle was marched to a cell down in the "brig," a dingy little shack built behind one of the barracks, with a dirt floor and a hastily constructed gridwork of iron beams around one corner of the room. Private Milo shoved him roughly into the cage, and Gentle did not struggle—his will to fight had left him the moment Emmanuel said his name. After twenty-four years, one withering glance from his brother had somehow reduced him to a child again, accepting his inevitable punishment.

It hadn't taken Emmanuel long to convince the Reverend Judge that he was Kitt's father. He produced the documents and explained the situation with his characteristic assuredness, relating how he and his son had had an *unfortunate altercation*, the likes of which one might expect between any father and his troubled child, after which the boy ran away to visit his uncle, who had estranged himself from the family decades ago. He described how he had followed his son's trail west and learned from the Sheriff in Dalton Lake that Kitt had left town with his brother after stealing a dead body from the local cemetery. Chance had brought him and Hercules together: He'd run into the hunter just outside the smoldering ruins of Cedarville. The hunter informed him of all that had happened in the forest, and the two, finding their purposes aligned, set out in pursuit together.

"My brother is deeply unwell," Emmanuel said, gesturing at Gentle as though he were a mad dog badly in need of a bullet. "And he has enlisted my impressionable son in his lunatic schemes. Something to do with a giant salamander."

"They've got unnatural feelings for the lizard," Hercules interjected. Kitt, shrunken in his father's grip, did not correct him. "Boy bit a chunk out of me when I tried to shoot it."

The Reverend Judge ordered Jenkins, now sporting a prodigious bump on his head, to search Gentle for any weapons. He discovered the Liber Alchimiae in his jacket pocket and passed it over to his superior. The man flipped through the book, dispensing scandalized little gasps at each new page. After a few seconds he snarled and tossed the thing onto his desk as if it had burned him. Gentle reached for it, but Hercules slammed a heavy hand on his shoulder and yanked him back.

"Pagan symbols," the Reverend Judge whispered, crossing himself. "Another one of Adam's spies, then. And to think I was about to give the man a room in my home. You've done me a great service, Mr. Montgomery."

After this, Gentle was taken down to his cell. Private Milo—who'd been ordered to keep watch over Gentle and the other prisoners that night, which meant he'd be missing the Thanksgiving banquet—made his disdain clear by bashing his boot into the back of Gentle's knees, sending him face-first into the muddy floor.

"Satanist," Private Milo said. "Hope the Reverend Judge strings the lot of you up."

The lot of you referred to Gentle and the two other occupants of the cage. One of them was Manon, hunched in the far corner of the shed. Her clothes were tousled and a purple bruise darkened the tip of her chin. At the sight of Gentle she gave an exhausted snort.

"Fancy seeing you here," she said.

"So it really is you," Gentle said. "Reverend Judge told us they'd captured a spy."

"Spy." Manon laughed. "Right."

"You left us," Gentle said.

Manon shrugged, wincing in pain. Gentle noticed more bruises around her neck and wrists. "When white folks start shooting at each other, I make myself scarce. Not that it mattered. Crane's posse got the jump on me when I was setting up camp for the night."

"You're hurt," Gentle said. He moved toward her, but Manon went tense, her eyes sharpening to slits.

"Just clubbed me a few times for putting up a fight," she said. "I'm fine. You want to tend to someone, help the old man."

She pointed at the other figure in their cell: an ancient-looking man draped in fern leaves and staring blankly through the cell's bars. His face dragged to one side and was bright red where blood vessels had burst beneath the skin, his eye so swollen that it resembled a split peach. The prisoner's features were so thoroughly mangled that Gentle nearly failed to see that he was staring at the same old man who'd told him about the salamander back in Cedarville.

When he noticed Gentle staring at him, the old man smiled dreamily, revealing a mouth of shattered teeth, and raised one of his hands, which was missing its thumb. Judging by the freshness of the wound, sloppily stitched up and crusted with blood, it had been taken recently.

"I know you," Gentle said.

"You've seen it," the old man said. "You carry the truth on you like a pox."

"Seen what?"

"The beast that will swallow the world. Leviathan."

"You mean the salamander?"

The man nodded blissfully. "*His head and his hairs were white like wool, as white as snow; and his eyes were as a flame of fire; And his feet like unto fine brass, as if they burned in a furnace; and his voice as the sound of many waters.*"

"Don't bother trying to make sense of it," Manon said. "I think the soldiers jangled something loose when they beat him."

"*There will be no more death or mourning or crying or pain, for the old order of things has passed away.*"

"No more talking," Private Milo barked. He sat on a chair by the door, taking glum drags off a poorly rolled cigarette. "Bad enough I have to miss dinner. Least you can do is shut your mouths and give me some peace and quiet."

The old man closed his eyes and continued speaking as if he hadn't heard Private Milo. "*For the Lamb at the center of the throne will be their shepherd; he will lead them to springs of living water.*"

Private Milo picked up a stone from the ground and hurled it at the bars of the cell. "I said shut up!"

The old man made a whimpering noise and clenched his eyes shut, shuffling up against the shed's wall. He stuffed his face against the rotting wood and began muttering to himself, his voice so low that Gentle couldn't hear him.

Emmanuel arrived two hours later. As he opened the door, the sounds of the feasting up on the hill—the shouts of the men, the twang of a guitar, the clattering of glasses and cutlery—filled the shack, only to be muffled again as the door swung shut. Private Milo, who'd been drowsing in his seat, was awoken by the noise and stumbled to his feet.

"Sir?" he said, bringing a hand up to salute and then stopping halfway, as if he wasn't sure of the proper etiquette for addressing Emmanuel.

"I'd like to speak to my brother," Emmanuel said. "Alone."

Hearing the threat in his voice, Private Milo left the shack without another word. Emmanuel grabbed the chair he'd been sitting in, dragged it over to a spot a few inches away from the bars of the cell, and sat down with a weary sigh.

Now that Emmanuel was closer, and the raw shock of his arrival had passed, Gentle could see the full extent of his brother's aging. The deep canyons carved into his once-sturdy cheeks. The sagging curve of his jowls. The gray mustache drooping beneath his crooked nose. And his skin: The Emmanuel he'd known was perpetually tanned, his flesh coarsened to brown leather from the hours he spent working with the cattle beneath the Ohio sun. But now Emmanuel was deathly pale, his skin so transparent Gentle could see the blue blood coursing beneath his cheeks. There was still strength in him, though. Gentle could see it in the way his shoulders and arms strained against the fabric of his coat. They were the muscles of a man who'd put his body to considerable use.

"*And I beheld, and lo a black horse*," the old man murmured from his corner of the cell. "*And he that sat on him had a pair of balances in his hand.*"

Emmanuel shot him a look. The old man giggled.

For the next several minutes, Gentle and Emmanuel sat in silence, listening to the muted reveries of the feast and the intermittent grunts of Manon's snoring. Despite his brother's age, Emmanuel's gaze still made Gentle feel like a very small insect having its wings and legs slowly wrenched from its body.

"You look like shit," Emmanuel said after some time.

"Could say the same to you," Gentle replied. "Did Kitt break your nose?"

Emmanuel smirked. "He did. Surprised the hell out of me. Never knew the boy could throw such a punch. Made me a little proud."

"I'm sure you had it coming."

The smile disappeared as quickly as it had arrived. "Don't pretend to understand the relationship I have with my son."

"The shiner you left on his eye tells me everything I need to know about your relationship. Did you shave his head, too?"

"A man has a right to discipline his children. But I wouldn't expect you to understand anything about that."

"Oh, I'm very familiar with your idea of discipline," Gentle said. His mind returned to the image of his brother bent over the bucking flank of his dying horse, the hammer raised over his head, the blank look on his face, as though his spirit had fled and left only the angry husk of his body behind. "Or did you forget why I left in the first place?"

"Mother never let me forget. Even in her final hours, she still expected you to come back."

"I always planned on telling her where I'd gone."

"Right. And never mind the years she spent waiting, without so much as a letter from you. Never mind the pain she felt, thinking her little boy was dead in a ditch somewhere."

"Is that why you're missing the Judge's feast?" Gentle snapped. "Came down here to shame me?"

"No," Emmanuel replied, slipping his pale hand into his coat. "I came to give you this. Kitt insisted. Called it your medicine."

Gentle's final vial of Sweet Vitriol glinted in the lamplight. Before he could think about what he was doing, he thrust his fingers through the bars of the cell, grasping desperately for the bottle, only for Emmanuel to pull it out of his reach.

"Just as I thought," Emmanuel said. He turned the vial ponderously in his hand. "You're a drunk. Just like Father."

Gentle settled back onto the ground, humiliated. "Father wasn't a drunk."

"How would you know what Father was? You were barely walking when he died."

"I know that he believed in justice. That he was willing to die for it."

Emmanuel laughed. "The only thing he believed in was himself. Dragging Mother and me from town to town. Starting fights with every man he met. He had more ideas than sense, which is why we very nearly starved to death on more than one occasion. And then, when we'd finally settled in Ohio, he abandoned us. Do you have any idea the debts he left behind? Do you have any idea how hard I had to work to turn Montgomery Beef into what it is today? The comfortable life you ran away from—that Kitt ran away from—was all built by me. Built to protect my family. And yet Mother, in the end, acted as though your leaving had been my fault. There's your justice."

"You always hated him," Gentle said. His head throbbed with intensified desire—knowing that the Sweet Vitriol was so close only worsened the ache of his cravings. More troubling, though, were the doubts now trampling through his thoughts. Had he ever seen his father drink? Most of what he knew about his father had come to him from his mother, and she had never said anything about him being a drunk. So: another one of Emmanuel's lies, then.

"Hate is more than he deserved," Emmanuel said. "I pitied him. Like I pity you. Kitt told me all about your little quest. Giant salamanders and—what was it—alchemy?" Emmanuel pronounced the word like it was something foul. "He told me about your friend, too. The dead fellow you've been carrying with you. I always knew you were a little soft, Sampson, but I never thought you'd take up with a man. Tell me: Which of you played the role of wife in your little arrangement?"

Blood rushed to Gentle's face. "He was my friend."

"I'm sure. Two grown men living alone in the woods together for so long? Must have been awfully lonely."

"I was never lonely with Liam," Gentle said, realizing after he spoke that this would only bolster Emmanuel's point.

It's not as though he'd never considered the peculiarity of his and Liam's closeness. They'd encountered many such men in their travels. Fellows who disappeared into the woods together after a few drinks, or pressed against one another in saloon halls, snickering and slapping one another's asses to hide their tentative graspings behind a pantomime of vulgar comedy. Once, he and Liam had been charged with embalming a soft-spoken horse rancher's wife, only to discover, after the beautiful woman's dress had been removed, that she had once been a man. Liam, far from being scandalized—as Gentle was—had been overjoyed. Here, he proclaimed, were citizens of the future, unencumbered by the illusory distinction between the sexes.

So, the thought had certainly occurred to Gentle that his feelings for Liam might exceed those of a regular friendship. After all, how else to explain the joy he felt in Liam's presence, the sense of *wholeness* that overwhelmed him when they were together? How else to explain the years they'd spent in that cabin, eating meals together, reading by candlelight, breathing the same air as they drifted off to sleep, their heads just inches apart?

Yet the physical longing Gentle associated with that sort of love never surfaced. For a long time, he wondered if he could not lust like other men—if that supposedly natural desire had somehow never taken root in him. But then, just a few weeks after he turned thirty, he'd lain with a woman, a lonely widow in Port Orchard who'd led him to her bedroom and helped him make his first fumbling incursion into that hazy world of carnal satisfaction, and he'd realized that the adoration he felt for Liam was a different species entirely. He was surprised by how much this disappointed him: Romantic love was a clear-cut institution, bolstered by orthodoxy and ritual. When a man lost his wife, it was expected that his world would unravel. But friendship? Friendship was a wilderness with no guide. There were no courting rituals one might follow to pursue it, and little sympathy for the gut-wrenching horror of its loss.

"I have to say," Emmanuel went on, "you certainly did a number on my son. He's been swept up in your stories about the philosopher's stone. But I suppose that's no surprise. He was always susceptible to Catherine's passing fancies."

"Catherine?"

"His mother."

"The one you hid away in a hospital?"

Emmanuel snorted, but there was something sad, something defeated, in the sound. "Catherine loved believing in things. She collected ideas like some people collect stamps. It strained her mind in the end. Did you know she dragged Kitt down to the Quaker congregation last year and had them both converted? Got my son quoting scripture like a good little choir boy."

"It's good to believe in things. Things other than money."

"Catherine thought as much. But as usual, she was wrong. Perhaps if I hadn't pampered her so, she'd have seen that. I might have spared Kitt the taint of her hysteria."

"Might have spared yourself that broken nose, too."

Finally, a shift registered in Emmanuel's rigid features—a crinkling of his brow, appearing for just a moment before it was subsumed again by his reptilian disinterest. "Our altercation revealed certain realities to me. I've neglected my duties as a father. Let myself get distracted with work, while Catherine filled the boy's head with all that religious nonsense. I won't make that mistake again. He'll be the focus of all my energies, now. I'll take a firmer hand with him."

Again, Gentle saw the flash of the bloody hammer, heard the frightened whinnies of the dying horse. *A firmer hand.*

"Never took you for the doting father, Emmanuel."

"He is my legacy."

"And what if he doesn't want to be your legacy?"

"It isn't up to him."

Gentle's brother rose from his chair. For a moment, he imagined Emmanuel would leave the room without giving him the Sweet Vitriol. His mouth parched at the thought.

"Will you at least let him see her?" Gentle asked, shuffling up to the bars again.

For the first time since he'd arrived, Emmanuel looked genuinely surprised. "What are you talking about?"

"Kitt says you won't let him visit his mother. In the hospital."

Emmanuel shook his head wearily, as if what Gentle had asked was impossible.

"The boy misses his mother," Gentle said.

"The boy's mother is dead. She hung herself her first night at the hospital. I'm currently suing her doctors."

Gentle was speechless.

Emmanuel turned toward the door and began to leave. Gentle, even in his shock, still managed to cry out after him.

"Emmanuel," he said, unable to hide the desperation in his voice. "My medicine."

His brother turned back. He smiled viciously, and Gentle knew, in an instant, that the man had never forgotten about the Sweet Vitriol in his hand. He only wanted Gentle to beg. Carelessly, he tossed the vial across the room. Gentle reached out and grabbed it, terrified that it would fall through his hands and shatter on the floor.

Gentle was just about to drink the Sweet Vitriol when the door to the brig swung open again. He thought Emmanuel might be returning to offer some final insult, but it was the Reverend Judge who walked through the door, followed quickly by Private Milo and Jenkins. The Reverend Judge stepped to the cell door and peered inside. The light from a lamp hanging from the wall severed his face in two, so that his eyes disappeared into the shadows while his mouth, grinning, seemed to hang in the air before him. His teeth, Gentle noticed, were as pristinely white as his suit.

"I'm going to open the door now," he said. "If any of you feel a sudden inclination to escape, I'd ask that you reconsider. Private Milo here has been given orders to shoot any prisoner who steps outside this cell. Understood?"

Neither Gentle nor Manon, who'd been awoken by the Reverend Judge's entrance, spoke. The old man, still tucked into the far corner of the cell, whispered. "*They have mouths but do not speak; eyes, but do not see. They have ears, but do not hear; noses, but do not smell.*"

"Quote scripture at me again," the Reverend Judge said, his voice surprisingly tender, like a father correcting an unruly child, "and I'll take your tongue."

The old man turned his face to the wall.

The Reverend Judge nodded at Private Milo and the young soldier unlocked the cell door. Gentle shuffled backward as they entered, but it was Manon that the Reverend Judge stepped toward. The woman remained kneeling on the floor. She glared up at the three men who now loomed above her, and though her face showed no fear, Gentle could see, by the frantic palpitations of her chest, how quickly she was breathing.

"Jenkins?" the Reverend Judge said. The little man stepped forward and held out a polished wooden box. The Reverend Judge opened the box, revealing a simple pair of gardening shears resting in plush velvet. He held up the shears to the light like an artist holding aloft his favorite brush.

"I'm a man who believes very firmly in mercy," the Reverend Judge said to Manon. "Unlike your people, I worship a God who extends grace at every conceivable juncture. I'd like to do the same for you, now. Tell me where the arsonists are hiding, and I'll give you a quick death and a proper Christian burial."

"I already told you," Manon said. "I don't know about any fucking arsonists."

The Reverend Judge's smile widened, as if he'd been hoping for this answer.

"It's easier than you think, you know," he said, looking over at the old man. "To keep a person alive once you start cutting bits off of him. The Lord in his wisdom has made the road to death a long one."

"Save yourself the trouble, then," Manon replied. "Put a bullet in my head."

The Reverend Judge shook his head and snapped the shears in front of Manon's face. She flinched, and the Reverend Judge laughed. "Hold out your hand."

Manon spit in his face. The Reverend Judge did not recoil, though Jenkins huffed at the offense. He pulled a satin cloth from his pocket and dabbed the saliva off the Reverend Judge's chin.

With the calculated speed and violence of a trained boxer, the Reverend Judge thrust out his wooden fist and punched Manon squarely in the chest. The woman sagged, gasping, and while she tried to catch her breath the Reverend Judge planted himself on her legs and waited while Jenkins grabbed her arm. The Reverend Judge brought the shears around the pinky on Manon's right hand.

"Tonight I just take the tip," the Reverend Judge cooed. "Tomorrow, I take the finger. Then I take your hand." He turned to

Gentle. "And then I'll start on you, while she recovers. We have many long nights ahead of us. As I said: The road to death is a lengthy one, and I will be there with you every inch of the way."

Urine trickled down Gentle's pantleg. He knew he should do something. Stand and attack the Reverend Judge, even if it meant getting shot. Because what did he have to lose, now? But he stayed where he was on the floor, frozen. And when the Reverend Judge snipped the shears through Manon's finger, and she began to scream with such force that Gentle thought her vocal cords might snap, he uncorked his Sweet Vitriol and finished what was left in the bottle. By the time he realized that such a dosage might be enough to kill him, the tonic had already done its glorious work. The nothing swallowed him up and he was gone.

Yet Gentle's nightmares were too strong to be sated by the Sweet Vitriol. They flung back the curtain of his oblivion and dragged him into the scalding light of other lives, each more alien and inscrutable than the last. He pawed through the dark bowels of a coal mine, his lungs burning from the particles he inhaled with every breath. He smelled the sour rot of a herd of dead bison, their massacred bodies littered over the plain like a fleet of dreadnoughts in a green sea, the rifle that had accomplished the deed still burning in his hands. He stumbled down the sides of mountains whose peaks had been scooped away and filled with hissing pools of green muck, and waded through shorelines where hulking ships wept black sludge from their rusting hulls.

He watched the salamander's green valley burn. Its splendor reduced to mere kindling. Its ancient, proud trees wreathed in crowns of blazing flame. Its herds of elk burned to scorched carcasses, its flocks of birds twirling down from the sky like hot embers, its fish boiled alive in their stagnant rivers. The heat was unbearable, the air pure smoke. The sun was a perfect red circle glaring down at them through the black sky.

"Deep waters," Gentle begged.

He longed for the flood—for the deluge that would wash it all away.

"Deep waters," he said again. But no waters came.

Just as the flames reached him, as his skin began to bubble and burn, he was jolted out of his dream. He awoke back on the floor in the brig, with the old man kneeling on his chest and shaking him, a wild smile spread across his face.

"I heard you," he said. "I heard you calling for them."

The prison was unnaturally bright, and for an instant Gentle thought it was morning. But the light burning through the window was too intense to be proper daylight, filling the brig with sharp lines of brilliant orange. Outside, he heard the shouting of men and the mournful bellowing of a hundred terrified cows.

"What's happening?" Gentle said. The words traveled slowly from his brain to his mouth, as if wrestling through the lingering muck of the Sweet Vitriol.

"It has begun," the old man said blissfully. "*The first angel sounded, and there followed hail and fire mingled with blood, and they were cast upon the earth: and the third part of trees was burnt up, and all green grass was burnt up.*"

Manon was slumped against the bars. Gentle was amazed to see that she was conscious at all, though this looked as though it might change at any second: Someone had bandaged her severed pinky, but her skin was deathly pale, and beads of sweat dotted her forehead.

"Hey!" she screamed at Private Milo, who'd fallen asleep again in his chair. "Let us out of here! Something's on fire."

The young man roused from his sleep. He ran to the window. "Christ," he said, the golden glow of the flames outside burnishing his face bright red. "Oh, Christ. They're back."

He ran for the door, leaving them locked in the cage.

"Bastard!" Manon said. She crawled to her feet and shoved herself against the rusty bars, crying out in pain, but the metal held.

"*And death and hell were cast into the lake of fire*," the old man said, rolling off Gentle's body. He clasped his hands in prayer and closed his eyes. "*This is the second death*."

Manon hurled her shoulder against the bars again. She spun toward Gentle and growled at him through gritted teeth. "Care to help?"

Gentle slowly pulled himself upright. His body felt gummy and unyielding, as though it were made of taffy. "Guh" was all he managed to say.

Manon thumped the back of her head against the wall and grimaced at the ceiling. "Stuck in a cell with a madman and a drunk. Just my luck."

Gentle was surprisingly at ease. The flickering golden light and smell of woodsmoke reminded him of winters he'd spent with Liam beside the fire. He might have fallen back asleep if the door to the shed had not suddenly blown open again, followed by a gust of cold air.

Kitt stood at the threshold, Gentle's leather embalming bag clutched in his hands. He was wide-eyed and harried, with a streak of ash smeared over his face like warpaint. Abe followed behind him, trying and failing to fit his massive frame through the shed's door.

"Uncle," Kitt said. He rushed across the room and gripped

the bars. "The Judge's house is on fire. We have to go."

"Kitt?" Gentle said. He tried to rise to his feet, but his legs would not steady beneath him.

"What's wrong with him?" Kitt asked Manon.

"Drunk, I think," she replied. "We need a key for the door."

"What happened to your hand?"

"Don't worry about it. Find us a key. Quickly."

Kitt hastily surveyed the rest of the room. But other than Private Milo's chair, there was no furniture in the space. No place to hide a key.

"Can we break the door down?" Kitt said.

"I've already tried," Manon said. "The bars are old, but they're holding."

Kitt made his own frantic attempts at banging down the bars, but he had no luck. The shouting outside was growing louder and more panicked. Gentle heard men calling for water. The smoke in the room thickened.

"Uncle," Kitt said, pressing the leather embalming bag between the bars. "Is there anything in there you can use to get out?"

Gentle stared at the bag, and then at Kitt. A thought stirred somewhere in the back of his head, but it was only a whisper, like something uttered from behind a heavy iron door.

"Uncle?" Kitt said. He began to cough.

"Come on, man!" Manon said.

"Acid," Gentle said warily.

A memory: Liam mixing a concoction together to melt a bar of iron. He'd spilled some on himself, and Gentle had sprinted down to the laboratory after hearing his screams. He'd been lucky: The liquid had only touched the edge of his finger, but it had eaten cleanly through the flesh.

Gentle's hands moved slowly in the bag as he fought the urge to close his eyes. He found the vials labeled BLACK SULFUR and ANTIMONY. Liam had forced him to memorize both names, so that Gentle would never accidentally place them anywhere near each other when he was organizing the chemicals on the shelf.

"Step back," Gentle said, waving at Kitt.

Kitt did as he was told. Gentle shuffled over to the gate's rusty hinges. He poured a few drops from both bottles onto the bottommost hinge of the cell's door. Together, they made a faint sizzling noise, but the metal remained unharmed.

"Is that it?" Manon said from behind him. "It didn't do anything."

"Water," Gentle said. Kitt retreated back through the door and returned with a canteen from Abe's saddlebags. Gentle took it and carefully poured a bit of water on the hinge. The fizzle intensified, and the hinge began to smoke and bubble.

"Should be weaker now," Gentle said.

Manon wasted no time: Again, she threw herself at the door. This time, the lock lurched, twisting and bending like a bit of rubber. With another shove from Manon, it broke free from the wall, allowing them to push the bottom half of the door aside and crawl through the opening. Kitt helped Gentle to his feet.

"Incredible," he said.

Gentle leaned against him. "The light is beautiful," he said.

Manon began to run for the door.

"Wait!" Kitt said. "Where are you going?"

"Somewhere safe," she said. "And far away from here."

"Will you take us with you?"

Manon pointed at Gentle. "He can barely walk."

"You'd still be in that cage if it wasn't for him," Kitt said.

"Wouldn't have wound up there if it weren't for him, too."

"Please. I'll carry him."

Manon gnawed on her lip. “Fine,” she said. “But if you slow me down, you’re on your own.”

Kitt heaved Gentle’s arm over his shoulders and helped him toward the door.

The world outside was all light and fury. Up on the hill, the Reverend Judge’s mansion blazed in a column of golden flame. As it burned the valley roared with the booming crackle of its immolation, the timbers belching up vortices of swirling flame that reminded Gentle of the infernal hellscapes from his nightmares. It may have just been the lingering effects of the Sweet Vitriol, but Gentle swore he could see figures twisting and dancing within the conflagration. They had lithe, fluid bodies and triangular heads and long tails that twirled around their legs in mesmerizing spirals. They leapt from shingle to shingle, flinging sparks behind them like confetti as they pranced and pirouetted to the swishing orchestra of the inferno.

“Salamanders,” Gentle mumbled. No one heard him.

Around the base of the mansion soldiers and servants, most stumbling from drink, attempted to fight the blaze with buckets of water from a nearby creek, while dozens of cows who’d escaped from their pens rampaged about in bovine distress. One of the soldiers stepped too close to the burning building, and his coat caught fire. He screamed and threw himself to the ground, where he rolled back and forth while his companions drunkenly laughed and pointed. One of them eventually wandered over with a pail of what Gentle assumed was water, but as he splashed its contents onto the screaming man, Gentle could see that it was milk. The white fluid doused the fire, leaving the soldier, who’d been badly burned in the time it took his inebriated companions to fetch the milk, moaning in a heap of charred flesh and sticky cream.

“Is Emmanuel still in there?” Gentle asked.

"I saw Father in the yard when I snuck out," Kitt replied.

"A shame."

"Come on," Manon panted, already moving toward the barricades. The entire Army of the Olympics seemed to be fighting the fire, and the barracks were completely empty. Still, just as they were creeping through the camp's front gate, a figure stepped out from behind the trunk of a tree. It was Private Boris, a rifle in his hands. The sight of the gun knocked the strength from Gentle's legs, but Kitt caught him, dragging him upright again.

Manon stopped. "Shit."

"Brother Buck," said the old man, who had been following them so silently that Gentle hadn't even known he was there. At the sight of him, Boris's face softened, and the two men embraced.

"Brother Owl," he said. "Glad to see you're still alive. I heard the soldiers gave you a rough time of it."

"Only my body," the old man replied.

"What did you tell them?"

"Nothing. Absolutely nothing." He held up his hand, displaying the bloody knuckle. "Even after they took my finger."

"You should have stayed in the mountains."

The old man did not reply. He only hung his head, ashamed.

"You're lucky this fire came along," Private Boris said. "The Judge spent half the dinner talking about all the wretched things he planned to do to you tomorrow. But you can't go this way. He's sent some men to patrol the trail. He thinks we started the fire."

"We?" Manon said.

Private Boris's smile widened. "The chosen. The Sons of Adam."

The Judge was right, Gentle thought. The man really was surrounded by spies.

"I started it," Kitt said, and the whole group turned to look at him. "I lit a curtain on fire when my father was out of the room and crawled out the window. I just wanted to distract them. I didn't think . . ."

He turned back to the burning mansion. A portion of the structure's roof buckled in on itself, crashing through the building and burping a shower of fiery particles into the sky.

"We don't have time for this," Manon said. "If there are soldiers in the forest, we need to find another way out of this valley."

"There's a trail, hidden in some rocks to the west," Private Boris replied. "We used it during the attack a few nights back. I can show you the way."

"Give me your gun, brother," the old man said suddenly. "I'll go and find the Reverend Judge. I'll make sure he's dead."

"No," Private Boris said. "You'll go to the forest and lick your wounds. Our brothers will come and find you when the time is right."

The old man looked ready to argue, but then the sound of approaching voices reached them through the trees. Private Boris pressed a finger to his lips and pointed in the opposite direction, toward a dense thicket of manzanita shrubs. Without another word, they headed into the forest.

Private Boris led them to the head of an overgrown path hidden at the base of one of the surrounding mountains and told them to follow it west. They were a good ways away from the fire by then, but they could still see its light in the distance, a false sunrise glowing above the tree line.

"It's tough going for a while," he said. "But you should get out of the valley without any soldiers troubling you."

"Why are you helping us?" Gentle said. As they'd walked, he'd felt life sluggishly returning to his limbs. By the time they reached the trail, he could remain upright without Kitt's help, though he still found himself struggling to overcome the hazy suspicion that all of this was a dream.

"You found the Leviathan," Private Boris said flatly, as though this explanation were obvious.

"So?" Gentle said.

"So you've seen the dream. You know about the deep waters. Yet you have not strayed. You have not closed your eyes to the truth. That makes you pilgrims. And pilgrims must be protected."

"We need to go," Manon interrupted. "Longer we stay, higher the odds are somebody finds us."

Gentle wanted to ask more. But Private Boris was already heading back the way they'd come—though not before pressing a crumpled ball of fabric into the old man's hand. As the old man gratefully slipped the filthy fabric over his head, Gentle understood that it was a mask, like the wolf mask on the man who'd captured them in the woods. This one had been stitched together to resemble an owl, with a crooked yellow beak and a head of chaotically arranged feathers plucked from half a dozen different species of birds. For a few moments, the man stared at Gentle, his eyes hidden behind the slits sewn in the mask's face. Then, with a slight tilt of his head, he gave a quiet hoot, as if testing the sound. And then another, more happily. Seeming pleased, he stepped past Gentle, and then Kitt and Manon and Abe, all of whom stared at him in disbelief.

After a moment, Abe sighed with uncannily human exhaustion. Manon shrugged. They followed the madman up the rocky trail and did not stop walking until dawn.

Just as Private Boris had warned, the trail into the mountains was steep and exhausting, a vertical mess of loose rocks and jagged boulders that rose directly into the sky. They climbed for hours, grunting and groaning in the dark, stopping every now and then to catch their breath. No one spoke, as if they all knew that the act of speech, here in the fast-thinning air, was an unforgivable waste of energy—though the old man did, on occasion, deliver one or two of his odd little hoots into the cold dark.

Eventually they'd hiked high enough that they could see, far beyond the trees below, the burning remnants of the Reverend Judge's mansion, flickering in the valley's center. From such a height, the blaze looked like nothing more than a dying ember lost at the bottom of a great black cauldron, waiting for a passing breeze to snuff it out forever.

It quickly became obvious that Manon was their leader. After a few miles of hiking, she seemed to have determined their location, and began ignoring the path entirely, scrambling up steep inclines with the unmistakable confidence of someone who'd summited the cliffs many times before. Though her wounded hand was still pressed against her chest, she moved with surprising speed, practically gliding over the crumbling stones while the rest of the group lurched and tumbled in pursuit. Poor Abe had the worst of it. Thanks to the casket on his back, he was perpetually under threat of losing his balance, so Kitt—and Gentle, who'd finally climbed out of his Sweet Vitriol–induced lethargy—had to keep shoving themselves at his prodigious backside to stop him from cartwheeling backward down the mountain.

It was not until they finally stopped to make camp that Gentle thought to ask Manon where they were going. They'd settled in a canyon near the mountain's peak, where a few thin pines jutted from the soil at odd angles and formed a protective canopy overhead. Above their branches, Gentle could spy the delicate violet of the coming dawn.

"Harmony," Manon said, crawling into her bedroll. She'd forbade them from making a fire in case any soldiers were close enough to see the smoke. "Not sure where the rest of you are headed, but that's my destination."

"But the Judge thinks they're helping the arsonists," Gentle replied.

"Nonsense," said the old man, his voice muffled. "The Sons of Adam work alone."

"I've business there," was all she said.

"We had a deal," Kitt said. He'd begun distributing some food he'd stolen from the mansion before making his escape. Gentle tore ravenously at the hunk of bread the boy handed him, while the old man plucked off crumbs and nibbled on them beneath his mask. "You promised to help us find the salamander."

"And I did," Manon replied, scarfing down the loaf Kitt passed to her in two large bites. "Not my fault you started shooting at each other."

"The offer still stands," Kitt said. "The rest of the money is yours if you help us track it down again."

"You mean the money you stole from your father?" Gentle said.

Kitt did not even try to defend himself. "Father always said that ownership was nine-tenths of the law."

"And what about attempted murder?"

The boy stared down at his hands. "I wasn't trying to murder anyone."

The canyon howled with the cold passage of the wind.

"I'll consider it," Manon said. "But first: Harmony. There's a doctor there I need to see about my finger."

"I'd be happy to look at it," Gentle said. But Manon only sneered at him.

"I've seen what your medicine can do."

The group settled down to sleep. Gentle considered confronting Kitt about all he'd learned that day—his mother's suicide, his attack on Emmanuel, his brazen act of arson—but the boy had retreated into himself, not once looking at Gentle as he went about the work of preparing his bedding. Gentle wasn't sure what he was going to say, anyway. What did it mean that the young man was capable of these sorts of deceptions? The most obvious answer was that Kitt was more like his father than Gentle had suspected. He should have known better, he thought, than to have trusted anything that sprouted from Emmanuel's seed.

With Kitt and Manon fast asleep, Gentle turned his attention to the old man, who'd curled up at the base of a dead fir. Gentle shook the man until he saw his startled eyes open within the folds of the owl's face.

"The deep waters," Gentle whispered. "What does it mean?"

The old man clucked and hooted a few more times. "If you've seen the Leviathan then you already know."

"But I don't."

"You will," the old man mumbled, already drifting back to sleep. Gentle shook him again.

"No," he said. "Tell me."

"They are what is to come. When our work is done, and our sins have been burnt away, the deep waters will rise to take us back to the green country."

"The green country?"

"A world unspoiled by man. Eden."

"So Old Lee has promised you paradise?"

"No," the old man said, shaking his head. "Not Lee. The Leviathan. We placed our hands upon its blessed hide and saw the truth of our lives. The sins that lived inside us like black slugs.

Each man a judgment, each man a mask. To hide the foul creature he once was. A man. Most pitiful of God's creations. Most wretched. Most spiteful. Leviathan showed us the truth: To be a man is to be cursed. So we've taught ourselves to be animals again. To be innocent again."

"I don't understand," Gentle said.

"But you do. That's why the Leviathan showed itself to you. Because of the darkness in your heart. I can see it, too."

"It killed my friend," Gentle said. "I don't know how, but it killed him."

"*I will sweep away everything in all your land*, says the lord," the man exclaimed. "*I will sweep away both people and animals alike. Even the birds of the air and the fish in the sea will die.*"

"Quiet down," Gentle said.

"We have been judged, and we have been found unworthy. We are less than the lowest creature. More miserable than the worms slithering in the muck."

"I said quiet. You'll wake the others."

The old man hung his head, as if exhausted. When he spoke again, his voice was low and contemplative. "I used to hunt otters when I was a young man," he said. "In Oregon. There weren't many of them left in those days, not like when the Russians could take hundreds in a single afternoon. But the fur would go for a good price down in California if you could get your hands on some. Amazing creatures, otters. Smart, like dogs. They knew to hide when men were around. Damned hard to catch them once they'd seen you. But we figured out a trick. You take a pup, leave it stranded on the beach, and let it cry. Mothers can't stand the sound. We'd hide in the trees and shoot them like it was nothing. You ever heard the sound an otter pup makes when it can't find its mother?"

The old man's voice cracked. "I hear it all the time, now," he said. "I hear it in my dreams, every night. I see them stacked up on the beach like little black logs."

The old man began to cry. He tore at his mask and shriveled into a tight ball, wracked by his weeping. Gentle retreated to the other side of camp, frightened by the man's madness. After he'd climbed into his bedroll, he turned his face up to the sky and felt a cold prick on his forehead. When he held out his hands, he saw small flecks of white melting in his palms. Unlike the ash back in Cedarville, these were genuine snowflakes, lilting down from the sky in lazy twirls.

Gentle nestled deeper into his bedroll, plugging his ears against the old man's sobs. When he awoke hours later into the gray dreariness of dusk, a thin layer of snow covered everything, and the old man was gone.

IV
Citrinitas

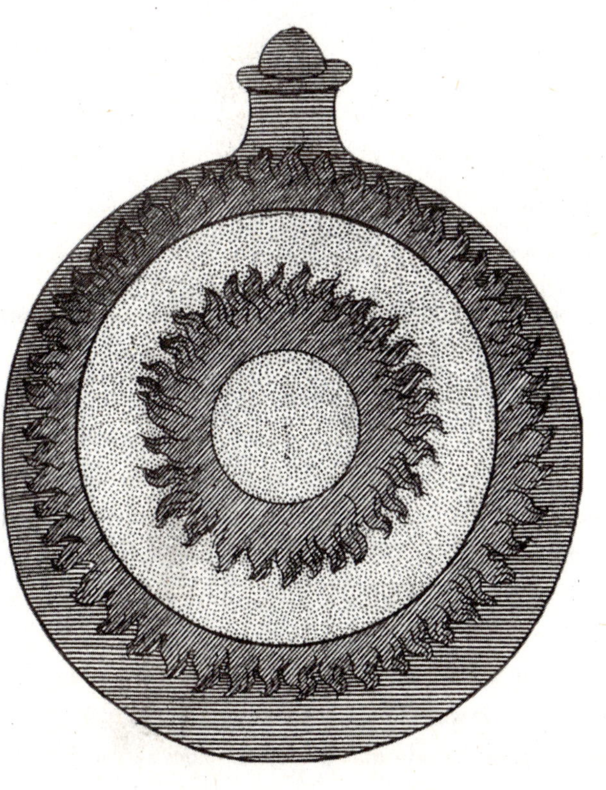

It took them a full night of hard hiking through the mountains to reach Harmony. During that time, the snow fell steadily, turning the surrounding peaks into silver fangs and filigreeing the trees with lumpy skirts of white that glittered like crystals in the moonlight. The route Manon led them through cleaved between the surrounding cliffs in a thin artery of frost and stone, and every few minutes the wind rushed through the canyon in a blast of frigid air, hurling icy flakes into their faces and stinging the skin of their cheeks.

Despite this, Gentle made no complaints about Manon's chosen path. It was obvious that following the woman was their only option—by midnight, the alpine valley below them had disappeared into a swirling vortex of black clouds. They seemed to be hiking through a boundless void. Even then, Manon never wavered in her course, as if she were following signs carved in the rocky earth that only she could see.

As the cold slipped beneath his coat, Gentle found himself obsessing over the old man's disturbing prophecies from the night before. Deep waters. The words quivered inside him with a kind of violence. He whispered them to himself, hoping they might conjure the salamander out of the fog, like a spell in a children's fable. Yet the creature remained hidden. Staring out into the blizzard, Gentle realized he was probably further away from finding the salamander, now, than when he'd first set out from Dalton Lake.

If Liam were here, he tried to remind himself, he would not despair at this detour. He would imbue their shivering march through the mountains with a contagious sense of adventure, remind them that adversity was merely God's way of testing our faith. He would have waved the Liber Alchimiae above their heads and stressed that the Great Work was never meant to be easy.

The Liber Alchimae.

Gentle stood there, frozen, as it dawned on him that he had no idea where the book was.

He patted his coat frantically, knowing even as he thrust his numb fingers into his pockets that there was no way it could be there. The Reverend Judge had kept it when Gentle was taken to the brig.

He ran to Abe and yanked his embalming bag off the animal's side. He turned it over, his bottles and tools rolling out in the snow, and fell to his knees. He pawed through the slush, ignoring the stinging cold as it soaked through his gloves.

"Where is it?" he said. "Where did you put it?"

"What's wrong?" Kitt said.

Gentle did not look up. He tore open the embalming bag, peering into its musty interior in the hope that the little book had somehow remained at its bottom. "The Liber Alchimiae," he said.

"Where is it?"

"We don't have time for this," Manon said. Gentle barely heard her voice above the howling wind.

"This is all we have time for!" he screamed. "This is all that matters! Kitt, tell me you grabbed the book before you left the house. Tell me you remembered."

The boy looked stricken. "I only grabbed the bag," he murmured.

Despair cleaved through Gentle like an axe through a rotten trunk.

The Liber Alchimiae was gone. Burned up, most likely, in the Reverend Judge's mansion. The one thing that Liam had left behind for him. His only hope. And Gentle had lost it.

"We need to keep moving," Manon said. "The storm is getting worse."

"I'm not going anywhere," Gentle said.

"Uncle," Kitt said helplessly.

"Have it your way," Manon said. "You want to stay here and freeze to death? Fine."

"Wait!" Kitt cried, just as Manon turned away from them. "Please, wait."

He reached down to touch his uncle's shoulder. The moment he did, something sprang loose in Gentle. He bolted upright and pushed Kitt up against the trunk of a tree, jostling a curtain of flakes loose from its branches.

"Enough!" Gentle screamed into Kitt's terrified face. "Why couldn't you have stayed in Dalton Lake, like I asked? Why couldn't you have let Hercules shoot the beast when we had the chance? We were so close! So fucking close. Now we're being chased by the Judge, and an army of lunatics, and your goddamned father, of all people. And we've lost the Liber Alchimiae.

We have no guidance on how to make the stone—how to bring Liam back. Haven't you done *enough*?"

There was a vicious pleasure in laying the blame at Kitt's feet. Even as the boy's eyes widened with guilt and fear, Gentle savored that ugly hurt like someone pressing pus from a boil.

Kitt pulled his leather sketchbook from his coat pocket. Shivering, he opened it to Gentle and held it up for him to see.

"Look," he said.

There, drawn on the page, was a crowned figure with two heads. A skeleton pierced by a curved dagger. A moon and a sun jostling for prominence in the sky. A raven, a lamb, an owl, and a salamander, boiling together in a cauldron. The Great Work, recreated with surprising skill in Kitt's own hand.

"See?" Kitt said, tears flowing down his cheeks. "We still have the instructions."

The boy must have made a copy back in the hunting camp. All at once, the anger powering Gentle abandoned him. He let go of Kitt's coat and stumbled backward, ashamed, not by his accusations, but by the look on his nephew's face—the submission he saw there, as if Kitt was already prepared to receive any punishment his uncle thought adequate. As if he thought he truly deserved it.

"Are we done here?" Manon said. Even in the darkness, Gentle could see the sheen of sweat on her forehead, could hear the ragged tenor of her breaths. The woman, despite her hiking speed, was clearly unwell.

Gentle nodded. He leaned down and gathered the things he'd hurled out of his embalming bag. After he'd secured it to Abe's saddlebags once again—the mule avoiding his eyes, Gentle thought, like a child embarrassed by his father's drunken outburst—they continued, silently, into the snow.

Harmony greeted them with gunfire. The sun had just begun to rise, and they'd finally begun their descent back toward the forest on the other side of the pass, the trail sloping down at such an extreme angle that they were forced to slide down through the snow on their asses. The country below them was still hidden behind a rolling curtain of white clouds, but the warped peaks of the Olympics rose all around them like a ring of volcanic islands. Staring down at the landscape, Gentle realized that this was the first time he'd ever laid eyes on the peninsula's interior. At first glance it looked like a vast inland sea, scooped out of the mountains and churning with foaming waves. But this illusion was quickly dispelled by the frosted tips of pines and firs poking up through the fog, fleeting glimpses of the mysterious country hiding below.

A gunshot rang through the mountains, echoing between the canyon walls.

"Down!" Manon shouted.

They slid behind a nearby boulder. Abe whinnied angrily as Gentle and Kitt tried to drag him into cover with them.

"Who goes there?" cried a voice—a boy's—from down below.

"Is that Peter?" Manon yelled from behind the rock. "It's Manon, you idiot!"

"Manon?" the voice replied. "Is it really you?"

Manon popped her head above the rock. Gentle peered over, as well. Down below them, farther along the trail, a boy Kitt's age peeked out from behind his own boulder. He wore a scruffy patchwork coat and clutched a rusty hunting rifle in his hands, though he gaped up at them in abject terror, as though he were the one who'd just been shot at.

He looked, Gentle thought, like one of the orphans who sometimes wandered into Dalton Lake from the surrounding lumber camps. Every now and then one of them would appear in town, usually some starved, half-feral whelp with sunken eyes and dirt on his cheeks who was promptly run out of every establishment and front porch until he reached Gentle and Liam's house. Gentle wasn't any fonder of the boys—and occasionally girls, though those were much rarer—than the rest of the townsfolk, but Liam never denied them. Even during the leanest years, he offered them a few stale rinds of bread or watery stew and a place for them to sleep by the woodstove.

"What the hell is wrong with you?" Manon roared, thrusting herself up from behind the rock and marching down the path. She tore the rifle from his grip.

"I'm sorry!" he said. "I thought you were one of the Sons. They've been all over the mountain. Judge's men, too."

Manon shook the rifle in his face. "Does Cora know you're out here shooting at strangers?"

"No," Peter replied. He pinched his lips defiantly. "You're not going to tell her, are you?"

"You'll be lucky if that's all I do," Manon said. She turned back to Gentle and Kitt. "Come on out. We're safe. Just a little boy playing soldier."

At the sight of Abe rising from behind the rocks, Peter seemed to forget Manon entirely.

"Abe!" he shouted.

The mule lowered his head for a pet.

"How do you know his name?" Gentle asked.

"How could I forget him?"

After a moment Gentle understood: The boy didn't just *look* like one of Liam's stray orphans, he *was* one of them. He'd collapsed on their porch just two years prior, a shivering pile of skin and bones with nothing but a pair of filthy overalls and a soiled hankie to his name. Another son of a dead lumberjack, wandering from town to town in search of food and shelter. Liam had carried him into the kitchen and served him their dinner, watching as the boy scarfed down an entire pot of stew and a loaf of bread, bristling over his bowl like a cornered porcupine. Liam only managed to get him to speak after introducing him to Abe, when the boy, mesmerized by the size of the animal, gave a brief recounting of the months he'd spent skirting violence at the fringes of various labor camps, a journey that had cost him a few teeth and a good portion of the vision in his left eye, the latter of which Liam cured by applying a salve of malachite pigment and tobacco.

Liam had offered to employ him, as he so often did, telling Peter he could clean Abe's stable each day in exchange for room and board. The boy had repaid this offer by disappearing sometime in the night with the rest of their bread and Gentle's favorite hatchet.

Peter grinned sheepishly up at Gentle, as if suddenly remembering his theft. "How's Mr. O'Kelly?" he asked with exaggerated concern. "I still tell Miss Cora the only reason I can see out of this eye is on account of that medicine he gave me."

"He's dead," Gentle said, pointing at the casket. "Murdered by a giant salamander. Don't suppose you've seen it around."

"Giant salamander?"

"Boys," Manon interrupted. Her voice was strained. "I think we should get going."

"You're bleeding," Peter said.

Manon looked down at the bandage wrapped around her hand. The fabric was drenched with bright red blood.

"Yes," she said.

As if she'd come to some conclusion, she closed her eyes and collapsed into the snow.

Gentle and Peter carried Manon—now drifting in and out of consciousness—the rest of the way, while Kitt hurried Abe along behind them. Thankfully Harmony wasn't far, and they reached the town in less than an hour.

The place was less impressive than Gentle had expected. He'd heard plenty of odd tales about the Harmonites ever since they'd settled on the peninsula five years ago: that they had sworn off clothes and frolicked about in the nude; that they'd forbidden property and lived together in great lodges, like the Duwamish; that they burned an effigy of the president each evening and engaged in all manner of exotic sexual practices under the moonlight. And though Gentle doubted the veracity of these stories, he had, at the very least, expected the settlement's outward appearance to reflect the peculiarities of its founders: tidy rows of white houses, perhaps, occupied by men and women in bohemian attire who lounged about quoting Aristotle and Socrates to each other all day.

Instead, they entered a township nearly indistinguishable from the ramshackle settlements that dotted the rest of the peninsula. Log cabins half sunk into the earth, their roofs so overgrown with moss that Gentle might have assumed they were abandoned if not for the clotheslines strung up in the yards behind them and the sooty drifts of smoke curling out from their crooked chimneys. Even the general atmosphere of the place—the smell of pig shit and firewood, the squawking of chickens and children—was no different from what Gentle might have expected on an average day back in Dalton Lake.

As the townsfolk rushed out to meet them, Gentle did notice two oddities: twenty or thirty women among the folks who came to greet them—about three times as many as one usually found in these sorts of towns—and a disproportionate amount of amputees among the men, many of them ambling over on peg legs and scratching at their dirty beards with curved metal hooks. Other than this, the citizens of Harmony were no different from the rest of the people who lived on the peninsula: their clothes all stitches and torn seams, their weary faces prematurely aged from toiling in the endless drizzle.

"Let me through!" cried someone from the back of the crowd. All at once the townsfolk parted, allowing the owner of the voice, a tall woman with spectacularly long limbs, to stride forth. She wore a simple cotton blouse tucked into a pair of denim trousers and possessed a face so peculiar that it somehow looped back around to being beautiful, with a wide-set jaw and furry eyebrows that looked like they might leap from her forehead at any moment. Though she moved quickly, she did so with a notable limp, which caused her to swing out her left leg with every step and pump out her elbows like someone wading through a stream.

"Is that Manon?" she said, her voice straining with concern.

"Her finger," Gentle said. "Tip's been cut off."

The fuzzy eyebrows crept inward, scrunching into a solid black line. "That wouldn't be your doing, would it?"

"Reverend Judge took it."

"This is one of the fellows I was telling you about, Cora," Peter added. "The ones that helped me with my eye."

Cora's eyebrows retreated, repelled by each other like two black magnets. She studied Gentle's face, lingering for a long time on his scar.

"What a coincidence," she said. "Let's get her back to my place. As if I don't have enough to worry about already."

Cora's "place" was a small hut perched precariously at the edge of a cliff over which a waterfall plummeted. Inside, the building was just large enough for a bed, a desk, and three stuffed bookshelves. Despite the lack of windows, the dwelling seemed cozy enough, especially after Cora lit the woodstove and filled the space with golden light. Gentle didn't have much time to appreciate the hut's other domestic accoutrements: After he and Peter had laid Manon out on the quilted bed, Cora ushered them outside and slammed the door shut behind them.

"Cora will fix her up," Peter said. "She always does."

"Does Manon live here?" Gentle asked.

"No. But she shows up every few months or so to do a bit of trading. She brought me a shark tooth once."

"And this Cora woman is your leader?"

"No leaders in Harmony," Peter replied indignantly. "No kings. No bosses. No gods."

"No gods?" Kitt said.

"Atheists," Gentle said. He did not try to hide his disdain. There was no one on earth more hopeless, Liam had once said, than the atheist, upon whom all the world's unending majesty was wasted.

"And proud of it," Peter added. "You all want a tour of town?"

Kitt, who'd turned oddly shy in the other boy's presence, looked pleadingly at Gentle. It was the first time he'd so much as glanced at his uncle since his outburst on the hike. "You all go ahead," Gentle said. "I need a rest."

As the two boys hustled back into town, Gentle went about unloading the casket from Abe's back. The moment the burden was removed, Abe trotted off after them, leaving Gentle by himself.

"You're welcome," Gentle called after the animal. Abe's only reply was an impish swish of his tail.

For the first time since he'd set out from Dalton Lake, Gentle unclasped the ropes around Liam's casket and pushed back the lid. His body tensed in preparation for the sight of his friend's corpse after so many weeks of travel. Thankfully, despite the days of rain and rough terrain, Liam had managed to remain mostly intact. His hair was tousled, and the skin of his face had bloated some, but otherwise he didn't look all that different from when Gentle had dug up his corpse all those weeks ago.

Nevertheless, Gentle found himself withering at the sight of Liam's stillness. His friend had been a creature of perpetual motion—even after he'd turned forty and Gentle had noticed a certain stiffness in his movements, the man could shuffle around his lab until sunrise if Gentle didn't descend the stairs to harangue him into getting some sleep. And when he did rest, his propensity for muttering and snoring and tossing about in bed ensured that, even then, he could never be mistaken for anything but a living being.

But to see him like this? So impossibly inert? A heaviness settled behind Gentle's eyes. He looked away from the coffin and took a deep breath, staring up at the mountainside they'd just descended, its upper reaches hidden behind a wet screen of passing clouds. After he'd calmed down, he reached for his embalming bag and commenced a round of cursory grooming, applying Macassar oil to Liam's faded red hair and freshening his cheeks with a layer of blush.

"I lost the Liber Alchimiae," he said. "I'm sorry. But I haven't given up."

And then, almost without thinking, he bent closer, so that his face hovered only inches from his friend's, and whispered, "Deep waters."

He leaned back and waited. Nothing happened, of course. Liam remained where he was, arms crossed over his chest, eyes closed. Gentle finished his work and closed the casket again. He wandered over to a stump and sat down to watch the river flow over the side of the cliff. It fell a good thirty or forty feet, carving a glossy chute down the stone face and into the overgrown valley below, where it erupted into a cloud of white mist that settled slowly over the surrounding vegetation, dappling the ferns with a thousand glinting gemstones. Somehow, the moisture reached Gentle's face, and no matter how fervently he wiped the droplets from his cheeks, they kept on falling.

Cora emerged from her hut a few hours later, just as it started to snow again. She wore an apron of sorts, its cotton front covered in streaks of fresh blood. When she noticed Gentle gaping at it, she laughed.

"Looks worse than it is," she said. "Manon will be fine."

"She collapsed," Gentle said, watching Cora untie the apron and fling it over a nearby branch.

"Overexertion," Cora said. "Along with malnutrition and dehydration. She just needs rest."

"And the blood?"

"Stitches were a mess. Had to pull them out and start over.

Whoever Crane has sewing up his victims these days is certainly no surgeon."

"But you are?"

"As a matter of fact, yes. Top of my class at Syracuse."

"A lady doctor," Gentle said. "You must be the first."

"Not quite. That honor goes to Elizabeth Blackwell. Trained with her during the war. Hell of a lady."

"You were a surgeon in the war?"

"A nurse, despite my training. We ladies weren't allowed to be surgeons. I worked at Satterlee." She eyed his scar again. "You serve?"

"My friend did," Gentle said. "He was an embalmer."

"He the one in that box? Manon mentioned you were carting a corpse. Something about a giant salamander?"

"It's a long story," Gentle replied.

"One I'm inclined to hear," Cora said. She looked skyward. "What do you say we get out of the snow? You a drinking man?"

"I've been known to dabble," Gentle said.

"Hope you like blueberries," she replied cryptically. "We keep the best stuff in the town hall. Come along."

They descended the dirt slope in front of Cora's house back into town, following the snaking pathways deeper into the clusters of overgrown homes. As they walked, the Harmonites glared at Gentle with unmistakable disdain, some of them going so far as to post up by their front doors with rifles and pistols.

"As you can see," Cora said, "we're all a little tense."

"Sons of Adam giving you trouble?"

"Already tried torching a few buildings, though we scared them off. Crane's men are the real problem. Keep showing up and threatening us."

"He says you're responsible for the mill burnings."

"He just wants a reason to start arresting folks. But unless he has proof of our involvement, he'd be wise to leave us alone. We aren't helpless."

"I'd heard you were pacifists."

"We don't go seeking out confrontations, but we aren't afraid to defend ourselves."

They'd arrived at a larger structure near the center of town—another moss-covered dugout, though this one was much larger than the surrounding buildings, with a bright red banner strung up above its doorway emblazoned with the same words Peter had said earlier: NO KINGS. NO BOSSES. NO GODS.

"You'll need to leave your weapons at the door," Cora said, gesturing at a rack positioned near the building's entrance, where a few handguns and knives already rested.

"Don't have any," Gentle said.

"Lost them in the mountains?"

"Don't carry a gun."

"A man without a gun, in this day and age?" Cora said curiously, more to herself than Gentle. "Wonders never cease."

Inside, the building was dark but spacious, with a dozen long wooden tables arranged around a central hearth already blooming with flame. Two men—one missing a foot, one missing a hand—sat close to the fire, smoking pipes. At Cora's entrance, they smiled brightly, though the expressions of goodwill disappeared when they caught sight of Gentle.

"Everything all right, Cora?" said the one without a hand. He was the larger of the two, a Chinese fellow with arms big enough to strangle a bull.

"Everything's fine, Mr. Li," Cora replied. "This gentleman means us no harm. Isn't that right, Gentle?"

"How do you know my name?" Gentle asked. He was already

calculating how long it would take him to reach the door in case Mr. Li wasn't soothed by Cora's promises. Despite his missing hand, the man was twice his size, and equally as mean-looking.

"Manon and I had some time to chat after she came back to her senses. Lots of interesting things to say about you and that nephew of yours. Kitt, was it?"

"That's right."

"Kitt and Gentle. Odd names. You'll fit right in. Everyone's odd in Harmony." Cora waved Gentle over to a bar on the far side of the room and practically shoved him into a chair.

"Mind if I pour us some drinks?" she called to Mr. Li. "You can put it on my tab."

Mr. Li grunted noncommittally. Gentle was amazed by this interaction—never in his life had he seen a Chinese man speak so casually to a white woman. Back in Dalton Lake, their presence together in this room would have been reason enough to run the man out of town.

Cora seemed entirely unperturbed, however. She walked to the other side of the bar and crouched down, giving Gentle a clear view of the shelves behind her. They were loaded down with odd sculptures: spiraling crescents that resembled the ridged horns of goats, flattened fish with exposed spinal vertebrae and spindly fins, starfish and crabs and something that looked like a very large centipede, all of them carved expertly from chunks of rock.

Cora returned with two full mugs and handed one to Gentle. She followed his gaze to the wall behind her and clucked happily.

"I see you've noticed our fossil collection."

"Manon had one of those on a necklace," Gentle said. "Told us some nonsense about them being millions of years old."

"She lets us keep the ones no one wants to buy. Lately I've been thinking they merit their own place in town. The Harmony

Natural History Museum. Has a nice ring, doesn't it?"

"Depends on your definition of history," Gentle said. He took a deep gulp from the mug. The stuff in the cup burned through him like liquid fire, though it left behind a sweet aftertaste that reminded him of jam. He'd imbibed some suspicious homebrews over the years, but whatever Cora had served might have been the most eye-watering batch of them all.

While Gentle coughed and sputtered all over himself, Cora laughed and took a few tiny swallows of her own drink. "I recommend small sips," she said.

"What is it?" Gentle finally managed to ask.

"Blueberry moonshine. They grow like mad up here."

"Like drinking turpentine." Gentle belched, though this assessment didn't stop him from taking another, albeit more conservative, drink. He could already feel the room's edges dulling.

"So," Cora said, voice dipping down to that pitch that told Gentle they'd moved on to more serious matters. "Mind telling me who you really are? Beyond someone who's interested in giant amphibians?"

Gentle gave her the condensed version: just another Western outcast, trying to scrounge out a living as an embalmer here at the edge of the world.

"And the salamander?"

"Killed my best friend," Gentle said. "So I'm returning the favor."

"With his dead body in tow?" Cora took a long sip of her moonshine, never taking her eyes off Gentle. "No," she said.

"No?"

"No, I don't think you're telling me the whole story. So why don't we try again?"

Maybe it was the fatigue, or the sleeplessness, or the calming sluice of strong liquor in his belly, but before he knew what he was doing, Gentle had told Cora all about Liam's conviction that the salamander's blood was the key ingredient in the Great Work.

Cora leaned forward, looking intrigued, and refilled his drink, which was barely half empty. "So you're trying to make the philosopher's stone?"

"You know about alchemy?"

"Sure," Cora said. "I've read all the greats. Böttger. Brand. Paracelsus, too. 'The dose makes the poison.' Rather ahead of his time in that regard."

"Yes!" Gentle said, unable to keep his voice down. "That's exactly what Liam always said. So you think it will work, then? You think the salamander is the key?"

"Oh, lord, not at all!" Cora said. She started to laugh but stopped herself when she saw the expression on Gentle's face. "Sorry. I'm not trying to condescend. It's just, well, alchemy isn't exactly the cutting edge of the medical profession these days."

"I saw Liam heal plenty of people using alchemy. Did a lot more for them than any country doctor."

"That I believe. Plenty of men in these parts think a scalpel and a couple bottles of opium are equivalent to a medical degree. Let me guess: He made tonics. Peppermint and honey for the treatment of colds. Witch hazel for rashes and sore throats. Dogwood for migraines. And mercury rubs for afflictions of the venereal variety. Am I close?"

Gentle hid his face in his drink. "And they all worked," he muttered.

"Maybe. I bet they did no harm, at least. Sometimes less is more."

"You think Liam healed people by not healing them?"

"We stand at a curious juncture in the history of medicine,"

Cora said. "Soon we'll know how to treat the *causes* of sickness, and not just how to alleviate the symptoms. Or, in the case of men like your friend, fill the body up with some harmless herbs while its natural defenses go about the work of repairing it."

"But Liam knew what caused their sickness," Gentle said.

"Did he? Or did he justify his treatments by referencing positions of stars and the dispensation of bodily humors?"

"Liam could explain it if he was here."

"You don't sound so certain of that."

She had him there. It was true—Liam had a way of confounding even himself when he went about describing why, exactly, a tonic of silver flakes and chamomile could help heal one person's stomachaches and not another's. He'd provided a number of explanations over the years, like how the roots of certain flowers mirrored the size and shape of the organs they were meant to heal, or how the astrological sign of the patient needed to be considered when choosing which minerals to include in their medication. The number and complexity of these considerations had grown considerably in the last few years, until it seemed that each and every individual required a highly specialized assortment of ingredients that only Liam could properly measure, no matter how many times he tried to explain his reasoning to Gentle. Even then, his efforts were inconsistent at best. One of the reasons he'd become so obsessed with finally unlocking the secrets of the philosopher's stone was that he was certain it was the only true path to counteracting whatever dark forces caused men and women to become ill in the first place.

"I've troubled you," Cora said, frowning at him. "It's none of my business, anyway, what a person believes. All worldviews are welcome here in Harmony, so long as they don't infringe upon the freedom of one's fellows."

"Funny," Gentle said. "Could have sworn the sign out there said 'no gods.'"

"More of a suggestion, really," Cora said. "People here can believe what they want about the fundamental nature of the universe, but we prefer they keep it to themselves. No justifying bad behavior by way of divine edict."

Gentle nudged his near-empty glass forward, and Cora refilled it. He was completely under the liquor's spell now, melting into his seat with the familiar, thoughtless elasticity that came over him during any good binge. "And you?" he said. "What is your explanation for our existence here on earth?"

Cora pointed a thumb at the fossils behind the bar. "I'm with Manon and Mr. Darwin," she said.

"Ah. So you're the one who got Manon hooked on all that rubbish."

"Not at all," Cora said. "She was already a staunch evolutionist by the time I met her. Manon has a rare mind for evolutionary biology. Her theories about the geological history of these mountains are fascinating."

"If you say so."

"I'm getting ahead of myself. I usually wait until my second glass to start in on matters of ideology," Cora said. "Let's start over, shall we? Why don't you tell me about that scar of yours? In my experience, there's nothing that puts a man at ease so much as discussing his scars."

Gentle's fingers crept up to his cheek, tracing the edges of the raised skin. "I've noticed you have your fair share of scars around here," he said, turning in his chair to glance back at the two men across the room, neither of whom had stopped glaring at him over the course of the conversation.

"The Judge's former employees. You'd be surprised at the

sorts of indiscretions he thinks warrant amputation. Took Mr. Li's hand because he oversalted his soup."

"Maybe he's just self-conscious," Gentle said. "You know, about that wooden fist of his?"

Cora scoffed. "You know it's a fake, right?"

"Impossible. I saw it myself."

"It's a glove," Cora said. "One of our residents here used to be employed as one of his maids. Said she saw him take it off every night before bed, and there was a perfectly good hand underneath."

"Why would he go to all that trouble?"

"Same reason you hear every rich fellow between here and New York pontificating on his humble beginnings as some lowly shopkeeper or stable hand. Makes them feel like real people—like the only thing separating them from their employees is a bit of gumption and good luck. Every fortune in this country is stained with the blood of innocents, and men like Malcolm Crane know it. That's why they insist on pretending to be normal men. Because if their workers knew what sort of devils hid behind their frocks and top hats, they'd burn every one of their lumber mills and cotton fields and gold mines to the ground within a week."

"Like the Sons of Adam?"

"Indeed," Cora said. "Those madmen are no allies of mine. Just a pack of killers with a penchant for self-aggrandizement. But if they aim to topple Crane's empire, more power to them."

"We were captured by one near the Judge's place," Gentle said. "Supposedly they're being led by Adam Lee."

Cora nodded. "I'd heard some rumors to that effect. Seems fitting that the man the Judge hired to map the peninsula is the one who finally ruins him."

"Even if the Harmonites are the ones who get blamed?"

"We get blamed for every ill in these parts. Nice to have our name attached to something I approve of for once." She took a sip of her drink and winked. "That was a clever trick, by the way."

"What trick?"

"Changing the subject when I asked about your scar," Cora said. "Must not be a story you like to tell."

"There's nothing to tell," Gentle said. "Got lost in the woods when I was younger. Fell and hit my head on a rock. Liam found me and patched me up."

Cora's eyes gleamed. She'd drunk just as much as Gentle, yet she seemed unfazed by the liquor, while Gentle had already started to notice a slight tilt to the bar's dimensions. "Strange," she said.

"How so?"

"I've seen wounds like that before," she replied, leaning over the bar to study Gentle's scar more closely. "But they're usually caused by guns. You sure you didn't fall on a bullet?"

"I'm sure," Gentle said. Cora was staring at him with newfound intensity. He could tell she wanted to pursue this subject further, but something about his face—a begging indifference he'd perfected over the years, dredged up whenever someone asked him questions he didn't much feel like answering—stopped her. She reached below the bar again.

"Another drink?" she said. "Looks like you need it."

Cora offered to let Gentle and Kitt sleep in one of the town's recently abandoned houses, a rotting shed only a little larger than their tent. It came equipped with a woodstove and a pair of frames for their bedrolls.

"Belonged to some fellow who only lived here a couple

weeks," Cora said as she showed them inside, lighting up a dusty oil lamp to reveal the shed's dingy interior, its dirt floor strewn with damp hay and its rafters thick with cobwebs. "He got handsy with some of the women, so we asked him to leave."

"And here I thought Harmony welcomed everyone," said Gentle, who by that time had drunk enough moonshine to set the world fully off its axis. He blinked every few seconds just to bring his sight back into focus, like a sea captain perpetually re-adjusting his spyglass.

"Even we heathens have our limits," Cora replied.

"Where did all the women come from, anyways?"

"Their mother's wombs, I would imagine."

"You know what I mean. Never seen a town with so many ladies this far west."

"They came from the same place as anyone," Cora said, fluttering a hand over her head. "Around. Some are widows of men who worked in timber and mining. Some were employed by the brothels over in Seattle. Easier for an unwed woman to build a life here than anywhere else. We don't have many rules in Harmony, but we do have this one: A woman has the same rights as any man. And anyone who questions that fact is welcome to leave. Which is worth keeping in mind if you plan on sticking around."

"Are you offering us citizenship?"

"Like I said: Everyone's welcome in Harmony."

"Except bosses," Gentle said. "And gropers."

"Goodnight, boys," Cora said, ignoring Gentle's goading.

Gentle and Kitt awkwardly went about preparing for bed, neither of them meeting the other's eyes as they shuffled around the cramped space. Later, after they'd finally put out the light and crawled into their bedrolls, Gentle spoke into the darkness.

"I'm sorry about how I acted last night," he said. "Losing the

Liber Alchimiae wasn't your fault."

"But it was," Kitt replied quickly, as if he'd been agonizing over Gentle's words all day, rolling them around in his head like a scalding ember. "I started the fire."

"If you hadn't, the Judge would be cutting me up right now."

"But you were in that cell because of my father."

"You're not responsible for Emmanuel's actions."

"And he never would have found us if he hadn't met Hercules, who wouldn't have been hunting us if I would have just let him shoot the salamander. Every rotten thing that's happened to us since we left Dalton Lake has been my fault. Everything is always my fault."

"That's just your father talking. Get some sleep. You'll be fine come morning."

"No," Kitt said desperately. "I won't. I haven't been fine since Mother went to that hospital."

Gentle hesitated for a moment before responding.

"Your mother," Gentle said, unsure how to proceed. Did Kitt know the truth? He wouldn't put it past Emmanuel to hide such a thing from his own son—to let the boy yearn desperately for the day she'd return to them, oblivious to the fact that she was never coming home.

"My father told you, didn't he," Kitt said. "That she killed herself."

"I'm so sorry, Kitt."

The boy did not respond. Gentle felt a part of himself yearning to remain in that silence, to end this conversation before it careened off the rails and carried them somewhere neither of them was ready to go. And yet he felt something else, too—a rising certainty that if he did not speak now, something between him and Kitt would be broken forever.

"I suppose you think that was your fault, too," he said.

"Father said she hung herself because of me," Kitt said, and already Gentle could hear the wretched self-loathing in his voice. The bandage pulled back from the old wound, so that he could stick his finger inside and plumb the bloody depths of his own pain. "He said she used to be happy, before I was born. He said I'd been a disappointment to her. And then he hit me. That's why I attacked him the way I did. I didn't want to kill him, I swear. But I was just so angry. And he looked so *surprised* when I fought back. Like he never expected someone like me to hurt him. It felt good to prove him wrong. But Mother hated violence. She'd never let Father hit me before. So maybe he was right. Maybe she was scared of me the same way she was scared of him. Maybe she wanted to get away from both of us."

"No," Gentle said. "That's Emmanuel's ugliness, not yours. You can't trust it. Don't give him the satisfaction."

"But," Kitt began. Gentle silenced him.

"I didn't know your mother," Gentle said. "But I know you never would have done something to hurt her. I can't speak to her reasons for doing what she did. But I don't believe, for a second, that she did it because of you."

Kitt was quiet again. They listened to the wind tugging at the roof, felt it slipping over the cracks in the walls and sliding its cold fingers over their faces. The trees creaked as they strained against it, joined by the murmuring voices in the nearby houses and the steady fizzle of the distant waterfall.

When Kitt spoke again, a long time had passed.

"It doesn't matter why she did it," he said. "Because I'm not like her. I'm not a coward, and I won't give up. We're going to bring her back. Her *and* Liam. We'll finish the Great Work and fix everything."

Gentle, who'd been hovering at the very edge of sleep, was stirred back into consciousness by Kitt's words.

"Right," he said, though there was an uncertainty in his voice that terrified him. Kitt didn't hear it—within a few minutes he was asleep, his breaths long and steady in the dark. It was Gentle's turn, now, to feel guilt riot through his insides, closing a tightening fist around his lungs until, breathless with dread, he sent out a hand in search of his Sweet Vitriol.

Around dawn, Gentle slipped out of bed, quietly added a few more logs to the fire, and left the cabin, careful not to wake his nephew. The snow had continued through the night, smothering Harmony beneath a sheet of fresh powder, and the air was sharp and frigid in his lungs. As he walked through town, Gentle encountered a few fellow early risers, busy clearing away the snow from their front porches and swiping it from their roofs with brooms and shovels. They nodded at him warily as he passed.

Cora was awake too, chopping wood in front of her house, dressed in a heavy woolen overcoat and knitted cap.

"You're up early," she said, leaning against her axe and wiping a sleeve against her forehead. "Cabin keep you warm?"

"Warmest place I've slept in a week," Gentle said. "You want some help with that?"

"Does it look like I need help?" Cora replied. There was a sharpness to her tone he hadn't heard yesterday. "To what do I owe the pleasure?"

"Was hoping to see Manon. She awake?"

"Sure is. Bad dreams kept her up most of the night."

"Bad dreams?"

"You'll have to ask her. She's being stubborn, as usual. Wouldn't let me give her anything to help her sleep."

That explained her tone, then, Gentle thought—it was the calculated indifference of someone trying to hide that they'd just been in a fight.

"All right if I go in?"

Cora nodded and returned to her splitting.

Inside the house, Manon lay in bed, glumly sucking one of her cigarettes and staring at the ceiling. Despite Cora's talk of her speedy recovery, the woman did not look much better than she had the day before: Dark circles carved shadowy crescents under her bloodshot eyes, and her skin was pale and clammy. A fresh bandage was wrapped around her hand.

Gentle caught sight of his own countenance in a small mirror hanging on the other side of the room. His dark hair lay over his face in a greasy cascade of tangles and knots. When he slicked it back over his skull in some vain attempt to appear more presentable, all he did was reveal the grisly condition of his face, a mess of muddy cheeks and unchallenged beard growth, his scar rising up out of his patchy salt-and-pepper facial hair like a streak of rotting fat. No wonder the Harmonites had looked upon him with such disdain; he resembled nothing so much as a shambling corpse.

Manon offered him some tobacco from a leather pouch, which he used to fill up his pipe—a slim and elegant thing carved from whale bone, which he'd received from a captain in Port Angeles as payment for piecing together the body of a man who'd been crushed between the side of a shipping vessel and a dock pylon. He stuffed it carefully, trying to find his words, while Manon watched him with unblinking eyes.

"So?" she said, after he'd taken a few long drags from the pipe and still hadn't spoken. "You come here to blow smoke in my face?"

"Wanted to see how you were doing," Gentle said.

"I'm alive."

"That's good."

Another few moments of silence passed.

"That all?" Manon asked.

"Wanted to say thank you, too."

Manon sat up a little in bed. "Now, that's a surprise."

"Wouldn't have made it over the mountains without you," he said.

Manon stared at him, cigarette hanging from her mouth. "Don't mention it," she said. "Far as I'm concerned, you all just followed me here."

"The Harmonites seem to know you well. You visit often?"

"Every now and again," Manon said noncommittally. "Sell them medicine and such. Cora likes to pretend that Harmony is self-sufficient, but there's still a lot they can't make for themselves. And it's a hell of a trek to the nearest town."

"That's kind of you. Given how the rest of the peninsula treats them."

Manon snorted two pillars of smoke from her nostrils. "Kindness has nothing to do with it. They pay a good price for what I bring them."

"Come now," Gentle said. "You mean you don't subscribe to Miss Cora's dreams of utopia?"

"Careful now," Manon said. "She'd give her life for these people if it came down to it. You notice that limp of hers? Pinkertons did that, back in Montana, on account of her riling up some mine workers. She isn't all talk."

"You two sure are protective of each other," Gentle said.

"We've known each other a long time," Manon said. Her eyes

shifted out of focus for a moment, lured inward by some memory. "She's been through a lot, trying to get this place up and running. Might not look like much now, but it was a whole lot less when she first showed up."

"I thought Harmony didn't have any leaders?"

"She'd never call herself one."

"Is that respect I hear in your voice? Surprised you haven't settled down here yourself."

"It won't last," Manon said. "Good things never last in this country."

"Awfully cynical."

"You disagree?"

"No," Gentle said. "Not at all."

The end of Manon's cigarette crackled as she inhaled more smoke, throwing the cratered scars on her cheeks into high relief. "So," she said.

"There's one more thing," Gentle said.

"The salamander."

"In the mountains you said you might be inclined to resume the hunt."

"For a fair price."

Gentle bit his lip. "Even now that you've seen it?"

"Why would that change anything?"

"You've been having nightmares, haven't you?"

"So?"

"You see it, don't you? The salamander. Does it speak to you? Does it talk about the deep waters?"

"They're just dreams," Manon said. Though Gentle noticed the uncertainty in her voice.

"Dreams must be heeded and accepted. For a great many of them come true."

"What?"

"Something Liam used to say," Gentle said. "Everyone who sees the salamander seems to have these nightmares. Maybe killing it is the only way to make them go away."

Manon's eyes stared at him, unflinching, through the smoke.

"Nightmares might be a novelty to you white folk," she said. "But they're nothing new to me."

"Kitt has the money. And I can't bring him along. Not if we're going deeper into the peninsula. It won't be safe."

"Then I suppose you'll have to ask him for a loan," she said.

Gentle sighed. He'd hoped that Manon had been as affected by the salamander as he—that she would feel, as he now did, that she could never rest until she'd laid eyes on it again.

"I'll get you your money," he said bitterly, rising to his feet. "When will you be ready to leave?"

"A week. At most."

"You lost a finger," Gentle said.

"The *tip* of a finger," she replied. "I've dealt with worse."

"Fine," Gentle said.

"And Kitt?" Manon asked. "What will you do with him?"

"The boy is none of your concern," Gentle replied. He opened the door and left, gasping at the sting of the cold air outside.

Kitt was awake when Gentle returned to the cabin, waiting for him with a bowl of porridge and a mug of coffee.

"They have a cafeteria here," he said excitedly. "And you take what you want and don't have to pay. Isn't that something?"

"Very civilized," Gentle said, settling down to eat.

"Where were you?"

"Checking in on Manon. She's doing better."

"Has she agreed to help us keep looking for the salamander?"

"She's considering it. Still wants her money, though. Despite us saving her life."

"That's all right," Kitt said. "She's a good guide, don't you think?"

"Sure," Gentle said. He stared down into his porridge, smushing the gruel around with his spoon. "You got that money in a safe place?"

"I keep it in my sketchbook," replied Kitt, patting one of the rotten slabs of wood that lined the room. "I'm hiding it in the wall."

"Good," Gentle said, still avoiding the boy's eyes. "Keep it there. No telling who we can trust around here."

For the next week, while they waited for Manon to recover, Gentle and Kitt settled into life in Harmony. Despite their status as temporary residents, Cora explained that they would still be expected to comport themselves like regular Harmonites and contribute to the town's general upkeep. For Gentle, this mostly meant clearing snow off the roads and helping various citizens with odd jobs around their homes—work he'd become quite acclimated to while living with Liam. With Gentle, the Harmonites were dour and tight-lipped, following closely behind him as he went about his work replacing creaky floorboards and insulating windows with tar, as though they feared he might steal the jars of pickled vegetables they kept on their shelves.

Kitt, on the other hand, went to work in the camp cafeteria, where his rosemary biscuits quickly elevated him to beloved status. The revelation that Kitt had started the fire that burned down the Judge's house solidified the Harmonites' admiration. After just a few days, the Harmonites had nicknamed him "Chef," and were greeting him in the street like he'd lived there his whole life.

Gentle went out of his way to avoid his nephew when possible, turning down alleys when he saw him strolling with Peter on the main avenue, or lingering in the town stable with Abe until he was sure that it was late enough that Kitt would be asleep when he returned. It caused Gentle no small amount of pain to return home each night and see the bowl of stew, now cold, that the boy had brought him from the cafeteria in hopes of them having dinner together. But Gentle felt too guilty in Kitt's presence. He did not enjoy having to lie to him about how they'd resume their search for the salamander once Manon's finger had adequately healed.

When Gentle wasn't playing handyman, he mostly sulked in the town hall, sipping blueberry moonshine and listening to the Harmonites argue over matters of local governance. He was audience to half a dozen such meetings, which were surprisingly organized affairs. Some of them regarded personal disputes—a pair of farmers who'd decided to manage a plot together, only to come to blows over what one of them saw as an uneven distribution of labor—while others pertained to the town's general upkeep. Gentle was surprised to discover that no subject was too small for discussion: One night, the townsfolk spent nearly an hour arguing over the cafeteria's menu for the next week, unearthing long-standing disputes about the souls of livestock and the future health of Harmony's soil, with a variety of clans and cliques chiming in to make their case.

The most popular subject of debate, though, was Reverend Judge Crane. There had been no word from the Army of the Olympics since Gentle and Kitt's arrival, and the town was split on how to prepare for the possibility of an attack by the Judge and his posse. Cora, and most Harmonites, wanted the town to make emergency plans, but no preparations to fight. But a smaller number wanted to reinforce the armory—at present a few old rifles and pistols—with a larger assortment of bullets and weaponry, and to construct and patrol a barricade along the main route between Harmony and Crane's camp. The only other way to reach town was farther south, a journey no one expected Crane's men to take since it would require hiking a significant distance around the mountains to reach them.

One surprising supporter of bolstering the town's defenses was the taciturn bartender, Mr. Li. One night, while Cora labored on and on about property rights and the rule of law, and how a man like the Reverend Judge would never risk outright war so soon after Washington had entered the union, he snorted audibly. The woman spun around at the sound, looking a little betrayed, while Mr. Li sighed and shook his head, as though disappointed that he'd allowed this vocalization of his disagreement to escape.

"Something to add, Mr. Li?" Cora asked.

"Begging your pardon," he said. "I only worry that the Judge has less respect for the law than you do."

"So we should arm ourselves and engage with this army of his in open combat?"

"Nothing so dramatic. But would it really be so foolish to have some folks patrolling the mountain trails? Just to sound the alarm if the Judge makes a move?"

"No one can match the state when it comes to violence," Cora said. "The more we act like a militia, the more justification the Judge will have to treat us like one. For better or worse, we must trust in the law."

"Easy for you to say," Mr. Li replied.

"Excuse me?" Cora said.

Mr. Li shook his head, as if merely broaching the subject exhausted him. “Meaning no disrespect, Cora,” he said. “But when people like me trust in the law, we end up hanging from trees.”

The blood drained from Cora’s face. For a moment she seemed lost for words, her lips forming and unforming syllables that never arrived.

“Of course,” she finally said. She turned back to the rest of the assembled Harmonites, many of whom had suddenly discovered something very interesting in the cloudy depths of their moonshine. “Shall we put it to a vote, then?”

As usual, the majority agreed with Cora’s position, though a few switched camps that evening, raising their hands uncertainly in support of organizing Harmony’s defense.

Mr. Li, Gentle noticed, chose not to cast a vote.

Most nights, the Harmonites argued for hours, while Gentle hunched in the corner of the hall and drank himself into a woozy stupor. Occasionally the debates became quite heated, with the participants lashing out at one another in full-throated diatribes, spilling their drinks and jamming accusatory fingers in one another’s faces. Gentle quickly came to understand why the Harmonites were asked to leave their guns at the door.

What was even more miraculous, though, was the manner in which these chaotic meetings came to a close. The townsfolk made their opinions known, put it to a vote, and then—once all the day’s issues had been discussed and put to rest—the Harmonites refilled their glasses, settled into their seats, and went about making civilized conversation with each other like regular saloon patrons, as if they hadn’t been hurling the gravest of insults at one another just minutes before.

“How’s it possible that you all haven’t killed each other?” Gentle asked Cora one night, after she’d saddled up next to him and commenced her own nighttime libations. As it turned out,

Cora enjoyed drinking nearly as much as Gentle, and they spent most of the evenings that week seated side by side at the bar, throwing back moonshine and engaging in a bit of intellectual sparring, though Gentle suspected Cora only joined him there because she couldn't stand to see someone sitting all alone in her town hall.

"We are all invested in Harmony's success," Cora said. "No matter our ideological differences. There are few problems that can't be solved by an involved discussion among equals."

"You should have shared this revelation with the nation back before the war began," Gentle said. "You might have saved a few lives."

"Sarcasm is a frail replacement for insight, Mr. Montgomery. Tell me: Are you capable of genuine belief? Or are you one of those sorts who revels in mere contentiousness?"

"I've pried enough bullets and blades out of men's bellies to know how folks in this country prefer to settle their disputes."

"And thus we are doomed to wrestle about in the mud and muck," Cora said. "Until we complete the Great Work, correct?"

Gentle scratched desolately at his beard and stared at the massive fossil of a curled nautilus looming over the bar. "Alchemy is an ancient science."

Cora snorted into her glass. "Ancient, yes. A science, hardly. A cabal of men who think that boiling bits of minerals and dunking them in dubious fluids gives them sovereignty over the universe. Boys on the beach, lording over sandcastles. Same as the Judge, with his little militia, and Adam Lee, with his army of madmen."

"Liam was nothing like that. Liam helped people."

"I don't question your friend's intentions. But did it ever occur to him that life wasn't something we needed to bring to heel? That we wouldn't one day be asked to pay some price for pruning back every wilderness into a more palatable shape? Manon's people lived here for who knows how long, and this place was like paradise to them. How much time did it take the white man to turn it into hell?"

"So you'd have us all sleeping in huts," Gentle said. "That's your answer? Cast off progress and live like animals?"

"Ah, progress," Cora said. "How kind has progress been to folks like Manon and Mr. Li?"

She had him there. "It doesn't matter," he said. "Man seeks dominion over nature. It's been that way since God put us in the garden."

"That's one story. But there are plenty of others."

"Like what?"

Cora leaned back and surveyed the surrounding patrons, all of whom were engaged in their own conversations. When she seemed confident that no one was eavesdropping, she hunched closer to Gentle and said, "You ever heard of the Leshy?"

"Sounds like something that gives you a nasty rash."

"Funny. But no. The Leshy is a kind of forest spirit. A protector, really. My mother grew up hearing stories about it, back in the old country. I've been thinking about this salamander of yours—its coloring, its size, its propensity for driving folks mad whenever it's nearby—and it's reminding me of the sorts of things she used to say about the Leshy."

"And this Leshy was a giant salamander?"

"It could take any form it wanted. Sometimes it was an old man covered in vines and moss. Sometimes it was a stag. Sometimes it was nothing more than a voice whispering the wind. What matters is that the people respected the Leshy. They didn't have a choice in the matter—if they upset it by disrespecting the forest, maybe by hunting too many animals, or cutting down too many trees, the Leshy would lash out and make life miserable. Crops would die. Farm animals would refuse to eat. The land itself would withhold its bounty. The Leshy loved tricks and illusions, too. It could appear and disappear at will. Make you hear and see things that didn't exist. Give you bad dreams. That sort of thing."

A shudder slithered through Gentle. He'd never told Cora about his nightmares, for fear that she might think he was losing his mind. Nor had he mentioned that strange dam they'd stumbled upon outside Cedarville—how his whole body had revolted at the sight of it. "You surprise me," he said. "For someone so quick to discount the hermetical arts, it seems awfully hypocritical of you to start proselytizing about forest spirits."

"I'm not so arrogant as to assume I know everything about how this world works. Maybe the Leshy is no different than the manatees sailors used to mistake for mermaids. Another animal made mystical by our own misunderstanding. What matters is what the Leshy represented. Respect for the forest. A warning that disregarding nature would not go unpunished. Maybe if the men of this country grew up with that sort of story, we wouldn't be in the trouble we're in now."

"You make it sound so easy," Gentle said.

Cora jerked her thumb at the fossils arranged on the wall in front of them. "It's no harder than a fish learning to walk on four legs. Is it so impossible to believe that we can change? That we could see ourselves as one thread of the world's tapestry, rather than its weaver?"

No, Gentle thought. It wasn't impossible. Liam had always said something similar, albeit in different words. *Man is not mere matter*, he once told Gentle. *He is spirit, first and foremost. The body might bind him for his short sojourn on this earth, but in par-*

adise he will change his shape as easily as a man slipping into a new suit. He will fly in the air if he so chooses, or swim deep in the sea. For man was never meant to be this single, bumbling creature. He was meant to be everything.

Liam would have loved Harmony, Gentle realized. It was he who should be sitting here, sparring with Cora over high ideas about humanity's place in the cosmos. The thought saddened him so terribly that tears began to gather in the corners of his eyes. He began digging in his coat for the final vial of Sweet Vitriol, desperate for that little sip of calm. Thus far, he'd been careful not to imbibe any in Cora's presence, but the urge this time was too strong.

"What's that?" she said as he uncorked the vial.

"Just some medicine," Gentle replied.

"Of what sort?"

"Nothing of interest to you."

"Few things fail to interest me," she said. "What's in it?"

Gentle considered lying to her. But then it occurred to him that Cora, being a surgeon, might have her own stash of Sweet Vitriol—or, at the very least, the ingredients necessary for him to make more, since he was down to his last few drops. Liam had never shared the exact recipe with him, but Gentle knew the approximate formula from watching him brew new batches over the years.

He shared the names of these compounds with Cora. She frowned. "What do you take this for?"

"I have nightmares. It helps me sleep."

Though this had proved less and less true with each night he'd spent in Harmony. Gentle had hoped that their relocation to the mountains might have reduced his nighttime terrors. After all, there seemed to be no evidence that the salamander had come anywhere near Harmony: None of the residents had seen the creature, and their drinking water remained untainted from its influence. Harmony, somehow, had been protected from it all.

And yet Gentle's dreams had only gotten worse. There were the images he'd come to expect—the boy with the obliterated face, the labyrinthine ice cave, the green valley sundered with fire, the monumental waves crashing over it all—but the endless stream of nightmare imagery that came after was becoming more varied and vivid. He spent his evenings grappling through the crowded streets of filthy shantytowns or scaling the girders and piping of machines that seemed to contain whole cities, Babels of shrieking steel that severed the sky with fissures of black smoke. One night he dreamed he was trapped in a warehouse of pigs, their bodies squeezed so close together that one could not move without sending a hundred more screeching in protest. Above him hung the bodies of countless swine, headless and pink in the darkness, blood dripping from their carcasses like rain.

He returned from these dreams filled with a guilt he could not name. It took him a long time to return to his body, to shake the sleep from his stiff limbs and settle back into his cold, aching frame. Even then, after he'd crawled out of his bed and stepped outside the cabin, the visions lingered behind his eyes, so that everywhere he looked he saw two different landscapes. The snowy green forests of the present, and the dry, lifeless horrors of that other place the salamander had shown him, that wasteland that seemed to be waiting behind it all like a sour, wrinkled pit in the center of a fruit.

"I should imagine it does a lot more than help you sleep," Cora said now, pointing at the bottle. "Based on its contents. Yet here you are, drinking it at the bar."

"It calms my nerves. So long as I don't drink too much."

Cora's eyebrows wiggled into an arrangement of concern. "You drink this every day?"

"Just about. Though my supplies are running low. Maybe you could mix up some more for me?"

"I don't have those sorts of substances available to me here. And if I did, I certainly wouldn't be using them to calm anyone's *nerves*."

"What do you mean?"

"Your Sweet Vitriol, as you call it," she said, "is nothing more than a witch's brew of ether and laudanum. Both highly addictive, I might add."

"Liam was always careful to moderate his doses," Gentle said. Though he was thinking, now, of the months leading up to Liam's death, when his friend had become increasingly reliant on the medicine.

"And how about you?"

"Perhaps less so," Gentle admitted. "Though I've a few more years of heavy drinking behind me than he did. I can handle it."

"The composition of these substances is nothing like conventional alcohol. Have you suffered any convulsions since you started taking it?"

"No," Gentle said. "Why?"

"Common symptom of ether overdose. Not a pretty sight. Have you given any to the boy?"

"Of course not."

"Well, I'll give you credit for that, at least."

"You sound awfully judgmental for someone who brews moonshine strong as this."

"Alcohol is a vice, I'll admit," Cora said. "But the stuff you're imbibing makes our moonshine look like mare's milk. I've seen what it does to those who overindulge. And I've witnessed the horrors endured by those who try and break the habit. You say that's your last vial?"

"It is," Gentle said.

Cora whistled and shook her head.

"I'll be praying for you, then," she said.

"I thought you were an atheist."

"I'll make an exception in your case," she said. "When that vial is empty, you'll need all the help you can get."

At the end of the week, just as Gentle had settled into his usual seat at the bar, a young man burst through the front door of the town hall, breathless and powdered with snowflakes. Gentle recognized him from around town: a scruffy twenty-year-old who wore a leather eyepatch over his left socket. A few Harmonites—Cora among them—rose from their seats and surged forward to meet him, leading him to a table near the fire and pouring him a drink. As they waited for him to catch his breath, a tense silence descended over the room. They expected the worst, no doubt—word of the Reverend Judge's posse marching over the pass.

But when the man finally began to speak, he delivered his news with a smile.

"They're gone," he said. "The Army of the Olympics is gone!"

For the next few minutes, the Harmonites stood in rapt disbelief as the man explained that he had just returned from the other side of the pass, where he'd been scouting out the Reverend Judge's valley. He'd found the property deserted, the Reverend Judge's scorched mansion standing silent over the empty workers' quarters. He stayed there for half a day, he explained, and didn't see a soul—not even one of the Judge's servants. The place was abandoned.

"How do we know they haven't set out over the pass already?" Mr. Li said from behind the bar. "Maybe that's why they were gone."

"I would have seen evidence of them on the trail," the man replied. "There was nothing up there but me and the squirrels."

"There's dozens of trails in those mountains," Mr. Li replied uncertainly. "You couldn't have checked them all."

The man shook his head. "No way the Judge could move so many men through the woods without me catching sight of some footprints, or at least a smoke trail. I'm telling you: The mountains were empty."

Gentle noticed a subtle change beginning to take hold of the Harmonites. Slowly, as if they couldn't quite trust their reactions, the townsfolk stared down into their laps, each man and woman lost in some silent contemplation too delicate to share. A faint breeze untethered in the air, as though all of them had let loose a single, collective sigh.

No one looked more changed than Cora. She glared at the ceiling, grinding her lower jaw back and forth, her face twisted into the jubilant concentration of a desperate gambler trying to hide their glee at the sight of a royal flush.

"I knew it," she said quietly. "Even the Judge isn't so foolish as to attack American citizens."

"You really think he's given up?" Mr. Li said.

"We could send some folks into the mountains tonight," Cora said, but Gentle could tell from her tone that she didn't really think this was necessary. "Check the trails. Just to be sure."

The man in the eyepatch jumped to his feet and spoke over her. "I saw it myself!" he shouted, striding over to Mr. Li and slapping his palm on the bar. "We won! By God, we won! Drinks are on me, Mr. Li. Tonight, all of Harmony drinks for free!"

The hall erupted into celebration. The Harmonites jumped out of their seats and threw their arms around one another. Some of them knocked over their drinks and fell, laughing, to the floor. A man with a wooden leg waddled over to the bar's piano and began to play.

They looked like souls returned from the dead. The Harmonites Gentle had worked beside since arriving in town, he realized, had been pale shadows of their former selves. The joylessness he'd observed in their labors, which he'd mistaken as a side effect of their late-night debates about who should be in charge of cleaning the latrines that week, fell away, replaced by a tender comradery far more intimate than the polite fondness he often encountered in frontier towns like Dalton Lake, where the most physical affection one could expect from one's fellows was a neighbor's handshake at church.

The Harmonites had no such scruples: They kissed one another's cheeks and ruffled one another's hair. As the man at the piano began to play a jaunty tune, they pushed the tables to the edges of the room and commenced a round of dancing with such natural ease that it was obvious such celebrations had been a common occurrence before the Reverend Judge cast his shadow over the town.

News traveled quickly through the rest of the settlement, and within an hour the town hall was stuffed to the brim with happy, sweating Harmonites. Kitt and the town cook, a German by the name of Hilda, brought in vats of steaming stew, baskets of bread still warm from the oven, and tray after tray of dried meats. When they saw Kitt, the Harmonites descended on him in an instant, hoisting him into the air and crying out "Chef! Chef! Chef!" The boy blushed madly while he was passed about by sturdy hands and wooden hooks—though, Gentle noticed, he always swiveled himself about so that he could keep his eyes on Peter, who smirked and waved at him from his place beside the door.

When the Harmonites finally let Kitt down and he returned, giggling, to Peter's side, Gentle hung his head and slid down to the bar's darkest corner, where he made the most of the open tab by waving down Mr. Li and purchasing a bottle of moonshine for himself.

Manon made an appearance later in the night. Gentle, who'd worked his way through most of the bottle by then, discovered that he was overjoyed by the sight of her familiar face, and would not stop waving at her and shouting her name until she acquiesced to sitting down next to him. Despite the hall's crowding, the stool had remained emphatically empty, as though even in the best of times the Harmonites could not bring themselves to take a seat next to the disfigured, brooding drunk who'd haunted their streets all week.

Gentle shook the bottle in her face.

"You're up and walking! Pour you a drink to celebrate?"

"I'm fine with water."

"More for me," Gentle replied. He refilled his glass. "I hate water."

"A shame," Manon said. "Looks like you could use a gallon or two."

"Never learned how to swim. Liam tried to teach me, but it never stuck." Gentle said, knowing, even as the words left his mouth, that the connection was nonsensical. But the moonshine had filled his head with thoughts of his friend—all those summers Liam forced Gentle to accompany him down to the lake, so that he could make yet another attempt at teaching him to float. What followed was an hour or two of fierce aquatic combat, with

Liam wrestling Gentle beneath the lake's surface while Gentle, screaming, tried to crawl back to shore. The lessons always ended the same way: with Gentle clinging to the rocks on the beach in panting desperation while Liam, knee-deep in the lake, clutched his belly and howled with laughter.

"Bad luck for you," Manon replied. "A man who can't swim hunting down a giant salamander."

"Liam didn't believe in bad luck. He had faith. More than enough for the both of us. Never had much myself."

"You seem awfully obsessed with this beast for a man lacking in faith."

"I want to leave tomorrow," Gentle said suddenly. "Will you be well enough?"

"Will you?"

"This is nothing," Gentle said, waving at the bottle. "I'll be ready."

"Have you told the boy yet?"

Kitt was standing on the other side of the room, laughing at something Peter had just said. The sight made Gentle's chest ache. He'd never seen his nephew so at ease.

"I told you: Kitt isn't your concern."

"My God," Manon said, shaking her head. "He doesn't know, does he?"

"Will you be ready to leave tomorrow or not?"

"Will you have my money?"

"I'll have your money."

"Then I'll be ready," Manon said.

"Ready for what?" said Cora, appearing suddenly beside them. Her face was flushed from dancing, or drinking, or both. She leaned herself against Manon's shoulder—a gesture, Gentle noticed, that brought a rush of scarlet to the other woman's cheeks.

"We're discussing the salamander," she said. "We'll be heading out tomorrow."

"Ah, yes," Cora said. "The Great Work. So we haven't enticed you into staying?"

"All that matters is the salamander," Gentle replied.

"And you have to take our Manon with you?" she said. She gazed down at Manon with half-lidded eyes. "After such a short visit?"

"About time I hit the road anyway," Manon said.

"Despite my best efforts," Cora said. Then, as if it was the most natural thing in the world, she pressed the tip of her finger to Manon's chin and tilted her face up for a kiss.

Gentle sat there in stunned silence. The nearby Harmonites seemed entirely unperturbed by this turn of events, glancing quickly away, not out of disgust, but out of what looked to Gentle like silent respect, as though they wanted to offer the two women as much privacy as was possible in that packed room.

When they were finished, Cora smirked at him provocatively, and Gentle had the sense that he was being tested.

"Something wrong?" she said.

"I'm only impressed," Gentle said, "that you feel comfortable performing your affections so publicly."

"Such affections aren't rare in Harmony," Cora replied, and as she did so she looked to the dance floor. Gentle followed her gaze, and, to his surprise, noticed other such pairings around the room: two gruff gentlemen swooning slowly to the music, their chins perched atop each other's shoulders. A pair of young women sitting together at a table, their hands entwined as they whispered into each other's ears.

Just behind them, Gentle noticed Kitt, standing beside Peter near the front door. They were surrounded by a gaggle of the town's other children—orphans, mostly—who Peter was regaling with one of his stories, which required him to leap about and toss out his hands with great enthusiasm. At one point, he threw an arm around Kitt's shoulder and pulled him close. Gentle watched his nephew turn bright red, but he seemed to find great comfort in the embrace, even going so far as to let his head rest against Peter's shoulder so that he could peer up at him with unabashed joy in his face.

"We'll be sad to see you go," Cora said. "Kitt fits in perfectly here."

And Gentle could tell, just by the tone of her voice, that she'd seen the truth of Kitt's affections the moment they arrived. That she had perceived, in a moment, what Gentle had failed to notice after weeks of traveling with the boy—a truth that Emmanuel had probably sussed out as well, and for which he had undoubtedly punished Kitt mercilessly. He recalled the disdain his brother had shown for the fact that Gentle and Liam had lived together for so many years. How would he react if he caught his own son staring, with such scandalous longing, at one of the farmhands back on the family ranch? There was no way Emmanuel could conceive of such desires as anything but the most severe aberration, worthy of torments Gentle couldn't even begin to imagine. Though Kitt had said his mother never let his father hit him, Gentle remembered Emmanuel's talent for leaving scars in hidden places. He forced down a mouthful of burning moonshine just to hold back the caustic surge of his own dismay.

"Yes, about Kitt," Gentle said. "I've a favor to ask of you."

He waited outside their cabin until Kitt returned home from the celebration, smoking endless bowls of tobacco in a fruitless attempt to sober himself. By the time Kitt appeared on the trail leading to the cabin, Gentle's throat felt as though it were made of brittle glass.

"Is everything all right?" Kitt said upon reaching him. The boy's face was dewy with sweat.

"Sit down," Gentle said. He used the sleeve of his coat to wipe away the thin layer of snow that had accumulated on the wooden chair beside him. "I've something to tell you."

"Can we go inside? It's freezing."

"Better out here. Where I can see the stars," he said. No stars were visible through the clouds, but Gentle knew if he tried to stand up, now, the liquor would sweep his feet out from underneath him. Better to sit here and get it all out while he still had the last bit of his wits about him.

"All right," Kitt said cautiously, sitting down. Gentle handed him the bottle of moonshine. There were still a few sips left at the bottom. "Are you sure?"

"We're celebrating, aren't we?"

He watched the boy uncork the bottle and venture a sip. Kitt scowled in disgust. "It burns," he croaked.

"It's supposed to burn."

Kitt tipped the bottle back again. No scowl this time. "There you go," Gentle said. "Feel a bit warmer now?"

Kitt nodded. He was smiling, no doubt surprised to find his uncle so talkative after days of silent shunning.

"Right then," Gentle said. "There's something I need to say."

Gentle stared at the sparkling patch of snow between his knees. He took a deep breath, and then another. Still he did not speak.

"What's wrong?" Kitt asked. The tenderness in his voice made

Gentle furious—reminded him, again, that a creature like Kitt had no right being out here in this squalid country. He belonged in a library somewhere, sitting beside a crackling fire with a mug of warm chocolate in his hands.

"It's not an easy story to tell," Gentle said. "And I've no practice in sharing it."

"Maybe you can share it another time?"

"No," Gentle said. "It's important you hear it tonight. Just give me that bottle, will you?"

Kitt passed the moonshine back to him, and Gentle drained the rest in one gulp. He tossed the bottle to the ground when he was finished, hissing through the scald it left behind in his throat.

"It concerns this scar of mine," he said. "And how I got it."

"When you ran away to join the army," Kitt said. "I remember. You fell and hit your head."

"Right. But that's a lie."

"What do you mean?"

"I didn't run away to enlist," Gentle said. "Or, rather, I told myself that was why I was running away. But it wasn't the real reason."

"What was the real reason?"

"My brother," Gentle said. "I just wanted to get away from him. Like you."

Kitt made a pensive noise. "Did you have a fight, too?"

Gentle shook his head. "Our mother was sick. Very sick. I thought she was going to die, and she was the only thing protecting me from him."

"I felt that way, too," Kitt said. "When Mother passed."

"Yes. I thought you might understand."

"That's your lie? That you left to get away from my father?"

"That's the *first* lie," Gentle said.

Kitt was silent. The sound of singing Harmonites drifted over on the wind.

"I did get lost in the woods," Gentle said. "For nearly a week. And I did go a little mad, from hunger and exhaustion. But I didn't hurt myself falling into any ditch."

Gentle took a puff from his pipe. Already, the words were carrying him backward, replacing the snowscape around him with the twisted tangle of that Ohio forest where he had wandered, alone, for so many days.

"I tried to cross a river," Gentle said. "Even though I couldn't swim. Even though I knew it was too deep. I'd lost all my senses by then. I was so tired. So hungry. I just wanted to keep moving. Away from Emmanuel. I'd started to imagine that he was following me. Felt his eyes on my back, like he was waiting until I was weakest to come and grab me. I just wanted to get away.

"So I waded through the river at a place that seemed shallow. But I miscalculated and lost my footing. I was swept downstream. There was nothing I could do but let the water carry me along, spinning me around like a log, dunking my head beneath the surface whenever it liked. At a certain point I just stopped struggling. I was sure I would die. But I didn't. Eventually the river just spat me out into some shallows, and I crawled my way to shore.

"I don't know how long I stayed there. It was daylight when I pulled myself out of the water. And night when I picked up the rifle I'd brought with me and turned it on myself. I knew I wouldn't survive out there on my own. I'd barely been away a few days, and already I was lost and starving. But I couldn't go back to Emmanuel. I just couldn't. So what other choice did I have? I was so afraid. So alone."

His fingers reached up for his scar. They traced the raised ridge of the flesh arcing over his cheekbone and sliding up his face, just missing his eye.

"Couldn't even manage my own suicide," Gentle said. "Lost my nerve at the last second. Jerked the rifle's barrel away, but not fast enough to save my face. Don't remember the shot itself. Next thing I knew, I was in Liam's cart, laid out next to a dead boy from Kansas. Liam had heard the shot from the road and came to investigate. He found an unconscious fourteen-year-old with a bullet wound in his cheek. He could have easily turned around and spared himself the trouble. But instead he took me back to his camp. Cared for me for a full week, even though he had a body to deliver. Even though I refused to speak to him about what had happened in those woods. He cared for me. Because that's the sort of man he was."

Though Gentle did tell Liam, eventually. At the end of the week, when the reality of what he'd nearly done finally overwhelmed him. He told him everything—about Emmanuel's abuse, and his flight from home, and his bungled attempt at taking his own life. He expected Liam to transport him to the nearest town and hand him over to the authorities. To unburden himself of the sobbing little lunatic he'd stumbled upon in the woods. But instead, after silently listening to Gentle's story and taking a moment to stare ponderously off into the distance, he sipped his coffee and offered to take Gentle along on his journey west. As if it were no more spectacular than offering the boy a second helping of oatmeal.

"He was nineteen," Gentle said. "He had his whole life ahead of him. He had no reason to become the guardian of a child whose only achievement in life was running away from home and failing to kill himself. Yet that's exactly what he did. He gave me a chance at a new start. A whole new life. And I took it."

"Why are you telling me this?" Kitt asked.

"Because you deserve to know what kind of man you've been traveling with," Gentle said. "The truth is that I don't know if I ever believed anything Liam said about alchemy. I only believed in him—because he saved my life. Because he showed me that there was a sort of person in the world who could move with such incomprehensible grace that you had no choice but to follow them wherever they went. To die for them, even, if they asked you to."

"I don't understand."

"The salamander, the Great Work—I have no reason to think any of it is true. And even if it is, it was Liam who was the alchemist, not me."

"What about the way you broke that door hinge back at the Judge's camp?" Kitt said quickly. "That was alchemy!"

"A simple reaction," Gentle said. "Not real alchemy."

"We can figure it out together," Kitt said. "We still have the picture from the Liber Alchimiae. And we've seen the salamander. We know it's real. We can't stop now."

"I can't, no," Gentle said. "I owe Liam that much. I wasn't there for him when he needed me most. I couldn't protect him the way he protected me. The least I can do is finish what he started. Even if it means I die up there in the mountains. Do you understand? I never thought this would be anything but a one-way trip. But I can't let you throw your life away, too."

"No one is *letting* me do anything," Kitt said. "I don't have anywhere else to go."

"That's what I told myself, too," Gentle said. "But that's not true anymore, is it?"

"What are you talking about?"

"I see the way you act here. How happy you are. How you care for Peter."

"He's my friend," Kitt said.

"But you think of him as more than a friend, don't you?"

Kitt's entire body tensed, like an animal suddenly alert to the presence of a predator.

"He's just a friend."

"Maybe so," Gentle said. "None of my business, really, what he is to you. But if there's more than friendship in what you feel, you'll get no judgment from me. I just hope you know that it's a rare thing, finding such feelings in this world. They're worth holding on to."

"I don't like this," Kitt said. "The way you're speaking to me—you make it seem like you're leaving."

"Manon and I are leaving tomorrow. You will stay here in Harmony. I've already spoken to Cora."

Kitt jumped to his feet. His hands clenched into fists.

"I'm not staying here," he said. "Manon won't take you anywhere unless you pay her. And I'm the one with the money."

"Not anymore," Gentle said. He reached into his pockets. When his hands returned, one held Kitt's sketchbook. The other held the money he'd hidden there.

"Those are mine," Kitt said.

Gentle stuffed the money back into his coat. He opened up Kitt's sketchbook to its most recent pages and held it out to the boy. Showed him the sketches Kitt already knew were there, scribbled in a hand so frantic that it had taken Gentle a few minutes to see the images hidden in the chaos of scrawling lines. A burning tree. A field of dead bison. A coastline heaped with piles of gasping fish. And salamanders. Dozens, maybe hundreds, of them, filling every inch of free space on the page.

"You've been having nightmares," Gentle said.

"So what? Everyone has nightmares."

"They're getting worse. And they'll keep getting worse if you go with me."

"You don't know that."

"You deserve to be happy, Kitt. You'll be happy in Harmony."

Kitt threw himself at his uncle. But Gentle was ready—he wrapped his arms around his nephew in a fierce hug, locking the boy's arms to his sides and holding him there as he struggled.

"Let me go!" he screamed, slapping uselessly at Gentle's sides. "You promised! You said we were a team. You're a liar, and a thief, and a bastard!"

"So I am," Gentle said. He tightened his arms. "All the more reason for us to part ways."

They stayed like that for what felt like ages, Kitt screaming all manner of abuses at his uncle and thrashing against his chest, while Gentle gritted his teeth and held firm. He did not loosen his grip until it seemed that Kitt had finally worn himself out, reduced to a limp body shuddering with sobs. But the moment he relaxed his arms the boy resumed his attack, punching him hard in the face. Gentle responded by shoving him away more roughly than he'd meant to. Kitt fell to the ground. Gentle rose up to help him, but Kitt responded by screaming for him to stay away. He shuffled backward and glared up at Gentle with incomprehensible hatred. The look twisted in Gentle's gut like a knife.

How many times, he wondered, had Kitt looked at his father this way?

"You're just like him," he said.

Before Gentle could respond, Kitt fumbled to his feet and ran back toward town, leaving Gentle slouched in his chair, his insides churning with shame. He pulled the final vial of Sweet Vitriol from his pocket—he'd been saving it for this moment—and drained it in one swallow. As serenity swept down his throat and trickled through his limbs, he thought of what Cora had said about the suffering he would soon endure, now that he had imbibed the last of his supply.

Good, he thought. He deserved whatever punishment was coming for him.

The sound of someone thumping on the cabin door awakened him. He'd somehow managed to drag himself inside the night before, though he hadn't bothered to light the fire, so now his body was stiff with cold. As he struggled to his feet, a wave of nausea overwhelmed him, and he stumbled back again, careening into his bedroll and thumping the back of his head against the wall. His entire body felt like a rotten bridge, ready to collapse under the slightest strain. He patted his coat in search of his Sweet Vitriol, only to remember that there was none left.

"Gentle?" said a voice on the other side of the door. It was Manon. "We leaving or not? It's nearly noon."

"I'm here," Gentle said. The act of speech was a precarious maneuver—expelling anything from his mouth, even breath, threatened to make him vomit.

Manon thrust open the door, unleashing a blinding burst of sunlight into the cabin. Gentle threw up his hands to protect his eyes.

"Lord," Manon said. "You look like a corpse."

"Death would be a relief," Gentle groaned.

"I take it we'll be delaying our departure? Shame—first nice day we've had all week."

"No," Gentle said. "I just need a few minutes, is all. Mind closing that door?"

"I fear the stench in here would overwhelm me if I did," Manon said.

Gentle pulled his hands away from his face and tried to open his eyes again. He managed a pitiful squint.

"Have you seen Kitt?"

"Not today."

"I told him I was leaving him here. He wasn't happy."

"No surprise there," Manon said. "But it's the right choice."

"That almost sounds like a compliment."

"You have my money?"

Gentle revealed the roll of bills. "Payment upon delivery of one giant salamander."

"If it's in those mountains, I'll find it," Manon said. "When can we leave? I don't want to lose any more daylight."

"Soon. Just need to drink some water and go find the boy. I need to say goodbye."

"Thought you hated water."

Gentle held his breath and rose to his feet. "Hilarious."

Manon stared at him, as if waiting to see if he'd tumble back to the ground. When he didn't, she gave a slight nod and turned away from the door.

"I'll be waiting near Cora's place," she said. "Come find me when you're ready."

Gentle watched her walk back into town, her breath trailing behind her in a thin wisp. When she turned a corner and disappeared, he hurled himself out of the cabin and fell to his knees. In a great burning gush everything he'd consumed the day before—the moonshine and the Sweet Vitriol and the stew he'd eaten for dinner—erupted from his mouth. He stayed there for a few more minutes, the muscles in his abdomen aching from the strain, until there was nothing left inside him but air and burning spit. Maybe it was just his nausea playing tricks on him, but before he looked away from his sick he could have sworn he saw strands of sticky black mucus threaded through the mess.

When he finally managed to rise to his feet again and begin his search, Gentle quickly discovered that the previous night's festivities had left Harmony in a state of slovenly disarray. Despite the sunshine, the streets were mostly empty, save for a few chilly souls who hadn't made it all the way home the night before and were sleeping off their hangovers on porches or curled up beside the livestock in their pens.

Gentle made his way through Kitt's usual haunts: the bunkhouse where the orphaned children slept, the library with its musty-smelling tomes, and the cafeteria, where a surprisingly jaunty Hilda was busy preparing a banquet of eggs and potatoes, though her only clientele were two dour-looking women nibbling despairingly on slices of bread, stopping occasionally to smile weakly at each other.

"No boy," the woman said in her thick accent when Gentle asked her about Kitt's whereabouts. "No cooks. No dishwashers. Nobody but Hilda. Little Harmonites cannot hold their liquor. Already twice this morning I beat men for making mess on my cafeteria floor."

This quickly devolved into a loud and boisterous speech about the superior drinking capabilities of the German race, which Gentle slunk away from as quickly as he could. Outside, he ran into Peter, who, despite standing firmly on his own feet, looked somehow worse than every other Harmonite Gentle had seen that morning. His face was red and splotchy from tears, and his clothes were disheveled, as if he'd been a fistfight.

"Peter," Gentle said. "Have you seen Kitt?"

Peter shook his head miserably. "He told me not to tell you."

"Told you not to tell me what?"

Peter hesitated, chewing on his lip. Gentle was surprised to see that the boy—who'd spent all week guiding Kitt about with the easy charisma of a young Napoleon—was capable of such distress. "He came and found me in the middle of the night. He said you stole his money and were planning on leaving him here."

"What didn't he want you to tell me, Peter?"

Peter's hands yanked at the bottom of his coat. "I told him not to go," he said. "He said I could come with him. But I was too frightened. I've heard about what the Sons of Adam do to people. How they cut out their eyes."

Gentle grabbed Peter's shoulders and began to shake him. "Where is he?" Gentle said. "Where did he go?"

"He took Abe and left at dawn," Peter said. "He told me he'd find the salamander himself."

Gentle's heart leapt up his throat. He let the boy go, afraid that he would vomit again. He needed to go and find Manon. He needed to leave Harmony this very instant. Kitt would have a few miles on them, but Abe would slow him down. There was still time to fix this.

Yet his body remained frozen, as though the speed of his thoughts had overwhelmed whatever mechanism controlled his limbs. He was only able to start moving again when a strange blast of sound swept through Harmony: a bugle call, descending from the mountain slopes above town and echoing through the streets. Gentle peered up at the ridgeline, where he could see movement in the trees. Three figures emerged from the forest, all on horseback: the Reverend Judge, Hercules, and Emmanuel. It was the

Reverend Judge who held the bugle, and as he appeared on the ridge he gave it another hearty blow, compelling the Harmonites out of their homes and into the street, where they joined Peter and Gentle. They squinted up at the pass, bleary and disbelieving.

The Reverend Judge shouted something into the trees behind him. Seconds later, a line of soldiers in gray fatigues emerged from the woods, the bayonets on their rifles glinting in the sunlight. They began the short march toward town.

The Harmonites scrambled to organize some kind of defense while the soldiers descended the mountainside. Cora, looking no less ragged than the rest of the townsfolk, sprinted through the streets shouting at every house she passed. She slapped those who'd fallen asleep in ditches and shoved weapons into the arms of those standing, dazed, outside their homes. By the time the Army of the Olympics entered the streets, she'd gathered a surprisingly sizable contingent of Harmonites in the town square. A hundred men and women stood under the burning brightness of the new day holding antique pistols and rifles, knives and clubs and rusty skillets.

Gentle found Manon smoking one of her cigarettes on a bench in front of the town hall, her scarred face oddly impassive given the chaos swirling around her.

"We have to go now," Gentle said. "Kitt has run off with Liam's body. He's trying to track down the salamander himself."

Manon shook her head. "Soldiers have the whole town surrounded," she said. "Unless you feel like jumping over the falls, we're trapped."

"This is insane," Gentle said. "It's going to be a bloodbath."

"Cora can handle it," Manon said. Though this didn't stop her, Gentle noticed, from removing her revolver from its holster and placing it in her lap.

Another bugle call shattered the frigid air. The three riders had reached the edge of town.

"Be calm, everyone," Cora shouted to the assembled Harmonites. Gentle was surprised by the lack of fear he saw in their faces—despite their pallid complexions and bloodshot eyes, the Harmonites stood steadfast in their positions, seemingly unperturbed by the frightening appearance of the soldiers descending toward them: forty or fifty dreary phantoms in ashen fatigues who stroked their filthy armaments and cackled like jackals.

The Reverend Judge pranced before them on a white stallion, his thin body erect in his saddle and bulked out by a general's coat, complete with tasseled epaulets and a tricorn hat. He rested his wooden fist on the polished pommel of his saddle and caressed the ivory-studded grip of his golden pistol with the other. Hercules, riding beside him on a muscular red draft horse with hooves the size of Gentle's head, looked similarly excited, though there was an element of derangement in his smile. His reattached ear, Gentle noticed, had only gotten worse, the flesh swollen to twice its normal size.

Emmanuel did not look nearly as ebullient as his companions. Gentle took trivial satisfaction in his brother's disheveled appearance, though any trace of pleasure was lost the moment Emmanuel's icy gaze found him in the crowd.

The Reverend Judge did not dismount from his horse when he reached the assembled Harmonites, presumably because he knew he would strike a far more diminutive figure when standing next to Cora. Instead, he led his horse as close as possible to where she stood at the head of the crowd and leaned over the edge of his saddle to address her.

"Cora Friedman, I presume?"

"Explain your presence here, Crane," Cora replied.

"That's *Reverend Judge* Crane," Hercules interjected. "This man represents the people of Washington. Show some respect."

"Not my people."

"Quite the contrary," the Reverend Judge said. "I bear the burden of vouching for all my constituents. Even those whose ideologies have led them to flirt with anarchy."

"No laws have been broken here," Cora said.

"I have it on good accounting that you played a role in the destruction of my property."

"Whose accounting would that be?"

"You really expect me to believe that you aren't aiding the Sons of Adam?"

"Unless you have evidence we are, you'd best be leaving."

"There are other crimes, as well."

"Such as?"

"The matter of your people's sartorial decadence, for starters." The Reverend Judge continued, his eyes lingering, suggestively, on Cora's trousers. "Women in men's clothing are an abomination unto the Lord."

"We are free citizens of the United States," Cora said. "Which, as you may recall, is a nation governed by the laws of human beings, not God."

"There is no law that does not find its root in God. And regardless of your ethical indiscretions, you have also run afoul of secular justice. You've been harboring criminals."

"What criminals?"

"The delinquent who burned down my house," Judge Crane replied.

"My son," Emmanuel interrupted, leading his horse forward and practically shoving Crane's own steed out of the way. The Reverend Judge wobbled momentarily on his saddle, yanking his hat down so that it didn't topple off his head. "Where is he?"

Gentle, still standing near the town hall with Peter, called out over the Harmonites. "He's run off," he said.

"You idiot," Emmanuel said. "What have you done?"

"As you can see," Cora said, "there are no arsonists here."

Crane, now recovered from Emmanuel's usurpation, shook his head and jabbed his wooden fist at Gentle and Manon. "Yet his coconspirators still walk free."

"Those people were wrongfully accused. If you wish to put them on trial for some crime, you will do so here in Harmony, where we can ensure the proceedings are fair. We know our rights."

Crane's face purpled with indignation. "I will let you know what rights you have, Miss Friedman."

Cora didn't move. "You aren't taking anyone from this town."

"Like hell I'm not," Crane replied. He plunged his arm down and grabbed the collar of Cora's jacket, dragging her forward and pinning her to the side of the horse. "You're under arrest."

Enraged shouts rippled through the crowd of Harmonites, who began to surge forward toward Crane and his soldiers. Cora held out a hand to stop them.

"No violence!" she shouted. "Not for my sake."

But the Harmonites were not subdued. At the edge of the crowd, Mr. Li and a few others began to wrestle with the soldiers.

"Let her go!" cried a voice from behind Gentle. He turned to see Peter holding his rusty hunting rifle. He aimed it at Crane.

"Peter!" Cora shouted. "Don't you dare!"

Crane's horse began to snort and tremble, unsettled by the screaming crowd. Crane wrestled with the animal while keeping his grip on Cora. "Order!" he roared. "I will have order!"

"I said let her go!" Peter yelled again. But in his distress, his finger must have tightened around the trigger. The weapon fired and leapt out of his hands.

Crane's wooden fist exploded in a burst of splintered pine and blood.

The Reverend Judge held the mangled stub up to his eyes, unbelieving, as if the reality of his hand's destruction was a riddle he couldn't quite wrap his mind around. As he did so, Gentle realized that the rumor Cora had told him was true: Beneath the shattered wood, Gentle could see bloody fingers. The wooden appendage had indeed been nothing more than a glove.

The townsfolk ceased their struggles with the soldiers, and the two groups seemed, for a moment, to hold each other in a silent embrace, every eye locked on the Reverend Judge. In that brief instant of calm, Gentle's senses brightened with newfound awareness. He heard the steady swish of the trees swaying in the wind, the gentle plink of the snow blowing over the shingles of the nearby roofs, the crackle of Manon's cigarette, inhaled in one long drag and then tossed to the ground as she rose to her feet.

The world was still. Peaceful, even.

Finally, the Reverend Judge looked up from his ruined fist and found Peter in the crowd. He raised his golden revolver and aimed it at the boy. Cora cried out. A gunshot rang through the town. The force of the blast hurled Peter back into the snow, his arms thrown wide to either side of him, and the fighting began.

By the time Peter's body reached the ground, Gentle had already begun to run. Bedlam engulfed Harmony in an instant, the streets exploding with the sounds of the mournful Harmonites as they hurled themselves at the Army of the Olympics. Gunshots echoed through the streets, whizzing through the air like lethal insects, shattering windows and ricocheting off corrugated roofs. The soldiers had entered the town from every direction, but the Harmonites had the advantage of fighting on familiar territory: They fired upon the soldiers from rooftops or charged out from the shadows, falling upon the men with hatchets and pitchforks.

Gentle sprinted through the avenues, slipping on slush and tripping over bodies, but no matter where he turned there seemed no escape from the horror. He watched a soldier pin another man to the wall with the bayonet of his rifle, only to have his head caved in a moment later by a woman with a skillet. He ducked as an oil lamp flew through the air and into a house, the occupants inside screaming in terror as flames burst from the windows. On every street bodies raged against one another in the thickening smoke, soldiers and Harmonites indistinguishable from each other in the frenzy. Gentle saw bleeding hands closing around throats, and bellies slit open in gory cornucopias. Grunts and shouts swarmed the air, embellished with the accompaniment of gunfire and the terrified whinnies of horses. Gentle could only make out flashes in the chaos. A dazed little girl wandering down a muddy avenue, clutching her face where a bullet had entered her eye. A soldier with a cleaver in his neck slumped against the base of a building and laughing at the sky. A mangy dog wagging its tail and gnawing happily on a severed arm. Each sight seemed a vision of Armageddon, dredged up from the brimstone and arrayed all around Gentle in garish brilliance.

Overwhelmed, Gentle ducked into one of the houses. He knew the place—had been there just a few days before, helping the couple who lived there put some legs on a new table. But as

Gentle entered the house, he found the table smashed beneath the husband's body. Beside him lay his wife, her white dress riddled with red bullet holes.

Gentle was staring down at the two dead Harmonites in shock when he heard a whimpering from the other side of the room. He turned to see one of the Judge's men—a boy barely older than sixteen—pointing a revolver at him. A gash in his forehead leaked blood down his face, though tears had left a streak of white running from his eyes to his chin.

"She came at me with a knife," he said, voice cracking. "I wouldn't have shot them if she didn't. I swear to God I wouldn't have."

"I believe you," Gentle said. Slowly, he raised his hands in surrender and tried to step back toward the door.

"It's just like the nightmares," the boy was saying. "The fire. The blood."

"Listen—" Gentle began, but a gunshot sent the boy flying back against the wall, killing him instantly. The bullet had come from the doorway behind Gentle, where one of the Judge's own soldiers now stood, a bearded man in a tattered uniform still holding a smoking rifle. He set down the gun and shoved past Gentle, unsheathing a knife from his belt as he approached the young man's body. When he reached him, he bent over the corpse and began, without hesitation, to carve out his eyes.

"What the fuck are you doing?" Gentle said.

The man ignored him. "He's seen the dream, but it did not change him," the man said, his voice locked in the same hypnotic cadence Gentle had heard from the man who'd taken him and Kitt hostage in the woods outside the Judge's camp. "He has eyes but does not see."

The man pulled a handful of dirt from his pocket and began

packing it into the boy's still-bleeding sockets. He turned to Gentle and pointed at the door with his chin.

"The way is clear now. Carry on, pilgrim."

To his disgrace, Gentle didn't try to stop him. He just stumbled back outside, to a street strewn now with groaning bodies and puddles of blood. Cora's hut stood on a small rise at the end of the road, and Gentle ran there, thinking there might be some hidden path beside the waterfall down to the valley. But once he reached the house it was obvious there was no such trail—just a plummeting descent to the river below.

Gentle stared down at the roaring depths and felt a chill spread through his stomach. He turned back to Harmony and saw that the whole town had now been engulfed in flames, the fire writhing on the mossy roofs like a thing in pain. At the end of the street Gentle had just run down, the gargantuan shape of Hercules emerged from the smoke, striding through the flames like some demon prince strolling through his private section of hell, a gun in one hand and a cavalry saber in the other. He lumbered between the bodies of the Harmonites on the road, kicking them over with his alligator boots to see if they were still alive. When he found an old man still convulsing from a gunshot wound in his belly, Hercules leaned down and plunged the saber through his chest with such force that Gentle thought he heard the man's sternum crack. Hercules gave the saber a good twist and, when he was certain the old man was dead, yanked it out of his body and straightened back to his full height. As he did so, his eyes fell upon Gentle, standing alone at the end of the avenue. A smile cracked open Hercules's lips, widening until it seemed his whole face was just one great laughing mouth. He raised his gun and fired.

The bullet grazed Gentle's cheek, barely missing him. He threw his body to the ground as more gunshots rang out, thunking against the building above him. He clawed through the dirt to the edge of the cliff, then peered over the edge at the roiling green waters below. All that waited for him down there was a slow death by drowning, that torturous struggle that had haunted his nightmares for so many years.

But Kitt was down there, too. All alone in the wilderness, with nothing but his prayers and a giant mule to protect him from the Sons of Adam.

Stupid child, he thought. Useless boy.

He took a deep breath and rolled over the edge.

As he flew toward the canyon below, Gentle remembered the words Liam had written in his note—*come and find me in the deep waters*—and allowed himself to imagine, for the instant it took him to reach the river, that his friend had predicted all of this. That Gentle, despite all his failures, despite the fact that he had now lost the salamander, the Liber Alchimiae, his nephew, his mule, and the body of his best friend, had still managed to follow the trail Liam had left behind for him. The thought purchased him a small slice of calm while he plummeted through the air.

But soon it was gone, replaced by the crash of his chest against the river's surface, the impossible frigidity of the water, the panicked contortions of his body as it tried to save itself.

The river carried him quickly away from the falls, hammering Gentle against roots and rocks and dragging him through a tangle of rapids. He made a few feeble stabs at salvation—clutching at the slippery branch of a tree, digging his nails into the side of a boulder—but each time the river yanked him away.

He didn't know how long he spent being battered about in

the raging waters, but it felt like hours. At one point, he wondered if the river might not have carried him all the way out to sea. But no: There were the trees, leaning over him like a crowd of ambivalent onlookers. There was the riverbank, just out of Gentle's reach.

Eventually the rapids did end, depositing Gentle into a comparatively calm stretch of river. Even here, the water was too deep for his feet to reach the bottom. He made one last attempt at some of the swimming techniques Liam had tried to teach him over the years, but he was too tired. His body surrendered to fatigue, hanging limp in the water while Gentle peered out at the murk surrounding him, the sun breaking through the gloom in hazy shafts.

How fitting, he thought, that he, like Liam, should die in a river. Even in death, he couldn't help but follow his friend.

A shadow plummeted into the river a few feet away. Out of the swirling torrent of bubbles a face emerged: wide and white, with dead, unblinking eyes.

The salamander.

It surged toward Gentle, who had no time to react before it reached out and grabbed him, its fingers—and they were fingers, Gentle could see, human ones—closing around the collar of his coat and dragging him back to the surface.

The salamander hauled Gentle onto the riverbank, where he collapsed, gasping for air. He pressed his forehead into the snow, gagging and panting, and nearly wept from the relief of it all. As his breaths deepened, he became aware of a piercing sensation in his chest. Each gasp left him feeling as though someone had smashed a cudgel in his side.

"Saw you fall," said the salamander, who was standing above him now.

Gentle rolled onto his back. He looked up at the salamander, who had the body of a wet, naked old man, with a concave chest and a limp, deflated penis. The salamander reached up and tore off its face—not a salamander's face after all, Gentle realized, but an owl's—and Gentle found himself peering up at the crazed, gray-bearded face of the old man he'd shared a cell with the week before.

"You," Gentle said.

"I thought of letting you drown," the old man said. "But you helped me escape. *The wicked borrow and do not repay, but the righteous give generously. For such as be blessed of him shall inherit the earth; and they that be cursed of him shall be cut off.*"

"Appreciated," Gentle said. He tried to rise to his feet, but fell back again almost instantly, stunned by the sudden jab of pain beneath his left arm. He tugged up his wet clothing and peered down at the spot—he could see no blood, but the skin was inflamed and red. When he placed his hand at the top of his stomach and applied a little pressure, a bolt of agony briefly blinded him.

The old man tilted his head and hooted. "Looks like a bruised rib," he said. "Broken, even."

Gentle clenched his teeth and tried to stand again. He was able to manage it, this time, though the effort left him breathless. "Kitt," he said. "I need to find Kitt. He's alone in the woods."

"I saw him," the old man said. "Last night. Him and the mule. Spotted them trekking through the dark. But I didn't reveal myself. I stayed still and watched, like a good owl."

"Where were they headed?" Gentle said.

The old man pointed to the cragged line of peaks above them. "Same place we're all headed: back to the deep waters. Back to the beginning. Before the end."

"Will your people hurt him?" Gentle said.

The old man shook his head. "The boy is safe," he said. "The Sons of Adam know what he did, burning down the tyrant's house. They know he longs to see the Leviathan. They have no right to stop him. They were like him, once. Sleepers without a dream. Lost and wandering, with no good Moses to take them to the promised land. Pilgrims, all. And pilgrims must be protected."

"Kitt is not a pilgrim."

"Yet he follows the pilgrim's path. Same as you."

The words seemed to carry the naked man's mind elsewhere. He flung out his arms and flapped them like wings and hooted three times, the loose skin around his neck trembling like a turkey's wattle.

"There are soldiers in the forest," Gentle said. "We need to find him."

"The soldiers are headed there, too. We will guide them. Play shepherd to their flock. Just as Adam commanded. The end is near. The final trumpet sounds. *And they have conquered him by the blood of the Lamb and by the word of their testimony, for they loved not their lives even unto death.*"

The old man began to prance into the woods. "Wait," Gentle said. "Where are your clothes? It's freezing out here. We need to make a fire and get dry."

The old man waved disinterestedly at a pile of furs and leaves heaped on a log.

"Take them," he said. "What use does an owl have for clothes?"

"We need to find Kitt."

"Follow the signs," he said. "We haven't tried to hide the way."

The old man pressed his hand against the trunk of a nearby pine. When he removed it, Gentle could see the shape of a salamander scorched into the bark. The old man's voice grew louder as he slipped the owl mask back over his head. "*Behold, I have set before you an open door, which no one is able to shut.*"

"Wait!" Gentle said, trying to follow. But the pain was so fierce that he could only limp. The old man moved with surprising speed up the side of the overgrown hill, bounding through the snow on all fours, his wide white ass bouncing through the air as he crawled over logs and ducked beneath branches, hooting all the while. "Wait, damn you!" Gentle said again, but the man was already gone.

V

Rubedo

Gentle slithered out of his wet clothes and dressed himself in the outfit the old man had left behind. It was one of the Sons of Adam's peculiar uniforms, a cloak made of ratty animal furs and leaves. The plants sewn into the fur scratched against his skin, but the clothes were warm, and included a pair of thick leather moccasins that were only a little tight on Gentle's feet.

With no other options available to him, he began the long trek up the mountainside. Despite the old man's insistence that he should *follow the signs*, there was no discernable trail leading into the snow-covered cliffs, and Gentle clambered up into the woods with no real sense of where he was headed, hoping that he would find another one of the salamander markings before he was completely lost.

After he'd dried off some, he began to notice a hot, itching insistence spreading through his body. At first he attributed this to his new clothing, but the more he scratched the worse the itching became. This was soon followed by a needling discomfort distinct from his aching rib. Within a few minutes, he had a raging headache so intense that he wondered, for a moment, if his brain might burst the confines of his skull.

When he noticed his hands unconsciously searching the folds of his outfit, Gentle finally understood he was suffering from the withdrawal Cora had warned him about.

It was amazing how quickly the change came. One moment, Gentle was struggling up the hillside, huffing against the pain in his ribs and the sting of the cold air that blew down from the mountains. The next, he found himself barely able to remain upright, overcome by a sudden urge to fall to his knees and begin weeping. He'd suffered feelings like this before—those clammy weeks of anger and desolation he endured each time Liam convinced him to forsake the bottle—but those were manageable, deeply uncomfortable but hardly paralyzing. The most disturbing symptom was the cruelty he was capable of unleashing upon his friend when denied his whiskey.

Gentle's current condition, on the other hand, seemed almost lethal. Was it possible to die from the lack of Liam's tonic? The landscape around him imbued itself with a newfound hostility, every tree and rock and passing cloud radiating with abject disdain. He felt like an insect squirming and scuttling in terror beneath the eyes of a cruel god.

He had no idea where he was going—the landscape blurred into one seamless stretch of pine and snow. Even after hours of swerving up the increasingly perilous incline, the peak overhead seemed no closer. But every so often, just as he was beginning to accept that he was hopelessly lost, he would spot one of the salamander symbols, carved into tree bark or chiseled into a stone.

If he could find them, he reasoned, then Kitt could, too, and though he'd seen no signs of his nephew on the trail, this thought was all the hope he needed to keep moving.

Near dusk, he spotted a thin wisp of smoke swirling from a patch of forest higher up on the mountain. Thinking it might be Kitt's campsite, he pushed past his pain and exhaustion and hurried his pace through the increasingly treacherous snowdrifts, which were now so deep they reached his knees. Each step was a grueling exercise, his thighs burning from the effort, his tendons like taut strings ready to snap, but Gentle refused to stop for even a moment to catch his breath. He was certain that the second he did he would collapse right there in the snow and die of cold, or shrivel into nothing for want of his Sweet Vitriol.

After another hour, he finally reached the source of the smoke: a large, recently doused fire whose embers still pulsed in the wind, surrounded by a trio of shoddy lean-tos. Gentle's heart sank. Kitt could never have constructed such a camp—and if he'd used it as he passed through, he was now nowhere to be seen. But why would Kitt have abandoned the camp so close to nightfall? The lean-tos, built from roughly hewn logs and insulated with mud, were excellent protection against the cold. There would be no reason for Kitt not to spend the night in one of the structures. Unless, of course, someone else had spotted the smoke and found him first.

Regardless, there was no way Gentle could hike any farther. He would just have to hope that the old man had been telling the truth, and that the Sons of Adam would leave his nephew alone. With the last dregs of his willpower, he plucked a handful of fern fronds from his clothing and tossed them into the fire's ashes. A few desperate breaths brought the flames back to life, and some more foliage from Gentle's cloak—as well as a couple of dry logs he discovered in one of the lean-tos—transformed the spent heap back into a serviceable conflagration. Gentle crawled into the nearest lean-to and fell immediately to sleep.

He'd only just begun to dream of the salamander—its pale face hovering in the murk of some depthless sunken trench—when he was shaken back into the waking world by three men grabbing his legs and dragging him out into the gray light of dawn. They dumped him in the wet snow surrounding the now-dormant fire and leaned over him in silent contemplation. A boar with yellow tusks jutting at savage angles from its prickly snout. A rabbit with long ears made from sticks wrapped in half-rotten furs. And a buck with real antlers strapped to the sides of its head.

"He's dressed like one of ours," said the boar. "But he has no face."

"I know him," said the buck, who was taller than the other two. Gentle noticed a dark patch of what appeared to be dried blood on his right shoulder.

"You know me?" Gentle asked, searching his mind for some face to attach to the low, formidable voice. But all he could conjure was the gruesome deer mask, with its deflated snout and concave eyes.

"Should we speed him along to the green country?" said the rabbit. He unholstered his gun, but the buck held out his hand.

"Not yet," the buck said. "He's seen the dream. We should take him to Adam."

"The soldiers are only a few miles behind us," the rabbit replied. "He'll slow us down."

"Can you walk?" asked the buck.

"Have you seen a bald boy with a giant mule?" Gentle said.

"I said, can you walk?"

Gentle crawled to his feet.

"If he's following the signs," the buck said, "then he's heading to the same place we are."

Gentle sensed sympathy in his tone.

"Will he be safe there?"

"No less safe than the rest of us," said the buck.

"You have anything to drink?" Gentle said.

The buck handed him a canteen. Gentle opened it and sniffed the rim. Water. Only a little soured by the coppery flavor that meant the salamander was nearby. "I was hoping for something a little stronger," he said. Now that he was fully awake, his thirst for the Sweet Vitriol had returned, speckling his forehead with sweat and making his teeth feel as though they were trying to wriggle out of his gums.

"He's a drunk," said the rabbit. "We don't have time for this."

The buck ignored him. "All we've got is water."

Gentle handed the canteen back. Though his mouth felt like it was coated in sand, he didn't trust his stomach to keep the water down.

"I'll be fine," he said, and began to walk.

They spent the rest of the day hiking up the mountain. Within a few hours they'd left the tree line behind, and with it the protective bulwark of the surrounding forest. Now, there was nothing to hold back the roaring gusts of mountain wind, which buffeted Gentle's exposed face with piercing needles of cold. The snow was deep enough to reach Gentle's waist, which meant wading through the powder like it was a creek. Not that his companions seemed to mind—in fact, more than once they stopped to stomp harshly on the snowpack, deepening the impression of their passage, so that they left behind a long, clear track behind them.

The landscape grew strange in proportions: Jagged black rocks jutted from the planes of white like the wrecked hulls of galleons on a white beach. The few trees that managed to grow at this altitude were warped and savage things, their twisting trunks leaning almost parallel to the ground. Some had curled branches that looked, to Gentle, like grasping fingers. Once, when he lost his balance and reached out for one to stop himself from falling, his hand returned from the bark a bright shade of crimson.

Blood. Just like in Cedarville.

But no, Gentle thought. It must be sap. It had to be sap. Some color he'd never seen.

He took a long, shaky breath and turned back to survey the route behind them. He was amazed by how high they'd climbed. A carpet of dense forest lay below them, cracked with silver streaks where rivers cut through the woodlands. The horned dome of Mount Olympus hovered in the distance, so tall it made the range they were currently summiting seem like a quaint gathering of hillocks.

To the east, Gentle saw smoke billowing up from a gap in the woodland—Harmony, still burning. Watching it, Gentle felt himself oddly lulled, as if by the hypnotic dance of a roaring campfire. The smoke seemed to move with a mind of its own, prowling through the streets with the plodding but deliberate gait Gentle had seen in the salamander. In fact, the longer Gentle stared at the smoke the more it resembled the pale amphibian, crawling over Harmony with webbed fingers of fog, slipping down the falls and into the valley below, where it continued west, growing as it went, until the entirety of the peninsula's interior had been engulfed beneath a curtain of ash. It stopped only when it reached the outer mountains, where it lay its flat face against the granite cliffs and disappeared, its white body dissolving as quickly as it had appeared.

As the air cleared and the landscape of the peninsula was revealed once more, Gentle gasped. Every tree in the smoke's wake had disappeared. The green hills were now a series of gray, forsaken humps pimpled with the stubby stumps of a million dead evergreens. The soil was dry and bereft of fern or flower, and the rivers—the few that still cradled some dribble of water—gushed with a sooty fluid that reminded Gentle of the trail of dark sludge the salamander had left behind in the forests outside Cedarville. In an instant, the verdant interior had been transformed into a jagged brown scar. Gentle recognized it immediately. It was the wasteland from his dreams, the same one the salamander had shown him every night for weeks.

He turned to the masked men. "Something's happened."

They stopped and looked at him.

"What is it?" said the man in the buck mask.

"The peninsula," Gentle said, and turned back to show them the desolation that had overtaken the valley below. But the peninsula he saw now had been returned to all its emerald glory, its trees and waters as pristine and untouched as they must have been on the day of creation. Harmony's smoke remained pinned to the burning town.

"The thin air is getting to him," said the man in the rabbit mask. "Told you we should have left him behind."

"I'm fine," Gentle said quickly. "Just tired. That's all."

But as they started to walk once more, he kept his eyes locked on the summit above and did not look at the valley again.

They stopped only once over the course of the day, squatting on a flat expanse of stone as the path they were following finally began to level out into flat ground. Though they still hadn't reached the peak, the ground here widened into a sort of valley, flanked on either side by sheer cliffs of basalt. The men sat down and passed around a few chunks of what appeared to be jerky, slipping it under their masks to eat. They didn't offer Gentle any. They whispered to one another and pointed to the forested hills east of them, where Gentle could see fluttering gray shapes moving amidst the green.

"The soldiers follow," the boar said. "Just as Adam said they would."

Now Gentle understood why the men had been so intent on leaving footprints in the snow. They wanted the Army of the Olympics to know where they were going.

"Why?" Gentle asked. But the men didn't answer.

They resumed their march into the cloud-shrouded cliffs. The snow here had clearly been walked over many times: There was a trail of packed snow running through the center of the valley, which tapered into a single point as it tunneled into the mountain, as though they were walking into the waiting jaws of a giant beast.

After another hour or so of walking, Gentle began to notice a strange shape emerging from the mist. At first he assumed it was just another natural rock formation, since it lacked the rigid geometry of a human structure. But as they came closer he saw that it was, in fact, a building of some kind, though it was covered in carvings that gave it the lumpy, organic texture of a barnacle or a clump of pumice. Gentle couldn't make sense of it until a passing break in the clouds allowed a spray of sunlight to illuminate the far corner of the valley, revealing the scene in its grisly entirety.

The first thing he noticed was not the building itself—instead, his eyes were drawn to the glittering sheet of ice that loomed over it. A glacier, shining bright blue under the sun like a polished sapphire. At its base, someone had built a broad, rounded structure. It was indeed a human creation—Gentle could see the strips of cut timber that made up its bulk—but what Gentle had initially confused for sculptures were, in fact, bones. Skulls of all varieties covered the walls of the building: The long snouts of deer hung beside the stubby, fanged visages of bears and wolves. Heaped atop its roof, where one might have expected shingles, rib cages and femurs and pelvic bones lay strung together into a gruesome canopy, some of them still streaked with bits of ligament and tufts of hair. Even the chimney, which was busy puffing a streak of gray smoke into the air, looked to be encased in a column of vertebrae and yellow jaws.

The only thing that stopped Gentle from turning around and fleeing the horrific sight was Abe, tied to a post near the structure's curtained entrance. The mule whinnied excitedly at their approach. Gentle raced to him, then pressed his forehead against the animal's wet snout and scratched behind his ear.

"You beautiful fool," he said. "Why did you follow that boy all the way up here?"

Abe snorted and placed his heavy chin on the top of Gentle's head. Gentle did a quick circuit of his body, checking for wounds. Excluding the layer of frost covering his coat, the animal was unharmed. Liam's casket was still tied to his back, and while Gentle went about the work of sliding it off, two more masked Sons of Adam—a beaver and a duck—emerged from the structure's entrance, immediately leveling their rifles at him.

The buck waved for them to lower their weapons.

"Peace, brothers," he said. He pulled off his mask. Now Gentle understood why he'd recognized his voice.

"Boris," Gentle said, recognizing the soldier by the scar on his face. "What are you doing here?"

"When the Judge attacked Harmony," said Boris, "those of us who had been hiding in his ranks took the opportunity to stage an assault of our own. While his men were busy with the Harmonites, we shot a few of them and made a quick retreat. But they know where to find us. We left a trail."

Gentle remembered the horrible sight of the old soldier digging out the boy's eyes. Had that been their plan along? To lure the Reverend Judge to Harmony and strike at him when he was distracted? Had all those innocent people died just so these madmen could fulfill their demented prophecies?

"You're taunting him," he said. "You want him to follow you. Why?"

"It's time for a reckoning," Boris said.

Gentle, who'd been about to unlatch the casket from Abe's back, stopped. Maybe it was better to keep the thing in place, in case he and Kitt needed to make a hasty exit. Whatever these men were planning, he didn't want to be around when it started.

"The boy who was traveling with this mule," he said. "Where is he?"

"He was shown Adam's truth," said the duck.

"And sent to see the Leviathan," said the beaver.

"What the hell does that mean?"

"Relax," said Boris. "You'll be joining him soon enough."

"If they've hurt him," Gentle began, but Boris ignored this threat, turning his attention to the other men.

"How many made it back?" he asked.

"Twenty in all," said the beaver, pointing at the surrounding cliffs. "They've taken the dynamite and headed up to their positions. Only ones left are us."

"And Brother Owl," said the duck. "Showed up here this morning, couple hours after the boy. He isn't well. Less so than usual, I mean."

"Dynamite?" Gentle said.

"You've done well," Boris said. "Go and join your brothers at the entrance to the valley. You know what to do."

"See you in the green country," said the beaver.

"See you in the green country," said Boris.

The men saluted Boris and set off. The boar and the rabbit headed for the cliffs, while the other two descended the trail back to the lower part of the valley.

"What the hell is going on?" Gentle demanded. "Where is my nephew?"

"Come inside," Boris said, holding open the filthy sheet that covered the building's arched entryway. "Adam will explain everything."

The structure's interior stank of death. Though Gentle's familiarity with the smell had dampened its impact over the years, he still faltered at the entryway as the sweet, rank aroma of rot filled his nostrils. The large room was filthy: a wide stretch of earthen floor littered with grimy bedrolls and dirty clothes, logs of wood stacked beside a small firepit, a table overloaded with plates and cutlery in desperate need of cleaning, their surfaces striped with hardened streaks of calcified food.

The man Gentle assumed was Adam sat at the far end of the long table that occupied the room's center. He was not dressed like the rest of his men: He wore a buckskin coat and a pair of leather gloves, though his face, too, was covered by a mask. It was sewn from sackcloth and featured a wide mouth and large, black eyes made from polished stone. A salamander, of course.

He did not stand to greet them as Boris shoved Gentle into a chair. He remained rigid in his seat, his hands languidly folded in his lap, like a statue. Gentle tried to find the man's eyes within the folds of his mask, but there was only darkness.

Beside him, huddled up in a shabby fur blanket, was the old man.

"Brother Owl," Boris said. "Glad to see you made it."

"You're alive," Gentle said, amazed that he had somehow managed to scale the mountain without any clothes. The old man smiled demurely and leaned back in his chair, revealing the thin legs that jutted out from beneath the blanket. Dark, frostbitten skin the color of coal covered his toes and the tops of his feet, all the way up to his ankles.

"Not all of me," he said.

Boris shook his head and walked over to the firepit, where a metal pot sat on an iron grill above the flames, hissing steam. "An unnecessary sacrifice, Brother Owl."

Boris grabbed a chipped mug from a hook on the wall, sniffed it, and then ladled some hot water out of the pot and into the cup. He rifled through a tiny wooden box on the floor by the fire pit, removed a teabag from its interior, and dunked it into the steaming water.

"Won't need feet where I'm going," the old man said. "In the green country, I'll have wings."

"My nephew," Gentle said. "Where is he?"

"Already gone when I got here," the old man replied. "Adam deemed him worthy to see the deep waters."

Adam neither confirmed nor denied this. He only stared at Gentle.

"And what about me?" Gentle said to the silent man. "Am I *worthy*?"

"Show some respect!" the old man shrieked. "*To him who sits on the throne and to the Lamb be blessing and honor and glory and might forever and ever*!"

Gentle stood from his seat. He had to hunch over as he rose—otherwise the pain in his rib was too great. "Where is Kitt?" he shouted.

"That's enough," Boris said. He returned to Gentle's side, put a strong hand on his shoulder and lowered him back into his chair. He set the mug of tea in front of Gentle and motioned for him to drink. "Dried apricot vine," he said. "Used to drink this when I was getting over the opium."

"I'm not getting over any opium," Gentle said, but he drank the tea anyway. He ignored the scald of the hot water, his nostrils flaring from the odd, mulchy taste of the stuff.

"I get it," Boris said. He stepped around Gentle and slid into the seat on the other side of Adam. "It's easy to pretend you're in control, especially in the early days. Then suddenly your supply is gone, and all at once it's like your whole body turns against you. Skin feels like it's gonna crawl off your bones. Head starts aching something awful. The cravings blot out everything else—next thing you know you're pondering all the ugly things you'd do just to get a little taste of the stuff. Start taking stupid risks. I just about died when I tried to quit."

"Yet here you are," Gentle said. The man wasn't lying—the tea helped a little. The wicked gymnastics in his guts were reduced to a few angry squirms.

"All thanks to Adam," Boris said, smiling at the silent man beside him. "Tracked me down in Montana, few years after we got out of the cavalry. Found me begging for scraps behind some shithouse, brains all fucked up from rotgut and opium. He dragged me out to some cabin in the woods and locked me in there for two weeks. Slipped me food from time to time and sat at the door with his gun. Said he'd shoot me if I tried to leave, and I knew him well enough to know he meant it."

"A man of infinite kindness," the old man added somberly.

"Old friends?" Gentle said.

"Brother Owl and I served under him, fighting the Sioux in the Black Hills," Boris said. "He came looking for us two years back. Saved me from myself, and rescued Brother Owl here from a life preaching in back alleys and brothels."

"Many are men's dens of sin," the old man said.

"Told us he had honest work lined up," Boris went on. "Said some rich man in Washington wanted the last bit of wilderness in the territories mapped out. Didn't matter to me. I'd have followed him to hell if he'd asked."

"What a man," Gentle murmured. "If only we could add the power of speech to his list of virtues."

Adam's unwavering stare prickled Gentle's skin with goosepimples.

"Adam is beyond speech now," Boris said.

"He's deep in the dream," added the old man. "Preparing the way for the rest of us."

"You keep talking about this dream," Gentle said. "What does it mean?"

"The dream is all that's left," Boris said. "Leviathan has returned. The end is at hand."

"You sound like a lunatic."

Pity flickered across Boris's face. "And yet you've seen it," he said. "Every night you've seen it. The deep waters. The green country. The wasteland that follows."

"I've always suffered from strange dreams."

"Not like these ones," Boris said, "and you know it."

"You said Adam needed to decide if I was worthy," Gentle said. "How does he plan to do that if he won't speak to me?"

"You'll hear our story," Boris said. "About the dream. And what it means. Then Adam will decide."

"That's all?" Gentle said.

"Hearing the truth is harder than you might think."

"For the testimony of Adam is the spirit of prophecy," the old man said.

"Fine," Gentle said. He brought the mug of tea up to his face—the loamy smell of the drink did an admirable job masking the stink of decay that pervaded the building. The pain in his head had subsided to a dull throb. Still, his rib ached with every breath. "Say what you need to say. And then take me to Kitt."

Boris swept back his hair, revealing the scar that swerved across his forehead. "We'd been trying to penetrate the peninsula for four months," he began, his voice dipping into the comforting familiarity men used when recounting a story they'd told many times before. "We'd wasted weeks trying to find a clear path through the mountains. When it became apparent that we wouldn't be able to cross before winter began, some of the men thought we should double back to Cedarville and wait until spring to make the crossing. But Old Lee would hear nothing of the sort. He was certain that if we waited, someone else would make the crossing first. That was the most important thing to him—he didn't care about the Reverend Judge's money. He wanted to be the first one to see what the peninsula was hiding behind all those mountains."

"A man with a vision," the old man said.

"I'll admit that even I was skeptical," Boris said. "I wasn't much interested in freezing my ass off in these mountains. And Adam was acting more brash than usual, like a man on the run from something. Suppose he saw the writing on the wall. End of the frontier and all that. Just wanted a piece of it for himself. Before there was nowhere left for men like us."

"Don't think the world will ever stop needing soldiers," Gentle said. Boris shook his head sadly.

"Men like Old Lee are more than soldiers," he said. "They're sin eaters."

"Sin eaters?"

"Adam spoke of it often, during the war. He said it was something they used to do in ancient times. Place a loaf of bread on the body of someone who'd just died—and then hire a holy man to come and eat the bread. He'd gobble up the dead man's sins with the loaf and take them upon himself. That's what we did, fighting the Indians. Took all that ugliness into ourselves, so people like you could sleep soundly at night."

"A clever justification for slaughter," Gentle said. Already, the tea's effects were wearing off, and Boris's romanticizing was irking him.

"You don't know!" the old man screamed. His bloated feet slipped from the table and thumped to the floor. "You weren't there! You did not face the terror!" The man's voice grew shrill and he thrust his hands up in prayer. "*Do not fear what you are about to suffer. Behold, the devil is about to throw some of you into prison, that you may be tested, and for ten days you will have tribulation. Be faithful unto death, and I will give you the crown of life.*"

Boris reached across the table and placed his hand on the old man's shoulder. The old man took a shaky breath and lowered his clasped hands back into his lap. Boris turned his gaze back to Gentle, a fire burning in his eyes.

"Have you ever seen a child die?" he asked.

"I've embalmed people of every age," Gentle said.

"But have you *watched* a child die? Have you seen the disbelief on their faces when they leave their bodies? Like death is a game they no longer want to play? They don't die easily, children. They cry out until the very end, certain that someone—anyone—will come and rescue them. It's not an expression you forget. No matter how much you drink."

"And who was it that killed these children?" Gentle said. "Who was it that stood by and watched them die?"

A thick vein pulsed on Boris's forehead. The muscles in his face tightened with anger. But when he spoke again his voice was flat.

"I won't argue morality with someone who's never been tasked with taking life," he said. "All I'm trying to say is that for a man who's seen something like that, the frontier is blessed relief. Open space and silence. Freedom from the judgments of 'civilized' men. So I understood why Old Lee didn't want to return to Cedarville. He wanted to go deeper. He wanted to know what the mountains were hiding. And we followed him. Even if it meant we might freeze to death."

"*For you have need of endurance*," said the old man. "*So when you have done the will of God you may receive what is promised*."

"We had a string of bad luck after that," Boris said. "Adam thought we could build a barge out of logs and float our supplies upriver before it froze over. Spent a week building the raft, and then lost it on the second day when it got caught in some rapids and flipped over. River took most of our supplies, too."

"A dire day," the old man added. "Though Old Lee was not dissuaded."

"No," Boris said. "If anything, I think he was a little excited. He started talking about how burdensome all those supplies had been. We were soldiers, after all. We'd fought the Sioux! What did we need a bunch of salt pork and sugar for? We'd hunt for our dinners. We didn't need the river, either. We'd head straight over the mountains."

He looked up at Adam, admiration pooling in his eyes. "It was a damn good speech," he said. "And you fooled all of them. All of them, except for me. I heard the doubt in your voice. Saw you pacing the camp at night. But I didn't tell anyone. Because I trusted you."

Gentle sensed bitterness in his voice. Adam did not respond.

"Blasphemy," the old man muttered.

"Oh, get off it," Boris said to him. "You were there, same as me. The long march up the mountains. The first blizzard, which lasted for nearly a week. Nothing to hunt. Nothing to eat. Through it all, he just told us to keep heading up the mountain. Once we got over the summit, he said, we'd be through the worst of it. And then we did—we made it to the top of the mountain. But instead of finding a path through, we found this."

He gestured behind him.

"The glacier. Solid ice, blocking our path. That's when the men began to lose hope. Some of them even deserted, disappearing in the middle of the night. Adam wouldn't leave, though. He found a cave, you see, leading under the glacier. Said he was certain it would take us to the other side of the mountains. Made us set up camp here and started leading groups inside. No one wanted to do it, of course—ice caves are hell. They can collapse in an instant. And these ones were particularly bad. They twisted and wound round themselves, led to dead ends and sprawling crevasses. Lost one or two men that way. Just fell into some crack in the ice. About two weeks in it finally happened: Adam sent a group of five men to explore a new section of the caves, and the tunnel collapsed around them. They were alive when it happened. Cut off. But there was no way to reach them. We could hear them screaming for days.

There were about thirty of us left by that point. Most of them turned against Adam then. Refused to go back in the caves. Called him a lunatic. Another storm came over the mountains and snowed us in—but they vowed to leave at the first thaw. Adam would hear none it. He called them cowards and scoundrels. He started going into the caves by himself. Sometimes for hours."

"We did not join him," the old man said. "We were weak."

Boris looked to Adam, ashamed. The man offered him no comfort. "I lost faith," he said. "Hearing those men, trapped in the ice. I lost faith."

"*Father, forgive us*," the old man wailed. "*For we did not know what we were doing*."

"Eventually, he disappeared inside the cave for nearly two days," Boris continued. "We thought he was dead. There was talk of going after him and trying to find out what happened. But none of us was brave enough to go back into the caves. Then, one morning, Adam returned. He seemed to have lost his mind entirely. Ranted about some monster—a giant lizard hidden away in a spring beneath the ice."

"Leviathan," Brother Owl said. "Slumbering in the deep waters. First of God's creations."

"He raved about the visions the beast had shown him. Said he'd seen a new world—a paradise, destroyed by men. He said the Leviathan wanted revenge. He said it would reward us by carrying our souls back to that green country. We'd never heard him talk this way. The man was a Christian, but he wasn't the preaching type. That was more Brother Owl's game."

The old man bowed his head in agreement.

"We were scared of him. We tied him up and put him in one of the tents. Figured we'd have to keep him like that till spring. Otherwise he'd just run back into the caves and get himself killed."

Boris turned from Gentle to stare at Adam, smiling sadly at the silent man. "But we didn't know you had a gun hidden away," he said quietly. "I suppose you could have tried to fight your way out. But that would have meant firing upon your own men. Way I see it—way we all came to see it—was that you wanted to send us a message. You wanted to prove your faith in the green country. Wanted us to see that the dream was bigger than the life of one man. We heard the gunshot near dawn."

Just as Gentle understood what it was that Boris was telling him—just as horror yanked at the hairs on the back of his neck—the old man reached out and tugged off Adam's salamander mask. Gentle cried out, because there, sitting at the other end of the table, was a dead man with a bullet wound in his skull. By the looks of the yellow rot seeping from the gaping crater in his forehead, he had been dead for a long time.

"Jesus Christ," Gentle whispered, but Boris was unperturbed by his horror. He took the mask from the old man's hands and slipped it back over Adam's decrepit skull.

"We understood his message," Boris said. "I only wish we'd believed him sooner. The next morning Brother Owl and I and a few of the other men went back into the caves. We needed to understand. We needed to know. What could make a man like Old Lee kill himself? Adam had left us signs, just like the ones you followed in the forest, so that we could retrace his steps. And we found it, just like he said. And when we returned to camp, and we led the others back inside, they saw it too. The Leviathan came to us while we were sleeping every night after we first laid eyes upon it. It showed us the green country, the new frontier. Our reward. We lasted out the winter, and built a camp here in the mountains, and as Adam had commanded, we prepared ourselves for the war to come. We protected the Leviathan, awaiting some sign. And a few months ago, when it emerged from the caves and headed for the river, we knew the time had come. We followed it, an army of God, just as Adam had predicted."

The old man raised his hands to the air. "*Count it all joy, my brothers, when you meet trials of various kinds, for you know that the testing of your faith produces steadfastness.*"

"You're insane," Gentle said. "All of you are insane."

Boris shook his head. "You've seen the dream. You know it's real. The Leviathan led us to war—but now it's returned. Our path is clear. Two armies must meet at Armageddon. We'll lure the Judge's forces into this valley, and when they've gathered here to slaughter us, we'll blow the whole mountain sky high."

"The dynamite," Gentle said.

"We'll release the deep waters from the glacier, send the ice hurtling down the mountainside. We'll clear it all away in a great deluge, just as God did once before. The grime and the blood and the shit—all the human filth of this world—will be made new."

"Where is Kitt?" Gentle said. "Where is my nephew?"

"In the caves, of course," Boris said. "He wanted to see the Leviathan. Why would we deny him, knowing he's seen the dream?"

A gunshot cracked in the distance. Another followed soon after. A few moments later the air was peppered with the sound of gunfire. Boris and the old man grinned at each other.

"It has begun," said Boris. "Just as Adam said."

"Praise be," the old man replied.

"You can't do this," Gentle pleaded. "You'll kill us all."

"It's already done," Boris said. "The others have their orders. Brother Owl and I will stay here and hold the line."

"Please," Gentle said. But the men ignored him. Boris placed his rifle on the table and began cleaning its barrel with a damp cloth he'd taken out of his pocket. The old man threw his hands skyward again and began to shout at the ceiling.

"*And he saith unto me, Seal not the sayings of the prophecy of this book: for the time is at hand. He that is unjust, let him be unjust still: and he that is filthy, let him be filthy still: and he that is righteous, let him be righteous still: and he that is holy, let him be holy still.*"

The man continued, but Gentle did not hear him. He jumped from his chair and fled outside, into the blinding glare of the sunlight and the snow. Neither man tried to stop him. In the distance, he could see the source of the gunfire: the Judge's gray soldiers, packed behind boulders and crouching in gullies, firing up at the hidden Sons in the surrounding hills. Tufts of smoke billowed from their rifles, hanging over them in gray drifts. Abe snorted and whinnied at his post, frightened by the noise. Gentle wasted no time in untethering the mule and slapping him on the rump.

"Get out of here," he said. "Go anywhere, just get out of here."

But rather than charging off into the distance, Abe turned around and trotted toward the glacier. Gentle tried to entice him back the other way by nudging his side, but the animal was far too large. Instead, he led Gentle the short distance to the face of the glacier, to a slim crack in the ice beside which someone had scrawled a salamander symbol in black charcoal. It was the passage into the caves, Gentle realized, the place Kitt must have entered hours before.

The space was not large enough for the mule to fit inside, and after some cajoling Gentle was able to maneuver around the animal and squeeze into the crack. He turned back, grabbed Abe's head in his hands, and pressed their foreheads together.

"Go," he whispered. "Please go. I'll find Kitt. I promise."

The mule, as if embarrassed by this display, yanked his head away and snorted a wet blast of air into Gentle's face.

"Fine," Gentle said. "Wait for us here, you stubborn bastard."

Gentle turned away and stared at the path before him: a bright blue tunnel of ice, just large enough for a single man to pass through, though only if he hunched himself over and shuffled sideways. The closeness of the passage elicited a shriek of protest somewhere in the deepest part of Gentle's mind. But Gentle had been here before. He'd crawled through these tunnels every night for a month now. He squeezed himself into the dark and began to walk. It felt a little like coming home.

The path to the salamander's lair would have been beautiful if not for the fear. Fear first of the space itself, so tight as to resemble the cold, coiling guts of some enormous monster, and then fear of the darkness, so impenetrable that Gentle had no choice but to wander forward into blindness, tracing a finger along the frigid wall and hoping he did not slip into one of the crevasses Boris had mentioned. Soon the tunnel began to widen, though, and here someone had lined the route with lanterns, whose flames drenched the icy walls with flickering light. As he walked, Gentle learned that these lanterns served another purpose beyond mere illumination—whenever one was placed in the path, he inevitably discovered a charcoal salamander drawn on the walls nearby, directing him where to go just as the tunnel forked off into any number of adjoining paths and channels.

Gentle could easily see how someone might get lost in the caves. They led off in every direction. Sometimes Gentle had to lie flat and shuffle through a gap so tight he could barely squirm forward, while other times he had to scale chinks in the frozen wall to reach some hidden shelf, where the path continued unobstructed. Despite the randomness of his progression, Gentle sensed some foreboding intelligence in the cavern's construction, as if someone had carefully carved out the caves to mock the human desire for wide-open spaces, forcing a person to hunch and scrape like an animal if they hoped to make any progress toward the glacier's center.

Once or twice, Gentle cried out for Kitt, but the tunnel muffled his voice in a way that made him all too aware that he was surrounded by layers of compacted ice. Meanwhile, the calm produced by Boris's tea quickly evaporated. The fits of shuddering that pulsed through him soon grew so intense that he sometimes had to stop moving entirely until they passed, forced into a coil of stiff shivering that left his body aching. During these moments the tunnel contracted around him, as though he really were in the intestines of a great serpent. Through the glacial walls he thought he saw the anguished faces of desperate men, their cheeks pressed up against the ice, mouths wide with pleading. Their cries echoed through the tunnel, joined by the frantic squeals and squawks of unseen animals, the crushing grind of screeching machines. Gentle pressed his hands against his ears until the sounds silenced themselves.

After half an hour of this slow, torturous progress, Gentle found himself sliding down a slippery incline into a vaulted room far larger than any he had encountered so far. The massive cavern was nothing like the cramped tunnels that preceded it. Daylight washed down from a crack in the ice thirty or forty feet above the cave, flowing down the chiseled columns and grooved walls and gathering itself in a pool of impossibly blue water that filled most of the space. Despite the fact that the water was unnervingly transparent, Gentle, from his place at the top of the slope, could not see its bottom—only a blue abyss deep beneath its surface.

Kitt was sitting at the bottom of the incline, near the edge of the pool. He turned at Gentle's approach, though he did not seem surprised by his uncle's arrival. Gentle marveled at the changes in his nephew's face. Any trace of the joy he'd seen there back in Harmony had been scoured away, leaving behind something hardened and exhausted. He held a long, dull carving knife in his hands, probably pilfered from Harmony's kitchen.

"What are you wearing?" he asked.

"No time," Gentle said. He shuffled down the icy slope, clenching his aching rib. "We need to go."

"I'm not going anywhere," Kitt said. "This is where the salamander lives. I just need to wait until it comes to the surface. And then I'm taking its blood."

"With that?" Gentle pointed at the knife. "You'd be lucky to slice butter with that blade."

"I've come this far," Kitt said. "I'm not leaving now."

Another round of gunfire thundered down from above. Kitt frowned up at the opening in the ceiling.

"What's going on out there?" he said.

"Crane's men are attacking the valley," Gentle said. He'd limped over to one of the cave's icy columns and leaned against it. His vision had begun to blur, and he was starting to worry that he might not even have the energy to make the trip back out of the caves. "The Sons of Adam are insane. They're going to try and blow up the mountain. It isn't safe here."

Kitt stared down at his knife. "They showed me Adam," he said quietly. "They showed me the hole in his head."

"Like I said: They're insane."

But Kitt didn't move. A vacant sorrow gathered in his eyes.

"Do you think God has abandoned us?" he said. "These dreams I've been having. They're so sad. So hopeless. Do you think we're being punished?"

"Kitt—" Gentle began, but he was cut off by another wave of nausea. His mouth filled up with saliva and his legs finally gave way, slipping out from underneath him and sending him down to the hard-packed ice. Kitt rushed over and kneeled beside him, speaking in a voice that had suddenly lost all traces of scorn.

"Uncle?" he said.

"We need to go," Gentle mumbled.

"I don't think you're going anywhere," Kitt said.

Just then, a pair of voices reached them from within the caves. Gentle recognized them right away.

"Hide," he said.

But there was nowhere to hide. The cave's columns were too thin to obscure Gentle's bulky frame, and the sloping sides of the cavern held no hidden passages or exits. There was only the single gap in the wall Kitt and Gentle had used to access the cavern, out of which now squirmed the massive body of Hercules Belmont. Somehow the man looked even worse than he had the last time Gentle had seen him: He'd lost his leather coat, and now wore only a heavy wool sweater drenched in dried blood. His infected ear had begun to burst from its stitches, wilting away from his face like the decaying head of a purple flower. All his pistols and knives were gone, though as he finally squeezed through the cave's exit and stumbled out into the cavern, Gentle saw the hulking barrel of Bertha gripped in one of his hands.

At the sight of them, he clapped his hands and whooped madly, turning back behind him to shout into the cave. "They're here!" he said. "I told you. Follow the drunk, and you'll find the boy! Didn't I say that? Didn't I tell you?"

Emmanuel slipped out into the cavern, cringing at Hercules's shouting. When he caught sight of Kitt, he sighed with relief.

"You're alive," he said. "Do you have any idea what sort of trouble you're in, Christopher?"

"My name is Kitt," the boy replied. He stepped in front of Gentle and held the knife out before him.

"Mr. Belmont," Emmanuel said. "Grab my son. I lack sufficient energy to cope with one of his tantrums."

Hercules easily smacked the knife from Kitt's hand. He grabbed the boy under his shoulder and began tugging him away, but Kitt, after a moment of hesitation, began biting at the man's hands. Gentle, his head still throbbing, tried to rise to his feet, only to fall again.

"Fucking cannibal!" Hercules shouted, shoving Kitt roughly away when the boy's teeth finally found his thumb.

"Careful!" Emmanuel said. "That's my son, you idiot."

"He bit me," Hercules said. "You saw it."

"Stop this," Gentle murmured. He'd finally managed to stand up and was trying to put himself between Hercules and Kitt, but the huge man just shoved him back down.

"Enough," Emmanuel said. "You're all acting like children."

While Hercules was distracted, Kitt picked up the knife again. He crawled forward on his knees and struck out wildly, plunging the weapon into Hercules's boot. The blade passed, with miraculous ease, straight through the eyes of one of the grinning alligators and into the giant's foot.

Hercules didn't scream. He only gaped down at Kitt, the blood draining from his face.

"Hercules," Emmanuel said, sounding like a man trying to soothe a wild animal. But the words didn't seem to reach Hercules. He raised Bertha in his arms and aimed its barrel at Kitt's head.

Gentle rallied his strength and lunged forward, wrapping his arms around Kitt just as the boom of a gunshot rang out. The sound was much quieter than Gentle would have expected from a gun of Bertha's size. When he looked up a few seconds later he saw the reason why: A hole the size of a quarter had appeared in the center of Hercules's chest. The giant man dropped Bertha and tumbled backward, the thud of his gargantuan body shaking the ground as he fell.

Gentle looked at Emmanuel. His brother was holding a tiny, single-shot derringer in his hands. His lips were pinched, as though he'd just taken a sip of some bitter medicine. He flung the spent pistol aside and sighed.

"Are you happy now?" he said to Kitt. He pointed to Hercules, who was probing at the wound on his chest and making wet gasping noises. "Do you see what lows you've brought me to?"

"What have you done?" Gentle said.

"I've protected my son," his brother replied. "And now I'm taking him home. I've had enough of the West for one lifetime."

Another blast of sound tore through the cave, shaking the cavern's walls and unleashing a shower of icy fragments from the ceiling.

"They're blowing up the mountain," Gentle said.

"Christopher, get up," Emmanuel said. "It's time to go."

"You've shot me," Hercules wailed, finally gathering his unintelligible groans into speech. "You've killed me."

"Shut up," Emmanuel snapped. "Christopher. *Get up*. Now."

But Kitt didn't move. He was staring at Hercules. The man had begun to cry—childish sobs that shuddered through his body like hiccups.

"Fine," Emmanuel said. "Do you think I won't drag you out of here myself?"

He stepped toward them. Kitt, moving as if in a trance, grabbed Bertha, stood up, and pointed the gun at his father.

"No," he said.

Emmanuel froze.

"Kitt," Gentle said. "Don't."

"Don't come any closer," Kitt said.

"You'll shoot your own father?" Emmanuel said. Though he wore a savage smirk, Gentle heard, buried beneath, some tremor of true distress.

"You're not my father," Kitt said.

"How I wish that were true," Emmanuel said. "But you and I are stuck with one another, Christopher."

"My name is Kitt!"

Another boom shook the cave. A large chunk of ice broke from the ceiling and fell into the pool, splashing them with a spray of frigid water.

"Are these hysterics really necessary?" Emmanuel said, glancing nervously up at the spot where the ice had broken free. "You're worse than your mother."

Kitt's grip suddenly tightened on the rifle.

"Don't talk about her," he said.

"Or what? You'll kill me?"

"Kitt," Gentle said again, more firmly. He reached out and clasped his nephew's ankle. The boy kicked his hand away. "Put the gun down."

"Why should I?" Kitt asked, despairingly, as if he really did want Gentle to give him a good reason. "Why should he live? When she doesn't get to?"

"Look at me, Kitt," Gentle said. "Please."

Kitt glanced down at him, though he kept the gun trained on Emmanuel. Gentle took a shaking breath and tried, again, to speak with Liam's voice. The voice of a man who could unlock that hidden room inside of anyone, that place where they bolted away their impossible dreams, their yearning conviction that their lives held some meaning beyond the drudgery and injustice of their everyday existence. The voice of a man who'd seen the absolute ugliness of the human spirit, had watched as the most wicked among them triumphed while the innocent were put to the flame, and still believed in the fundamental goodness of every person he met. The voice of an alchemist, who could spin the dull, base materials of the world into glittering gold.

"That isn't your way," he said.

Kitt and Gentle stared at each other. After a few long seconds, Kitt cried out in rage and tossed the gun to the floor.

"I'm not coming with you," he said to his father. "I'd rather die here, with Uncle Gentle, than come with you."

Gentle could not remember ever having seen his brother look genuinely hurt. But after he heard Kitt's words, something inside Emmanuel seemed to shatter. He shook his head in disbelief, and when he spoke again, his voice cracked on the first words.

"How easy it is for you people," he said. "How easy it is for you to judge me. You want to make a monster out of me? Fine. Fine! Lord knows your mother did. Never mind that I gave her the sort of life she never could have dreamed of. Fucking women. Fucking hysterics. Fucking children! Ever since I was a boy, you've all treated me this way. All because I wanted a little *safety*. A little *security*. All because I was willing to accept the basic truth about the world—that the strong thrive, while the weak suffer—so the rest of you could kneel and pray, so that you could have your fancy little ideas about magic and redemption. Where would you be without me? What sort of life would you have? You know who you would be?" Emmanuel pointed at Gentle. "You would be him. A poor, stupid drunk, chasing impossible dreams."

"You killed me," Hercules wailed again. He kept repeating the words, as if he was only now beginning to understand their meaning. "You killed me. You killed me."

"Shut the fuck up!" Emmanuel screamed. He walked over to Hercules and stomped on the man's stomach. Hercules screamed in pain. "Just shut the fuck up!"

"Stop," Kitt said. "Please stop."

But Emmanuel was lost in his rage. "Isn't this what you want?" he said, kicking Hercules again. "A sick little villain? Fine. I'm happy to oblige."

Hercules squealed, curling up on his side in an attempt to protect himself from Emmanuel's attacks. Emmanuel spat on him, and then leaned down to pick Bertha up off the ground.

"I can be a villain," he said bitterly. "It's the easiest thing in the world."

"Don't," Gentle said—but he knew there was no hope of stopping his brother now. In an instant, Emmanuel's fury disappeared, and what was left was something worse. The same silent, indifferent creature Gentle had seen all those years ago, when he watched his brother cave in the skull of that horse, bringing the hammer down in steady slams long after the creature had stopped squirming beneath him.

Emmanuel raised Bertha up to his shoulder and aimed at

Hercules's head. He pulled the trigger, and a thunderous explosion shook the cavern. A flash of light detonated in Emmanuel's hands, sending the gun—or what was left of it—twirling over his shoulder and down into the snow in front of Gentle's feet. The weapon's barrel had burst into a tortured tangle of scorched metal.

For an instant Gentle could hear nothing but a painful ringing in his ears. But he could see just fine: could watch as his brother, wavering on his feet like a drunk, spun around to face him. His hands were scorched and raw where the gun had gone off, and his face—Gentle tried to grab Kitt and pull him away to save him from the sight of it, but he was too late—had been peeled back by the blast, the bone pierced by the bits of metal that had flown off the gun's barrel. The only part of his brother's face that was still intact was one bright blue eye, staring out at them from the bloody disarray of his skull.

For a few seconds Emmanuel stood there, swaying. Then he collapsed.

If Kitt screamed, Gentle couldn't hear him. The cave shuddered once more, and the ice above them began to collapse in earnest. A bolt of adrenaline fired through Gentle's body, providing him just enough strength to grab Kitt and rush him toward the cave's exit.

Just as Gentle pushed Kitt into the tunnel, and began crawling in himself, his nephew turned around and stared up at the cavern behind them. His eyes widened, and he cried out, but Gentle couldn't hear him. All at once the light from outside disappeared. Something heavy collided with the back of Gentle's head and he was plunged into black.

When Gentle opened his eyes again, he was surrounded by darkness. An immense weight held him in place. The pressure on his chest made breathing nearly impossible. After a few brief moments of confusion, his brain finally understood that he was trapped beneath the cave's frozen rubble.

He began flailing in the dark, with no sense of what direction might be up or down, his grunts and moans muffled by the snow and ice surrounding him. Soon, he knew, his air would be gone, and this realization only intensified the urgency of his thrashing.

After a few seconds of wild contortion, one of Gentle's arms miraculously pierced the outer reaches of his icy cocoon. He used it to scrape the snow away from his face, momentarily blinding himself. After his eyes adjusted, he could see he was still in the cavern, the crack in its roof now reduced to a slim sliver of sunlight. The bulk of the ceiling had crumbled inward, filling the space with huge boulders of ice and mounds of snow, though the frigid pool in the cavern's center had remained strangely undisturbed, its depths swallowing up whatever rubble plummeted into its waters. The bodies of Hercules and Emmanuel were nowhere to be seen.

Gentle had no sense of how much time had passed since he'd pushed Kitt into the tunnel, though the light from overhead seemed to be fading. Now that he knew he wouldn't suffocate, he lost whatever energy had animated his limbs just moments before, and he lay still, completely exhausted, his bottom half still submerged beneath the snow. If the soldiers were still fighting outside, he couldn't hear them. His few strangled calls for help went unanswered.

More time passed. Hours, Gentle thought, of cold silence punctuated by the occasional crinkle of ice falling from the ceiling. Gentle called out a few more times, but the ache in his rib was nearly too much to bear.

Night descended overhead, filling the collapsed cavern with the blue light of the passing moon. Gentle, who'd been shivering against the cold for hours, began to notice a numbness spreading through him, followed by a pleasant gush of warmth: the telltale signs, he knew, of hypothermia. Yet just as he began to settle into a comforting drowsiness, he was jolted awake by a bubbling noise from the pool of water in the center of the cave.

At first he thought another hunk of ice had splashed into the pool. But when the sound continued, growing from a faint gurgle to a crescendo of slapping waves, Gentle opened his eyes and peered down at the pool, where a massive, rounded shape was slowly rising from the water. It floated there at the surface for a few moments before drifting toward the shore, where it slid from the depths like a huge seal beaching itself on a sandbar. Its immense, webbed feet carried it over the snow with steps so heavy they sent more ice crumbling from the cave ceiling, the moon reflecting off its wet, alabaster flesh in dripping waves of bright mercury.

Gentle's breath caught in his throat as the salamander crawled up the bank and set its black, depthless eyes upon him. Somehow the creature seemed even larger than it had the last time he'd seen it, its body so huge that it barely fit inside the cavern. The monster did not move with the same easy grace as before; instead, it lumbered toward him like a thing recently awoken from a fitful slumber, every step accompanied by a deep, resentful sigh. Once the creature even seemed to lose its balance, the legs on its right side slipping out from underneath it and sending it to its belly, where it lay panting for a few moments before groaning and raising itself up again.

Eventually the salamander's head loomed over Gentle, puffing cold wafts from its nostrils that passed over Gentle like a heavy gale. Its giant jaw opened slightly, and Gentle heard the hiss of its breath, saw the tip of a long tongue hover momentarily in the air, as if tasting the breeze. Black bile gathered around its lips, and with a great cough the salamander sent a spray of the stuff into the snow by Gentle's face, where it sizzled in the ice, smelling of coal and gunpowder. The monster's mouth was more than large enough to swallow Gentle in one bite, yet the salamander made no move to consume him. Instead, it just remained there, staring down at him while the water dripped off its body.

Gentle found himself incapable of looking away from the salamander's white flesh, his vision absorbed by that unnatural shade of white, so bereft of any tint or hue he associated with the ordinary world. Now that Gentle was closer, he could see strange quivers and bulges in the skin, like he was studying the vast surface of an alabaster sea, its shifting currents and whirls beckoning Gentle deeper and deeper into its depths, until he gradually became less and less aware of his surroundings, the icy cavern and the weight of snow on his legs replaced by a cold, floating sensation, as though he had somehow slipped into a dream while still awake. He had never experienced anything like it—this abrupt weightlessness and loss of self—though the closest approximation he could recall was the blissful emptiness he'd felt after a heavy dose of Sweet Vitriol.

While the patterns flickering on the salamander's pale flesh initially looked like abstract, random shapes, they soon gathered themselves into figures Gentle recognized: the curled lips of crashing waves, the swaying fronds of bull kelp, the shuddering flanks of schools of fish. He saw creatures that seemed to have arrived from another world, covered in plates of thick armor and surveying the ocean floor with prodding antennae. He felt the gentle tug of currents carrying him vast distances through the hazy cerulean, the warmth of the sun filtering down from the water's surface, the vibrant kaleidoscope of greens and blues and violets exploding up from teeming reefs. And he felt time, passing with impossible speed, like someone flipping too quickly through a picture book. He saw mountains rise from the sea, watched them drape themselves in landscapes of steaming alpine wilderness, watched wildflowers erupt into fields of color only to wither a few seconds later.

His webbed feet made their first tentative steps onto a newborn coastline. His wide nostrils sniffed the salty air and quavered at the smell of pine and cedar, of seaweed drying in the sun and mushrooms sprouting in the soil. He watched shaggy giants commence a new kind of dance amidst the whispering trees: elephants and rhinos covered in burly cloaks of fur, hunted by fanged cats the size of horses. He gorged himself on river fish and sunned his damp body on flat stones and felt at peace there in the strange, new land.

Then, he felt fear. New animals, lithe and hairless, prowled the forest, calling out to one another in warbled clicks and grunts. They brought down the woolly giants with spears, trapped the colossal cats in pits and slaughtered them with stones and knives. They sailed down the rivers in hollowed-out logs and plucked nets of fish out of the crisp waters with impossible ease. Their hands, so delicate and thin, frightened him with their dexterous reaching, their gripping and grasping.

He hid from them. From their hunger and their cleverness. He slithered through rivers and streams, slept for what felt like years in the deepest depths of lakes. But even there he felt them, their presence spreading through the river like murky ink. He tasted them in every drop of water, their dreams and their stories carried along by the bitter tang of their sweat. He drifted upstream, into the mountains, lured by the memories of the oceans that lived in the stones, and by a newfound need for solitude. Caverns and tunnels latticed the landscape, secret places that eventually led him to the pool beneath the glacier, so quiet and still, so safe. And there he lived, for how long he didn't know, while the land below him changed, ravaged by fires and earthquakes, its waters soured by poisonous new tastes and smells.

It was a man who shattered his seclusion. A desperate-looking man, so much paler than the ones he knew, who broke through the walls of his secret cavern. He felt the man's hands upon him, felt the man's memories—memories of war and cruelty, of despair and shame—enter the delicate layers of his flesh. He felt their thoughts mingling, took in the man's oppressive concept of time and life, of God and virtue. There was relief when the man ran away, and then agony when more of them came, their hands reaching out for him. Infecting him. He fled again. Followed the tunnels to the old valleys and streams. But the water had changed. They were in it now, polluting his thoughts with things he did not wish to know. What had once been only sensations were given strange names—tree, stone, boot, and bullet. Safety. Danger. Home. Relief. Water. Deep waters. Waters deep enough to hide from them.

He felt rage at this new vocabulary. He felt despair. He felt the sheer vulnerability of his body, so tender and delicate despite its size, like a tapestry of the finest silks, muddied by every human eye that gazed upon it.

He slunk through the peninsula, fleeing and hiding, hungry and lost, until he reached a stream that Gentle—his consciousness bobbing to the surface of the salamander's vast intelligence—recognized. A little creek not far from Dalton Lake. He saw Liam, alive, peering down into the waters at him from atop a little boat.

He saw Liam the way that only the salamander could: a trembling network of nerves and arteries, floating in the air like the shimmering roots of a fantastic tree. He felt Liam's memories scorching off him like the sun's rays: the horrors he'd seen in Andersonville, the joy he'd felt passing those years with Gentle in their little cabin, his growing certainty that the Great Work was his only hope in turning back sickness and death. He saw the blood pumping through Liam's veins—all except one, where a tiny clump of fat slowed the flow. He watched in horror as a bit of the clump tumbled away, as the blood crowded around the craggy wall, forming a dam that cut off the flow to Liam's thumping heart. He saw his friend's face go pale. Saw him collapse off the side of the boat and onto the shore. And the salamander, frightened by what Liam had seen in him—a thing to be captured and killed, an ingredient to be collected—turned and fled farther upstream.

"Go back!" Gentle cried, and felt himself return, suddenly, to his own body, still prone beneath the salamander. "Go back and help him!"

But the salamander didn't go back. And within seconds Gentle felt himself submerged beneath the amphibian's heavy thoughts once more, even as his own mind struggled to escape, even as he began to whimper and moan, because the things the salamander showed him next were somehow worse than anything that had come before, worse even than Liam's death. He saw cities of glass and steel submerged beneath frothing waves. He saw legions of starving men and women scrambling over piles of trash beneath an unrelenting sun, their skin burned to boils as they wrestled with one another for scraps. He saw lakes of brown waste, wildfires of incomprehensible ferocity, whole continents composed of nothing but ash and scalded earth.

He saw the salamander's truth: that there would never be a place free of them now. They would cut down every tree, uproot every flower. They would poison the water and fill the air with smoke. He saw the salamander's green valley reduced to the cracked wasteland from his dreams, tasted dust on the hot air, ached with the hopeless yearning for deep waters, any deep waters, where he could be free from the horrors of the monsters that stole the land and the sea and the sky.

In the face of all this, Gentle knew now, the salamander had unyoked itself from some primal vitality, surrendered itself to decay after eons of careful equilibrium. The salamander had chosen to die.

Gentle could stand it no longer. He tore his own hand from the snow and flung it upward, to try and push helplessly against the salamander's cold, wet stomach. But as his fingers reached its flesh, a bolt of lightning seemed to pass from the salamander into his own body, a blinding white light that eviscerated his sight and filled his mouth with the taste of metal and reduced his mind to a single black dot in an endless expanse of white nothing. The salamander's white skin burned and bubbled away from its bones and slid down Gentle's arm like hot wax, searing itself into him, mixing its flesh with his until that whiteness was his whiteness.

Gentle screamed. And then he was gone.

When he opened his eyes again, he found himself staring up into the distant branches of trees. Dusty columns of light hung, suspended, between the needles. He could tell that the sea was close by the familiar scent of salt water on the breeze and the distant shrieks of seagulls in the air. His body was bundled in a heavy quilt, and his muscles felt as though they were made of stone. He opened his mouth to speak, but instead of words his throat produced only a garbled arrangement of vowels.

"He's awake," said a familiar voice.

Kitt's face blocked out the trees. The boy threw his arms around Gentle's shoulders, stuffing his face into the crook of his neck. Gentle wheezed at the boy's weight against his rib.

"Give him some room," said another voice. "You're crushing him."

Kitt pulled away, looking a little abashed. Cora leaned over his shoulder. A bandage encircled her head like a grimy halo, hiding her prodigious eyebrows. When she spoke, her voice creaked like an old bedframe, as though she hadn't stopped shouting for days.

"Welcome back," she said.

"Water," Gentle finally managed to say. His throat felt like it was packed with sawdust.

"Of course," Kitt said, uncorking a canteen and tilting it over Gentle's cracked lips. The water within was pure. Gentle suckled desperately on the leather pouch. When he was done, he pushed Kitt's hands away and said, "Liam."

"Don't worry," Kitt said. "He's safe. Abe carried him all the way here."

"No," Gentle said. His memories of his encounter with the salamander returned slowly, like fragments of a dream. "I saw him die. Something in his blood."

Kitt frowned and turned to Cora. The woman shook her head, as though nothing Gentle said made any sense.

"Must have hit his head pretty hard in that cave-in," she said. "It'll take him some time to reclaim his senses."

"No," Gentle said again. "The salamander showed me. It showed me everything."

And then the sensations returned—the feeling of his long, amphibious body slipping through those ancient waters, the water tainted with humanity's taste. A strangled noise escaped his lips. It was too much. It was all too much.

"It was horrible," he said.

"Uncle?" Kitt said. "What are you talking about?"

"The burning air," Gentle said. "The boiling seas."

Kitt spoke but Gentle couldn't hear him. His eyes filled, again, with the horrible visions the salamander had shown him. The world that had been lost, and the world that was coming. He gasped for breath, but no air would come. He disappeared again.

For hours, Gentle dipped in and out of consciousness. Kitt came to him each time he returned, offering water and soft words, until Gentle was overcome, once more, by the immensity of what he'd seen. Each time he stayed awake a little longer, until finally, after the sun had set, he managed to sit up and resist the temptation to drift back into oblivion.

Crouched around a motley gathering of tents and cooking fires, the weary refugees of Harmony sniffled and groaned. There were only about twenty of them, their heads and arms enveloped in bandages. A few men and women—some of whom had already lost a hand or a foot to the Judge's cruel justice in years past—now nursed fresh amputations, with stumps bound tight by rags and strips of cloth. Gentle saw Mr. Li among them, hobbling about on newly hewn crutches. Though none of them spoke, a hum of activity hung over the otherwise gloomy scene, with the few

Harmonites still capable of locomotion attending to those whose bandages needed changing, or carrying water to those who'd been laid out on makeshift stretchers. Beyond the lights of the camp, the gray shadow of the Pacific striated the horizon into two different shades of black. Gentle could hear the crash of waves against the shore.

"Where are we?" he called out, his voice weak. "Where is the salamander?"

The Harmonites glared up at him like monks interrupted in deep prayer. Cora emerged from one of the tents, followed by Kitt, who held a pot of bloody dressings.

"Up again?" Cora said.

"Where are we?" Gentle said once more.

"The coast," Cora said. "About a day's ride west of Port Townsend."

"How?" Gentle said.

"They rescued us," Kitt said, pointing at Cora. "After you pushed me out of the cave, just before it collapsed. I barely made it out myself. I tried to get back inside. I really did. But all the passages were closed off."

While she kneeled down and checked Gentle's temperature, Cora explained the rest. She and her people had lost the fight back in Harmony. Those who hadn't been slaughtered by the soldiers were rounded up and taken as "prisoners of war." The Judge had completely lost it, she said. Supposedly a number of his soldiers had actually been Sons of Adam in disguise, and they'd killed some of his men and set fire to a good portion of the posse's munitions before disappearing into the woods. The Reverend Judge was so enraged by this betrayal that he didn't even let the Harmonites linger and care for their wounded: Instead, he marched them deeper into the peninsula, following the deserters' trail to

Adam's hideout in the mountains.

"I suppose we're lucky he didn't execute us on the spot," she said bitterly. "We lost good people in those woods. We're still losing them."

"Peter is dead," Kitt said quietly. "Miss Cora told me how he took off the Judge's hand."

"Little fool," Cora said. She began pressing against different parts of Gentle's chest, paying close attention to the spots that made him pull away from her touch. "He survived for longer than I expected, despite the bullet in his belly."

Kitt turned away, hiding his face.

"I don't understand," Gentle said. "How did you find me?"

"The Judge made camp at the foot of the valley. Left us there with a couple of his soldiers. It's the only reason we aren't dead. We could see the avalanche from where we were camped."

"Avalanche?" Gentle said.

"That's right. Heard a giant crack, and suddenly the whole face of the mountain buckled. The Judge and his soldiers just disappeared, swallowed up by a wave of snow. The men that were left to guard us didn't hang around after that. Just ran back the way we'd come. We were getting ready to leave when Kitt here wandered out of the valley with that mule of yours in tow. Told us about how you were trapped in a cave under the ice. Raised such hell that we had no choice but to send some folks to look for you."

She pressed her hand beneath Gentle's left arm, and he gasped in pain.

"That rib is definitely broken," she said.

"I don't understand," Gentle said. "What happened to the salamander?"

"What do you mean?"

"It was there with me, in the cave."

"I never saw any cave," Cora said. "We found you passed out on top of the mountain. You don't remember climbing out?"

"I couldn't have. I was stuck in the ice."

"Amazing, the things people will do to survive."

"I saw the deep waters," Gentle said. "I saw how things used to be. How they're *supposed* to be. It was beautiful. And now it's gone."

"Kitt," Cora said, her voice sharp. "Will you go and get some soup for your uncle?"

"I'm not hungry."

"And some water, too," Cora said. Kitt cast a concerned glance at his uncle, and then turned and headed back to the fire. After he'd left, Cora leaned closer to Gentle, her face grim.

"Enough," she whispered.

"What?"

"I said *enough*. No more talk of salamanders."

"But I saw it—"

"I don't give a shit what you saw. Or what you think you saw. Take a look around you—do these people look edified by your visions? Ever since we rescued you from that mountain, you've been mumbling about death and despair. I chalked it up to all that laudanum you've been drinking, but now that your senses are returning, I need you to pull yourself together. If not for your own sake, then for Kitt's."

"The boy is fine."

"The boy is *not* fine. He told me what happened in that cave. How you stopped him from shooting his father. You're all he's got, now."

"But it was so beautiful," Gentle said, unable to speak without sounding desperately, pitifully afraid. "And we ruined it." His heart began beating faster in his chest. His breathing grew shallow and quick. His eyes jittered in their sockets, like copper balls shaking in a tin can.

Cora slapped him.

"I'm sorry," she said. "Really, I am. But we don't have time for this."

"Is everything okay?" Kitt had returned with a bowl of soup. Gentle looked up at him, hand pressed against his stinging cheek.

"We're fine," Cora said. "Just testing your uncle's reflexes. Isn't that right?"

Gentle stared at them. There was no use trying to explain. They had not felt what it was like to inhabit the salamander's body—did not feel decades, centuries, passing by them like so many clouds drifting through a blustering sky. They would only think he was mad if he tried to put it into words.

"I want to see Liam," he said.

"Maybe you should eat first," Kitt said.

Gentle rose to his feet, wavering on his legs like a foal fresh from its mother's womb.

"Take me to him."

Cora sighed. "Can you show him the way, Kitt? I've more important things to do."

"Follow me," said Kitt.

Liam's body was on the far side of camp, where the forest met the beach. Abe was keeping watch over the casket, grazing on the tall, willowy grasses that grew in the sand. As Gentle came closer, the mule backed away, shaking his head and rolling his eyes as though he smelled a predator.

"He hasn't been the same since we left the mountains," Kitt

said. "The avalanche must have really frightened him."

But Gentle knew the truth. Abe could smell the salamander on him.

"Must have been quite the hike."

"It wasn't too bad," Kitt said. "Manon knew a trail that ran straight through the mountains. I don't think we would have made it if it weren't for her. She was the one that found you on the glacier. It was strange: All the snow near you had melted away, like someone had set off some kind of explosion there. Manon said it must have been the dynamite."

"She still around?" Gentle asked.

"She's out checking traps, I think," Kitt replied.

"I'll be sure to thank her when she returns," he said.

Gentle kneeled down beside the casket. The wood was scuffed and powdered with dirt, and half of the loops holding its lid in place had been torn away. But the structure itself remained miraculously intact.

"They wanted to leave it in the mountains," Kitt said. "But I insisted."

"Kind of you," Gentle said.

"I thought maybe you'd still, well . . ." He hesitated, fingers finicking at the buttons of his coat.

"Get the salamander's blood," Gentle said.

"Right. But you didn't, did you?"

"No," Gentle said.

"I'm sorry."

"That's all right."

The salamander's visions tugged at Gentle's thoughts again. He remembered those ancient seas, full of living fossils. Millions of years passing before his eyes—yet he had seen it all happen in seconds. How was it possible that the world was so old? Had Liam seen it, too? The uselessness of it all? The utter inconsequentiality of their lives?

Because it *was* inconsequential, wasn't it? Hadn't the salamander shown him as much? The world was older than humanity, much older, and it would persist long after men had finished scratching out their feeble marks on the planet. There was no dream great enough to rescue them from this truth: not Liam's Great Work, or Crane's tyrannical plans for a civilized frontier, or Cora's flowery words about some new, enlightened society. Even Adam had it wrong in the end: He'd twisted the salamander's visions into yet another self-edifying legend, one in which he and his men would overcome destruction by embracing it, by becoming its champions. But destruction needed no champions. It required no great armies or honey-tongued prophets to proclaim its sovereignty over the creatures of the earth. All it had to do was wait.

There had never been any grand purpose to their lives. Not even their suffering. Their torments were neither a testament to the strength of their faith, nor evidence of some vicious, uncaring god. Though they had fled west in search of fresh stories—had seen, in these vast tracts of wilderness, a blank page waiting for their pens—they had accomplished nothing new. They'd merely gussied up the same old conquests and cruelties with novel justifications, made heroes of themselves and monsters of the ones they aimed to destroy. They had torn up the land, tainted its waters with blood and sickened its skies with ash. As if they would not one day taste the fruit born from that foul soil and putrid air.

What would they do, he wondered, now that there was no West left to run to?

Make a new myth, he supposed. Another lie to quiet that dark, squirming terror in their bellies. They would collect the senseless horrors of this century and write them off as one more cantankerous interlude in their tireless pursuit of paradise.

But it would not save them. Not from what the salamander had shown him.

Gentle took a deep breath. Blinked his eyes a few times. He listened to the wind rustling the highest branches of the trees and pressed his fingers into the dry grass beneath him.

Kitt was watching him. "Uncle?" he said. "Maybe you should go back to bed."

"I think I'd like to be alone with Liam for a little while," Gentle said. "Would that be all right?"

"Of course," Kitt replied. "I'll just leave your soup here. Be sure to eat it before it gets cold."

"Right. Thank you."

The boy turned and headed back toward camp, but Gentle stopped him.

"Kitt," he said. "I'm so sorry about Peter."

Kitt nodded. The coldness of his response surprised Gentle.

"We've still got his body, at least," he replied. "We're going to bury him once things have settled down."

"That's good," Gentle said. "I'm sorry about your father, too. For what's it worth."

"I'm not," Kitt said. Not maliciously, Gentle noted, but wearily, as though the words were heavy stones he'd had to haul a great distance out of himself. "I'm not sorry at all."

Cora's voice called out for Kitt. The boy turned and left, his little body sharpened to a thin black stalk by the light of the campfires.

Gentle did not eat the soup. It would only be a waste of good food. He did take a few sips of the water Kitt had brought, if only to moisten his lips and throat.

He pushed back the lid of the casket. Somehow, Liam seemed older than he had back at Dalton Lake: The wrinkles around his eyes and across his forehead were stiff as old leather, his hair wispy and thin. He looked, Gentle realized, like an old man.

He considered searching for his embalming bag—certainly Kitt must have placed it somewhere nearby—so that he could return some of the blush to his friend's cheeks, and grease back the few sprigs of red that had sprung out from his hairline. But given what he was planning to do, he saw no reason to waste time with any cosmetic modifications.

He slipped his hands under Liam's armpits and hauled him out of the coffin, amazed at how light he'd become. He rose painfully to his feet, Liam nestled in his arms like a sleeping child. Abe watched him from the other side of the clearing, his expression unreadable in the darkness.

"I'm sorry," Gentle whispered.

The mule's ear twitched. He turned his head away.

Gentle headed down the gravel slope that led to the water, trying not to slip on the rocks. The moon was full and bright, its light drowning out the surrounding stars and glinting over the water's surface in silvery ripples. The beach was mostly pebbles, and as Gentle tried to keep his balance, the pain in his rib grew more pronounced, until each step left him feeling like someone was twisting a knife in his side.

When he reached the water's edge, and the first blast of ocean waves crashed against his shins, he gasped at the cold of it. Within moments everything below the water's surface was numb. But he pressed on until the water had reached his chest, and Liam's body began to float easier in his arms. He was amazed by the force of the waves, which kept knocking him off his feet and forcing him to let go of Liam's limp corpse. Each time he waded back to his friend and took hold of him again, pushing farther out into the waves, until soon they began crashing over his head, stinging his eyes with salt.

All at once the seafloor fell away, and Gentle was set adrift in open water. The buoyancy of Liam's dead body kept them afloat, but the cold was unbearable. At first it hurt tremendously, like being pricked by thousands of icy needles, but this soon passed, replaced by a disconcerting tightness, as if his body were being slowly squeezed by a giant hand.

The whole process had seemed so peaceful in his mind: He would carry Liam's body to the sea and they would wait for the tide to carry them out to the depths. The cold would sap the energy from his limbs, and he would drift off into a deathly slumber. He would drown for the last time. Just as he was meant to drown all those years ago, in Ohio.

But suicide, he should have remembered, was difficult. The ocean was more cantankerous than he'd expected, so that he was constantly fighting to keep his head above water. A few times he tried to finish the job himself, dunking his face beneath the surface and expelling all the air in his lungs. But the moment he began to twitch and shake from his desperate need to breathe, he surged back above the water, gasping for air.

Behind him, the Harmonites' camp was a faint glow flickering behind the trees. Even if he changed his mind now, there was no chance he'd make it back to shore. He tried to retain the certainty he'd had, back on land, that this was the only conceivable action left to him. How could he be expected to go on living, after what he'd seen? There was no Great Work. No redemption for the pain he'd endured when he was a boy. Just time and decay.

Who would blame him for ending things now, when all he had left before him were a few decades of lonely nights in the woods, entombed in the silence of his empty cabin?

But what had been so obvious on the shore was rendered absurd—insane, even—by the violence of the frigid waves and blistering air. Gentle's mind was accosted by images of life. A warm fire crackling in a stone hearth. The smell of Liam's pancakes. Kitt, drawing some flower in his sketchbook, his face locked in a tight expression of concentrated joy.

Gentle did not want to die. The recognition boomed through him like the sound of a train howling through the woods in the middle of the night. He did not want to die. Even if his life was one long string of disappointment and pain, even if he didn't feel an ounce of happiness for the rest of his years, his body—every drop of blood and bile, every screaming tendon and muscle—wanted to go on living.

"Help!" Gentle yelled, but the crashing waves drowned out the sound of his voice. His fingers, cramped from the cold, could no longer keep hold of Liam's clothes. His friend's body slipped out of his grasp and began to float farther out to sea. Gentle desperately clawed after him, but within moments he was slipping down into the darkness.

Something grabbed him from behind, hauling him back toward the surface. For a moment, Gentle wondered if the salamander had returned to save him. But when he turned around he saw Kitt, shaved head glistening like sealskin in the moonlight, his thin arms hooked under Gentle's armpits. The boy shouted something at him, but the words were drowned out as another wave crashed over them.

When they returned to the surface, Kitt yelled, "Kick!" and

began dragging Gentle slowly toward the shoreline, his own legs fluttering beneath them.

"Where's Liam?" Gentle yelled. "We can't leave him!"

But Kitt ignored him and kept kicking. So Gentle, too tired to struggle, tried to kick as well, though his legs were so heavy that he did little except splash the water behind them.

They continued like this for what felt like hours but couldn't have been more than a few minutes. The waves swallowed them and spit them back to the surface. A few times they lost hold of each other in the tumult, but Kitt always found his way back to his uncle, grabbing him again and resuming the slow float back to shore.

Eventually Kitt's legs found solid ground. He dragged Gentle back onto the beach. Once they were both free of the waves, he dropped him onto the gravel and collapsed to his knees. They stayed like that for a long time—Gentle staring up at the impossible brightness of the moon, and Kitt, still kneeling, taking long drags of air through his nose and coughing up seawater while the tide splashed against his heels.

Once the shock and adrenaline had drained away, little whimpers began to flutter from Gentle's lips. Soon, he was crying. His broken rib ached with each shuddering sob, but he could not stop. It was like he'd swallowed some great portion of the sea, and now it was all draining out of him at once.

He heard Kitt shuffling through the rocks toward him. The boy tugged Gentle's head into his lap and cradled his skull. He leaned forward and wrapped his arms around his uncle, protecting him from the wind. Gentle laid one of his hands across his chest, and Kitt took it in his own. They remained there, holding each other while Gentle cried, until sunrise drained the dark from the sky.

They returned to camp looking like the beleaguered survivors of a shipwreck, stumbling past the gawking Harmonites to the tent Cora had lent them. There, they changed into some dry clothes and crawled into their respective bedrolls.

But Gentle quickly discovered he was incapable of sleep. He was too frightened of what dreams might come for him when he closed his eyes. So he found his pipe in Kitt's satchel and settled onto a stool outside the tent to smoke. When he realized he didn't have any matches, or any tobacco, he sighed and began to stand again, only to find himself staring up into Manon's face.

"Need a light?" she said.

She was dressed as she always was: same thick wool coat, same muddy trousers, same wide-brimmed hat. She didn't look to have sustained any wounds in the attack on Harmony, though there was a new weariness to her posture, a slight slouch of the shoulders and a slanting lilt to her right foot, that implied some unseen damage.

"Excellent timing," Gentle said.

Manon offered him some of her own tobacco, as well as a match, and while Gentle took greedy gulps of smoke, she settled onto the stool beside him and began rolling a cigarette.

"Heard you went for a swim last night," she said.

"Tried to drown myself," Gentle said. "But the boy wouldn't let me."

Manon didn't seem surprised by this. "Awful rude of you, given all the trouble we took hauling you out of the mountains."

"Kitt said you were the one who found me. Thank you."

Manon shrugged. "Kid wouldn't shut up about it. Figured

finding you was easier than listening to him weeping and moaning all the way to the coast."

"And here I figured you just wanted to be paid."

"You don't owe me anything," Manon replied. "I didn't find your salamander."

Gentle pulled on the pipe, trying not to breathe too deeply. When he exhaled, he noticed Manon staring at him with uncharacteristic interest.

"So why'd you do it?" she asked.

"I didn't see much point in living."

"And Kitt?" she asked. Gentle thought he heard anger in her voice.

"Figured the Harmonites would look after him."

"Not many left. And they're practically strangers."

"He doesn't know me all that well, either."

"But you're family."

"It's more complicated than that."

Manon stared at him through the smoke.

"No," she said. "It really isn't."

"The salamander showed me things. The same things it must have shown the Sons of Adam. The truth of the world. It was just like you said. These mountains used to be underwater. The oceans and the land were full of strange monsters. And then they died, or changed, and the things that came after that died, too. We killed them, and we'll keep killing them. And then we'll die too. Just like every other animal."

Manon was silent for a moment. And then, a tremendous laugh shivered up from her belly. A few of the Harmonites down in camp looked up, surprised. Gentle thought he noticed a few of them smiling wearily at the noise.

"That's funny to you?" he said.

Manon waved her hand in the air between them, struggling to catch her breath. She shook her head.

"I'm simply amazed," she said. "Your great unraveling was the realization that human beings are animals? That we shit and fuck and die like everything else?"

"But we *aren't* like everything else. There is a cruelty inside of us that isn't like other beasts. Look what we've done to the world. What we're going to do. And none of it—none of the horror and the pain—will have meant anything."

Manon replied without hesitation. "Why does it have to mean something?"

"Because it's only going to get worse! You've seen the dream. All of that ugliness to come, and for what? Our grand reward, our triumph, will be the end of the world."

"The world is always ending for someone," Manon said.

Gentle didn't know what to say. Seagulls circled in the air above them, crying out in joy or terror. Manon slapped her legs and rose to her feet.

"Anyway," she said. "I didn't come here to philosophize. Cora thinks it's time we buried the dead. We've got half a dozen bodies that need tending to. Now that you're healthy enough for moonlight swims, she figured you could help with the preparations."

"I don't have my embalming fluid," Gentle said. "I can't preserve anyone."

"She doesn't want them preserved. She just figured you might be able to make them a bit more presentable. So that folks can have a nicer image of them before they're buried."

"I see," he said. "I suppose I can do that."

Manon lingered for another moment, looking uncertain.

"What's wrong?" Gentle asked.

She bit the inside of her lip and pulled something from her

pocket. A vial of light brown fluid. Gentle's pulse quickened at the sight.

"Cora thought you might need something for your rib," she said. "It's laudanum. Watered down something fierce, but it should help with the pain. She said there'd be no more of it for you after this."

"Back in Harmony she told me she didn't have any."

"She isn't one for cultivating unhealthy habits. Not in others, anyway. She wouldn't offer this unless she thought you needed it."

Gentle stared at the vial. The fluid seemed to sing to him—he swore he heard a new frequency in the air, a humming lullaby pulsing from the golden heart of the little tube. And for a moment he felt himself beginning to reach out for it. But he stopped.

"That's all right," he said. "The pain isn't so great."

Manon looked relieved.

"Are you ready to get started?" she asked.

"Let me go and wake the boy."

"You sure that's a good idea?"

"It's the only skill I've got worth teaching," Gentle said. "If we're to keep on together, he may as well start learning now."

Manon nodded. "We'll be waiting."

After she left, Gentle finished smoking his pipe. He took his time, hoping to give Kitt as much rest as he could before the day's work began. More than once he contemplated leaving the boy to his sleep. But he thought Kitt would want to be a part of preparing the bodies—especially Peter's. Even if the sight of the other boy's corpse hurt him, Gentle thought there might be a kind of peace in tending to his friend. In combing his hair and stitching up his wounds. Wiping away the blood. Massaging a bit of tenderness back into the limbs. Even amidst death, Gentle thought, there was room for care. For kindness, even. And perhaps there was some small triumph in that fact. What else could they do, really, but look after one another?

His rib cried out as he rose, but he paid it no mind. He turned back the tent's heavy flap and peered inside, where the light penetrated the deepest shadows and fell, warm and soft, over Kitt's sleeping face. The bruise around his eye, Gentle noticed, was finally gone.

How Gentle would have liked to let him linger in his dreams a few minutes longer. But then he noticed a crinkle in Kitt's brow, a choked whimper in his throat. The boy began to struggle with some unseen phantom, pushing away his blanket as though it were trying to smother him. Gentle wondered if the salamander's visions had come, once more, to haunt the boy's dream, or if these were just the normal nightmares that stalked anyone foolish enough to keep on living in a world so suffused with suffering. Gentle called out his nephew's name, first quietly and then a little louder, and watched the boy's bright blue eyes flutter open. For a moment he looked puzzled, maybe even a little afraid. But then his surroundings came into focus. He saw his uncle and smiled in drowsy astonishment. As if he couldn't believe how lucky he was to finally wake up.

THE END

ACKNOWLEDGMENTS

Thank you to Caroline Eisenmann, for your intelligence, thoughtfulness, and tenacity, as well as your unwavering support of my weird stories.

Thank you to Jess Zimmerman, for your always-astute edits, your boundless creativity, and your humor. This book would not exist without you.

Thank you to Scott Broker, my forever first reader and greatest inspiration. I would have given up writing long ago if it weren't for you.

Thank you to Maryann Held, for the incredible cover art.

Thank you to Sarah Clark, for your invaluable insights.

Thank you to Quirk Books, for proving there's a place for unconventional stories in publishing.

Thank you to the faculty and my cohort at Ohio State's MFA program, for three years of feedback and friendship.

Thank you to Mom and Dad, for giving me reading and appreciating my creativity, even when it meant I spent a lot of time hiding in my room.

Thank you to Piper, Greta, and Grey, for the never-ending delights and distractions. Cats are a writer's best friend, and I've been lucky enough to live with three of the best.

Thank you to Eliza Smith Costa, for a love that couldn't possibly fit into words. Every day I wake up excited to spend the rest of my life with you.

SHELDON COSTA is an award-winning fiction writer who has been published in the *Georgia Review*, *Conjunctions*, *Electric Literature*, and other outlets. He holds an MFA from the Ohio State University and lives in rural Missouri with his wife and three cats. This is his debut novel.

QUIRK BOOKS